THE ENDS OF THE EARTH

THE ENDS
OF THE EARTH

Robert Goddard

The Mysterious Press
New York

First Grove Atlantic hardcover edition: May 2017

Printed in the United States of America

First published in the United Kingdom in 2015 by Transworld Publishers, a division of the Random House Group

ISBN: 978-0-8021-2656-6
eISBN: 978-0-8021-8953-0

The Mysterious Press
An imprint of Grove Atlantic
154 West 14th Street
New York, NY 10011

Distributed by Publishers Group West

groveatlantic.com

17 18 19 20   10 9 8 7 6 5 4 3 2 1

THE ENDS OF THE EARTH

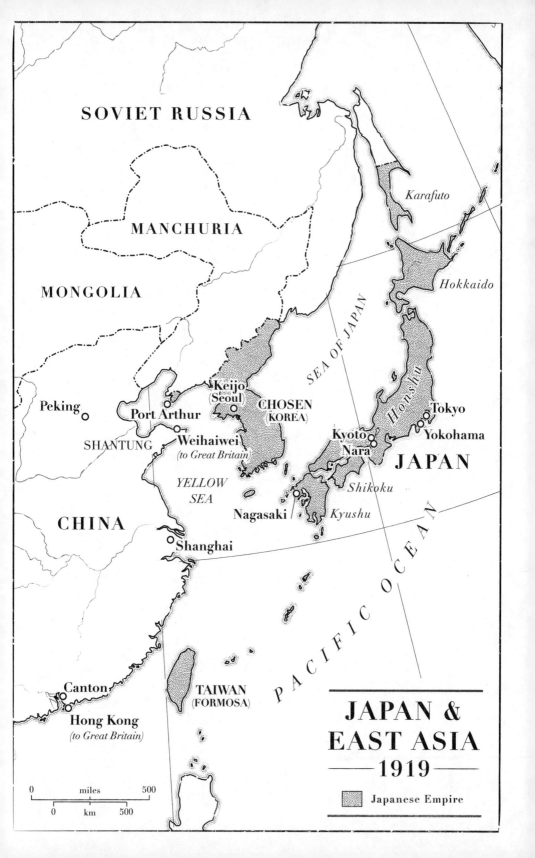

SOVIET RUSSIA

MANCHURIA

MONGOLIA

Karafuto

Hokkaido

SEA OF JAPAN

Keijo
Seoul
CHOSEN
(KOREA)

Peking

Port Arthur

SHANTUNG

Weihaiwei
(to Great Britain)

YELLOW
SEA

Honshu

Kyoto
Nara

Tokyo

Yokohama

JAPAN

Shikoku

Nagasaki

Kyushu

CHINA

Shanghai

PACIFIC OCEAN

Canton

TAIWAN
(FORMOSA)

Hong Kong
(to Great Britain)

JAPAN &
EAST ASIA
—1919—

Japanese Empire

0	miles	500
0	km	500

SAM TWENTYMAN WAS A LONG WAY FROM HOME. HE HAD NEVER imagined he might stray so far from his Walthamstow roots. He was not by nature the straying kind. Yet here he was, sitting on a bollard smoking a cigarette while people of several races and numerous nationalities swarmed around him on Yokohama pier. They would have taken him for some species of idler, if they had paid him any attention at all. But they would have been mistaken.

It was a hot Saturday afternoon in early July, 1919, the sun blazing down from a deep blue sky. Sam was seated on the shady side of the pier, beneath the vast hulk of a moored liner, but even where he was the heat was stifling. Nothing in the way of a cooling sea breeze reached him from the bay. Past him streamed passengers leaving or joining ships. Most of them were Japanese, some clad in kimonos, some in Western clothes. There were Europeans as well, sporting boaters and loose linen suits and dresses. Sam studied them with particular care as they passed. He was looking for one familiar face among the throng. But he did not see it.

Eight weeks had passed since Sam had sailed from Brest with Schools Morahan and Malory Hollander aboard a French liner bound for New York. Those weeks had required little more of Sam than to while away a succession of days at sea and wander the streets of New York, Chicago and San Francisco, gaping at the sights. But they had allowed him ample time to reflect on what had led him to embark on such a journey.

Less than four months ago, his life had seemed to be reverting to a humdrum form of normality, working in the family bakery business, after his years on the Western front as an engineer in the Royal Flying Corps. Then James Maxted, known to all as Max, the finest pilot Sam had encountered in France, had proposed they open a flying school together. Sam had jumped at the chance. But Max had been summoned to Paris to investigate the mystery of his father's sudden death in a roof-fall while serving as an advisor with the British delegation to the post-war peace conference. Sam had followed, eager to help Max settle the matter quickly.

Since then, the intrigue surrounding Sir Henry Maxted's murder – for murder Max had proved it was – had several times threatened to claim Sam's life as well as Max's. The truth, it had finally become clear, could only be found in Japan, destination of Sir Henry's old enemy, Count Tomura, following his sudden departure from Paris. Max had engaged former soldier of fortune Schools Morahan to recruit a team of hardened men to travel to Japan and await his arrival, before they went in search of the secret Sir Henry had been killed to protect.

Prior to leaving Paris, Max had emphasized to Morahan that whoever he took to Japan, Sam should not be among them. 'I want Sam kept out of this,' Morahan had quoted him as saying. But Sam was not out of it. Thanks to the force of his own argument that his mechanical skills might well be needed, he was very much in the middle of it.

Someone, possibly Jack Farngold, for long a thorn in Tomura's flesh, was held prisoner in Japan on the Count's orders. That someone was the key to the secret Max was determined to unlock. Morahan was to hire the sort of men whose expertise would be needed to free Tomura's prisoner. He had reckoned he could find them in circles he had previously moved in, in New York and Chicago. Once assembled, the team was to travel to Japan and meet Max in Yokohama.

Morahan's friend, Malory Hollander, had gone with them. She had spent some years in Japan as a young woman and knew a little of the language. She had also, to Sam's surprise, urged Morahan to accept Sam's offer of his services.

2

'We don't have a clue what sort of rescue we'll need to attempt, Schools,' she had said. 'A plane is the quickest getaway I can imagine. You'll have a pilot on hand in Max. I think you should have someone who knows how a plane engine works as well, in case you decide to use one.'

The discussion had taken place in the offices of Morahan's deceased business partner, Travis Ireton, a few hours after Ireton's funeral. News of another death – that of Commissioner Kuroda of the Japanese police, an old friend of Sir Henry Maxted, drowned in unexplained circumstances on his way back to Japan – had convinced Sam he could not sit tight in Paris.

'I don't know as I'll be any safer here if it comes down to it,' he had pointed out. 'Count Tomura doesn't seem to be the kind to let people who've crossed him live to tell the tale.'

'And you have crossed him,' Morahan had admitted. 'We all have.'

'So, we'd better all go, hadn't we?'

They had left Paris the following day.

Morahan's assembly of his team had been done through a series of meetings at undisclosed locations to which neither Sam nor Malory had been invited. Three men – Lewis Everett, Al Duffy and Howie Monteith – had left New York with them. Another two – Grover Ward and Gazda Djabsu – had been picked up in Chicago.

During the two-day train ride from there to California, Sam had spent much of his time gazing out at the Wild West he had only ever imagined courtesy of his favourite Tom Mix movies. He had even seen what the guard had assured him was a pair of genuine Red Indians lolling by the tracks at a one-horse watering-stop somewhere in southern Wyoming.

His travelling companions had seemed unimpressed by the scenery. They tended to the laconic, as Sam supposed such men should. But the three-week voyage across the Pacific from San Francisco to Yokohama had nevertheless enabled him to form some opinion of their individual characters.

Everett naturally defined himself as Morahan's deputy. Sam

judged he was a few years older than the others and he was certainly the best looking of the bunch: dark-haired and moustachioed, with a ready smile and fluent turn of phrase – a marksman by all accounts. Duffy was a big, muscular redhead possessed of a prodigious capacity for sleep, who oozed reliability. Monteith, a leaner, less imposing man, cracked passable jokes when the mood took him and spent much of his time aboard ship seducing female passengers. Ward was a stern, ruthless-looking fellow, the sort Sam would not have liked to find himself on the wrong side of. He came as some-thing of a pair with Djabsu, a large, usually genial but occasionally morose Serb, who spoke little English but evidently understood what was required of him. Sam had thought his name was spelt as it was pronounced – *Jabzoo* – until he had seen it written down in all its Serbo-Croat glory. 'Nots worry' was his all-purpose saying.

Sam trusted Morahan to have chosen these people wisely, probably for reasons that would only become clear in Japan. None of them knew exactly what would be required of them. Sam guessed their principal qualification was an ability to tackle just about any-thing. They were being paid well. But they would not begrudge earning their money.

The task ahead would only become apparent when Max joined the party. Nothing had been heard from him since his departure from Paris on May 3. Today, Sam needed no reminding, was July 5. The Paris peace conference was a week over, the treaty bringing the war to a formal close signed and sealed. There had been no way for Max to contact them in the interim. His instructions had been that they should simply wait for him in Yokohama, although Sam's assumption – and Morahan's too – was that *he* would actually be waiting for *them*. Sam had braced himself for Max's angry reaction to his presence. He suspected Morahan and Malory had braced themselves too.

But there had been no such reaction, because Max had not been waiting for them. They had been in Yokohama since Wednesday without word or sign of him. 'We sit tight,' was Morahan's response. 'He'll be here.'

In truth, sitting tight was all there was to do. They had booked into hotels and waited. 'We do nothing to attract attention to ourselves,' was Morahan's repeated injunction.

As far as Sam could tell, it was an easy injunction to follow. Yokohama was a bustling port city, awash with foreigners. A whole community of expatriate Europeans and Americans dwelt in Western-style villas up on the Bluff, above the harbour. And there were as many Chinese as Japanese on the streets. There was plenty to see even if there was little to do.

Loitering on the pier in the hope of seeing Max disembark from one of the ships that arrived at frequent intervals was an activity Sam knew Morahan considered neither necessary nor wise. 'Max will have no trouble finding us when he arrives. The last thing he'll want is a pier-head reception committee.' Sam had in fact tried to stay away, but his eagerness to have done with the moment when Max caught a horrified first sight of him had proved too powerful. And so, here he was, watching the latest disembarking crowd thin as the ship that had brought them steadily emptied.

Sam's war had been full of waiting. A forward base was a quiet and pensive place when the squadron was out. At least then, though, he had known there was a term to the waiting. This vigil in Yokohama was open-ended and insidiously unnerving. With each day that passed, the question of why Max had not yet arrived grew more insistent.

Pitching the butt of his cigarette into the oily width of water between the pier and the moored liner, Sam stood up and ambled off towards the Bund. Rickshaws and motor-taxis were heading in all directions from the passenger terminal. The hotel where he was staying with Morahan and Malory, the nostalgically named Eastbourne – the others were staying elsewhere – was not far, but he was in no hurry to return there.

He stopped and sat on one of the benches along the esplanade and squinted out into the bay, where launches and lighters and bigger steamers were criss-crossing the sparkling water. He lit another cigarette, wishing it was a Woodbine rather than whatever this rubbishy Japanese brand was called.

'You are Sam Twentyman, yes?'

The words were spoken by a man who had sat down on the bench beside him: a lean, round-shouldered fellow dressed in a rumpled cream suit and boater. He had dark, grey-flecked hair and a full moustache. His cheeks were hollow, his gaze wary, his skin sallow. He would have looked like any other European of the clerking classes but for the ghost of a knowing smile at the corners of his mouth.

'You *are* Sam Twentyman?' His English was good, but there was a French accent bubbling beneath it.

'Who wants to know?'

'My name is Pierre Dombreux.'

'*What?*'

That was impossible. Pierre Dombreux was the late husband of Sir Henry Maxted's mistress, Corinne Dombreux. He had died in Petrograd, by all accounts, more than a year ago, a French diplomat turned German and/or Russian spy, killed by his paymasters when he had outlived his usefulness.

'You heard, I think. I *am* Pierre Dombreux. And *you* are Sam Twentyman. Hoping to see Max get off that ship, were you?'

'I don't know what you're talking about,' Sam blustered, certain that admitting anything would be folly. 'But I do know you can't be Pierre Dombreux. He's dead.'

'No, I am not dead. As you can see, I am very much alive. But I must tell you . . . Max is not.'

RETURNING TO JAPAN HAD REVIVED MANY LONG-BURIED MEMORIES for Malory Hollander. She had first arrived there in 1893 as an eighteen-year-old assistant to the redoubtable Lutheran missionary Miss Dubb, with whom she had toured the country, armed with translated biblical texts intended to convert Japanese womanhood to the path of righteousness.

Whether she had lost her illusions before her faith or the other way round, Malory could hardly say now. She still burned with shame when she recalled how naïve she had been. The parting of the ways with Miss Dubb in the wilds of Hokkaido remained for Malory the end of a life she could barely imagine having led and the beginning of the one that had finally drawn her back to Japan.

She had taught for two years in Tokyo before leaving the country, as she had supposed, for good. Falling into and out of love during that time with a Japanese man, Shimizu Junzaburo, had shaped the character she now possessed: cautious, precise, self-reliant; or bossy, as Schools would have it.

Malory was no happier than Sam about kicking their heels in Yokohama. The pier where Sam had spent so much time that afternoon was the scene of her final parting from Junzaburo. She remembered with terrible clarity seeing him running helplessly along the pier after her ship – a ship that had already sailed, bound for San Francisco. He had learnt of her departure just too late, although there had been a moment when she had thought he might jump into the bay and swim after her.

But he had not. One small figure at the end of the pier, vanishing slowly from sight, was the last she had seen of him – and of Japan. Now, twenty-three years later, for good or ill, she was back.

She had decided to occupy herself that afternoon by walking up to the Foreign General Cemetery on the Bluff and seeking out the grave, which she felt sure must be there, of the parents of Jack Farngold and his sister, Matilda. Dredging a few appropriate phrases of Japanese from the depths, she had solicited the help of a solemn caretaker, who had consulted a dusty ledger before leading her to the spot.

The Farngolds' last resting place was in the middle of the cemetery, one among many kerb-bound graves, decorated in their case with a weeping angel and inscribed in the stately prose of the era.

GERTRUDE MARY FARNGOLD, NÉE HOLTON
BORN PENSHURST, KENT 16TH JANUARY 1842
DIED YOKOHAMA, 14TH JUNE 1886
MOURNED BY A LOVING HUSBAND

CLAUDE ASHLING FARNGOLD
BORN CHATHAM, KENT 4TH JUNE 1828
DIED YOKOHAMA, 26TH OCTOBER 1889

THE LORD WAS NOT IN THE FIRE
                              1 KINGS 19:12

Lapsed Lutheran though she might be, Malory could have recited the whole of the passage from the First Book of Kings there and then. *And, behold, the Lord passed by, and a great and strong wind rent the mountains, and brake in pieces the rocks before the Lord; but the Lord was not in the wind: and after the wind an earthquake; but the Lord was not in the earthquake: and after the earthquake a fire; but the Lord was not in the fire: and after the fire a still small voice.*

Claude Farngold had died in a warehouse fire, in the same year, Malory now knew, as his daughter had married Count Tomura. It was likely Matilda Farngold had chosen the words from the Bible to memorialize her father. But what did she mean by them? What did she intend to convey?

The Lord was not in the fire.

Suddenly, Malory became aware she was not alone, though the caretaker had left some minutes before. Turning, she saw a woman standing a few yards away from her, on the path between the graves. She was wearing a pale pink dress, a loose pale blue coat and a generously brimmed straw hat. Her face was heavy-featured, Slavic, Malory sensed. She had intensely black hair and her skin, even in the shade of her hat, was milkily pale. There was something about her men would find irresistibly attractive. This Malory knew because, whatever it was, she did not possess it herself.

'You are Malory Hollander?' The woman spoke English with a subdued but definite Russian accent.

'Have we met?' Malory asked, defensively.

'No. But I think you know who I am.'

'Pardon me, but I don't.'

Although Malory did not yet know for certain who the woman was, she strongly suspected she was Nadia Bukayeva, close confidante of Fritz Lemmer, who had killed one of Lemmer's spies in Paris to ensure he could not be arrested and interrogated. She had tried to kill Sam Twentyman as well, as Sam had several times recounted.

'Since you evidently know who I am,' Malory said coolly, 'perhaps you'd like to introduce yourself.'

'I am Nadia Bukayeva. I know a great deal about you and you probably know a little about me. I am here with a message for you and your friends: Schools Morahan and his American associates – and dear Sam, of course. We have been watching you since you arrived.'

A chill ran through Malory. How could they have been detected so easily? 'Who is *we*?'

'You know who I represent. And we know who asked you to come here. Everything is known. Everything is foreseen.'

'I have no idea what you mean.'

'I would not expect you to admit it. But, after all, your choice of

9

grave to visit gives away the game. Farngold. Dead names from thirty years ago.'

'You know something about them, Miss Bukayeva?'

'This is what I know. The man who asked you to come here is like the Farngolds. Dead.'

Malory exerted her considerable will not to react. Nadia Bukayeva was capable of telling many lies. There was no good reason to believe a single thing she said.

'Yes. Max is dead. He was killed in Marseilles on the sixth of May by Pierre Dombreux, who is not dead but with us here, in Japan. Before he died, Max revealed what he had asked Morahan to do and where you were to meet him. I was not there, but I suppose he did not give the information easily. Probably Dombreux had to torture him before he killed him. That death would not have been good. I am sorry for him. But it was his own fault.'

Still Malory said nothing. She held Nadia's gaze and tensed every muscle in her face to suppress the least sign of a reaction.

'This is the message I have for you. With Max dead, your mission here is over. There is nothing for you to do. And if you try to do anything you will be stopped. There is an NYK steamer leaving for Seattle Tuesday. You will be on it. All of you.'

'Why would I leave so soon after arriving?' Malory asked, slowing her words so that none of her alarm inflected them.

'For your health. You will be on that ship. Or we will come for you.'

'I'm not going to Seattle, Miss Bukayeva.'

'Because you do not believe me?'

'Why would I?'

'Proof, then. Here.' Nadia took an envelope from an outer pocket of her coat, stepped forward and offered it to Malory.

'What is this?'

'A photograph taken by Dombreux of Max dead. You will not believe me without, will you? So, you must have it. Take it, please.'

Reluctantly, Malory took the envelope. The flap was not sealed. She saw the border of the photograph inside. She slid it out. And gasped.

'There. That is your reason to go to Seattle. That is how it ended for Max. And that is how it will end for you. If you stay.'

10

THE PHOTOGRAPH SHOWED MAX LYING ON HIS BACK, HIS ARMS spread, his head angled to one side. There was a bullet hole in his right temple and his head was resting in a pool of blood. In the open palm of his right hand was a revolver, his fingers curled around the butt and trigger.

Malory and Sam each had a copy. Dumbstruck by the photographic evidence of Max's death, they had hardly noticed the departure of their informants – Nadia slipping away between the gravestones, Dombreux hailing a passing taxi. The proof had been supplied and the message had been delivered: abandon their mission and leave Japan as soon as practicably possible. That was Lemmer's generous offer.

Malory had hurried back to the Eastbourne Hotel, struggling to compose herself as she went. The caretaker, who had come upon her at the grave, had invited her to his hut to recover from what he had assumed was grief for the long-deceased Farngolds. She had declined, assuring him she would soon be herself again.

But there was little prospect of that. And she saw her reaction mirrored in Sam, red-eyed from his own tears. Shock, disbelief and disabling sorrow had assailed them both.

They told Morahan what had happened and adjourned to his room, where he poured stiff whiskies for all of them and heard their stories in solemn silence, staring at the photograph as they spoke.

'My God,' he said at last, 'I never imagined it would turn out like this. Max always seemed to have enough resourcefulness to see him through any challenge.'

'Dombreux said he arranged it to look like suicide,' murmured Sam. 'But he also said it was an empty house. You don't think . . . Max is still there, do you, waiting to be found?'

'We must pray not,' said Malory, her head drooping.

'They said this happened May sixth?' Morahan asked.

'Yes.'

'That was the day Lemmer and Tomura sailed from Marseilles. Their ship arrived here June twentieth. So, chances are they know what the French police have done about this. We should find out too.'

'How?'

'We'll cable Yamanaka in Paris. With Tomura out of his hair, he'll be free to get the information for us.'

Sam groaned. 'All those times I saw his plane flying back to base in one piece. It often seemed like a miracle he'd survived when so many others didn't. Some miracle, hey? He didn't survive the war by so much as a year.'

Malory grasped his hand. 'I'm sorry, Sam,' she said softly. 'Your loss is much heavier than ours.'

'What will I tell his family?'

'That he died taking risks he believed worth taking.'

'But it wasn't a clean death, was it? He wouldn't have given us away without a struggle. I don't like to think about how hard that was for him.'

'We only have their word for it Max gave us away,' said Morahan. 'It's possible they guessed what was going on after hearing we'd left Paris.'

'You reckon?'

'I reckon it's possible. Nadia and Dombreux do as they're told. It's clear now Dombreux must have been Lemmer's man all along and Nadia's as close to Lemmer as anyone. They do his bidding. Which, remember, doesn't necessarily involve telling us the truth.' Morahan glanced at his watch. 'Everett should be here soon.' He slipped the photographs into the drawer of the desk. 'Say nothing about this to him – or the others.'

'You're not going to tell them?' asked Malory in surprise.

'Not yet. We have until Tuesday at least.'

'But what can we do without Max?'

'That's what we have to decide, Malory – you, me and Sam. We're here because we chose to be. The others are here because they're paid to be. It's for us to say whether we pull out or go on.'

'I'd like to go on,' said Sam. 'Otherwise Max died for nothing.'

'With Lemmer and Tomura on our tail,' said Morahan, 'we could easily finish up dying for nothing ourselves.'

'*How* would we go on?' Malory pressed.

'There's a lead I haven't mentioned to you. Everett's been following it up for me.'

'What kind of lead?'

'Jack Farngold's been a sailor most of his life. He's skippered vessels for Jardine Matheson all over the Far East. A lot of people in the shipping world would know him – crew and owners. So, while we were in San Francisco, I reckoned it was worth asking a few questions round the docks. Everett had been given the names of some people to talk to by his contacts in New York, a few of them Japanese. Anyhow, the sum of it was that Farngold never made many friends, but one of them is the woman who runs a notorious *chabuya* here in Yokohama.'

'What's a *chabuya* when it's at home?' asked Sam.

'Restaurant, teahouse, bar, dance-hall, gambling den, brothel. Any and all of those. There are dozens of them in the city. They cater mostly for foreigners. Tarazumi Yoshiko runs one of the older established *chabuya*s: the Honey Bee. She met Jack Farngold when he went there to bail out members of his crew who couldn't pay their debts. Over the years, they struck up some kind of friendship. The word is that if anyone knows how to find Jack Farngold it's Tarazumi Yoshiko. I sent Everett to see her because he fixed an introduction for himself with an acquaintance of hers in San Francisco, who told him she speaks serviceable English.'

'What will he have told her?' asked Malory.

'That James Maxted, son of Sir Henry, wants to speak to Jack Farngold.'

13

'But Max—' Sam cut short his objection. It hardly needed spelling out.

'I'll decide what to do when we hear how far Everett got with her. Their little tea-time tête-à-tête had to be agreed in advance with her assistant. These things have to be handled delicately here. I'd hoped to have some progress to report to Max' – Morahan's voice dropped – 'when he arrived.'

It was Sam who broke the silence that followed. 'Isn't Jack Farngold locked up in a lunatic asylum?'

'Maybe. Maybe not. But, in Kuroda's report to Marquess Saionji, Kuroda said he couldn't confirm Farngold's current whereabouts. So, he may be on the loose. And Tarazumi Yoshiko may know where he is. It's a long shot, I admit, but—'

The knock at the door was only just loud enough to be heard. Sam and Malory both looked at Morahan, who signalled for them to be calm.

'Remember,' he whispered, 'not a word about Max. Unless and until I deem it necessary.'

They nodded and Morahan stepped across to open the door.

Lewis Everett entered smiling, as usual. He looked his normal relaxed and confident self. It appeared his visit to the Honey Bee had been a success, though he might well have carried himself in much the same way even if it had not been.

'Someone died?' he remarked casually, noting their subdued expressions.

Sam flinched, but fortunately Everett was looking at Malory, whose face gave nothing away. Sam admired her more in that moment than ever.

'If it's Wilson, we should break out the champagne.'

Everett had recorded his loathing of President Wilson – 'puritanical sonofabitch' – on more than one occasion. Morahan sighed in a way that implied impatience and said, 'How'd you get on at the Honey Bee?'

'Well, I sure wasn't stung like most of their customers. It's a high-class clap-house, if you'll pardon my French, Malory. As for Tarazumi-san, she ain't exactly what you'd call garrulous. I wouldn't

14

have got a word out of her but for the intro from friend Higashida in Little Osaka, San Fran. And you'd never have heard of Higashida, Schools, but for my New York connections.'

'I'm impressed, Lew, OK? But there's no bonus clause in your contract.'

'Maybe there should be.'

'Maybe you should just get on and tell us what you found out.'

'All right.' Everett flung himself into an armchair and lit a cigarette. 'The Tarazumi dame didn't deny knowing Captain Jack, even though she didn't exactly admit it either. She claimed she couldn't understand everything I said, although her grasp of English seemed pretty damn good to me. Eventually, after a lot of tea-sipping and brow-beetling, during which I lost all feeling in my legs thanks to kneeling on her damn mats, she said it was *possible* she could get a message to him.'

'How did you leave matters?'

'I – we – call round tomorrow afternoon for news.'

'Did you mention the report we'd had that Farngold was being held in a lunatic asylum?'

'I hinted at it.'

'And?'

'She said, "I am sure Farngold-san is where he wants to be."' Everett shrugged. 'You can make what you like of that. One thing, though.'

'What?'

'I was followed part of the way to the Honey Bee. Japanese and not bad at the job, but not quite good enough. I lost him, obviously, but considering no one's supposed to know we're here . . .'

'We'll have to take extra precautions.'

'How would they have got on to us so quickly, Schools?'

'I don't know. I hope none of the team has spoken out of turn.'

'You know us better than that. Maybe Max has given himself away.'

'And maybe you'd like to take that back,' snapped Sam, suddenly angry.

15

Everett looked at him in surprise. 'No need to be so prickly, Sam. We all make mistakes.'

'It's true,' Morahan said, shooting a warning glance at Sam. 'We shouldn't jump to conclusions. I told you the people we're up against are well resourced, Lew. Maybe this proves it. There's nothing we can do but tread carefully. We'll go visit Madam Tarazumi tomorrow and see what she has for us.'

'No word from Max yet, then?' said Everett, who was still eyeing Sam curiously.

'No,' said Morahan. 'No word.'

A CABLE WAS DESPATCHED TO YAMANAKA AT THE HOTEL BRISTOL IN Paris, where Morahan judged he would still be, despite the formal end of the peace conference. Such an event was bound to leave a lot of clearing up to be done in its wake, certainly enough to keep Yamanaka busy for a while yet. PLEASE CONFIRM REPORT OF DEATH OF JAMES MAXTED MARSEILLES MAY SIXTH was the simple but desperate message.

Malory went to the NYK offices to book eight berths on the *Iyo-maru*, due to sail for Seattle on Tuesday. Morahan's reasoning was that they should at least be seen to be complying with Lemmer's demands even if they had no intention of doing so. As it turned out, eight berths had already been reserved in Morahan's name. It had been made as easy as possible for them to accept defeat.

But the contemplation of defeat only sharpened Sam's anguish. Considering the number of fine and noble pilots he had seen take off and never return during the war, he was dismayed by the force of his reaction to the news of Max's death.

'Give me something to do, Schools,' he pleaded. 'I'll go mad just sitting around here.'

Fortunately, Morahan did have a task for him. 'I want you and Malory to take Ward, Duffy, Monteith and Djabsu to Kamakura tomorrow. It's an easy trip on the train. Highly recommended for sight-seeing, I'm told. Shrines, temples, a giant Buddha: the full works. Make a day of it.'

'I'm not in the mood for sight-seeing.'

'If there's a tail on us, Sam, as there evidently is, we should lead them astray. While you're wandering around Kamakura, towing one or more of Tomura's people on an invisible line, Everett and I will have less to worry about when we pay a call on Madam Tarazumi. OK?'

Sunday was as hot and sunny as Saturday had been. The sights – and the beaches – of Kamakura had lured many Tokyoites out from the city. Anyone delegated to follow Sam and his companions through the crowds had his sympathy. Only Djabsu and Monteith gave any sign of enjoying the excursion, Djabsu because he took a child-like pleasure in seaside attractions, however alien they might be, and Monteith because of the prospect of seeing Japanese women taking a dip in the ocean. Duffy and Ward kept their thoughts to themselves, though well aware they were serving as decoys. Whatever came with the job was all in a day's work to them.

Aside from strolling on the waterfront, they visited a few Shinto shrines and Buddhist temples, which, in a different frame of mind and on another day, Sam knew he would have found fascinating. Japan, he already realized, was like nowhere else he had ever been. But too much had travelled with him to be cast aside. The splendour of the place was lost on him.

Even standing before the Great Buddha, all fifty bronze feet of him, up in the woods above the shore, failed to move Sam. Malory was clearly appalled when Djabsu scrambled up on to the Buddha's left knee, but to Sam this and everything else that occurred passed by him beyond a gauze curtain. He saw it, but could not engage with it.

'Cheer up, buddy, for Pete's sake,' Monteith said to him at one point. 'Or if not for his, then Buddha's.'

But Sam did not cheer up. And knowing he could not explain why he was so downcast only made it worse. The one meagre consolation he could find was to hope that Morahan would have something promising to report when they returned to Yokohama.

The Honey Bee was located on the other side of the Bluff, over-looking Mississippi Bay. Its boundary wall was high and plain, but its front door was decorated with a luridly painted beehive and the young woman who greeted Morahan and Everett was clearly no demure miss. It was doubtful if she was even Japanese.

A few customers lingered in the main salon with attentive hostesses. A man of Scandinavian appearance was playing a ballad very slowly on an out-of-tune piano. Morahan and Everett were required to wait while Madam Tarazumi prepared herself to receive them.

In his pocket Morahan had the reply from Yamanaka, delivered to him as he was leaving the Eastbourne. WILL INVESTIGATE AND REPORT SOONEST. He would do his best, Morahan knew.

He had detected no sign of a tail. Perhaps whoever had tried to follow Everett the previous day was panting round Kamakura to no purpose. The thought gave him some meagre satisfaction.

The call came after they had toyed with bowls of green tea for twenty minutes or so. They were fetched by an English-speaking assistant, who led them up to Madam Tarazumi's sitting room.

It was tatami-matted and entirely Japanese in style, with panels thrown open to admit as much of a cooling breeze as there was. A balcony gave the proprietress of the Honey Bee an imposing view of the bay, on which she had chosen to turn her back.

She was an elegant, kimono-clad figure, of some age between forty and sixty, carefully made up and immaculately coiffured. She spoke English more than adequately, but very slowly, as if weighing every word – as she well might have been. Her expression gave nothing away.

Morahan treated her to several respectful bows as Everett introduced him, without any discernible effect on her demeanour. More tea was served. They knelt either side of a low table. The air, even when it moved, was damp with heat. Morahan felt like a giant in a doll's house – and about as comfortable.

'Where is James Maxted?' was Madam Tarazumi's opening question.

'He is on his way,' Morahan replied.

'When will he arrive?'

'When can Jack Farngold see him?'

19

Madam Tarazumi pursed her lips. 'What are you to James Maxted?'

'Friends. Advisors. Representatives.'

'What do you know about Farngold-san?'

'That he's an enemy of Count Tomura Iwazu. That his sister was married to the Count. That he blames the Count for his father's death and probably his sister's too.'

'Only a fool makes an enemy of Count Tomura.'

'We can't always choose our enemies.'

'Have you spoken to Jack Farngold since we met yesterday, Tarazumi-san?' asked Everett.

She did not answer directly. In fact, she said nothing at all for fully half a minute while she scrutinized each of them in turn. Then: 'What kind of women do you like?'

If she had hoped to embarrass them she had mistaken their character. 'The young and willing kind,' Everett replied with a laugh.

Madam Tarazumi did not laugh. 'You prefer Russian to Japanese? I have Russian women here. Born in the nobility. They came to Japan after the Revolution. Some men like their ways. But you cannot trust them. They are greedy for their old life. They are . . . ruthless.'

Morahan had the distinct impression she was talking now about one Russian woman in particular. 'Have you ever employed a woman called Nadia Bukayeva, Tarazumi-san?' he asked.

'Perhaps. I do not remember their names.'

That struck Morahan as highly unlikely. 'But you'd recognize her – if she'd worked for you – if you saw her again, here in Yokohama?'

'I see many things that I do not speak of. I see you before me. I will never speak of that.'

'Jack Farngold is a friend of yours?'

'I trust Farngold-san. He trusts me.'

'Sounds pretty much like friendship to me,' said Everett.

Madam Tarazumi glanced expressionlessly at him, then sipped her tea and said, 'Will James Maxted be here tomorrow?'

'Yes,' said Morahan, sensing the lie needed to be told if they were to have any chance of meeting Jack Farngold.

'Near Shimbashi station, in Tokyo, there is a bicycle repair shop run by a man called Sakashita. He hangs a red bicycle outside when it is open. Above the shop is a room. He will let you go up to it if you show him this.' She handed Morahan a slip of paper with Japanese writing on it. He bowed awkwardly in thanks. 'Wait in the room after nightfall tomorrow. Sakashita will be open late.'

'Jack Farngold will come to us there?'

'If he chooses. If you are not there – you and James Maxted – you will not see Farngold-san.'

'We'll be there,' said Morahan.

'You *and* James Maxted?'

Morahan nodded. 'Yes.'

'Kind of risky, wasn't that, Schools?' said Everett as they walked away from the Honey Bee. 'You can't be sure Max is going to join us in time to keep our appointment with Farngold.'

'Jack Farngold doesn't know what Max looks like. If he doesn't arrive between now and tomorrow night, we'll take Sam in his place.'

'Sam isn't going to convince anyone he's the son of an English lord.'

'Sir Henry wasn't a lord. Besides, once we're in the same room as Jack Farngold, I back myself to talk him into levelling with us.'

Everett digested the answer for a few moments, then said, 'You know Max and I don't, but is this really how he'd want you to play it, Schools?'

'Yes. I think it is.'

Everett shrugged. 'OK. Well, you're the boss.'

And so he was. For the time being, at least.

ANOTHER CABLE FROM YAMANAKA EISAKU WAS WAITING FOR Morahan at the Eastbourne. CANNOT CONFIRM DEATH JAMES MAXTED MARSEILLES MAY SIXTH BUT UNIDENTIFIED MALE BODY FOUND IN BURNED HOUSE SAME DATE. He decided to disclose the contents only to Malory, fearing how Sam might react to the possibility that Max's corpse had been incinerated.

'You think that's how Dombreux covered his tracks?' Malory asked.

'Could well be. Maybe we should ask Yamanaka to go down to Marseilles and see what he can find out.'

'Surely there isn't time for him to travel there and learn anything valuable before we're supposed to board the *Iyo-maru*.'

'No. There isn't.'

'Which leaves you meeting Jack Farngold tomorrow under false pretences.'

'However you cut it, we're here to help him. He should appreciate that.'

'Will you tell him Max is dead?'

'I'm not sure what I'll tell him. I'm not sure what kind of man he is.'

'And Everett and the others? Will you tell them?'

'Not before I have to.'

'Will you take Sam along?'

'Oh yes. He looks the right age to be Max and if Farngold's watching out for us, that could be crucial.'

'So, it'll be you, Everett and Sam?'

'No. I'll take Duffy as well. I'll need someone to cover our backs.'

'Are you worried this might be some kind of trap?'

'Hard to see how. They already have us where they want us. But it could be a trap for Farngold. And I don't want us to spring it. As for worried, you bet I am. This wasn't how it was supposed to be.'

Sam was glad when he heard he would be one of the party rendez-vousing with Jack Farngold. It would give him what he had asked for: something to do. He was less glad when Morahan insisted he visit the hotel barber for a haircut and buy a white linen suit to make him look 'better bred'. Performing as a stand-in for Max only sharp-ened his sense of loss, grateful though he was for the role allotted to him. Memories of all those narrow escapes from the jaws of death Max had pulled off in the war filled Sam's mind. If only he could have done it again.

Morahan and Sam left a couple of hours before Everett and Duffy, with a plan in place to meet at Shimbashi station. Morahan led Sam through a maze of streets in Yokohama's Chinatown that evidently satisfied him they were not being followed before they made for the station and caught the next train to Tokyo.

Tokyo Central was seething with Japanese workers heading home at the end of the day, a surging, sweating mass of humanity that, to Sam's amazement, left Liverpool Street in the rush hour looking quiet by comparison. The crowds were another safeguard against being followed, of course, although even Sam, no more than average height by English standards, towered above most of the people around him, which left Morahan resembling a sunflower among daisies.

Trams were loading and disgorging passengers outside the station. Beyond lay European-style red-brick office buildings, park-land and thicker woodland than Sam would have expected to see in the centre of Tokyo. 'That'll be the Imperial Palace,' said Morahan. 'Follow me.'

They walked as far as the moat separating the palace from the city, though the palace itself remained screened by trees. The heat was far more oppressive than in Yokohama, the atmosphere damp and heavy, crows cawing lazily, trams filled to overflowing rattling by at intervals.

'We're both a long way from home, Sam,' said Morahan, drawing on a cigarette. 'About as far as we can be, if it comes to it.'

'Are you really going to go on without Max, Schools?'

'That's my intention. But the risks are greater than ever. You understand that, don't you?'

'Yes. I do.'

'See that building along there – the one with the policeman out front?' Morahan pointed to an imposing pile just past a kink in the moat.

Sam squinted through the glare towards it. He saw a group of men in morning suits and top hats exit the building, saluted by the policemen, and climb into waiting cars. 'What about it?'

'That should be the Home Ministry, if I've remembered Yamanaka's directions right.'

'Yamanaka?'

'I had a word with him before I left Paris. Contacts can be the difference between life and death in a strange city, Sam, so take note. Yamanaka's elder brother, name of Fumiko, is some kind of Home Ministry bigwig. We can turn to him for help if we need it. He'll have had a letter from Eisaku by now, assuring him we're owed a lot of favours by the Yamanaka family.'

'Why are you telling me this?'

'Because we're in enemy territory. There's no knowing what might happen.'

They walked south-west along the line of the moat as far as the Imperial Hotel, a slice of Paris to Sam's eyes, then headed for the elevated railway line and followed it through a noisy, crowded shopping district to Shimbashi station, where, amid the swirling mobs and rumbling trains, they found Everett and Duffy waiting.

'I propose an early supper, gentlemen,' said Morahan. There were no objections.

Supper was taken in the cramped booth of a noodle restaurant virtually underneath the railway line. Afterwards they adjourned to a café, where the demeanour of the waitresses suggested some of the establishment's services were not listed on the menu. There they drank coffee while darkness fell over Tokyo.

When they left, the lanterns were lit outside the numerous eateries and drinking dens of the neighbourhood. This was Tokyo as Sam had imagined it: the sing-song alien language; the kimono-clad women with their glossy hair and child-like faces; the rickshaws and bicycles weaving between the pedestrians; the clacking of wooden sandals on the pavements; the fluttering of gigantic moths in the humid air.

It took them about half an hour to find Sakashita's shop, with the red bicycle suspended outside and Sakashita working on repairs at a small bench by the dim light of an electric lamp, surrounded by bicycles in various stages of dismantlement and reassembly.

At this point Duffy drifted away across the street, there to keep watch, on Morahan's instructions, for any kind of dangerous development. Sam and Everett followed Morahan into the shop. Sakashita, a thin, wizened little man with a nervous smile, looked up at their approach and greeted them in Japanese.

'Mr Sakashita?' asked Morahan.

'*Hai.*' This was one of about three words of Japanese Sam had so far learnt.

'Madam Tarazumi sent us.' Morahan handed Sakashita the note.

It appeared to require lengthy study despite the brevity of its contents. Sakashita twirled a tiny screwdriver in his fingers as he read the message. As he did so, he kept glancing at Sam in a far from reassuring fashion.

Eventually, he laid the screwdriver and note aside, stood up and moved round the edge of the shop to a far corner, where he pulled back a curtain to reveal a steep and narrow flight of steps. There

25

was no handrail, only a rope stiffened with wooden rings. He pointed up the steps and said something in Japanese.

'Let's go up and take a look-see,' said Morahan.

THE FLOOR DIRECTLY ABOVE THE SHOP WAS IN DARKNESS, BUT there were a couple of green-shaded electric lamps lighting the floor above that, little more than an attic in effect, with a sloping ceiling and small paper-panel dormer windows. Furnishings were few, comprising a couple of battered cabinets and some dusty tatami mats. A curtain was drawn across the other end of the room, which was in deep shadow.

'We can disport ourselves on the chaise longue until Farngold shows up,' quipped Everett.

Morahan moved to one of the windows, slid open the panel and glanced down into the street. 'Everything normal out there,' he announced.

'Al in sight?'

'No.'

'I told you he was good. Don't worry. He'll have seen you.'

'How will he warn us if there's trouble?' asked Sam.

'A pebble at the window,' said Everett. 'He has a pitcher's arm.'

'So, we just—' Sam broke off. They all stood stock still. A sound – a groan – had come from the curtained-off part of the room.

Morahan padded silently across to the curtain and pulled it back. The other two caught up with him and gasped at what they saw.

A thin futon had been spread on the floor beneath a bamboo wall-hanging. On the futon, wrapped in a threadbare green kimono, lay a European man, grey-haired and bearded, his face haggard and marked with scars and bruises. His eyes were open but unfocused, his gaze drifting. His mouth was open, his lips encrusted with dried spittle. He looked to Sam to be a man of sixty or more. On the street he could have been taken for a vagrant, insensible with drink. But there was no smell of alcohol on him, only stale sweat and a strange chemical odour.

'Is that . . . Jack Farngold?'

'Could be, Sam,' said Morahan. 'In which case friend Sakashita has some questions to answer, because this man didn't climb up here without help.' He crouched beside the occupant of the futon and patted his cheek. 'Hey, feller, can you hear me?'

The eyes moved woozily in Morahan's direction, but no words came.

'Jack Farngold?'

Sam thought he saw some reaction in the man's face. His lips quivered. He was surely trying to speak.

'Are you Jack Farngold?'

The mouth wavered. The gaze wandered.

'He is Jack Farngold,' said Everett suddenly. Sam heard the click of a gun being cocked and turned to see that Everett had retreated to the centre of the room, from where he was training his revolver on them. 'So I'm told.'

'What in hell are you doing?' Morahan stood up and glared at Everett.

'Sorry, Schools, but I don't work for you. I never did.'

Sam saw by the heave of Morahan's chest how shocked and angry he was. 'Whose payroll *are* you on then, Lew?'

'Lemmer's. Seems he guessed you'd be the man Sir Henry asked to organize this little rescue party. So, he sent one of his agents to New York to offer attractive terms to the kind of people you'd be likely to use, me included. Looked like it wasn't going to happen when Sir Henry was rubbed out, but then Max turned up at your end and here we are. Like I say, I'm sorry. Herr Lemmer just pays too damn well.'

'The lead you picked up in San Francisco . . .'

'Bait, Schools. Which you swallowed.'

'Who's in this with you?'

'Al and Howie. Ward and Djabsu are on your side, for all the

28

good it'll do you. We never foresaw the Chicago diversion, I'll give you that.'

'And Farngold? What's been done to him?'

'How the hell should I know? He looks drugged to me. They've had him over a year. Forced him to sign a confession to God knows what crimes. Crimes they're going to lay at your door as well. Along with one other. Stand away from him.'

Morahan took a single long stride away from Farngold – and closer to Everett. Sam edged back.

'It's time to put the old salt out of his misery.'

Everett aimed the gun and fired. Sam flung himself in shock against the wall. Two more shots followed. A smell of cordite filled the air. And blood oozed from the wounds in Farngold's chest. A sound came from his throat, choking and guttural. Then his head lolled to one side and he was silent.

Morahan made a move towards Everett, but stopped short when the gun swung back in his direction. 'Don't do it, Schools. I don't want to kill you. They mean to take you alive. And while there's life, etcetera.'

'I'll make you pay for this, Lew.'

'I've already been paid. And you and I are never going to meet again. The police will be here any minute. They'll only have been waiting to hear the shots. You and Sam are going to be arrested for the murder of Jack Farngold – among other things.'

'They'll never believe we killed him when you're holding the only gun that's been fired.'

'Yes they will. They have their instructions too. This is a Kempeitai operation. Know who they are? Japanese Secret Police. Not nice people. Not nice people at all.'

There was a sound from the window of cars drawing up outside, followed by a slamming of doors and a jabber of voices.

'Here they come. Nearly time for our goodbyes.'

It was only a fleeting glance Everett cast towards the window, but it was enough for Morahan. He lunged forward and felled Everett with the force of his attack. The gun went off, the bullet splintering the bamboo on the wall behind Sam. The two men crashed to the floor. In a second, Morahan had a grip on Everett's gun-arm and they were wrestling for control.

In the same second, there came the sound of heavily shod men running up the stairs. Sam took a step towards Morahan and Everett, intending to intervene in the struggle, but Morahan caught his eye as Everett pushed his head back with the heel of his hand and the gun waggled dangerously between them.

'Get out, Sam,' Morahan shouted. 'Save Malory.'

But there seemed nowhere for Sam to go. The shadow of the first man up the stairs loomed into view ahead of him. Then Sam noticed the bullet hole in the bamboo. He could recall no sound of impact with the wall behind it. He tore the bamboo aside. It screened a paper-panel gable window. The bullet had gone straight through.

Sam glanced round at a shout from the head of the stairs. '*Tomare!*' Two burly policemen were in the room. Morahan and Everett were still grappling on the floor. There was no time to wonder or calculate. There was time only to act.

Sam flung himself at the window. The paper panels and flimsy wooden bars gave way. He was through it and falling.

Then he struck the roof of a lower building next door. His momentum carried him in a crazy slide down the roof and over the eave. His flailing hand caught a chain suspended from the corner of the eave that arrested his fall, aided by the lid of a water-butt into which the chain fed.

There were shouts from behind and above him. He knew it could not be long before he was pursued. He also knew Morahan was right: Malory was in as much danger as they were. He had to get to Yokohama.

He was in a courtyard to the rear of the building next to Sakashita's shop. There were ramshackle structures visible in the gloom, a pond and a low-growing tree. More buildings lay beyond, with lights showing. He headed towards them, following his instincts in the absence of any other guide. Flight was his sole recourse.

He wrenched open a sliding door and entered what looked like someone's home. A woman rounded a corner and cried out in alarm. He ran through a couple of rooms, blundering past a goggle-eyed old lady. He could not grasp the internal layout of such a house. He could only aim to hold his course.

Another door, stouter than the others, yielded to his tug. Then he was out in the next street, where lanterns blazed and crowds milled. He plunged in amongst them, trying to remember the direction of the station.

Sam bitterly regretted abandoning Morahan, but he knew there was no one better equipped to look after himself. According to Everett, Morahan would be taken alive, which was a blessing to cling to. Sam did not understand the entirety of the trap they had walked into, but Jack Farngold's death would be blamed on them. That much seemed clear. And Malory would surely be arrested, along with Ward and Djabsu, as their accomplices. Still, it was likely that would only be done after confirmation had been received in Yokohama that the operation in Tokyo had gone according to plan. If Sam could warn them of what was afoot—

He stumbled, believing at first he had been jostled by another pedestrian. But then he realized how light-headed he felt. Raising a hand to his brow, he winced at a stab of pain and felt blood on his fingers. He must have hit his head at some point during his escape, perhaps when he was descending from the roof. He could not recall the exact sequence of events. Everything had happened so quickly.

Ahead, to his relief, he saw the lights of Shimbashi station and staggered in among the throng. He bought a ticket for Yokohama, needing only to state his destination and dole out coins until the clerk signalled enough. Then he climbed to the platform.

The light-headedness was growing worse. There was a sharp pain now, whether he touched the wound or not. The wary glances other people on the platform were giving him suggested he was not a pretty sight.

A train drew in and he clambered aboard. It was only when he had sat down that he wondered whether he could rely on all south-bound trains going to Yokohama. '*Sumimasen*,' he said to the man sitting opposite him, deploying one of his very few words of Japanese. 'We go . . . Yokohama?'

'Yokohama?' The man shook his head. 'Kofu.'

Wherever Kofu was, it was evidently not to be reached via Yokohama. The train had only just jolted into motion. There was still time for Sam to jump off. He leapt to his feet.

That was when the pain hit him like a fist. And he went down into darkness.

MALORY DINED ALONE AND FRETFULLY AT THE EASTBOURNE Hotel. She could only pin her hopes, as Schools was pinning his, on the rendezvous with Jack Farngold. What worried her most was how little they knew. They had relied on Max to tell them more when he arrived. But now he would not be arriving. Jack Farngold was merely a name to them.

It was all very well to declare their determination to carry on. Malory had recoiled from the notion of retreat. But Everett and the others did not know Max was dead. Sooner or later, they would have to be told. And then . . .

'Message for you, Miss Hollander,' interrupted the bellboy, a Portuguese youth called João who had displayed a consistent eagerness to please her throughout her stay. 'From a Meester Monteith.'

'*Obrigado, João.*' Expressing her thanks in Portuguese delighted him mightily and he grinned widely.

Since the note was written on Eastbourne Hotel headed paper, it was hard to understand why Monteith had not come into the dining room and simply spoken to her, though the contents hinted at special circumstances.

Malory – Please meet me out front immediately you get this. I need to see you very urgently. Howie

'Where is the gentleman now?' Malory asked, considering whether she should send João to fetch him.

'The street. I theenk.'

'Very well, thank you. That's all.'

As João capered off, Malory took a sip of her wine, then rose and went to find out what Monteith could possibly want.

He was standing in the shadow of one of the bushes that flanked the entrance to the hotel, smoking one of his cheap cigars. She had never liked their scent. She was not sure she liked the smoker any more than the cigar, if it came to that. Monteith was the sort of smooth-talking, apparently good-humoured man she had often found to be at heart faithless and deceitful. But Schools had not chosen him for his gentlemanly qualities. She was aware of that.

'Can we take a ride, Malory?' he said at once.

'A ride where?'

'It doesn't matter. Away from here would be healthy.'

'Healthy?'

'Let's get a cab.'

He grasped her elbow and piloted her towards the first of several taxis parked in front of the hotel. 'What's this about, Howie?'

'I'll explain as we go.'

'You'll have to explain now.' Malory pulled up. 'I'm not going anywhere unless I know why.'

Monteith frowned at her in the lamplight. 'I'm trying to help you, God damn it. There isn't much time.'

'Why isn't there?'

'Because— Will you just trust me, Malory? This once?'

The sincerity of his tone moved her. Something was clearly wrong. But it seemed she would have to board the taxi to find out what it was. 'All right. But I won't be going far if you don't spell out what's going on.'

Taking that for as much in the way of consent as he was likely to get, Monteith virtually manhandled her into the taxi and instructed the driver to head 'towards' – rather than to, Malory noted – Yokohama station.

'Don't get off there,' Monteith advised her in an undertone as the

taxi started away. 'Have him take you on to the next station north
– Kanagawa.'

'What on earth are you talking about?'

'I'll be getting out soon, so we'd better keep this snappy. It's over,
Malory. Truth is, it was over before it started. We sold you and
Schools out before you even reached New York. Lemmer's been in
control all the way along.'

'*What?*'

'The show closes tonight. The meeting with Farngold was a trap.
Schools and Sam will already have been arrested. The police will be
picking up Grover and Gazda right around now. Then they'll come
for you. I don't know the charges and it doesn't really matter anyway.
They'll stick. You can be sure of that.'

'Are you insane?' But Malory could see the truth written in the
shadows on Monteith's face. He had never been saner. 'You gave us
away?'

'We gave nothing. We were bought in advance. Lemmer foresaw
this whole operation. You were never going to achieve a damn thing.
Even if Max had got here alive. Which we know he isn't going to,
don't we? Now listen. You probably think I'm the lowest form of life
there is, but it's lucky for you I'm not. And that Schools didn't ask
me along on the trip to Tokyo. He can cope with what's coming his
way. Maybe he'll strike a deal with them. I hope so. But surren-
dering a lady like you to the Japanese Secret Police doesn't sit well
with my conscience. So, I'm giving you a chance. How much of a
chance I don't know. But you said you know the country, so maybe
you can get clean away. I can't risk helping you any more than this.'
Monteith stretched forward and tapped the driver on the shoulder.
'Stop here, pal. I'm getting out. *Tomare! Koko.*'

Malory was too horrified to react. Schools and Sam under arrest;
Ward and Djabsu likewise. And everything anticipated and orchestrated by Lemmer. He had won. And they had lost.

'We could all have gone home on the *Iyo-maru* and no harm done,
but you and Sam and Schools between you wouldn't let it rest,
would you?' The taxi jerked to a halt and Monteith jumped out. He
glanced back at her and touched his hat. 'Good luck, Malory.'

35

He slammed the door and the taxi pulled away. Malory's breaths came in shallow draughts. Her heart was pounding. What was going to happen to Schools and Sam and the other two? What could she do to help them and to save herself? Her mind threw back no answer, only doubts and desperation. *What could she do?*

She looked out of the rear window at Monteith's retreating figure. She should be grateful, she knew, for the atom of decency that had prompted him to give her a chance of escape. But all she felt was fear and loathing. The men they had trusted had betrayed them. And their enemy had prepared this fate for them.

She leant forward. 'Take me to Kanagawa station,' she said to the driver. '*Kanagawa-eki.*'

'No Yokohama?'

'No. Kanagawa.'

Then she leant back and tried to force herself to think. Max was dead. The fact that Monteith had taken pity on her meant she had to believe him about the comprehensiveness of their defeat. There might be some way for her to leave the country. Her passport was in her room at the Eastbourne, but travelling under her real name was hardly feasible anyway. Besides, her instinct was to stay and do what she could for Schools and Sam. It was the same instinct that had landed them all in so much trouble. But it was the instinct she was bound to live by.

To survive, if not to escape, she needed an ally. That very day, Morahan had told her where she might find one. Yamanaka Eisaku's elder brother, Fumiko, was an official in the Japanese Home Ministry.

But how was she to contact the elder Yamanaka? It was not likely he would still be at his desk at such an hour. She had to find shelter – somewhere to hide – until morning. No hotel would take her in without requesting sight of a passport. She could hardly pretend to be Japanese and they would be bound to report an undocumented foreigner, especially a woman, to the local police station.

Where could she go, then? Where could she turn?

There was only one answer. In other circumstances, the irony of it might have induced a smile. But there was nothing for her to smile about now – nothing at all.

36

MORAHAN HAD NO IDEA WHERE IN TOKYO HE WAS. THE VAN THAT had taken him to the building had been blacked out and he had been bundled down a narrow flight of steps to a basement entrance before he could take any note of his surroundings. His guess was that he was in the headquarters of the secret police Everett had mentioned: the Kempeitai.

The organization clearly did not believe in supplying comfortable accommodation for those they detained. He had been placed in a cage in the middle of a dank, bare, ill-lit chamber, which he shared now with Ward and Djabsu, who had been seized in Yokohama.

They were still enraged by the treachery of Everett, Duffy and Monteith. 'I kills them,' was Djabsu's simple assertion. 'I kills them slow.' Morahan's own anger had given way to self-reproach. He had been taken in completely and he had withheld from his companions the news of Max's death. Ward assured him this was a small matter compared with the deceit practised by the others. 'We've been shafted, Schools,' he said. 'And not by you.'

Morahan took some small comfort from Sam's escape and the possibility that Malory too had slipped through the net. Ward and Djabsu had seen nothing of her, although it was hard to imagine how she might have eluded the police. Sam surely could not have made it to Yokohama in time to render her any assistance. She might be in custody elsewhere, of course, meriting softer treatment as a woman. There were other less pleasant possibilities Morahan tried not to dwell on. He could only trust to her oft-demonstrated resourcefulness.

His biggest regret, aside from walking straight into a trap, was that he had not managed to wrench the gun out of Everett's hand and put a bullet through his head before the police pulled them apart. If he ever regained his freedom, he would track Everett down and finish the job. He made that a solemn promise to himself.

Where Malory might have gone, or Sam for that matter, he had no idea. He had no idea about far too much, in fact, including the exact nature of the trap Lemmer had prepared for them. Everett had spoken of charges, but what would they be?

The answer promised to become clear when the door of the chamber opened and two guards carrying rifles came in, followed by a young, upright, hard-faced man in military uniform – Kempeitai, Morahan assumed. He had no knowledge of the Kempeitai. But he suspected that if he did he would be even more worried than he was.

The young officer walked slowly across to the cage and stared in at them, his arms folded behind his back. His expression was calm but contemptuous. He did not look like a man from whom much mercy was to be expected.

'I am Captain Mikanagi of the Tokubetsu Koto Kempeitai.' He slipped their passports out of the pocket of his tunic and opened them. 'You will answer your names. Thomas James Morahan?'

'I'm Morahan.'

'Grover Francis Ward?'

Ward raised his hand.

'Gazda De . . . jabsu?'

Djabsu grunted.

'Why are you holding us?' Morahan demanded.

Mikanagi gave no immediate answer. He carefully replaced the passports in his pocket, then said, 'Where are Samuel Twentyman and Malory Hollander?'

Morahan had to stop himself smiling at this confirmation that Sam and Malory were still at liberty. Before he could speak, Ward said, 'In a better hotel than this one, I hope.'

Mikanagi's mouth twitched. He did not appear to be a connoisseur of sarcasm. 'It will be better for you if you cooperate.'

'Why are you holding us?' repeated Morahan.

'The man you murdered, Jack Farngold, confessed to us he was part of a plot to assassinate Prime Minister Hara. You were his accomplices. We allowed him to meet you to find out whose orders you were acting on. But, when you realized he was not loyal to you, you killed him. You would have killed Lewis Everett also if the police had not stopped you.'

'This is bullshit,' pronounced Ward, accurately enough.

'It was Everett who killed Farngold,' said Morahan. 'The bullets were fired from his gun.'

'His gun? Your gun?' Mikanagi shook his head. 'It does not matter. Everett and Duffy and Monteith will swear to everything I have said.'

'How exactly will they swear we planned to assassinate the Prime Minister?'

'You sent Farngold here to watch Hara-san's movements. He was to tell you where and when to strike.'

'And why should we want to kill Hara?'

'You will tell me, Morahan. You are American. Perhaps your government paid you to do this. Perhaps they fear us. Perhaps they think we will be their enemy one day and want to weaken us.'

'We're not working for the American government and you know it.'

'You will admit you are before we are finished with you.'

'Everett, Duffy and Monteith. What's happening to them?'

'They have helped us. Therefore we will help them.'

'Why not ask them who paid us?'

'They do not know. They say you, Morahan, organized everything. These two will say the same soon. And you will confess the truth soon also.'

'I'd tell you the truth, but somehow I doubt it would satisfy you.'

'We're American citizens,' said Ward. 'We demand to see someone from the US Embassy. You can't hold us without consular access.'

Mikanagi almost smiled as he looked at Ward. 'There will be no
. . . consular access. We operate under the Special Higher Law. Our
powers of arrest, detention and interrogation are unlimited when an
act hostile to the Emperor is committed – such as a conspiracy to
assassinate the leader of His Imperial Majesty's government.'

Djabsu, who had said nothing so far, chose that moment to
declare his feelings, by sending a well-directed jet of spittle through
the bars of the cage on to the glistening toecap of Mikanagi's left
boot.

One of the guards raised his rifle and stepped forward, but
Mikanagi gestured for him to stay where he was. 'Thank you,' he
said. 'Your insolence will make me a better interrogator. Our
methods ensure cooperation, sooner or later.' He glared at Morahan,
whom he seemed to hold responsible for Djabsu's behaviour. 'Make
it later, please. I would like that.'

'We know nothing of a plot to assassinate the Prime Minister,
Captain Mikanagi,' said Morahan. 'You know that, I'm sure. Your
people have had Jack Farngold killed to protect Count Tomura.
And we're to be blamed for it while some accusation's put together
to be thrown at the American government. That's how it is. And
we're not going to tell it any other way.'

'Your questioning will begin tomorrow. I give you tonight to
think about it. Think well.'

With that Mikanagi turned and strode from the chamber. The
guards swiftly followed.

'Sorry, boys,' said Morahan, breaking the silence that followed
the slamming and bolting of the door.

'They're going to torture us, Schools,' said Ward. 'And eventually
we'll say whatever they want us to say.'

'Yes.' Morahan sighed. 'Eventually.'

AFTER HER CRISIS OF FAITH AND TERMINAL LOSS OF PATIENCE WITH the privations of missionary life, the nineteen-year-old Malory Hollander gravitated to Tokyo, where she took a teaching post at Silvers' Academy in the Tsukiji foreign settlement. The area was an architectural simulacrum of an English Home Counties town, with row upon row of Victorian villas, occupied in several cases by schools specializing in English language lessons for the children of Japanese parents willing and able to stump up a yen a month.

It was there that Malory met the precocious Shimizu Chiyoko, one of the few female pupils the school had. Her father was reported to be so impressed by her intelligence that he wanted her to learn English, perhaps in the hope she would snare a wealthy British or American husband.

Chiyoko was sometimes delivered to Silvers' by her older brother, Junzaburo, a handsome young man in his early twenties. Malory, for long starved of much that was pleasurable in life, did not resist his early advances. Their first kiss was on the top floor of the Twelve Storeys building in Asakusa. She was intoxicated by all things Japanese at the time, as well as by Junzaburo. He introduced her to the delights of Kabuki theatre and Sumo wrestling and the hot springs beyond the city. The weekend they spent at an *onsen* hotel in Hakone marked for her the point of no return, as she saw it, in her immersion in the country and her union with Junzaburo.

But what she saw was not all there was to be known. She detected a gradual change in the Japanese after they emerged victorious from

41

their war with China – and she did not care for the resulting strain of strident nationalism. Then Mr Silvers, a man whose perceptiveness was usually confined to precariously balancing the school's books, decided he should inform her that her beau had associations that were, to put it bluntly, criminal. 'He is being groomed by the Yakuza, my dear. This is what I hear. And I hear it from reliable sources.'

How Mr Silvers had any connection, however indirect, with the Yakuza, Malory never discovered. But Junzaburo did not deny the report when she confronted him. He saw membership of the Yakuza, she realized, as a way of earning enough money to maintain her in luxury as his wife. And, more disturbingly still, he did not believe she was entitled to an opinion on the subject.

He changed his mind about that when she ended their relationship. He offered to turn his back on the Yakuza and do whatever she wanted him to do. But it was too late. 'The question you must ask yourself, my dear,' advised Mr Silvers, 'is whether you wish to become a Japanese woman, with all that entails.'

There could be only one answer.

More than twenty years had passed since Malory had last set foot in Tokyo. The station she arrived at from Kanagawa that night had not existed when she left. A whole area of the city she remembered as an empty quarter considered dangerous after dark had been filled with office buildings. And streetcars had arrived, screeching and rattling through the evening heat.

A letter Malory received from a fellow teacher, Miss Gibson, about five years after leaving Japan, told her Mr Silvers had died and the school had closed. Miss Gibson was heading for another teaching post in Shanghai. She said nothing of Junzaburo, although she must have known of their affair. Malory was ashamed to recall just how notorious she must have been in the small world of Tsukiji.

One person Miss Gibson did mention was Chiyoko, whose father had died suddenly, obliging their star pupil to abandon her education and help her mother run the family's toy and confectionery shop in

Fukagawa. Malory had been there once, with Junzaburo, and could remember only too well Chiyoko's confusion about what had brought Miss Hollander to her humble home.

She would be confused tonight too, if she still lived there. But this time Malory would have to explain herself. She took a taxi to Eitai-bashi, one of the bridges over the Sumida river, and walked from there.

Fukagawa was, as she remembered, a fetid warren of tenements threaded by narrow alleys and murky canals. Little had changed in the area. She tried not to attract attention and had left it late enough to ensure most of the residents were asleep. The canal water slopped with the occasional passage of barges and small boats. Cats slipped in and out of openings and the few people still out and about cast her odd, quizzical glances. She knew she looked out of place, but it could not be helped. She *was* out of place.

Junzaburo had brought her by *choki-bune* – canal taxi – from Asakusa. She remembered a tavern next to the landing-stage. The Shimizus' shop was one alley back from there. The boat had turned off the river just before the bridge. By following the canal it must have used, and retracing her steps several times after realizing she was on the wrong track, she eventually found what she thought was the tavern she had seen that night.

She was close now, to help or the discovery that there would be no help. The alley was even narrower than she recalled, the roofs of the buildings either side almost meeting in the middle. The boards covering the central gutter sounded to her footsteps. People unseen in the paper-walled homes jumbled together around her coughed and muttered and cursed. The smell was of stale cooking and smoke and sewage and cramped humanity. Moths fluttered round the lamps. Gnats and mosquitoes swirled in the air.

The door of the shop was closed, but through its bamboo bars she could see confectionery cases and spinning tops and kites hung up behind them. She tapped on the door so quietly, in order to avoid rousing any of the neighbours, that she doubted anyone inside would hear either. She tapped again, more loudly.

There was movement within. A figure came into shadowy view,

holding a lantern. Could it be Chiyoko? She would be a woman in her mid-thirties now, vastly changed from the bright, smiling young girl Malory had taught. There was no way to tell. The woman in the kimono holding the lantern might be her – or a stranger.

'Chiyoko?' Malory called softly. 'Is that you?'

'*Donata desu ka?*' came the response. *Who is it?*

A hesitant breath. Then: 'Malory Hollander.'

Silence and stillness. The lantern did not move. Malory did not know what to do or say. Then the lantern was set down. The door slid open.

Chiyoko looked out at her. In the gloom, with the lantern behind her, it was impossible to see the expression on her face. 'Miss Hollander?' she murmured, disbelievingly.

'Yes.'

'What . . . are you doing here?'

'May I come in?'

'But—'

'Please, Chiyoko. I need your help. May I please come in?'

The Shimizus' home was even smaller than Malory's memory of it. Beyond the tiny shop, overflowing with stock, was an even tinier kitchen and another room, the door to which was closed.

'We must be very quiet,' Chiyoko whispered. '*Haha* is sleeping.' So, her mother was still alive. Chiyoko looked slightly younger than her age in the lamplight, however disappointed she might be by what life had allotted to her. 'Why are you here?'

'I'm in trouble. There's no one else I can ask for help.'

'You said you would never return to Japan.'

'I never intended to. I'm sorry. I have no right to ask you for anything. I'm desperate, Chiyoko. Tell me to go and I will. But what will happen to me then . . . I don't know.'

'How can a person like you be in trouble? You are American.'

'That means nothing. I came to Japan with friends, also American. They've been arrested by the Secret Police.'

'Not possible.'

'It's happened. And they're looking for me.'

'Kempeitai? Looking for you? I cannot believe this.'

'You must. I'm telling you the truth, Chiyoko. I've done nothing wrong except take a stand against a cruel and ruthless man.'

'What man?'

Mentioning Lemmer would require too much explanation. But his Japanese partner in crime was a different matter. She might well have heard of him. 'Count Tomura.'

Chiyoko did not respond at first. A look of amazement crept across her face. 'Count Tomura?'

'You know him?'

'Has someone told you what happened to Junzaburo . . . after you left?'

'No. But when I met Count Tomura recently, in Paris—'

'You met him?'

Suddenly, the door from the other room slid open. Chiyoko's mother, a little bird-like old woman, stared out. If she was surprised to see Malory, there was no hint of it in her voice. '*Hollander-san,*' she murmured.

Chiyoko engaged her mother in urgent, whispered conversation. Mrs Shimizu frowned suspiciously throughout. Malory could not follow the exchanges, but noted Chiyoko's frequent instruction. '*Nete.*' Go to bed. Eventually, Mrs Shimizu obliged, after a parting glare at Malory.

'You look tired, Miss Hollander,' said Chiyoko, returning her attention to Malory. 'And worried.'

'I'm both.'

'Because you and your friends have become enemies of Count Tomura?'

'Yes.'

'How did that happen?'

'Do you want me to explain? Once I do, you will know things it may be dangerous for you to know.'

'Things about Count Tomura?'

'Yes.'

'Then I want to know them. He is my enemy also.'

45

SAM WOKE TO A DULL ACHE IN HIS HEAD AND A GENERAL SENSATION of disorientation. For a moment he was unsure if he was in Paris or Walthamstow. Then he remembered he was actually in Tokyo.

It was dawn, as he could discern by the grey light seeping through the shutters at the windows and the fine mesh of a mosquito net. He was in bed in a large dormitory. Other men were sleeping in the beds around him. The patching together of his memory of the previous night soon enabled him to deduce he was in hospital. His head was bandaged, the bandage low enough to restrict the vision from his right eye.

Experimentally, he flexed his limbs, then pulled himself up on the pillow. The pain in his head was not a great deal worse than a Bass hangover. He must have been brought to the hospital after collapsing on the train. But there were no policemen sitting at the end of the bed, so he could only suppose no one knew who he was. Fortunately, he had left his passport at the Eastbourne Hotel, so they would have had no way of identifying him.

Consciousness brought little in the way of consolation. Malory had probably been arrested, along with Ward and Djabsu. Max was dead. Schools was in custody. The game was up.

Except that Sam himself had still not been apprehended. And he intended to spite Lemmer and Tomura by staying at liberty as long as he possibly could. If he could find any way of freeing his friends or punishing their enemies, he would take it. But to do that he had to avoid capture. And the longer he remained in hospital the harder that would be.

He parted the mosquito net and swung his legs to the floor, which met them rather sooner than expected because of the lowness of the bed. Then he slowly stood up. He felt a little unsteady, which he attributed to hunger as much as concussion. A big fried breakfast appealed mightily to him. He rated his chances of obtaining it at zero.

He was wearing a thin white kimono-style gown. Someone had tied a label to his wrist, on which there was a jumble of Japanese characters. A narrow cabinet stood beside the bed. Easing the door open, he found his suit and shirt hung inside, with his socks and underclothes neatly folded on a shelf. His shoes were propped on a piece of bamboo at the bottom. He glanced around, but the other patients all seemed to be asleep. Moving as quickly and quietly as he could, he took the gown off and dressed himself. Then he tore the label off the piece of string round his wrist and slipped it under his pillow.

He reckoned a hat to cover his bandage would be useful, but he had lost his own at some point during his escape from Sakashita's shop. Then he noticed a straw hat resting on top of the cabinet serving the next bed. With apologies to the oblivious owner, who looked more dead than asleep, he tried it on. It fitted loosely, which did the job.

Sam headed off, treading carefully, along the ward. Outside, a nurse was sitting at a desk, dozing gently. The building was bathed in silence and the lingering warmth of a hot night. The clock on the wall above the nurse's head showed the time as just short of 4.30. It would be another four or five hours before Sam could hope to find Fumiko Yamanaka, the man Morahan had recommended he turn to for help in an emergency, at his desk in the Home Ministry. Where Sam could spend those hours he did not know. For the moment, he could only think about making a swift and inconspicuous exit from the hospital.

He padded past the dozing nurse, to reach a landing and an unshuttered window through which he saw what looked like warehouses beyond the hospital grounds and the silvery curve of a river. He had no knowledge whatever of the geography of Tokyo and therefore no idea where in the city he might be. He would just have to trust his own judgement.

He started down the stairs.

Around the same time, Malory woke from the few hours of sleep she had managed on the futon Chiyoko had laid in the kitchen for her. A cockerel in some nearby tenement was celebrating the dawn, as yet a grey and grudging affair. Through the open doorway, in the shop, Malory could see the shadow of the bamboo branch hung with strips of paper Chiyoko had pointed out to her the night before.

'Today was the star festival. Shopkeepers hang out a branch for people to tie their wishes to. If I had written one, it would have been a wish to never have heard the name of Count Tomura Iwazu.'

The two women had sat for hours in the kitchen, sipping tea as they each revealed a little, and then a little more, of their dealings with Count Tomura. They had spoken in a whisper, anxious not to be overheard.

'Fukagawa is a bad place to bring a secret, Miss Hollander. We are as close almost to our neighbours as I am to you.'

'There's nowhere else I can bring it. And no one else I can bring it to.'

'You should not stay here long. You will be seen. Someone will report you to the police. Then Kempeitai will come for you. And for me.'

'I'll leave in the morning. There is a man at the Home Ministry who may agree to help me.'

'Does Tomura know who he is?'

'Possibly,' Malory had admitted. And it was true. Yamanaka's brother would probably be suspect in Tomura's eyes.

'Then his men will watch for you there. You must stay here. I will go to the Home Ministry. *Haha* will serve in the shop. She will say nothing. She will make an evil face at you. But she will say nothing.'

48

Malory had told Chiyoko the full truth of her presence in Tokyo because she could conceive of no way to enlist her aid without being completely honest. Her position was too perilous for any other course.

She had feared on her way to Fukagawa that Chiyoko would denounce her as the treacherous foreigner who had broken her brother's heart. But the tragedies and misfortunes of Chiyoko's life had deeper causes, as she had acknowledged. And one of those causes was Count Tomura.

Listening to Chiyoko, Malory had finally understood how Tomura knew of her years in Japan. The realization that he had been aware of her existence for some time had dismayed her during their encounter in Paris. Now all had become clear.

'It was not you who broke Junzaburo, Miss Hollander. He was sad after you left. Oh, he was very sad. Yakuza had no use for him. He had not much use for himself. Our uncle is a servant at Count Tomura's house in Tokyo. He arranged for Junzaburo to work for the Count. Not in Tokyo. In Chosen. In Taiwan. And other places. I did not know what the work was. Later, when he came back to us, wounded in his mind, he told me. Count Tomura sent him to assist a man called Muraoka Iheiji. Muraoka ran a gang that kidnapped Japanese women, in Kyushu and Shikoku mostly, and sold them in China, for men to use. You understand, Miss Hollander? You understand what this was?'

'Forced prostitution.'

'Yes. That was the work Count Tomura gave my brother. I could not believe it. It was horrible. And I was worried Tsuyoshi, the man I was to marry, would reject me if he knew. He was a soldier. Lieutenant Misora Tsuyoshi. I loved him very much. In his uniform, he looked so fine.'

'Did he find out what Junzaburo had been doing?'

'No. But I lost him anyway. He was killed in the war against Russia. Battle of Mukden, March first, 1905. That was when he died. That was when I knew I would never leave this place.'

'And Junzaburo?'

49

'He is a monk, Miss Hollander. At a temple in Nara. I have not seen him for more than ten years. I pray he is happy.'

'So do I.'

'You were right to leave. I know that now. I think Junzaburo knows it also. You should not have returned.'

'I had to.'

'To help your friends – Mr Morahan, Mr Ten . . . Tooen?'

'Twentyman. Sam Twentyman. And Schools Morahan. I can't let them die like Max.'

'Perhaps you cannot stop them dying.'

'I have to try. But you don't have to.'

'Oh yes. Your enemy is Count Tomura Iwazu.' A steely gleam appeared in Chiyoko's gaze. 'Therefore I also have to try.'

Malory took courage from Chiyoko's resolve as she lay listening to the tenements stir slowly around her. There was nothing to be gained by dwelling on the awfulness of the situation. The little she could do to help Schools, Sam and the others she would do. As for herself, she was not yet ready to admit defeat, however starkly it stared her in the face. It was a new day. And she would not shrink from whatever it held.

S AM HEADED WEST AS HE WALKED AWAY FROM THE HOSPITAL, STEERING by the swollen red sun rising over the city. He made eye-contact with no one and moved as fast as his throbbing head and general weakness allowed. Tokyo was utterly alien to him in its sights and sounds and smells and he did not doubt he looked utterly alien to it. All he could do was put one foot in front of the other and hope he was going in the right direction.

Confirmation that he was came with the welcome appearance ahead of the elevated railway line. He began to suspect he was not far from Sakashita's shop. He had no wish to return there, of course, but the railway line would take him to Tokyo Central, where he could at least lose himself in the crowd. He followed the narrow street beside it, past mostly shuttered businesses trading in the arches beneath the line.

One restaurant was open, serving what Sam assumed was break-fast. Hunger drove him to mime his need for food until something edible – a bowl of rice and beans – was supplied in exchange for a handful of coins. Tea of a kind he would have discarded as dish-water in England accompanied the food. He gulped it all down gratefully, then pressed on.

Central Station was still relatively quiet. He bought an English language newspaper – the *Japan Mail* – and hid behind it in a café where he ordered coffee on the basis it was a safer bet than the local tea.

There was nothing in the paper about the arrest of American

51

would-be assassins the previous night, nor about the hunt for one of them who had eluded the police. Sam derived some relief from that, but another problem was already weighing on his mind. Count Tomura knew Yamanaka had been in cahoots with them in Paris. He might easily deduce Sam would turn to Yamanaka's brother for help in Tokyo. The Home Ministry might therefore be under watch. He could be arrested as he entered.

A taxi would safely take him as far as the door, of course. But he began to wonder if he could disguise himself in some way. The hat he had stolen from his fellow patient at the hospital had a conical, oriental look about it. What he needed was the sort of loose, enveloping garment he saw many men walking around in, although he drew the line at the wooden pattens they clunked along on.

Spying a clothing emporium among the several shops inside the station, he waited for it to open at nine o'clock, then hurried in and pointed out the sort of thing he wanted, generously sized. It was, he gleaned, called a *yukata*. To the assistant's obvious horror, he put it on over his suit after paying and went straight out.

He loitered in the waiting room for another hour, where he pretended to read a Japanese language newspaper someone had left behind, although he soon realized he was spoiling the effect by turning the pages in the wrong direction. He abandoned the pretence and concentrated on smoking until ten o'clock came and went, giving him some confidence that Yamanaka the civil servant would have arrived at work if he was ever going to. Then he set off.

The taxi ride to the Home Ministry was short and stressful. The driver understood not a word of English, so could not grasp where Sam wished to be taken. Eventually, they settled for Sam sitting in the front with him and pointing the way.

The driver was clearly surprised when they reached their destination so quickly. Sam handed him more than enough to cover the fare, jumped out and rushed straight into the Home Ministry building.

He slowed to a seemlier pace in the high, hushed foyer. A reception desk stood ahead of him, with an impassive, frog-like man behind it, dressed in a morning suit. Sam held out little hope he spoke English either.

'I'm here to see Yamanaka Fumiko,' he ventured, congratulating himself on remembering the correct order of the names in Japanese usage.

But the congratulation was premature. The man behind the counter frowned at this uncomprehendingly.

'Yamanaka Fumiko. It's very important.'

The frown deepened. '*Yamanaka-san?*'

'Yes. Yamanaka-san.'

'*Nanji no goyoyaku desuka?*'

'Just tell him I'm here. My name's Twentyman. I know his brother Yamanaka Eisaku. This is urgent. You understand? *Urgent.*'

'Excuse me,' came a voice from behind Sam.

Turning, he found himself looking down at a small, bright-eyed woman with shorter hair than he had seen on most Japanese women. She was wearing a flower-patterned kimono and a wispy scarf. Her face was kind and soft-featured. Bewilderingly, she was looking at him with apparent recognition – and surprise.

'You are Sam Twentyman?'

'Yes.'

'So, you are free.'

'I . . . Who are you?'

'Shimizu Chiyoko. I have been waiting to speak to Yamanaka-san. Shall I explain to this gentleman for you?'

'Well, thanks, yes. I suppose so. But . . .'

She rolled off a statement that appeared to satisfy the frog-like man entirely. He plucked the receiver from the telephone beside him and dialled a number.

'I am here on behalf of Miss Hollander, Mr Twentyman,' Chiyoko said in an undertone, stepping closer to Sam to ensure he could hear her.

'Malory?'

'She also is free.'

'How?'

'Later I will explain.'

The man was speaking on the telephone now. Sam heard his name mentioned as '*Two-enty-man*'. Then there was a pause.

'What is it you are wearing, Mr Twentyman?'

'Disguise.'

'Is that a bandage under your hat?'

'Yes. But it's just a scratch.'

'You are very pale.'

'That'll be the lack of beer.'

'You are trying to be funny?' She appeared perplexed by the notion.

'Not hard enough, obv—'

The man with the telephone interrupted with a stream of Japanese, to which Chiyoko responded. 'Mr Yamanaka's secretary will come down,' she explained. 'Your arrival has made a difference, I think. I expected to wait much longer.'

'Pardon me, miss, but I really don't understand who you are or what you have to do with Malory.'

'I am a friend. And you both need a friend, yes?'

'You can say that again.'

'So, be glad I am here.'

YAMANAKA FUMIKO WAS A PUDGIER, OLDER, BALDER VERSION OF his brother, though equipped with an uncannily similar pair of circular steel-framed glasses. He received his visitors in a dark, heavy-marbled office, wearing a morning suit, complete with carnation buttonhole. Apart from the fact that the photograph over the mantelpiece was of the Taisho Emperor rather than King George, Sam might have suspected they were in a ministerial building in London rather than Tokyo.

But Tokyo it was. And amid his troubles Sam now had two unlikely, though as yet untested, allies. Shimizu Chiyoko, who had so far told Sam only that she was a friend and former pupil of Malory's; and Yamanaka Fumiko, who looked an improbable saviour to say the least.

Early signs were encouraging, however. He thanked Sam profusely for helping his brother emerge unscathed from their clash with Count Tomura in Paris and spoke fondly of the late lamented Commissioner Kuroda. 'I do not believe he drowned accidentally, Mr Twentyman. We live in dark times.'

Sam's account of the events of the previous night, supplemented by Chiyoko's explanation of how Malory had escaped arrest, hardly made the times sound any less dark. Mention of the Kempeitai in particular threw Yamanaka into head-shaking despondency.

'If Kempeitai have your friends, they will be forced to confess to whatever crimes they are accused of. Kempeitai are . . . *yabin-jin*.'

'Savages,' said Chiyoko for Sam's benefit.

Yamanaka nodded. 'Yes, savages. They get what they want. Always.'

'Isn't there anything you can do?' Sam pleaded.

'For you and Miss Hollander, perhaps. I have an idea.' Yamanaka pressed a buzzer on his desk. 'I saw nothing in *Asahi Shimbun* this morning concerning the arrests you describe, Mr Twentyman, but—' His secretary looked round the door. There was an exchange between them in Japanese. The secretary withdrew.

'I've told you the truth, sir,' said Sam.

'Please.' Yamanaka looked appalled at the implication that he doubted Sam's word. 'I believe you. Eisaku has vouched for you. Also for Mr Morahan and Miss Hollander. And the gratitude Eisaku owes you I owe you also.'

Chiyoko asked something then in Japanese, at considerable length, and with head-bowed deference. As far as Sam could judge, the issue was a delicate one. Yamanaka gave his reply after much thought.

'Shimizu-san wishes to know the office I hold here, Mr Twentyman. She wonders if I can use my position to help you.' Yamanaka smiled, apparently amused by the notion. '*Osaraku, osaraku.* How would you say that in English, Shimizu-san?'

'Probably. Possibly. Perhaps.'

'Which is it?' asked Sam.

'We will find out,' said Yamanaka. 'The office I hold is less important than the people I know.'

'Do you know Count Tomura?'

'I have met him.'

'What d'you think of him?'

'A bad choice of enemy.'

'It wasn't exactly a choice.'

The secretary returned. There were further exchanges in Japanese. He withdrew again.

'The police confirm the arrests last night,' Yamanaka announced. 'One in Tokyo, two in Yokohama. Two fugitives are sought, one male, one female. All are accused of involvement in the murder of an Englishman named Farngold. The three men arrested were taken by the Kempeitai because they believe the murder was part of a plot against the government.'

'There's no plot against the government, sir,' said Sam. 'I swear it on my mother's life.'

'Not necessary, Mr Twentyman. Once again I believe you. But that does not help you and your friends. What will help is action.'

'You've got something in mind?'

'I have a question in mind. When did you first see an aeroplane fly?'

'Me? Why?'

'Because I would like to know.'

'Well, that would have been . . . Hold on.' Sam snapped his fingers. 'I told your brother this, when we were trapped in Schools' apartment in Paris. Thought it'd take our minds off the stew we were in.'

'And what did you tell him?'

'Summer of '09 it was. Walthamstow Marshes. Aviator by the name of Vernon-Roe. There was a big crowd.'

'Eisaku did not remember his name. But date and place, yes, those are as he said in his letter.'

'You're checking up on me, Mr Yamanaka?'

'Eisaku said I should. Though I do not think anyone could pretend to be you successfully, Mr Twentyman.'

'What's that supposed to mean?'

The telephone rang at that moment, sparing Yamanaka the need to reply. He picked up the receiver and spoke for some minutes to someone he seemed to know well. There were many uses of *hai* and *arigato gozaimasu – yes* and *thank you*. Eventually the call ended.

'What—' Sam began. But Yamanaka cut him off with a gesture. He seized a sheet of notepaper, dipped his pen in the inkwell and began writing at a furious pace.

'The man he spoke to is an old friend,' whispered Chiyoko. 'He has asked him if he will allow you and Miss Hollander to stay in his house for a few days. The old friend agreed.'

'What's he writing now, then?'

'A letter for Shimizu-san to take to Commissioner Fujisaki at Police Headquarters,' said Yamanaka, without looking up. 'He was trained by Commissioner Kuroda, so he will help us as much as he can, I think.'

Yamanaka finished the letter, then wrote another, briefer note, clipped the two together and handed them to Chiyoko. 'You are willing to do this, Shimizu-san?'

'Yes. I am.'

'What are you asking this Fujisaki to do for us, sir?' asked Sam.

'As much as he can. Now, the friend I spoke to? He is Professor Nishikawa Hideoto. We were students together. He teaches at Tokyo University. At least, he teaches there when he does not have something better to do. He is . . . *fugawari na hito*. He does not . . . play the game.'

'Is that good?'

'It is good for you, Mr Twentyman. And for your friend, Miss Hollander. Nishikawa-sensei is the only man I know who will enjoy keeping a secret such as this. If he believed you were plotting against the government, probably he would congratulate you. His house is in Sendagi, north of the university. You will be safe with him for a while. I will order a car to drive you there now, Mr Twentyman. We will collect Miss Hollander tonight, when it is dark.' Yamanaka said something to Chiyoko in Japanese, to which she nodded her assent. 'It is settled, then.'

'All this is very kind of you, I'm sure, Mr Yamanaka,' said Sam, 'but we can't just hide in your friend's house.'

'For the present, you must.'

'What about Schools and the other two?'

'I hope Commissioner Fujisaki can do something. But they will not be set free. It has gone too far. A man is dead.'

'Killed by Lewis Everett. I'd be happy to sign a statement saying that.'

'Again I believe you, Mr Twentyman.' Yamanaka looked pityingly at Sam. 'But no one else will. I am deeply sorry. What you came to Japan to do you will not be able to do. Count Tomura is too strong for you. He is too strong for all of us. That is the truth. And you must accept it.'

MORAHAN, WARD AND DJABSU HAD EATEN AND DRUNK NOTHING for more than twelve hours when they were taken from the cage, chained hand and foot, and led to separate rooms along a corridor off the chamber they had been held in overnight.

Morahan did not delude himself about what lay ahead. Mikanagi required confessions and would relish doing whatever was needed to extract them. But confessions to complicity in a plot to assassinate the Prime Minister guaranteed they would be executed. Morahan had emphasized the point to Ward and Djabsu during the long, hot, thirsty night.

'Whatever they do to you, don't give them what they want,' had been his parting remark when the guards came to fetch them.

As he was well aware, however, that was much easier said than carried through. The windowless cell he was marched into contained a low table long and wide enough to accommodate a spreadeagled man and furnished with sinister gutters and drainage holes that fed into a runnel in the floor. There were hooks in the ceiling at several points and the peeling walls were stained with blood and excrement. A foul smell lingered in the stale air, along with the silent echo of screams uttered by other men who had been led into this room.

The guards fastened his wrist-chain to one of the hooks in the ceiling, then tore off the thin cotton *yukata* he had been given to wear, leaving him naked. His arms were stretched so far above his head that he was standing on his toes to spare his wrists. But this, he knew, was a minor discomfort compared with what was to come.

59

Mikanagi entered with the air of a man looking forward to his day's work. He had removed his tunic but was still wearing his cap. He was carrying a long bamboo cane. And his hands were gloved. That last detail struck Morahan as particularly ominous.

'How did you sleep, Morahan?' he asked, with no hint of irony.

'Like a babe.'

'Have you decided to confess?'

'I was raised a Protestant. It's a Catholic you'd want for confession.'

'You think being funny is the same as being brave?'

'Maybe it's possible to be both.'

'Not for long. And we have as long as we need.' Mikanagi flexed the cane and prodded him in the stomach with it. 'You are old, Morahan. You are not as strong as you were.' He moved the cane lower and pushed it against Morahan's genitals. 'You are not even as strong as you think you are.'

'We'll see.'

'Yes. We will. And the other two – Ward and Djabsu – will hear.' Morahan did not doubt that. Sound would carry well in the bare stone corridor and they were only a few cells away. 'They will hear you beg me to let you sign a confession.'

'You think they'll hear that?'

'I know they will. Now, are you willing to confess?'

'Guess.'

The morning passed in an agony of inactivity for Malory. She could not leave the tatami-matted rear room of the Shimizus' tenement and she had to make as little noise as possible for fear of attracting a neighbour's attention. Mrs Shimizu played her part doggedly, but made it clear by her scowling expression that she considered her daughter's behaviour madly imprudent. And Malory strongly suspected she still hated her for breaking her son's heart – or for engaging his affections in the first place.

The scowl lifted only once, when she noticed Malory's embarrassment at being supplied with a chamber-pot to spare her risking a visit to the communal latrine behind the building. Their proximity and their complicity were otherwise unbearable for both.

But borne they had to be.

On Yamanaka's advice, Sam spent much of the car journey from the rear entrance of the Home Ministry to Professor Nishikawa's house in Sendagi crouched out of sight. He consequently had little idea of where in relation to the centre of Tokyo the house was, although it was certainly some way off. Stillness and silence were the dominant features of the residence, a large, traditional Japanese house of carved wood and paper walls and narrow corridors and tatami-matted expanses of quietude.

Dispossessed of his shoes and supplied with ill-fitting slippers by a mute manservant, Sam was briefly received by Nishikawa in his book-crammed study. The Professor was a stooped, hawk-nosed little man with a grey beard and an air of distraction, clad in a kimono speckled with ink stains around the sleeves. 'You are welcome, Mr Twentyman. Stay as long as you need to. But, please, do not disturb me.'

Sam had the impression when he left the study that he had just had the longest conversation with Nishikawa he was ever likely to. The manservant popped up and led him to the bathroom, where the floor-sunk tub was full and waiting for him. Sam could not deny he probably needed a bath.

He gingerly removed the bandage from his head before climbing in. He could not find a mirror, but there was no fresh blood, which he took as a good sign.

He was drying himself after the bath when the manservant's wife – or so he assumed she was – appeared in the room, ignored his flusterings and applied a fresh and rather smaller bandage to his wound. '*Kurushi?*' she asked several times. The word sounded a little like excruciating. He shook his head and smiled, which seemed to satisfy her.

Professor Nishikawa had one room in his house furnished in Western style, with table and armchairs. There Sam was served a meal of grilled eel and noodles. Afterwards he sat out on the verandah. The garden of clipped trees and ornamental ponds was a restful sight, but Sam felt only a gnawing anxiety.

'*You should never have left home, Sam, my boy,*' he could imagine his mother saying. And for once he would have had to agree with her.

Chiyoko's return to the tenement on Fukagawa was a relief to both Malory and Mrs Shimizu. There was a whispered conversation between mother and daughter – with an argumentative edge to it – before Chiyoko entered the room where Malory was waiting.

'Is there good news?' Malory asked at once, for Chiyoko looked slightly less sombre than when she had left.

'There is some, Miss Hollander. And there may be more to come.'

Morahan lay chained to the table, face down, his legs and arms stretched taut. He was breathing shallowly and gingerly after repeated beatings with the cane. The pain he felt was both general and specific, beating to its own pounding rhythm in his head and his lungs and his limbs.

Mikanagi had alternated between insisting Morahan confess to plotting against Prime Minister Hara's life and demanding he reveal where Malory Hollander and Sam Twentyman might be hiding. Morahan had held his tongue on both counts. So far.

'Tell me, Morahan,' said Mikanagi, appearing above him, 'is Miss Hollander your woman?'

'She's no one's woman.'

'I do not believe you. She is yours. But you will be no use to her when I have finished with you.'

There was a dimming of the light. Morahan's chains were loosened and the guards pulled him over on to his back before tightening them again. He heard something being plugged into one of the overhead lamp sockets. A few seconds later, an electric shock coursed through his genitals. His back arched with the pain.

'That was just a few seconds,' said Mikanagi, stooping close to his ear. 'Longer and your flesh will begin to burn. You want that, Morahan? You want—'

He broke off at the sound of the door opening. There was an exchange in Japanese with someone who entered. The exchange grew heated. The newcomer stepped into Morahan's field of vision. He wore Kempeitai uniform and looked older than Mikanagi. He handed Mikanagi a piece of paper, then glanced down at Morahan. '*Amerika-jin*,' he said, in a fatalistic tone.

There was nothing fatalistic about Mikanagi's response to whatever the document was. He glared at the newcomer and gabbled some angry words, then stalked out of the room.

'What's going on?' asked Morahan.

The newcomer ignored him. He said something to the guards, then left.

Nothing happened for a moment. Then the guards moved to either end of the table and began to release the chains.

MALORY FINALLY LEFT THE TENEMENT AT TEN O'CLOCK THAT NIGHT. Chiyoko walked with her to the street, where the car promised by Yamanaka was waiting. Malory had already thanked Chiyoko profusely for her help, but it was unclear if they would meet again and she felt the moment of parting keenly. The car drove away towards the river. A tram passed between it and the receding figure of Chiyoko. When Malory looked again, she was gone.

Her reunion with Sam at Professor Nishikawa's house was ambivalent for both of them. If Schools had been there, they could have congratulated each other on a narrow escape. As it was, they were free, at least for the time being, but Schools was not. They regretted Ward's and Djabsu's incarceration as well, but it was Schools they truly missed.

There were grounds for hope, though, according to Chiyoko. Commissioner Fujisaki had said he would do all he could. 'He is not frightened of Kempeitai,' Chiyoko had said of him. 'He will try to help.'

Yamanaka arrived shortly before midnight. He cut a less dapper and dignified figure than when Sam had visited him in his office. A long day of discreet and difficult negotiations had left him worn and weary. He eagerly accepted a glass of *shochu* from their host and suggested Malory and Sam should join him.

'You will be pleased to know,' he announced, 'that Commissioner Fujisaki has arranged for Mr Morahan, Mr Ward and Mr Djabsu to be transferred from Kempeitai custody to normal police custody.

They are being held at Sugamo prison, charged with the murder of Jack Farngold. There is no other charge – nothing concerning a plot to assassinate the Prime Minister. The prison is run harshly but correctly. There will be no torture – no forced confessions. This is very good for your friends.'

'How did Commissioner Fujisaki achieve this?' asked Malory.

'Like you, Miss Hollander, your friends are American citizens. If the US Embassy learnt three of its citizens were being mistreated by the Kempeitai, there would be protests at the highest level. It is only twenty years since all British and American citizens were exempt from Japanese law. In Commissioner Fujisaki's opinion, this Kempeitai operation was arranged by Count Tomura without the approval of the Justice Ministry. Difficult questions would be asked if your friends remained in the hands of the Kempeitai.'

'But they're still charged with murder?' put in Sam.

'Yes, Mr Twentyman. They are. It is *dakyo* – a compromise. The police will investigate the case against them and the US Embassy will be notified of their arrest. The investigation will take many weeks – or months. In the end, they will be released without a trial. Commissioner Fujisaki believes Count Tomura left Paris before the end of the peace conference because he has urgent business – political business – to conduct here in Tokyo and that, once he has dealt with it, he will allow your friends to be deported quietly.'

'Don't think we're not grateful, Yamanaka-san,' said Malory, 'but is this the best we can do for them?'

'Commissioner Fujisaki has probably saved their lives, Miss Hollander. I am sorry their freedom will take so long to achieve, but I am certain this is the best for them. The *dakyo* has been agreed and must be respected. As for you and Mr Twentyman . . .'

Sam looked at Malory, then at Yamanaka. 'Yes, what about us?'

'You will be arrested on the same charge of murder if the police catch you. I advise you not to let that happen. Commissioner Fujisaki can delay the investigation for a few days. You should leave Japan as soon as you can.'

'Leave?' Malory shook her head. 'We can't abandon Schools and the other two.'

'You must. You cannot hide here – or anywhere else – for long. If you stay, they will find you. Then you will go to prison also. What good would that do, Miss Hollander?'

She pondered the question for a long, silent moment, then said quietly, 'None.'

'I have arranged for you to leave Yokohama tomorrow evening on a Dutch freighter bound for Shanghai.'

'You want us to run away?' asked Sam despairingly.

With a solemn nod Yamanaka acknowledged that he did. 'It is what I advise.'

The night was hot and humid. A soft rain was falling like a murmur in the garden. After Yamanaka had left, Malory and Sam stood out on the verandah, smoking cigarettes. For a while, they did not speak. Then Sam said, 'We should never have come to Japan, should we?'

'It seems not,' Malory admitted.

'It's all been for nothing. Max's attempt to nail Lemmer. Our long journey here. Now Schools and Grover and Gazda are stuck in the clink. And we're going to be smuggled out of the country like two barrels of contraband.'

'I don't think we can stay, Sam. It wouldn't be fair to the people who've helped us.'

'Schools would want you to leave, that's for certain. Me too, probably.'

'We could hire a lawyer in Shanghai and send him here to press for their early release.'

'And wait in Shanghai to see what happens?'

'I don't know what else to suggest. We're lucky to have the chance of going. If it hadn't been for Monteith's perverse brand of gallantry . . .'

Sam groaned. 'I'm trying to think what Max would do.'

'He wouldn't give up.'

'No. But sometimes you have to.'

Silence fell between them again. The rain continued to fall.

'This is one of those times,' said Malory, her voice catching.

*

At Sugamo prison, Morahan slept fitfully but gratefully on a thin quilt in a twelve-man cell, wrapped in a threadbare red *yukata*. The heat that was such a trial for the other occupants of the cell was actually soothing for him, easing the pain from the bruises and weals on his back and buttocks. He did not want to move. He did not even want to think.

Ward and Djabsu lay alongside him, Djabsu sporting a few cuts and bruises of his own after quelling attempts by some of their Japanese cell-mates to intimidate the newcomers. No one had told them anything they actually understood about why they had been transferred here from Kempeitai HQ. But clearly external pressure of some kind had told in their favour.

'We're not on our own, boys,' Morahan had mumbled before falling asleep, and he had not been referring to the moody and malodorous prisoners they had been thrust in with.

The thought greeted Morahan when he stirred and saw, through the gloom, the huddled sleeping shapes around him. He inhaled slowly, to avoid any jabs of pain. Then he exhaled, equally slowly.

He was alive, breathing in and breathing out. It was not much to rejoice in. But he allowed himself a grim little smile. Everything had gone wrong. But all was not lost.

WITH THE DECISION TO FLEE JAPAN TAKEN, MALORY AND SAM spent the next day waiting in enforced idleness at Professor Nishikawa's house until it was time to depart. The Professor himself left early to attend to commitments at the university. Malory managed communication with the two servants in her rudimentary Japanese. Sam, whose head no longer ached and whose wound was healing well, felt physically better than he had the day before, but could not shake off the sense that he had failed first Max and now Schools as well. Malory assured him that was not the case. In reality, they had little choice in the matter. But that was no consolation.

Nishikawa returned in the late afternoon. He and Yamanaka had conferred during a lunchtime rendezvous. A car would collect Malory and Sam at seven o'clock and drive them to Yokohama, where they were expected aboard the *Star of Batavia*, due to sail on the evening tide.

'Payment has been made,' Nishikawa reported. 'There will be no difficulty.'

'I'm not sure we thanked Yamanaka-san enough last night,' said Malory. 'Will you tell him how very grateful we are?'

'I will. You are sad also, I see. You feel you will be leaving your friends in trouble.'

'We *are* leaving them in trouble,' said Sam.

'It is true.' Nishikawa smiled philosophically. 'But truth is neither good nor bad. It simply is. I spent an hour in the university library

68

this morning. It holds a large collection of newspapers. I read the reports printed concerning the death of Claude Farngold in October of Meiji twenty-two – 1889, as you would date it. A fire in his warehouse, as you know. But there was mystery about why he did not escape. No one knew he was there until his body was found in his office. It was badly burned, of course, probably too badly for signs of violence to be seen. If there were any.'

'You don't believe it was an accident, do you?' said Malory.

The philosophical smile broadened. 'Beware convenient accidents. None of the articles mentioned Claude Farngold was Count Tomura's father-in-law. Tomura was indebted to Farngold for allowing him to marry his daughter. Tomura does not like to be indebted to anyone. *Gen'in sei moto.* Farngold dead. Debt dissolved.'

'And Farngold's son as well as his daughter is dead now.'

'They are. Count Tomura is a dangerous man. Not just to you and your friends. To my country. He and people who think like him are determined to lead us on a path to war.'

'War against who, Professor?' Sam asked. 'Germany's been beaten.'

'And after our delegation's good work in Paris, Japan now has Germany's colonies in the western Pacific. There is a border out in the ocean, between the empires: Japan and America. It is a border Count Tomura and his friends plan we will cross one day. That is the next war. The war that will destroy us.'

'If you're right . . .' Malory began.

'Sad to say, I am.'

'What can be done to stop them?'

'By you and me, nothing. That is why I will lead the quiet life of a professor, thinking more than I speak or write. And why you will leave Japan tonight and never return.'

The afternoon faded into evening. The car arrived on schedule at seven o'clock. Nishikawa saw them off without a spoken farewell, merely moving his hand in a gesture of benediction as he stood in the portico of the house, watching as they were driven out through the gate.

69

The driver spoke no English and neither Malory nor Sam found anything to say during the journey south through Tokyo and on towards Yokohama.

The sky was a bruised grey, turning slowly blue-black as nightfall advanced. In the wide puddles left by earlier rain, distorted reflections of telegraph poles passed before Sam's gaze like Japanese characters of unknown meaning: the squiggles and serifs of a language and a country he could not hope to understand.

This, he realized, was what failure felt like. This was what being outmatched amounted to. They could hide from Tomura and Lemmer. And they could escape them. But there was no hiding from the knowledge that Tomura and Lemmer had defeated them. And that knowledge would sail with them into the night.

Yokohama pier was a quieter, stiller place without a liner alongside. Of the merchant vessels moored there, only one had steam up. The name on its bow, visible in the lamplight, was a reassuring sight: *DE STER VAN BATAVIA*. It looked ready to sail, with loading complete and only one gangway still in use. A man in an officer's cap and uniform stood by it, smoking a cigarette and glancing impatiently towards Malory and Sam as they hurried along the pier from where the car had delivered them.

'We're the two passengers you're expecting,' said Malory when they reached him. 'Mr Yamanaka sent us.'

'*Ja*,' the officer responded, none too genially. '*Yamanaka. Ja, ja. Gaan, OK?*' He motioned for them to step on to the gangway.

'*Sam. Malory.*'

They stopped in their tracks. Then turned in the direction from which they had been hailed.

A figure moved in the deep shadow of the darkened vessel moored on the other side of the pier.

'Who's there?' called Sam. He had felt an instant, instinctive recognition of the voice. But he had dismissed it as a hopeless flight of fancy. The impossible was always tempting him in dreams and fantasies. But dreams and fantasies had no place on Yokohama pier.

'It's me.'

The figure moved into the lamplight. Sam's mouth fell open in disbelief and astonishment. Malory gasped and clutched at his wrist. It could not be. But it was.

The man standing before them was Max.

Villa Orseis, Marseilles, early morning, Tuesday 6th May, 1919

MAX FELT THE BARREL OF THE GUN PRESSING INTO HIS TEMPLE AND his index finger being folded round the trigger.

He had always feared dying in a flying accident, as too many RFC pilots had, rather than in combat. It would have been both stupid and futile, a waste of his life as well as a good aeroplane. What was about to happen to him was similar in its unfittingness – and in the shame he felt on account of it. He had failed. He had fallen short. He had made a fatal mistake.

It could not be helped. At least, as when things went disastrously wrong in the air, it would end quickly. There was that to be said for it at any rate.

'We are ready, yes?' Dombreux nodded in evident satisfaction with his handiwork, then drew back and grimaced as he began to squeeze Max's finger against the trigger. '*Adieu*,' he murmured.

A click sounded in Max's ear. Then—

Nothing. No flash. No roar. No pain.

The gun had not fired. Dombreux grunted in annoyance and squeezed Max's finger against the trigger again, the drug he had been injected with ensuring he was helpless to resist. Another click. Then—

Still nothing. '*Merde*,' muttered Dombreux. He withdrew the gun and opened the chamber. '*Vide? Impossible. Qu'est-ce qui se passe?*'

Then he tossed the weapon aside. Max heard it clunk against the floor.

Dombreux glared suspiciously into Max's eyes. The gun was empty. But that was none of Max's doing. The realization of what that might mean dawned in Dombreux's gaze. He rose and stepped out of view.

Max could hear the Frenchman's footsteps as he hurried from the room. He had remembered the gun Max had left on the arm of one of the chairs in the music room. Max knew better than he did that it was loaded.

But before Dombreux had gone far enough to reach it, something happened. There was a strange, whipping noise. Dombreux cried out, then muttered several oaths. A door, or something like it, creaked.

'*Mon Dieu*,' Dombreux shouted. '*Qui êtes-vous?*'

Max could not imagine what had just occurred. But it was clear Dombreux had been waylaid in some way – by someone.

'*Dégagez-moi.* Let me go. *Vous êtes—*' Dombreux's protests were cut short, his words descending into a stifled moan. Several more moans followed.

Max heard footsteps, lighter than Dombreux's. A faint shadow moved at the edge of his vision. He heard something – a heavy object, he sensed – being placed softly on the table above him. Then the shadow moved away.

Time passed. Dombreux's muffled, unintelligible protests grew fewer. The creaking slowed, then stopped. Silence followed, spreading through the house, broken only by the clock striking the half hour.

Max could do nothing but reflect on the folly of allowing Dombreux to lure him to the villa with the promise he would learn the truth about his father at last: the great secret concerning the Farngolds, supposedly contained in the letter Jack Farngold had sent to Sir Henry in Petrograd, where Dombreux had intercepted it; the letter Max had not had the chance to read before Dombreux drugged him.

73

Then, slowly, feeling began to seep back into Max. He became aware of the discomfort of his position, his left shoulder propped against the leg of the desk. A tingling began in his limbs. He looked up at the camera on the tripod, positioned there to record his death, and was able to form a smile. He was not dead.

Dombreux's plan – Lemmer's plan – had miscarried. How – at whose hands – he did not yet know. But he was alive. For the moment, nothing else mattered.

The tingling became a flood of sensation spreading through him. He rolled awkwardly away from the leg of the desk and lay, his face resting on a rug, as his limbs and his mind reconnected.

Within a few minutes he was able to rise, albeit unsteadily. He leaned on the desk for support and saw what had been placed there: his gun. He picked it up and opened the chamber. It was fully loaded.

Clutching the gun in his hand, he pushed himself fully upright and began to walk towards the door.

He saw Dombreux's shadow in the music room before he saw Dombreux. The Frenchman was hanging upside down by one ankle, held by a rope stretching from a hook fitted in the double-height ceiling that supported a large wooden-armed chandelier. The other end of the rope was fastened to the bracket of a wall-lamp.

Dombreux's hands were tied together behind his back and a rag was held in his mouth by a rope gag. His face was flushed a deep red. A comb and some coins had fallen from his pockets on to the floor below him. Seeing Max, his eyes widened. He mumbled some kind of appeal for mercy.

Max's response was to raise the gun and aim it between Dombreux's eyes. Execution was all he deserved, as he must have known. He shook his head desperately.

Slowly, Max lowered the gun. Who had done this? Max could guess, but Dombreux could tell him. 'Make one wrong move and I'll shoot you,' he rasped, his voice hoarsened by the drug. 'It'd be no hardship, believe me.'

Dombreux nodded. Max stepped behind him, untied the rope gag and pulled it away. Dombreux spat out the rag, coughing thickly. It took him several moments to find his voice. 'Untie me, Max. Please.'

'Why would I do that? You planned to kill me.'

'I'll tell you everything you want to know. Just untie me.'

'No. Tell first. What happened?'

'Your friend— Is he your friend?'

'Describe him.'

'Arab boy. Berber, maybe. Small. But strong. And quick. Who is he?'

'Le Singe. Tomura's people hung a friend of his upside down before they killed him. In Paris, last week.'

'Soutine?'

'You're well informed, aren't you? Now, what happened?'

'He must have emptied my gun and set this trap for me. I didn't see the rope. Suddenly, it was round my ankle and I was hoisted up.'

Le Singe had used the ceiling-hook to haul Dombreux up to the desired height. Then he had delivered Max's gun and . . .

'He left me here. I don't know where he went. He may still be in the villa.'

'I don't think so.' Le Singe could still be in the building, of course. But Max had the very clear sense he was not. He had done what he meant to do and gone. He had saved Max's life for a second time and left him to decide Dombreux's fate.

'Let me go, Max. *Pour l'amour de Dieu.* I'll tell you everything.'

'You don't need to. I have the letter to my father from Jack Farngold, remember?'

'No. You don't.'

'What the hell do you mean? It's in the study.'

'Le Singe took it. I saw it in his hand when he walked past the doorway.'

Max hurried back to the study without another word. He had seen the envelope when he picked up the gun, but had not thought to check if the letter was still inside. He cannoned against the doorpost as he went, his legs still rubbery from the drug, his movements clumsy.

It was as Dombreux had said. The letter had gone.

Max made his way back slowly to the music room, where he stared at Dombreux thoughtfully for a moment, before untying the rope from the lamp-bracket and lowering the Frenchman none too gently to the floor. Then he re-tied the rope, ensuring Dombreux could crawl no more than a foot or so in either direction.

'Thank you,' Dombreux murmured.

Max crossed to the armchair he had occupied earlier and sat down. 'Tell me the secret, Dombreux. Now.'

'I can't.'

'I *will* shoot you if I have to. Painfully to start with, rather than fatally. You understand?'

'The letter did not reveal the secret. Farngold said he could not risk writing it. He wanted Sir Henry to know he had information about Count Tomura and the deaths of his father and his sister that Sir Henry would be "greatly disturbed by. Things did not happen as you believe they happened." That is what Farngold wrote. "You will not want to let matters rest when you hear what I have to tell you. We must meet."'

'You said it contained the whole story,' Max protested, 'which you revealed to my father when he visited you in prison in Petrograd.'

Dombreux tried to roll over on to his back, but could not, his hands tied together behind him as they were. He groaned. 'I said what I had to say to draw you in, Max. But this is the truth. It is what I told Henry that day he came to see me in my cell at the Peter and Paul Fortress.'

'Why should I believe you?'

'Because, thanks to le Singe, you have won and I have lost. The truth is all I have to trade with you. In the letter, Farngold asked Henry to travel to Japan and help him "undo what Tomura has done". That is what he wrote. It was not enough to make Henry go. He can only have learnt what Farngold had found out later, in Paris, which was lucky for him. Farngold had already been captured by

76

Tomura when the letter arrived. Henry would never have been able to speak to him. It would have been a wasted journey – or worse.'

Le Singe's removal of the letter meant Max could not be sure Dombreux was speaking truthfully, plausible though his version of events was. The man was a practised liar – a dissembler by trade as well as nature. 'You informed Lemmer of the contents of the letter?'

'Yes. Of course.'

'And no doubt he warned Tomura.'

'No doubt.'

'So, you're responsible for whatever's happened to Farngold since.'

Another groan. 'We are all responsible for ourselves. *Chacun pour soi.* I do not know the secret. I cannot give it to you. But there are other things I *can* give you.'

'If I let you live?'

'It would be foolish to kill me, Max. Then I could not meet Lemmer at the port a few hours from now and tell him you are dead. Your best chance of defeating him is to have him believe that.'

There was truth in that, Max could not deny. But there was an obvious objection. 'He required you to supply photographic evidence of my death. You can't do that now.'

'I believe I can. It is a myth that the camera never lies. We could take a photograph showing you with an apparently fatal bullet wound in the head, using the blood from MacGregor's very real wound. It would work. It would convince Lemmer.'

William MacGregor. It came as a shock to Max to realize he had actually forgotten that the private detective set on him by Susan Henty was lying dead in another room of the villa while they debated what to do. 'You're suggesting I let you take this faked photograph to Lemmer and then . . . walk away?'

'If I don't, he'll send someone after me – and you. You may not want to let me go free, but this is actually the best chance you have of gaining an advantage over Lemmer.'

'How could I be sure what you'd say to him – if I let you go?'

'I would be mad to admit I had failed. He does not tolerate failure. You know that.'

'And what if he learnt later that my body hadn't been found here?'

'I will tell him my plan to involve MacGregor miscarried. Therefore I had to improvise. I will set fire to the villa before leaving. MacGregor's body will be burned beyond recognition. There will be nothing to prove he is not you.'

'Maybe I'd sooner put a bullet through your head and take my chances with Lemmer.'

'*Peut-être*. But I can give you more than a faked death. I can give you a secret that is all Lemmer's. A weapon . . . to use against him.'

'What secret?'

'He has a son. Born Berlin, 1904. The mother is dead. Suicide. Who can be surprised? The boy is at a private school, in Switzerland. His name has been changed. But I know what it has been changed to. And where the school is. What favour would British Intelligence show me for that information, do you think? What favour would they *not* show me?'

'How did you find out about this?'

'I am a spy, Max. Finding things out is what I do. Anyone who works for Lemmer is well advised to learn as much as they can about their master.'

'Give me the boy's name. And the name of the school.'

'*Non, non*. You let me go. We fake the photograph. I take it to Lemmer. Then I take you to the boy.'

'*Non, non* to you, Pierre. Do you seriously think I'd trust you to turn up to whatever rendezvous we agreed?'

'My word as a gentleman?'

'Worthless. Since you aren't one.'

'If that is what you think of me, why would you believe what I said? I could invent a name for the boy. I could invent a school.'

'Convince me you haven't invented them, then.' Max rose, walked across to where Dombreux was lying and stared down at him. 'Everything you have, Pierre. Those are my terms for letting you go. Remember, it's in your best interests to be truthful. One way or another, I'm going after Lemmer. So, sooner or later, he'll learn you failed to kill me, then lied to him about it. You need me to win. Otherwise we both lose. It's as simple – and as certain – as that.'

THEY HAD A DEAL. BUT IT WAS NOT ONE MAX HAD ANY INTENTION of implementing impetuously. Leaving Dombreux trussed up in the music room, he searched the villa thoroughly. There was no sign of le Singe, though he soon found MacGregor's body, covered by a dust sheet, in the drawing room. Dombreux had assured him he had acted alone. Lemmer wanted there to be no possibility of a connection being made between Count Tomura and Max's death. Using Dombreux, a man himself officially regarded as dead, he had deemed the best way of ensuring that.

Max moved the camera to the drawing room and satisfied himself as to how a photograph could be taken of him lying on the floor with his head next to the pool of MacGregor's blood. He reckoned he could fake an entry wound using sealing-wax he found in the study. Only when he was completely satisfied did he release Dombreux.

He kept the gun trained on Dombreux more or less throughout. But the Frenchman was disarmingly philosophical about his situation. 'I owe Lemmer no loyalty, Max,' he emphasized. 'I will carry this through.'

That was patently disingenuous, of course. He had no choice but to carry it through. The beauty of their deal was that Dombreux gained as much from deceiving Lemmer as Max did. There was no question of them trusting each other. Trust simply did not exist in the reasoning of Pierre Dombreux. But he had committed himself now and there was no going back.

The photograph was taken. According to Dombreux, looking

through the camera's viewfinder, it would convince anyone he showed it to that Max was dead. He was pinning his own fate on the judgement, so Max was inclined to believe him.

That done, there was no time to be lost. Dombreux was certain Lemmer had not set a watch on the villa, for the simple reason Dombreux had not told him where the villa was. But still Max could hardly leave the way he had arrived. He could not risk being seen by anyone who might be able to identify him.

In a wardrobe Dombreux found a loose coat and slouch hat that served as disguise. There was, he said, a lemon grove to the rear of the villa, and a lane beyond that led to the south-eastern outskirts of Marseilles. It was vital Max draw no attention to himself, at least until the *Miyachi-maru* had sailed at noon.

Their parting was soberly unceremonious, with no handshake. Their alliance was one of strict necessity on both sides.

'We will meet in Lausanne two days from now,' said Dombreux, looking Max in the eye. 'Hotel Meurice, Ouchy.'

'I'll be there,' Max declared. He might have added, though he did not, 'But will you?'

In truth, Max reckoned it was quite likely Dombreux would go to ground rather than travel to Switzerland. Max sensed the information the Frenchman had supplied about Lemmer's son was accurate. But he might prefer to be far away when it was put to the test. And his freedom of movement was limited anyway. He could not be certain what Lemmer had in mind for him.

Letting Dombreux off the hook did not sit well with Max. But reason it through however he pleased, their deal offered him his best chance of outmanoeuvring Lemmer. There were too many imponderables for him to be certain he was acting for the best. Le Singe had twice saved his life, but what he was seeking to accomplish remained obscure. Sir Henry's elusive 'great secret' was altogether a threat as well as a lure. In pursuing it, Max was aware he might easily be pursuing his own destruction.

In the end, though, the imponderables could not be helped. He slipped out of the villa, scaled the rear wall into the lemon grove and headed for the lane.

He had covered perhaps half a mile, when, looking back, he saw smoke climbing into the sky from the Villa Orseis. The breeze from the sea carried a crackling of burning timbers on the air. So far, if no further, Dombreux was as good as his word.

The smoke was also visible from the front seat of a dusty Panhard saloon parked out on the headland at Malmousque. The driver was a smartly dressed man of sixty or so, with white, wavy hair and a slightly less white moustache. His features were soft and dimpled, his gaze contemplative. He folded the letter he had been reading in half and slid it into the pocket of his dove-grey jacket, then nodded in the direction of the smoke.

'*La villa est en feu,*' he murmured.

Le Singe was sitting in the seat beside him. He remained silent, but looked at the driver as if expecting a decision or instruction of some kind. When none came he raised his hands and posed a question in sign language.

His companion smiled reassuringly at him. '*Non, non, Seddik. C'était bien fait.*'

Another sign.

'*Oui. Maintenant.*' The man started the car, swung it on to the road and drove away north towards Marseilles.

Max took care to stay clear of the centre of the city until early afternoon, by which time the *Miyachi-maru* had set sail for the Far East, with Lemmer, Nadia and Anna Schmidt among the passengers, along with Count Tomura and his son.

Max travelled into the Gare St-Charles on a local train from a suburban halt and switched there to a mainline train to Aix, where he arrived an hour later and despatched a cable to Horace Appleby at Secret Service Headquarters in London, using a pre-arranged alias and terminology.

FAMILY ILLNESS REQUIRES YOUR PRESENCE LYONS
URGENTLY. WILL AWAIT YOU THERE TOMORROW
WEDNESDAY PM. GREAVES

He had chosen Lyons for their rendezvous because Appleby could get there within twenty-four hours and no one could deduce from the choice that Switzerland was their ultimate destination.

Max himself travelled to Lyons by an overnight train that delivered him to the Gare de Perrache in time for breakfast at the Hotel Terminus. He booked a room for himself and enquired if a Mr Brown had cabled through a reservation. He had. Appleby was on his way.

While Max took a relaxing bath at the Hotel Terminus in Lyons, the NYK liner *Miyachi-maru* was steaming sedately through calm Mediterranean waters on the second day of its scheduled forty-five-day voyage to Yokohama, by way of Port Said, Colombo, Singapore, Hong Kong and Shanghai. Pierre Dombreux was standing by the rail on the first-class deck, smoking a post-breakfast cigarette and gazing towards the coast of Sardinia, which had recently loomed into view on the eastern horizon.

'It's too far to swim,' said Nadia Bukayeva, causing him to start as she materialized with characteristic stealth at his elbow.

Dombreux brushed a scatter of spilt ash off his sleeve and turned to face her, taking care to keep his back to the sun. 'Nadia Mikhailovna.' He smiled. 'You are well this morning?'

'Thank you, Pierre, I am. But I am worried about you. It has seemed to me you are not pleased to be aboard.'

'I do not look for pleasure in the arrangements of my employer.'

'How wise. But, still, we have . . . hopes, do we not? You hoped to be allowed to go your way, I think, after solving the Max problem so . . . efficiently.'

'I hope only when I dream. I dream only when I sleep.'

'And do you sleep soundly, Pierre?'

'I have always slept soundly.'

'Because of a clear conscience?'

'Conscience?' Dombreux chuckled. 'What would I – or you – know of conscience? We were both born without one, I suspect.'

'A defect?'

'Or an asset.'

83

MAX DID NOT MEET APPLEBY OFF HIS TRAIN, BUT WAS WATCHING from the window of his room at the Hotel Terminus at what he judged would be the right time. He was rewarded by the sight of the weary old bull terrier of British Intelligence crossing the road from the station. It was late Wednesday afternoon and Max's summons had been answered.

He gave Appleby an hour to settle in, then called at his room with a bottle of whisky to ease the stresses of the long journey.

'This had better be worth my while,' was Appleby's gruff greeting. 'There's plenty for me to be doing in London.'

'It's worth your while, I promise.' Max poured them both a generous measure of Scotch. 'Cheers.'

'What are we drinking to?'

'The snaring of Fritz Lemmer.'

'A heart-warming toast. But how do we achieve it?'

'I tried to inveigle my way back into his circle – the strategy we agreed with C – but Lemmer had other ideas. He had Krenz send me off in pursuit of Anna Schmidt to Marseilles, but it was a trap. The plan was to kill me in a faked suicide, attributed to remorse following the murder of a private detective who'd followed me from Orkney. You should hold on to your hat, because the agent Lemmer entrusted with my elimination was Pierre Dombreux.'

Appleby reacted to this announcement with a measured frown. 'You keep yourself busy, Max, I'll say that. Dombreux?'

'It was somebody else's body in that canal in Petrograd. He's working for Lemmer. And now he's working for us as well.'

85

'How did you pull *that* off?'

Max recounted then all that had happened to him in Marseilles. Appleby listened patiently and thoughtfully, slowly filling and lighting his pipe as the story proceeded. He raised his eyebrows occasionally in a signal of surprise and smiled once, when Max mentioned shooting Meadows in the foot.

'Lemmer is en route to Japan with Tomura,' Max concluded. 'He thinks I'm dead, which is how I'd like it to stay until I catch up with him. I believe Dombreux, with his life depending on it, will have pulled off the deception. Letting him go was a risk, but I secured more than just his cooperation in return. I secured something I reckon we can use to bring Lemmer down, scotching his plans to sell his network of spies to the Japanese and identifying those spies into the bargain.'

'And what might that be?'

'His son, Horace. Fritz Lemmer's son.'

At last, Appleby looked impressed. 'Lemmer has a son?'

'According to Dombreux, yes. Born in Berlin in 1904 to a mother now deceased. He goes by her maiden name: Hanckel. Eugen Hanckel. He's been a pupil for the past three years at Le Rosey, a private boarding school at Rolle, on Lake Geneva, ten miles or so west of Lausanne.'

Appleby chewed vigorously on his pipe. 'We've never heard a whisper of there being a son. Lemmer's rumoured to have visited Switzerland quite often in recent years. I saw nothing significant in that. The country was an intelligence gold mine during the war and a lot of wealthy Germans salted money away there as insurance against defeat. But a son installed at a Swiss boarding school would also explain it, of course, if we can believe Dombreux.'

'I believe him,' said Max. 'What's the alternative? That he made it up to talk his way out of trouble? I doubt even he can think that fast. A name. A year of birth. A specific school. And the address of a Lausanne lawyer who pays the fees and reports back to Lemmer. Marcel Dulière. *Notaire* of discretion.'

Appleby took a prowl to the window and back again, then said, 'If it's true, we may just have him. Ties of blood are the ties that bind. A son?' He nodded approvingly. 'That would be more than a chink in his armour.'

'Dombreux's offered to meet us in Lausanne tomorrow.'

'You think he'll turn up?'

'I don't know. But we should.'

'How did he come by this information?'

'He wouldn't say.'

'No. Of course he wouldn't. Dombreux's clearly a slippery customer. We can't rely on him, Max. You understand that?'

'I'm relying on him to save his skin along with mine.'

'Mmm. We'll go to Lausanne and look for supporting evidence. If I'm satisfied, on a balance of probability, that the boy exists and is Lemmer's son . . .'

'Yes? What then?'

'We'll be able to apply more pressure than Lemmer's used to bearing. The result could be . . . gratifying, let's say.'

'I'll follow him to Japan. I'll be happy to apply that pressure. Once he's recovered from the shock of realizing I'm not dead.'

'Japan's a long way. Coordinating our actions won't be easy.'

'What sort of action do you have in mind?'

'When the time's right, we take the boy.' Appleby looked squarely at Max. 'We can't afford to be squeamish.'

Max nodded in appreciation of the point. 'Until then, I need Lemmer and everyone else to think I'm dead.'

'I'll do what I can on that front. Some false sightings of the private detective – MacGregor, did you say? – in Nice, perhaps. A forged letter to his client reporting he's on your trail there. Whatever's needed to stop the French police suspecting his is the body in the villa. Lemmer may have left someone in Marseilles to confirm Dombreux's version of events. Meadows, maybe. You can't go back there. And you can't contact anyone other than me. Dead men have to keep to the shadows.'

'I can do that.'

'No need to hide in a corner here, though. I think we owe ourselves a good dinner, don't you?'

*

They did not have to go far to find that good dinner. Hearty food and heady wine at the Brasserie Georges answered their needs amply. But they did not ease all of Appleby's anxieties.

'In ordinary circumstances, Max, I'd condemn this scheme as crazily risky. Dombreux will use us for his own ends, no question about it. We have no way of knowing what le Singe is up to either. I'm sure he's set on doing more than saving your bacon at convenient intervals. And then there's Morahan and his crew. I haven't dared tell C about the money I've paid that man on your behalf.'

'It was my money, Horace.'

'Considering how your father came by a lot of it, I'm not sure that's strictly true. The Service can't be party to a feud between you and Count Tomura. Try to remember that.'

'But if we land Lemmer and Tomura in the same net?'

'No one will complain. On the other hand, if it goes wrong . . .'

'You had nothing to do with it. I acted on my own initiative. I've never been employed by the Secret Service. You'll disown me. And I won't object.'

Appleby studied Max over a half-raised glass of Burgundy. 'Maybe you won't. But I will, even while I'm disowning you.'

Max raised his own glass. 'Thanks, Horace. That's nice to know.'

It was a short walk back to the hotel through the mild night air. When Appleby delved in his pocket, Max assumed he was looking for his pipe. But he produced an envelope instead, which he thrust into Max's hand.

'Bedtime reading for you.'

'What is it?'

'A report by our ambassador in Tokyo on the ramifications of the attempt on the Tsarevich's life in 1891. There was no Secret Service then, of course. I had to pull a few strings to extract it from Foreign Office files. I'm breaking every rule in the book by showing it to you, so I'd be grateful if you let me have it back in the morning.'

'Why *are* you showing it to me?'

'Because it contains some interesting information about your father. And Tomura. And Lemmer. See what you make of it.'

IN CONFIDENCE

TOKYO, 8th June 1891

Ref. HF/MEB/TODM/CAH

For the personal attention of the Permanent Under-Secretary of State, LONDON

The events that so seriously marred the Tsarevich's visit to Japan last month have significant potential adverse consequences for British interests in this country, which this report summarizes, together with actions taken to limit the effect of those consequences.

Hopes were high that the Tsarevich's visit would markedly improve Russo-Japanese relations, thereby alleviating tension between the two powers in Manchuria and Korea. Extensive preparations were made in Tokyo to receive and entertain him. He was due to arrive in the capital on Tuesday 12th May, after landing at Kobe a few days before and proceeding to Kyoto, the former capital.

On Monday 11th May, he took an excursion to Lake Biwa, lunching after a cruise on the lake at Ohtsu. It was while his party was leaving Ohtsu to return to Kyoto, travelling in rickshaws, that he was set upon by a policeman wielding a sword, who struck him on the head. Fortunately, the injury was not serious and the assailant was swiftly overpowered by the rickshaw drivers. The Tsarevich's advisors nevertheless recommended he abandon his tour and a few days later he sailed home from Kobe without visiting Tokyo.

The Japanese government apologized fulsomely for the outrage. The Emperor visited the Tsarevich before he left Kobe. A woman committed suicide, leaving a note expressing the hope that her act would atone for the shame brought upon her nation. Several ministers resigned. Yet the damage was done. A genuine rapprochement with Russia has at the very least been delayed, which will inevitably encourage Germany to resume its efforts to foster conflict between the two countries. This cannot be to our strategic advantage.

The Japanese authorities have been quick to cast the Tsarevich's would-be assassin, Tsuda Sanzo, as a madman acting alone, but there are indications they do not necessarily believe this to be the case. An Inspector Kuroda has been detailed to investigate Tsuda's background. His inquiries have led him to contact officials at several foreign legations. It appears he suspects active collaboration between the German Naval Attaché, Fritz Lemmer, and a militaristic Japanese politician, Baron Tomura Iwazu. This, at any rate, is the conclusion of 2nd Secretary Maxted, who was deputed to deal with Inspector Kuroda on our behalf.

Maxted believes Tomura to be a leading member of Dark Ocean, a secret society of ultranationalist persuasion founded in 1881 following the suppression of the Samurai revolt led by Saigo Takamori. Dark Ocean is believed to have been responsible for the attempted assassination of Foreign Minister Okuma in October 1889. The man who attacked him, Kurushima Tsuneki, committed suicide immediately afterwards. Tsuda Sanzo may have intended to do the same after attacking the Tsarevich, but was apprehended before he had the chance. He has not, so far as we are aware, admitted Dark Ocean membership. But the organization represents a serious attempt to steer Japan on to a more aggressive path in its relations with the Western powers. The Germans may see assisting its endeavours as a way of weakening the position of Russia – and Great Britain – in this region. From our point of view, this would be a very serious development.

Much of this is supposition, although there is general consensus that Herr Lemmer represents a new force in Germany's pursuit of her interests, reflective perhaps of a greater degree of assertiveness on the part of the Kaiser following his removal of Bismarck from the chancellery last year.

The Japanese authorities will obviously handle their investigation of the assassination attempt against the Tsarevich as they see fit, although Maxted reports that Kuroda appears doubtful he will be allowed to take his inquiries to a proper conclusion. The balance of power within the Japanese government is, as ever, difficult to assess. Dark Ocean may well enjoy sympathy for their cause in high circles.

The decision to send Maxted back to London at short notice, for reassignment elsewhere (as per legation cable 91/471), was taken when it became apparent he could be accused of a conflict of interest and might also be in some personal danger. His acquaintance with Baron Tomura and his late wife, who was of English birth, could be seen in some quarters as a reason to doubt the validity, or at the very least the impartiality, of his assessment of the situation.

Account was also taken of the death of Baron Tomura's English father-in-law, Claude Farngold, in a fire at his warehouse in Yokohama in October 1889. Some of the circumstances of the fire were suspicious and it occurred only eight days after the attempted assassination of Foreign Minister Okuma. If Mr Farngold was killed because he had learnt, perhaps through his daughter, of Tomura's involvement in the outrage, it would suggest Tomura is capable of extreme ruthlessness.

There is no solid evidence to be offered in substantiation of these speculations. Nor as yet are there grounds for complaining to the Japanese or the Germans about Herr Lemmer's activities in this country, although we have taken steps to discourage members of the British community from entering into any dealings with Lemmer, or, indeed, with Baron Tomura.

Vigilance will be maintained on the issues raised and an early report made of any significant developments.

    H. FRASER

Max felt the report raised more questions than it supplied answers. It was far from clear to him, for instance, whether the Ambassador intended any criticism of his father, although he supposed compromising oneself to the extent of being sent back to London post haste

91

was not the best way to manage a diplomatic career. Lady Maxted had never said anything implying they had left Japan under a cloud.

Given her reticence on many matters, however, that meant little.

Their train left Lyons so early a hurried cup of coffee at the station was their only breakfast. Appleby had to follow that with a pipeful of tobacco before he could offer much in the way of conversation.

'Spot anything useful in the report, Max?' he asked, glowering out at the mist-wreathed French countryside.

'Well, it appears Lemmer and Tomura may have been helping each other for a long time.'

'And your father was the man who uncovered their collaboration.'

'Yes. Small thanks though he got for it.'

'You don't believe he was sent home for his own safety?'

'I don't know what to believe. The report skates over quite a lot.'

'It does, doesn't it? Perhaps you should press the author for more details.'

'The Ambassador?'

'No, no. Fraser's long dead, I'm afraid. But he didn't write the report. A lesson in bureaucracy for you, Max. The first set of initials in a ministerial reference is the name of the fellow whose signature the document's going out under. The last set is the name of the fellow who actually wrote the document. The number of initials between the first and last tells you how many levels in the hierarchy the writer is from the signatory. That report was written by Second Secretary Cyril Hodgson.'

'OK. So, do you know where I can find him?'

'Tokyo. He's still on the staff there. Risen since to the dizzy heights of First Secretary. Due to retire soon. Whether he'll leave Japan then I couldn't say. He has a Japanese wife, apparently.'

'You seem to know a lot about him.'

'I made it my business to, once I read that report and noticed how much more he seemed to know than he was actually saying. The FO regard him as dull but dependable. I think there may be hidden depths. You should look him up. Plumb some of those depths if you can.'

'I will.'

'Steer clear of the embassy. We have a man there, obviously, name of Reynolds, but it's all too possible he's on Lemmer's payroll, so don't have anything to do with him. Approach Hodgson at home. I think it's safe to assume he's loyal. As for what he may be keeping under his hat about your father . . .'

'Where do I find him?'

'Uchida Apartments, Ginza. How easy that address will be to track down I don't know, but it's all I've got.'

'It doesn't matter. I'll track it down.'

'Yes.' Appleby nodded. 'I'm sure you will.'

THEY HAD AN HOUR BETWEEN TRAINS AT GENEVA AND WENT TO THE buffet in search of lunch. It seemed a decision they could take without weighing the risks. But, as it transpired, it was not.

A figure caught Max's eye as soon as they entered. He was seated at one of the gingham-clothed tables, sipping a glass of white wine. He was a handsome, elegantly dressed man of sixty, with greying hair and rugged features, English to his cosmopolitan fingertips. He was Lionel Brigham.

A chance meeting with the man who believed himself – wrongly, according to Lady Maxted – to be his natural father was very nearly the last thing Max would have wanted to occur. He had once suspected Brigham to be something much worse than his mother's former lover, but their violent encounter with the hired assassin Tarn in London five weeks ago had demonstrated that for all his many faults Brigham was not a traitor to his country.

That did not mean Max wanted to clasp the fellow's hand and confide in him. Nor was it likely Brigham would be pleased to see him in the company of Appleby, who had subjected him to some aggressive questioning in Paris.

'James, my boy,' said Brigham, rising from his seat. 'What are you doing here?' He looked at Appleby. 'With this fellow?'

'Passing through,' said Max. There were no moves to shake hands. 'You?'

'A house agent was supposed to meet me off my train. He seems to be late.'

'A house agent?'

'I've been told I'm to be part of the British presence at the League of Nations.' Seeing Max's puzzled look, he went on, 'You're aware it's to be based here in Geneva?'

'So it is,' said Appleby. 'Maybe you didn't hear about that, Max.'

The note of familiarity appeared to nettle Brigham. 'I thought you'd have quit meddling in this young man's life by now,' he said, glaring at Appleby.

'I don't meddle, Mr Brigham. I serve my country.'

'So do I. Where are you passing through *to*, may I ask?'

'We don't need to trouble you with our itinerary,' said Max.

'Whatever it is, why not let Appleby go on alone? Spend a few days here, James. Help me find somewhere to live.' Brigham looked pitifully hopeful for a moment that Max might actually accept the invitation.

'I couldn't do that, I'm afraid.'

'Because Appleby has something else in mind for you?'

'Could I have a word with you outside, Max?' said Appleby.

'Certainly.'

'That's it, then?' Brigham grimaced. 'You've no sooner arrived than you're leaving?'

Max mixed an uneasy smile with a shrug. 'You'll have to excuse us.'

'Sorry,' said Max, once they were out on the platform. He felt he owed Appleby some kind of apology for the awkwardness that had been all too apparent. 'Brigham and I . . . Well, the fact is he's convinced himself he has a right to take a paternal interest in me.'

'Paternal?' Appleby cocked one eyebrow curiously.

'Do I have to spell it out?'

'Not on my account. Matter of fact, I'm sorry too. The choice of Geneva as headquarters for the League of Nations should have put me on my guard. Missing breakfast must have made me careless.'

'What do we do now?'

'About Brigham? Well, we can't just leave him to his own devices. If he tells anyone he met you in Geneva, two days after you're supposed to have been killed in Marseilles, your goose is likely to be cooked well before you reach Japan. Worse still, Lemmer may guess where we're going – and why.'

Max sighed. 'I could ask Brigham to keep it to himself. I think he'd agree to do that for me.'

'I think he might agree to do rather more.'

'What do you mean?'

'The best way to keep him quiet is to keep him close. I've been worrying about who I can use in any operation I decide to mount in Lausanne. As things presently stand, there are precious few people in the Service whose loyalty I can rely on absolutely. And it would be next to impossible to deploy them in Switzerland without one of Lemmer's spies becoming aware of it. If Lemmer really does have a son at this Le Rosey place, it's vital he doesn't get wind of our interest in him.'

'You're not saying what I think you're saying, are you?'

'Whatever we think of Brigham, Max, we know he doesn't work for Lemmer. He nearly paid for that with his life when you ran into Tarn. Would you say he was a patriot?'

'I suppose so. But—'

'So would I. And a patriot is what we need. Ask him to step out here.'

By the time Max returned with a clearly bemused Brigham, Appleby had retreated to the distant, deserted end of the platform, where he was smoking his pipe and gazing into the middle distance.

'What the devil's going on?' Brigham demanded as soon as they reached him. 'James says you want to speak to me. I can't imagine what about.'

'The defence of the realm. And I suggest you call him Max from now on. Otherwise you'll confuse me.'

'Confuse you? *You're* confusing *me*, Appleby. What on earth's going on?'

'We're after Lemmer. He has spies everywhere and we need to find out who they are as a matter of urgency.'

'What do you mean by "everywhere"?'

96

'I mean that every government department is compromised, including the Secret Service.'

'Good God. That's appalling. And much worse than I was given to understand. Is the PM aware of the scale of the problem?'

'He is.'

'Then what's being done?'

'All manner of things. But, since we don't know who works for Lemmer and who doesn't, there's a good chance everything we do will be at best undermined, at worst sabotaged.'

'This is what comes of setting up a Secret Service in the first place. Teach people to spy on your enemies and before you know it they're spying on you.'

'You may be right.' Appleby looked at Brigham squarely. 'C has given me full authority to pursue Lemmer and the people who answer to him by all necessary means. Do you know why he chose me, Brigham? And why I engaged Max to assist me?'

'As to the first, I'd suggest poor judgement. As to the second, I assume James – Max as you call him – is naïve enough to do your bidding. Unfortunately for him.'

Appleby smiled wearily. 'I was chosen and I chose Max because our loyalty's been tested in the fire. The irony is – and it's quite some irony, considering your opinion of me and mine of you – that your loyalty's been tested too.'

'We need your help,' said Max simply, drawing a look of some astonishment from Brigham.

'We do,' Appleby confirmed with a sigh. 'You're still officially on leave?'

'Yes.'

'For how much longer?'

'It could be months. There'll be nothing up and running here before the autumn.'

'Then no one would miss you while you did some work for me, would they?'

'Possibly not. But—'

'Your country needs you, Brigham. As never before.'

'You're the most confounded fellow, Appleby, you really are. Is what he says true, James?'

'Yes,' said Max. 'It is.'

'I'd need some verification.' Brigham looked doubtfully at Appleby.

'There'll be no verification. You're either with us or not.'

'With you in what?'

'Disagreeable business that needs to be done – and that no one else can do.'

'Hardly an enticing prospect.'

'But a chance for you to earn that generous salary HMG has been paying you all these years.' Appleby looked Brigham in the eye. 'What's it to be?'

WHEN IT CAME DOWN TO IT, BRIGHAM SEEMED DISAPPOINTED THAT initially nothing was required of him beyond a vow of silence. 'Lemmer thinks I'm dead,' Max explained. 'He must go on thinking that as long as possible.'

'My lips are sealed, my boy.' It was touching, in its way, to see how eager Brigham was to protect Max. It was also infuriating, since Max had no wish to lend credence to Brigham's conviction that he was his father by exploiting it. But exploit it he had to.

'We'll leave you to your house-hunting for the present,' said Appleby. 'I'd like you to stay in Geneva until you hear from me again.'

'Very well. I'm putting up at the Beau Rivage.'

'I won't keep you waiting long.'

'Where are you going now?'

'East.'

'Is that all you're going to tell me?'

'I'll tell you what you need to know when you need to know it and not before. That'll be in your best interests as well as ours.'

'There's something in your tone I'm never going to grow fond of, Appleby.'

'But you'll play your part?'

'Whatever it is, yes.' Brigham was looking at Max when he added, 'You can count on me.'

Max did not conceal his doubts about the wisdom of enlisting Brigham in their cause. He could not deny the logic of the decision, however, and it was obvious Appleby derived no pleasure from it. 'Adversity acquaints a man with strange bedfellows,' he remarked as their train headed out along the shore of Lake Geneva.

'It's misery, not adversity.'

'What?'

'"Misery acquaints a man with strange bedfellows." *The Tempest*, I believe. Shakespeare.'

'I know who wrote *The Tempest*, thank you.' Appleby chewed irritably on the stem of his pipe. 'He obviously never tried his hand at intelligence work.'

'No. That was Marlowe. It got him killed.'

'What a ray of sunshine you are, Max.'

Max shrugged. 'I try to be.'

The train stopped at Rolle before it reached Lausanne. As it slowed on its approach to the station, it passed an imposing building set in its own grounds, part of which had been turned over to sports pitches. On one of them two teams of boys were engaged in an energetic game of hockey.

'Le Rosey, I assume,' said Appleby.

'Looks like it. Just think, Horace, Lemmer's son could be in our sight at this very moment.'

'Yes. I'd have him down as a games-player.'

'It's not his fault Lemmer's his father.'

'There are many things we suffer for that aren't our fault.'

'He won't come to any harm at our hands, will he?'

'Of course not. What do you take me for?' Appleby looked across at Max. 'No. Don't answer that. I'd rather not know.'

From the Gare Centrale in Lausanne they took the funicular down to Ouchy, a genteel lakeside resort, and booked into the Hotel Meurice. A swift scan of the register as they signed it in the names of Greaves and Brown revealed no other arrivals that day. Dombreux was not there.

Appleby remained sceptical about Dombreux's intentions, but acknowledged he could not afford to betray Max. 'His hands are

100

tied, I'm glad to say.' There remained the possibility he had despatched Max to Lausanne on a fool's errand, but Appleby intended to test the possibility without delay.

They passed much of the afternoon loitering in a café near the entrance to the offices of Marcel Dulière, *notaire*, at the southern end of the Avenue d'Ouchy, facing the lakeside promenades. Decorative stained glass and a wide marble staircase visible within suggested a prosperous practice, which the dowagers of Lausanne, pottering past in the sunshine in impressive quantity, went some way to explaining. The insulation of Switzerland from the convulsions of the war hung complacently in the spring-scented air.

At length, a man looking very much as Max imagined a Swiss lawyer would look – portly, fussy and morning-suited, with a trimmed moustache and a weathered briefcase – exited the building. A passer-by helpfully greeted him with a '*Bonjour, Monsieur Dulière,*' to remove any doubt in the matter.

'What are you planning to do, Horace?' Max asked as Dulière bustled off towards the funicular station.

'Nothing until tonight.'

'And then?'

'An office call, without an appointment.'

The evening elapsed with no sign of Dombreux. Max acknowledged, first to himself, then to Appleby, that he was not going to arrive. As to why, they agreed there was nothing to be gained by trying to guess.

There was a small courtyard behind the building housing Dulière's office. At gone midnight in tranquil Ouchy, silence and solitude were nowhere more abundant. Appleby entered the premises via a rear door after a masterful display of lock-picking, leaving Max on guard.

Aside from a couple of flashes of torchlight in windows overlooking the yard, Max saw nothing that could alert anyone to Appleby's presence. And there was no one about to be alerted anyway. Guard duty was chilly but uneventful.

101

Appleby emerged after half an hour or so, locking the door carefully behind him. 'We can go,' he murmured. They headed back to their hotel, where they treated the night porter to a tale of losing their way while returning from a late evening stroll. Then they adjourned to Appleby's room.

'You could have had a successful career as a burglar, you know, Horace,' said Max as he accepted a glass of whisky.

'I learnt from a master. Charlie Leggatt was burgling the homes of wealthy Londoners for most of the old Queen's reign. I felt his collar several times in my early days with the Met. Some of his victims didn't even realize they'd been robbed, he was that careful. Breaking and entering without breaking was his forte.'

'So, Dulière won't know anyone's been through his files?'

'Not a chance.'

'And what did you learn?'

'Enough to confirm Dombreux's story – as far as it can be confirmed. Dulière has a file on Eugen Hanckel, a pupil at l'Institut Le Rosey, Rolle. Date of birth twenty-fifth of February, 1904. The school's fees – and Dulière's – are paid through a lawyer in Munich. There's no information about the boy's parentage. In fact, beyond bills submitted and settled, there's no correspondence at all other than letters between the headmaster and Dulière, who's the school's only point of reference regarding the boy. That was laid down when he was enrolled. And he's a permanent boarder. "*Compris les vacances scolaires.*" School holidays included.'

'Surely Lemmer wants to see him from time to time.'

'He probably arranges visits by telephone. The dearth of documentation is telling in its own right. Eugen Hanckel is no ordinary schoolboy. That's clear.'

'You believe he's Lemmer's son?'

Appleby considered the question over a long swallow of Scotch. Then said: 'Yes. I do.'

THEY BREAKFASTED LATER THAN MOST OF THE MEURICE'S GUESTS. Appleby had left Max wondering what their next move would be. He announced it over coffee and toast. 'A trip on the lake, Max, before we go our separate ways. I've made some inquiries. An Italian liner, the *Perla*, sails from Genoa for Shanghai next Wednesday. You'll be able to find a passage from there to Japan. So, it's Genoa for you. And the sooner the better. We should be seen together as little as possible.'

'What will you be doing?'

'Groundwork.'

'Beginning with a pleasure cruise?'

'Who said anything about pleasure?'

The boat trip Appleby had in mind was a steamer crossing to Evian-les-Bains, on the French side of the lake. The weather was cool and cloudy, with specks of rain. Takers for the trip were few. And even fewer ventured on to the open deck to watch Lausanne receding behind them as they drew away. Max and Appleby had the stern rail to themselves.

'I'm going to base the operation in Evian,' Appleby explained between puffs on his pipe. 'If anything goes wrong, the French will be more accommodating than the Swiss. The *Deuxième Bureau* wants Lemmer just as badly as we do. I'll recruit a local boatman. And whoever else I think I'll need.'

'You intend to take the boy to France?'

'I do. And hold him there while you present Lemmer with our terms.'

'The key to the code of the Grey File?'

'Exactly. The names of all his spies, checked and verified before we release the boy. After that I doubt the Japanese will have much use for Lemmer. But he can stay there if he wants.'

'How do you propose to capture the boy?'

'I'm not exactly sure yet. Leave me to worry about that. It'll be best you don't know the details. Rest assured I'll be ready to strike when you give me the word. I'll rent a box at the post office in Evian. Cable me there when you're ready to move. I'm relying on you to judge the moment, Max. I'll be on hand here from late June waiting to hear from you.'

'What will you ask Brigham to do?'

'Take the lease on a house near Evian where we can keep the boy. And anything else I think he's suitable for.'

'How will you convince Lemmer we have his son?'

'Dulière will do that for us.'

'Managing this when we're thousands of miles apart isn't going to be easy, Horace.'

'No. It isn't. But it's our best chance of defeating Lemmer, so it has to be done.'

'Have you ever met him?'

'Lemmer? Yes. Once. If you can call it a meeting. One of his underlings tried to recruit me for his network. We met at a café in The Hague. October 1915, it would have been. His name was Bakker. He lured me there with an offer of information on German shipping movements out of Zeebrugge. But that wasn't what he had to offer me at all. I turned him down, of course. It was only later I realized Lemmer had been at another table in the café, watching the whole thing. I barely noticed him.'

'This would have been shortly after the Battle of Loos, yes?'

Appleby glanced at Max suspiciously. His son had been killed at Loos, as he had once divulged in a sentimental moment. Max wondered if Lemmer had known that and chosen to approach Appleby when grief might have weakened his defences.

'Is Bakker still active?'

'No.'

'What happened to him?'

'He died.'

'Natural causes?'

'An accident. In the docks at Rotterdam.' A distant look came into Appleby's eyes. 'Dangerous places, docks.'

All was quiet in Evian-les-Bains. They walked from the jetty past imposing buildings dedicated to its spa town economy: Palais Lumière, Theatre, Casino. At the post office, Appleby took a three-month rental on a box. Their next call was a house agent, where Appleby set out his – officially, Brigham's – requirement for a small, secluded dwelling near but not in the town. The gentle implication that money was no object had an electrifying effect on the agent, who expressed his confidence that several possibilities would be available for viewing within days. Would the gentlemen be taking the waters while they were in Evian? Appleby assured him they would.

Lunch at the Grand Hotel and a train ride west to Thonon-les-Bains was what actually followed, with Appleby's attention switching between a map he had bought and the topography of the lakeside. They took a late afternoon steamer back to Lausanne from Thonon.

'Everything falling into place, Horace?' Max asked as they sat this time in the warmth of the passenger cabin.

Appleby nodded. 'Success in something like this turns on logistics.' He lowered his voice confidentially, though there was no one within earshot. 'Remember that when you're in Japan, Max. Don't rush in. Prepare the ground. Assess the possibilities. And have an escape route in place. You may need one.'

'You think so?'

'I do. Though whether you'd use it if the need arose . . .'

'I'm certainly not going all that way just to turn tail and run for it at the first sign of trouble.'

Appleby sighed and shook his head despairingly. 'If you live to be my age, Max, you'll understand not every risk is worth taking.'

'How d'you tell the difference between those that are and those that aren't?'

'Experience.'

'Well, I'll come back with plenty of that, I imagine.'

Neither of them added the obvious corollary: *if* he came back.

Max had held out the unspoken hope that Dombreux might still put in an appearance. But the lapse of another day with neither word nor sign of him told its own story. He was not coming. As Appleby made it clear he had all along suspected would be the case.

'Fortunately,' he added, 'he's already given us something far more valuable than his presence.'

They parted the following morning with a handshake and a growled 'Good hunting' on Appleby's part in the ticket hall of Lausanne's Gare Centrale. Appleby was heading for Geneva, to confer with Brigham; Max for Milan and thence Genoa – and Japan.

THE VOYAGE EAST WAS SUSPENDED ANIMATION FOR MAX. HE existed in a condition of enforced idleness, overlain by the uncertainty of what awaited him at journey's end. He largely shunned shipboard society, aside from a few late-night poker games, which left him, rather to his surprise, marginally in profit. He several times yielded to temptation in the attractive form of an unhappily married woman who joined the ship at Port Said and left it at Colombo to be reunited with her husband. He dealt deftly with a few other minor difficulties. He read his way assiduously through the ship's library of detective novels. And he paid regular visits to the ship's gymnasium, overseen by the prodigiously muscular Massimo, whose advances he courteously declined.

All did not go smoothly, however. The *Perla* limped into Singapore several days behind schedule on half-power, thanks to mechanical problems which it took several more days to solve. They eventually reached Shanghai over a week late.

It was from a newspaper bought within minutes of leaving the ship that Max learnt of the final signing of the peace treaty amid much ceremony at Versailles on June 28 – and of the scuttling of the German High Seas Fleet at Scapa Flow a week before. All the struggles and intrigues in Paris had led at last to signatures on a piece of paper that would shape the post-war world, for good or bad. While somewhere in Scotland – or England – Lothar Schmidt, former captain of the SMS *Herzog*, one of the ships listed as sunk, was contemplating that world as a prisoner of war, no doubt satisfied he had done his patriotic duty.

But Max had more immediate issues to worry about. He was concerned Morahan and his crew would already be in Yokohama, waiting for him. There was nothing he could do but press on.

It was the concièrge of the Astor House Hotel who advised him that the quickest way to reach Yokohama was to take a berth on one of the many cargo ships heading for Japan, disembark at Nagasaki and travel on from there by train.

So it was that early in the morning of Saturday 5th July 1919 Max returned to the country of his birth: the homecoming of a stranger, standing alone on the small passenger deck of the merchantman *Groundsel* as it nosed into Nagasaki harbour. He looked at the houses and the hills of an alien land and felt relief mixed with exhilaration. The waiting was very nearly over.

Max saw more of Japan than he might have wished over the next three days. He took a slow train across the island of Kyushu to the port of Moji, then a ferry to Shimonoseki on the main island of Honshu and an overnight train from there to Kyoto.

Steam-bath heat prevailed by day and night. The overnight train was crammed with travellers. Max had to share a sleeping compartment with a garrulous businessman who spoke not a word of English. The corridor seemed the coolest part of the train and Max spent a good deal of time standing in it, gazing out at the passing scenery: forested hills and mountains; rice-fields; bamboo groves; glimpses of the Inland Sea, studded with islands; pagodas; temples; huddled townships of wood-and-paper houses; men and women in kimonos, glancing up as the train sped by. The strangeness of the country – and its beauty, especially in the pink, fading light of evening – disclosed itself to him as the journey proceeded. He had been born there, true enough. But he did not belong. And those who did paid him no heed.

The only book about Japan he had found in the *Perla*'s library had told him Kyoto was the former capital, supplanted by Tokyo when the Emperor was restored to direct rule at the end of the Shogunate in 1868. The vagaries of the timetable meant he had several hours to wander its streets, marvelling at the abundance of temples, before resuming his journey. He reached Nagoya that night and experienced the unfamiliar but agreeable customs of a *ryokan*, communicated to him in mime by the smiling owner. Sharing a bath with two women who appeared amused by his embarrassment was only one of its novelties.

He slept so well and so late on the *ryokan*'s floor-level bed, without the slightest twinge from the old wound in his side, that he missed the first train to Tokyo next morning. When he finally reached Yokohama at close to ten o'clock that evening, he instructed the taxi driver to take him to the best hotel: the Grand. No one called Morahan or Hollander was staying there, which did not surprise Max, given Morahan's cautious ways. But he was confident his friends would not be far away. He was tired and hungry. His only food since breakfast had been bought from a platform vendor during one of the train's many lengthy stops. He decided to have supper and a night in a Western-style bed before going in search of them.

Tuesday morning revealed the hotel's setting to Max as soon as he pulled back the curtains of his room. It faced Yokohama harbour, thronged with shipping, sunlight sparkling on the wavetops out in the bay. The air carried gull shrieks and ships' horns and the distant shouts of stevedores. He had reached the rendezvous at last. The search for his father's secret in the land where it had long lain buried was about to begin.

The Eastbourne was the third hotel he tried. He noticed something odd about the atmosphere of the place as soon as he entered the foyer. The staff looked distracted and several were huddled behind the counter, where a man with a managerial cast to him was answering questions on their behalf put by a small, insistent individual Max instinctively identified as a policeman.

A couple of uniformed policemen descended the stairs from the upper floors while Max lingered just inside the door. He had no clue as to what might be going on, nor any reason to think it concerned his friends. On balance, though, he reckoned it would be wise to call again later.

As he walked back out, he felt a twitch at his sleeve and turned to find a smiling bellboy, who looked more Hispanic than Japanese, close behind him.

'You friend of Miss Hollander?'

'What if I am?'

'I think you are friend she waited for. You look for her now?'

'Maybe.'

'Bad time, meester. Police look for her too. Also Meester Twentyman.'

'Twentyman?' Max was taken aback. Sam was not in Japan. He could not be. Max had explicitly told Morahan to leave Sam out of it. And yet . . . 'What's your name, son?'

'João.'

'So, what can you tell me, João?' Max fished a few yen out of his pocket, but João waved them away and shot an apprehensive glance over his shoulder.

'Post Office, Nihon-odori, half hour,' he whispered. '*Sim?*'

'*Sim,*' Max found himself saying. 'Yes. I'll be there.'

Max was loitering by the telegram form counter when João entered the post office, still in his bellboy's uniform, clutching several parcels. He joined a queue at one of the windows. Max stepped in behind him and opened a murmured conversation.

'I'm Max, João. Did Malory – Miss Hollander – ever mention me?'

'I heard her say your name to Meester Twentyman. They wait for you. Since Wednesday. Miss Hollander nice lady. All this with police not right.'

'All *what* with police?'

'They arrest Meester Morahan in Tokyo last night, I hear. They are looking for Meester Twentyman and Miss Hollander. I do not know about Meester Twentyman, but Miss Hollander left hotel just before police came last night. She had message to meet someone.'

'Who?'

'Meester Monteith.'

The name meant nothing to Max. But the rest spelt a catastrophe he could not quite come to terms with.

João reached the head of the queue at that point. He broke off to deal with the clerk. The parcels were weighed and João paid for them. Then they moved away from the counter.

'Mr Morahan's been arrested, but Mr Twentyman and Miss Hollander are still free,' Max pressed. 'Is that right?'

'I think yes. The police ask all about them.'

'Are they together?'

'I do not know. The police arrested two men at other hotel in Yokohama last night also, I hear.'

'What are they charged with?'

'The police say Meester Morahan murdered man in Tokyo. But he is not murderer, I think. Miss Hollander would not have friend who is murderer.'

'No more she would, João. Who's Mr Morahan accused of murdering?'

'Farngold.'

'*What?*'

'That is what I hear. Name is Jack Farngold.'

A meeting with Morahan and his team, followed by a dispassionate assessment of how they were to set about uncovering the truth and defeating the combined forces of Lemmer and Tomura, was what Max had foreseen. Instead, all their plans and preparations were in disarray. How and why, Max did not know. But it was clear disaster had overtaken them.

Thanks to Appleby, Max had a couple of false passports to travel under and he doubted the police had a photograph of him. He had to assume Farngold's murder and Morahan's arrest had been orchestrated by Tomura, however, acting at Lemmer's direction. It was likely they would be looking for Max as well. All in all, he should probably leave Yokohama as soon as possible. But to go where? And to do what?

He needed hard information and he needed it quickly. Without it, he was flying in fog. Only one way of obtaining any occurred to his mind.

He hurried back to his hotel and put a call through to the British Embassy in Tokyo.

'Hodgson speaking.'

'Good morning, Mr Hodgson. My name is Taylor. I'm writing an article for a London magazine on the challenges of a diplomatic career in this part of the world.'

'You are?' Hodgson sounded as if a sense of irony lurked beneath the crustiness of his voice.

'I'm told you've worked at the legation here for many years.'

'Too many.'

'Since Mr Fraser was ambassador.'

'Ah, poor old Fraser, yes. Worked himself into an early grave. Didn't call himself ambassador, though. Envoy Extraordinary was the formal title in his day.'

'Of course. Sorry. A slip of the tongue. Nomenclature is very important, isn't it?'

'I wouldn't go that far.'

'Could we perhaps meet for lunch? You could set me right on a few things.'

'Lunch? Well, I . . . what magazine is this for?'

'*Cartouche.*'

'Never heard of it.'

'It's quite new. So, could I buy you lunch?'

'Oh, well . . .'

'Anywhere you like. The editor will want me to entertain you properly.'

'Will he? That's decent of him.'

'Are you available today by any chance?'

'Today?'

'My schedule's rather . . . tight.'

'It is?'

'Yes. So . . . can we meet?'

THE PROSPECT OF LUNCHING AT ONE OF HIS FAVOURITE RESTAURANTS at someone else's expense clinched the matter for Hodgson. He doubted 'Mr Taylor' could locate the establishment unaided – 'the city's rather a maze, you'll find' – so they agreed to meet in the central hall of Tokyo station. Max had explained he would be arriving by train, though arriving from *where* he did not specify.

He booked out of the Grand and dropped his bag at the left luggage counter when he reached Tokyo Central. He did not want Hodgson to conclude he was without accommodation. Then he made his way to the rendezvous.

He spotted Hodgson from some way off – a fleshy, jowly, ruddy-faced Englishman in a loose linen suit and panama, leaning on a cane and perusing, with apparent comprehension, a Japanese newspaper.

'Mr Hodgson? I'm James Taylor.'

'Pleased to meet you.' They shook hands. 'Hope it's not too hot for you.'

'I wouldn't object if it was cooler.'

'I dare say. Japanese summers are gruelling affairs. But one gets used to them eventually. And old Nakahara has some ingenious arrangements with fans and trickling water to keep his restaurant cool. Let's take a cab there.'

Hodgson began to question Max about how long he had been in Japan and what sort of magazine *Cartouche* was, but was easily persuaded to talk about himself instead. A potted autobiography was delivered during their taxi ride, which, by Max's hazy concept of Tokyo's geography, took them into the Ginza district, where he knew – though could not admit knowing – that Hodgson lived.

'Grew up in Essex. Constable country. Father was a land agent. Can't tell you how pleased he was when I passed the Civil Service exam after I left Oxford. "You're made for life, my boy." Well, I'm not sure he was right about that. I thought I'd see the world, not just this corner of it, but apparently my expertise in the language makes me indispensable. Not many fluent Japanese speakers in the FO. Never have been.'

'Speaker *and* reader, I see.'

'Ah, the paper? Just perusing an editorial. Got to keep in touch.'

'What's the subject?'

'Candidates for the governor-generalship of Korea.'

'A new broom needed after the first of March riots?'

'Yes. Hasegawa's out and—' Hodgson frowned quizzically at Max. 'You seem to have done your research.'

'A little. Who would you blame for the problems in Korea?'

'Hold up, young man. I can't discuss policy with a journalist for a magazine I know nothing about. I thought you wanted to hear about the life and career of an average Far East dip.'

'Dip?'

'Diplomat.'

'Yes. I'm sorry. You're right. I do.'

And Max dutifully pretended to for the first half hour or so of their presence in the agreeable cool and quiet of Nakahara's restaurant. Hodgson was evidently a regular and valued patron. They were shown into a private room, where they sat at a sunken table and were attended by flower-scented waitresses in rustling kimonos. The sound of water wafted in from somewhere on the breeze of the fan. Filtered sunlight fell mellowly on panelled walls bearing artful depictions of cherry trees and cypress groves.

Apparently forgetting his bar on discussing policy, perhaps under the influence of several thimblefuls of Nakahara's most select sake, Hodgson revealed he actually blamed 'the militarists' for the disturbances in Korea. 'The sooner Saionji returns from Europe the better.' He felt obliged to explain who Saionji was, just as Max felt obliged to nod gratefully.

Hodgson's evident approval of Saionji and his comments on the situation in Korea implied to Max he was no better disposed towards Tomura than when he had written his report to the Permanent Under-Secretary back in June 1891. It was time to test the water.

'When were you first posted here, Mr Hodgson?' Max asked as he maladroitly manoeuvred a piece of raw soy-dipped fish to his mouth with his chopsticks.

'Autumn of eighty-seven. I've had plenty of time to accustom myself to Japanese cuisine and master the jolly old *hashi*.' Hodgson grinned and waggled his chopsticks by way of translation.

'You must remember Sir Henry Maxted, then.'

'Maxted?'

'Here from eighty-nine to ninety-one, I believe. Not *Sir* Henry then, of course. Just plain Mr Maxted.'

Lulled as he was by fine food and smooth sake, Hodgson looked nevertheless to be on his guard. 'Why d'you mention Maxted?'

'He was murdered in Paris a few months ago, while serving with the British delegation to the peace conference. You must have read about it. And been saddened to learn of the death of a former colleague, I imagine.'

'I was. But there was no question of murder, surely.' The assertion sounded half-hearted. Hodgson was evidently well aware of the eventual verdict of the Paris police.

'Count Tomura wasn't in Paris at the time. But he arrived shortly afterwards. He's recently returned to Japan, I believe.'

Hodgson laid down his chopsticks and looked searchingly at Max. 'What prompts you to mention Count Tomura?'

'Sir Henry crossed swords with him while he was posted here. You wrote a report explaining why he was sent home in the summer of ninety-one.' Max sat back and stretched his legs as best he could. He met Hodgson's gaze. 'Complications arising from a police investigation of the attempted assassination of the Tsarevich at Ohtsu on the eleventh of May that year. That was the nub of the matter, wasn't it?'

Hodgson was probably astonished. But his diplomatic training enabled him to hide it well. 'The magazine you're writing this piece for, Mr Taylor . . .'

'It doesn't exist.'

'Are you in fact a journalist?'

'No.'

'Is Taylor your real name?'

'No.'

'You've persuaded me to meet you under false pretences using an assumed name and fictitious credentials.'

'I have.'

Hodgson's face had flushed a worrying red. But his voice remained steady. 'I'll give you one minute to explain yourself before I ask Nakahara to have you thrown out.'

'My real name is James Maxted.'

'Good God.'

'Sir Henry's son.'

'Yes. Of course. I see now . . . You have his eyes.' Hodgson shook his head in bewilderment. 'What in heaven's name possessed you to come to Japan?'

'I followed Tomura. Lemmer's with him. They're working together. Just as they were twenty-eight years ago. Lemmer was responsible for my father's death, you see.'

'Lemmer?'

'You named him in your report, Mr Hodgson. Tomura too. The German working with Dark Ocean to—'

'Don't mention Dark Ocean here.' Hodgson looked alarmed. He raised one hand to silence Max. 'And don't mention my report. You shouldn't have been able to get hold of that.'

'But I was able to. I mean to bring them down – Tomura and Lemmer. It's time someone did, don't you think?'

'You can't bring Tomura down. Not here, in Japan. He's too powerful. As for Lemmer—'

'I need your help, Mr Hodgson. I'm very much hoping you'll give it. But I'll go on without it if I have to.'

'And get yourself killed?'

'Maybe.'

'Like Henry.' Hodgson leant forward and massaged his forehead. 'He should have left well alone.'

'What should he have left?'

'We can't talk about this here. The staff don't speak a word of English as far as I'm aware, but even so . . . We should leave.' He picked up his cup of sake, emptied it and reached for a small bell to summon the waitresses. 'You shouldn't have come, young man.'

'Call me Max. Everyone does.'

'Max? Very well. You should have stayed in Europe, Max. There's nothing for you here.'

'Except the truth.'

'You think so?'

'Yes. And I think you know what that truth is.'

THEY TRAVELLED BY RICKSHAW TO HIBIYA PARK, THE OTHER SIDE OF the Imperial Hotel from Ginza. As if to prevent Max mentioning sensitive subjects during the journey, Hodgson sustained a monologue about how much he preferred rickshaws to motor-taxis and trams. It seemed to Max he was simply playing for time.

The park offered patches of welcome shelter from the baking sun, but naturally that was where most of its visitors had chosen to sit, so Hodgson piloted them to an isolated, unshaded bench near the empty bandstand. He took a handkerchief from his pocket as he sat down and wrapped it loosely round his neck as protection against the sun. Max hardly noticed the heat.

'Some of the trees in this park are older than the city,' said Hodgson, squinting around. 'It used to be a parade ground. I saw the old Emperor reviewing troops here once. And later I watched his funeral procession from this very spot. That was only seven years ago, though oddly it seems longer. The whole Meiji era has vanished into a distant past. And its values with it.'

'You're not intending to tell me you've forgotten the events of 1891, are you, Mr Hodgson?'

'No. Certainly not.' Hodgson looked upset by the suggestion. 'If you've read my report, though actually I merely drafted it for—'

'You wrote it, yes or no?'

'In effect, I . . . suppose I did.'

'Kuroda suspected a connection between Tomura and the attempted assassination of the Tsarevich. He suspected Lemmer

118

was involved as well. My father was giving him what assistance he could when you intervened to have him sent home.'

'I didn't intervene. I was asked to assess the situation and that's what I did.'

'My father went back to London and Kuroda was called off by his superiors. Tomura *and* Lemmer were allowed to continue with their scheming.'

Hodgson lifted one end of his neckerchief to wipe some sweat from his upper lip. 'You've got the wrong end of the stick . . . Max. When I said you shouldn't have come here, it wasn't because I was worried about myself. It's because I'm worried about you. You really shouldn't have come.'

'Kuroda's been killed now as well as my father. You know that, don't you?'

'I heard of Kuroda's death, yes. Officially, an accident . . . I believe.'

'Do you believe it?'

More mopping of the lip. 'No,' Hodgson murmured. 'Of course I don't.'

'Did you recommend my father be sent home?'

'Yes. I did.'

'Why?'

'Tomura was and still is a dangerous man. Doubly so when collaborating with Lemmer. I was genuinely concerned for Henry's safety. He and your mother knew the Tomuras socially. They also knew Mrs Tomura's father.'

'Claude Farngold?'

'Yes. They met him aboard ship on their way here in eighty-nine. He joined the voyage at Hong Kong. Business often took him there, I understand. Henry told me – and Kuroda – that Farngold expressed grave concerns to him about Tomura's political activities. His daughter had only been married to Tomura a matter of months then. It was rumoured Farngold had agreed to the match to gain a commercial advantage. Army supply contracts: that kind of thing. Then came the attempted assassination of the Japanese Foreign Minister, Okuma. And, shortly afterwards, Farngold's death in a fire at his warehouse. Well, you've read the report. Kuroda said there was a strong possibility Farngold was already dead when the fire began. It looked to him like murder concealed by arson. His superiors disagreed. Just as they disagreed with his suggestion that Lemmer encouraged Tomura to move against the Tsarevich in order to poison Russo-Japanese relations. Henry offered to help him out by making a statement to the police putting on record his suspicion that Tomura had ordered Claude Farngold's murder to prevent him disclosing evidence connecting Tomura with the attempt on Okuma's life. That would have made it very difficult for Kuroda's superiors to stop him investigating Tomura's role in the attack on the Tsarevich. But London had insisted no legation personnel were to become personally involved in the matter for fear of provoking a full-scale diplomatic row. So, Henry was told to keep quiet, which he wasn't at all happy about. Since there was a distinct possibility Tomura was aware of his willingness to speak out, it seemed to me he was bound to be in danger. The boat home was the obvious answer.'

'My father learnt something in Paris earlier this year that made him determined to come here and right a great wrong dating from that period. Any idea what it might've been?'

'None. It's far too late to make accusations against Tomura about Okuma and the Tsarevich. I can't imagine what might have got into Henry's head. It's all water under the bridge.'

'Evidently not, since it's got my father killed – and Kuroda too.'

Hodgson could not refute that. 'Something to do with Lemmer, perhaps?' he offered.

'He's certainly involved. But Tomura's at the centre of it. It's about the Farngolds.'

That drew a doubtful look. 'Really?'

'Have you ever met Claude Farngold's son, Jack?'

Hodgson conducted further mopping with his neckerchief while he mulled the question over. Then: 'Yes. I have. Several times. He came to the legation seeking information about his father's death. Late eighty-nine, that would have been. He was referred to the legation by the consulate in Yokohama. Personable young fellow. I sent him to see Kuroda. The next occasion was shortly after Henry

120

went home in ninety-one. Young Farngold was hoping to speak to him. It was obvious he hated Tomura. Small wonder when you consider he had cause to suspect Tomura had murdered his father and also blamed him for his sister's death. He seemed to think she'd been neglected, whether with good reason or not I couldn't say. At all events, he continued to bear a grudge against Tomura. Some years later, I heard he'd been arrested for making a nuisance of himself at Tomura's house here in Tokyo, though I don't think any charges were levelled. The last time I saw him would have been . . . the autumn of 1917. He was looking for Henry – again. He'd changed a lot, I remember. Not simply older, but . . . worn out, dishevelled, a little deranged, it seemed to me. I told him Henry was with the embassy in Petrograd. He said he'd write to him there. What about I don't know.'

'That's the last you heard of him?'

'No. Kuroda came to see me late last year. He said he was looking for Jack Farngold, who was reported to be in Tokyo, possibly as a patient in a lunatic asylum. He hoped I might have heard something about him. I hadn't. Kuroda explained he was making his inquiries on behalf of Marquess Saionji. That struck me as odd. We didn't know then Saionji was going to head Japan's delegation to the peace conference. He was semi-retired, although still officially an advisor to the Emperor. I wondered why he should be interested in Jack Farngold.'

'Because he was interested in Count Tomura and the threat posed by Dark Ocean.'

'Yes.' Hodgson nodded, conceding the point with a downward glance. 'I suppose so.'

'Now Kuroda's dead. And so is Jack Farngold.'

'What?' Hodgson looked at Max in obvious astonishment. 'Jack Farngold's dead?'

'Murdered last night. Here in Tokyo.'

'How do you know this?'

'That doesn't matter. What matters is that Tomura's back in Japan and so is Lemmer. Now Jack Farngold's dead and a friend of mine is in custody charged with his murder. Two other friends are being sought by the police. They came here to help me get to the bottom of the Farngold mystery. Killing Jack Farngold is the last thing they'd be party to. They must have walked into a trap: Tomura disposes of an old enemy and blames it on them.'

'Are the police looking for you as well?'

'No. No one knows I'm in Japan – except you.'

'Good Lord.' Hodgson shook his head thoughtfully. 'This is . . . frightful.'

'I need your help, Mr Hodgson. So do my friends.'

'Well, I . . .'

'Do you know anyone senior in the police force?'

Hodgson nodded. 'Fujisaki. He worked under Kuroda for a number of years. A sound fellow.'

'Can you speak to him and find out exactly what happened? That would be a start.'

'I'll telephone him as soon as I get back to the embassy.'

'It might be wiser to call on him in person.'

Hodgson frowned at Max. 'Why?'

'Lemmer must have got wind of what my friends were doing here and alerted Tomura. There was treachery somewhere along the line. It's impossible to say who is or isn't one of Lemmer's spies.'

'How do you know I'm not?'

'Are you?'

'No. Of course not. But—'

'I had to take the risk of confiding in you, Mr Hodgson. I have nowhere else to turn. Will you help me?'

'I'll . . . do what I can, certainly.'

'Don't mention me to anyone. Lemmer mustn't learn I'm in Tokyo.' Or alive, Max refrained from adding, assuming Dombreux had persuaded Lemmer he was dead. 'When did you last meet Lemmer yourself?'

'I'm not sure. Probably at some reception or other back in ninety-one. He left Tokyo not long after Henry.'

'And you've never seen him since?'

'No. Heard of him, of course, by reputation. And there were reports he was in this region a couple of years back. Why he'd risk a journey to the Far East in the middle of the war I can't imagine. Rumours put him in China, which didn't declare war on Germany until August of 1917. And that only held for the Peking government. Sun Yat-sen down in Canton stayed neutral. There were suggestions the Germans were funding his régime. Perhaps that's what Lemmer was up to.'

'It won't have been all he was up to.' Max turned over in his mind what Nadia had told him about working for a Japanese businesswoman based in Korea known as the Dragonfly. One of Nadia's tasks, arranged by the Dragonfly to oblige Lemmer, had been to lure Jack Farngold into a trap. He had been seized and sent to Japan. And now he had been killed. 'Lemmer remains an active enemy of His Majesty, Mr Hodgson. Remember that. It's not just me you'll be helping. It's your king and country.'

'But the government Lemmer served no longer exists. The Germans have accepted defeat. They signed the peace treaty.'

'Which is why he's here, seeking another government to serve.'

'The Japanese wouldn't do that.'

'Which Japanese do you mean? Marquess Saionji – or Count Tomura?'

Hodgson took a moment to absorb the enormity of what Max had said. 'If this is true . . .'

'It's true.'

'I must alert my superiors.'

'Not yet. I need you to promise me you'll alert no one until we've learnt what happened last night and have had a chance to decide the best course of action.'

'But this is a gravely serious matter.'

'Yes. Which is precisely why it must remain between us for the moment. You'll be in danger yourself once you show your hand.'

'Like Henry.' The possibility dawned darkly on Hodgson's countenance. 'And to think I expected my last few months before retirement to be uneventful.'

'I'm sorry, Mr Hodgson.'

'You'd better call me Cyril, Max. Now we're in this together.'

'You'll speak to Fujisaki this afternoon?'

'If I can.'

'Then we should meet later. Shall I come to Uchida Apartments?'

Hodgson arched his eyebrows in surprise. 'You know where I live?'

'I know your address, yes. It came from the same source as the copy of your report I read. But I'll need directions.'

'Where are you staying?'

'Not sure. Let's say I'll be starting from here.'

'And we are starting from here, aren't we, Max?' Hodgson glanced around the park. 'I suppose I should have known, when I heard of Henry's death, then Kuroda's . . .' He rubbed his forehead. 'Perhaps I did know, on some level I preferred to ignore. The past, hey? It remembers you better than *you* remember *it*.'

MAX COULD SEE NOTHING FOR IT BUT TO BIDE HIS TIME UNTIL HE spoke to Hodgson again. He booked into the Station Hotel at Tokyo Central, using one of the several fake passports. He was James Greaves as far as anyone was concerned, occupation unspecified.

An anxious afternoon and early evening slowly passed. It was stiflingly hot in his room, but he knew unnecessary wandering was a risk he could not afford to take. Waiting was one of the hazards Appleby had warned him about, without offering anything in the way of a solution. 'You'll get used to it,' he had said. But Max had not got used to it – yet.

Uchida Apartments were part of a large red-brick Western-style building on a corner site one street away from the main shops of Ginza. The walk there had reminded Max how much more foreign he felt in Tokyo than he had in Shanghai. Japan was a world he knew little of. A misstep would be easy to take. A woman had caught his eye at the last crossing and he had not been sure why, though he felt he should have been. The city was crowded. But he knew he was conspicuous nonetheless.

He pressed the bell numbered six and heard the door-latch click. Entering, he was mildly surprised by the modesty of the interior. There was a line of mail boxes and a flight of plain stairs. He started up them.

A Japanese woman who was clearly Mrs Hodgson was holding

the door of the apartment open when he reached it. She was wearing a richly patterned kimono and looked much younger than her husband, though Max allowed for the possibility she had simply aged better. Her open, smiling features would once have been quite lovely. And some of their loveliness remained.

'Maxted-san,' she greeted him with a bow. '*Yokoso*. Please come in.'

The apartment he entered was a mixture of Japanese and Western in its furnishings and decorations. He was relieved of his coat and hat and shoes. Mrs Hodgson showed him into a drawing room, where Western style prevailed, though the feeble tinkling of a wind-chime out on a balcony, to which the doors stood ajar, conveyed a hint of the Orient. He politely declined the offer of tea.

'Hodgson-san is not here,' Mrs Hodgson explained. 'But soon he will be back. Will you wait for him here?'

'Certainly.'

'There is whisky.' She pointed to a drinks tray on a table in a corner of the room. 'Please have some.'

She left then and Max went to help himself to a Scotch. The wind-chime stirred only occasionally. There was noise of traffic beyond it: the rumble of tyres on cobbles, the squeal of a tram, the blare of a horn.

He sat down and drank some of his whisky. His gaze wandered to the pictures on the wall. There were several framed photographs of Europeans gathered in a social setting. Max rose and took a closer look, pondering whether they were of Hodgson's colleagues at the British legation. He suspected they were, these smiling English gentlemen and ladies in their smart evening dress. Differences in the men's beards and moustaches and the cut of the ladies' gowns suggested the photographs had been taken some years apart, perhaps spanning the thirty years or so of Hodgson's time in Japan.

Max wondered if he would see his parents' younger faces staring back at him from one of the groups. He inspected what appeared to be the earliest photograph. It showed a group of twenty or thirty couples in evening finery, assembled before the camera in a brightly lit ballroom decorated with ribbons and balloons. The ladies were arrayed in elegant silk dresses of varying shades, bustled and bowed and cinch-waisted, with generous displays of décolletage.

Suddenly, he saw his mother, looking young and grave and icily beautiful. There she was, with her hair drawn up as Max could only remember seeing it in her wedding portrait. A brooch he did not recognize was gleaming at her breast. Her gown was dark and lustrous – purple, perhaps, a colour she had always liked.

And there too, beside her, her arm in his, was his father, clearly younger, but also somehow less confident than the man Max had last seen in Paris four months before. He was glancing away from the camera a little oddly, as if distracted or simply unprepared for the closure of the shutter.

'Max,' came Hodgson's call from the doorway, breaking into his reverie.

'Ah.' Max turned away from the photograph. 'There you are.'

'Sorry not to have been here when you arrived.'

'No matter. I was looking at these pictures.'

'Ah, those. A few of the legation's New Year's Eve balls. It's become something of a tradition, actually. We've held it at the Imperial ever since . . . well, ever since the hotel opened.'

'I see my parents in this one.'

'Yes. That would be right.' Hodgson walked across to where Max was standing and looked hard at the photograph. 'Their . . . first year in Tokyo. 1889, it must have been. The others take us through to just before the war.'

'Are you in all of them yourself?'

'Yes. I think so. But we've rather more important matters to discuss, haven't we?' Max noticed then how flustered Hodgson appeared. There was a visible sheen of sweat on his forehead. 'Sorry,' he said, dabbing himself with his handkerchief. 'It's been a hectic evening. Shall we sit down?'

'By all means. Would you like me to fetch you a drink?'

'Thanks. I would. Scotch and soda.' Hodgson subsided into an armchair. Max poured him the drink and topped up his own whisky, then opened the door to the balcony a little wider before sitting down himself.

Hodgson took a swallow from his glass. 'You met my wife. Perhaps I should have mentioned the fact that she's Japanese.'

'There was no need.'

'Asking me if I'm in all of those photos touched a raw nerve, I'm afraid. I mean, I am, in the ones hanging on the wall. But I missed a couple of balls after we married. My wife wasn't made to feel entirely welcome, you see.'

'Sorry to hear that.'

'Best forgotten.' Hodgson took another swig. 'Now, to business. I've just come from a meeting with Commissioner Fujisaki. He keeps rather late hours. And he's a cautious fellow. Preternaturally so, some might say.'

'Was there anything he could tell you?'

'Yes. Some bad news and some good. The Kempeitai – the Japanese Secret Police – apprehended three men last night and charged them with murdering Jack Farngold in pursuance of a plot to assassinate the Prime Minister.'

'*What?*'

'Their names are Thomas Morahan, Grover Ward and Gazda Djabsu. You know them?'

'Morahan, yes. The others will be people he's recruited since we last met.'

'The police are looking for two other people: Samuel Twentyman and a Miss Malory Hollander. You know them as well?'

'Yes. They're friends. But the idea that any of them was plotting to assass—'

'I know. So does Fujisaki. Thanks to his intervention, the assassination charge has been dropped. Morahan, Ward and Djabsu have been handed over to the regular police. They're being held in Sugamo prison. It's not exactly the Ritz, but it's vastly preferable to being in the hands of the Kempeitai, let me assure you.'

'That's something, I suppose. But did Fujisaki intervene just to oblige you? I had no—'

'He was already involved when I spoke to him, Max. A senior official at the Home Ministry he declined to name asked him to help your friends as best he could. Which he was happy to do

128

once he realized Tomura was mixed up in what had happened.'

'And what exactly *had* happened?'

'It seems someone called Lewis Everett, who was working with Morahan, betrayed him to the Kempeitai. The police were called to a shop here in Ginza last night. They found Farngold shot dead in an upper room with Morahan and Everett engaged in a struggle. A third person – Twentyman – escaped at that point. Morahan was arrested. Ward and Djabsu were arrested at their hotel in Yokohama soon afterwards. Miss Hollander was to have been arrested as well, but couldn't be found. So, it was just the three of them who were handed over to the Kempeitai – and not for long, fortunately.'

'We need to know who this senior official at the Home Ministry is, Cyril.'

'Fujisaki wouldn't be drawn on the point. And he knew I was protecting someone's identity as well, of course.'

'Mine, you mean?'

'I couldn't account for knowing anything about the affair without admitting I was acting on behalf of someone else. I assured him of your bona fides and he accepted my assurance. He hazarded a guess that you were a friend of the men detained and the two fugitives. I could hardly deny it. But nor, in the circumstances, could I press him for further details of who he was cooperating with at the Home Ministry, or what more he was doing for him.'

'He is doing more, then, you think?'

'That's the impression he gave me. Fujisaki started out working under Kuroda, remember. He knows more about Tomura than most and probably believes he was responsible for Kuroda's death – the death of a man Fujisaki respected immensely. He won't shy away from tackling Tomura if he can. But as far as I can tell he has nothing he can actually tackle him *with*.'

'Maybe I can supply something.'

'I'm glad to hear you say that. Because Fujisaki wants to meet you.'

'But he doesn't even know who I am.'

'"Tell your anonymous friend to wait by the statue of Saigo Takamori in Ueno Park at four o'clock tomorrow afternoon.

Perhaps we can help each other." That's what he said.'

'Saigo Takamori?'

'You've heard of him?'

'You mentioned him in your report to the Foreign Office, Cyril. The one I've read.'

Hodgson looked bemused by his own forgetfulness. 'Of course. So I did.'

'The defeat of his rebellion . . . in 1881 . . . led to the foundation of Dark Ocean.'

'Actually, it was Dark Ocean that was founded in 1881 – reportedly. Saigo Takamori's rebellion was put down in 1877. Dark Ocean adopted him as a posthumous hero. Of course, dead heroes are the most convenient kind. They can't object to the values and opinions attributed to them.'

'If he was a rebel, why has a statue been erected in his memory?'

'After his defeat, he took his own life in an honourable fashion. The Emperor decided to rehabilitate him. Shortly after the attempt on the Tsarevich's life, as I recall. He may have hoped to detach Saigo's name from Dark Ocean's cause. Unlike him, they're certainly not trying to turn the clock back to the days of the Samurai. Still, Fujisaki's choice of rendezvous does seem oddly symbolic for a man who I'd have thought had no time for symbolism. I take it you will meet him?'

Max nodded. 'Of course.'

'I told him I was sure you would. His proposal surprised me, though. It's out of keeping with his cautious nature. As you say, he doesn't know who you are. So, meeting you is something of a risk.'

'One he won't regret taking.'

'I hope not. Just as I hope I won't regret keeping all this to myself a little longer.'

'You won't.' Max smiled encouragingly. 'You have my word.'

WEDNESDAY WAS STIFLINGLY HOT. MAX KEPT MOSTLY TO HIS ROOM at the hotel, bar one excursion to the main post office in Nihombashi, where he rented a box in the name of Greaves. Time dragged slowly by. At three o'clock, with enormous relief, he set off for Ueno.

The taxi set him down at Ueno station, next to the park, within sight of Saigo Takamori's statue. The old samurai was cast in bronze atop a high pedestal, clad in a *yukata*, pet dog by his side and a sword at his waist. Some children were sitting on the railings around the pedestal, engaged in a game that involved snapping and tossing twigs. There was no sign of anyone looking like a senior police officer.

But Max was early for his appointment, so he was not surprised. He walked on past the statue to the tree-shaded bank of Shinobazu Pond, lit a cigarette and wandered along its perimeter, donning a pair of sunglasses he had bought in Shanghai to shield his eyes from the bright pink glare of the lotus flowers covering much of the water. After a while he turned back.

Walking towards him was a middle-aged Japanese man in a worn grey suit and fedora. He was taller and broader than the average Japanese, with a grizzled beard and separate moustache. He looked directly at Max and nodded.

Max did not know how to react, but was spared the need to ponder the point when the man stepped directly into his path. He flicked a card out of his pocket and showed it to Max. It bore an insignia of some kind and a quantity of Japanese script.

'I am Fujisaki,' the man said. 'You will have to believe me that this is my police warrant-card.'

'I believe you,' said Max evenly.

'I saw you pass the statue and I thought: he is right; it will be better to talk while walking by the pond.' Fujisaki bowed slightly. 'It is a pleasure to meet you, Maxted-san.'

Max was taken aback. Hodgson had assured him he had withheld his name. 'You know who I am?'

'Commissioner Kuroda wrote to you from Marseilles. He wrote to me also. He predicted you would come to Japan. When Hodgson told me of a young man trying to help his friends, I knew it must be you. Even though your friends believe you are dead.'

How they had been given Dombreux's account of his demise Max could only guess, but, though he regretted the distress they must have been caused by it, he took some consolation from this confirmation that his survival was not yet suspected. 'How do you know what they believe?'

'I have had confidential discussions with Yamanaka Fumiko of the Home Ministry. He is the elder brother of Yamanaka Eisaku, who gave assistance to Mr Morahan and Mr Twentyman in Paris. He is sheltering Mr Twentyman and Miss Hollander. We have done as much as we can for Mr Morahan. As for Mr Twentyman and Miss Hollander, arrangements have been made for them to leave Japan tonight. I cannot protect them from arrest otherwise. And I cannot protect you, if Count Tomura learns you are alive.'

'Where are Sam and Malory? I need to speak to them.'

'They are in a place of safety. And by tomorrow they will be out of the country. Mr Morahan and the two other men arrested will be freed eventually, I think, though it may take many months. My advice to you is to leave Japan as quietly as you entered it. There is nothing you can do here.'

'How much do you know about Count Tomura, Commissioner?'

'Enough. He has formed an alliance with Fritz Lemmer. I know of what they intend.'

132

'Their plans will damage your country.'

Fujisaki nodded solemnly. 'So Kuroda believed. So I believe.'

'I mean to stop them.'

'It is foolish to attempt what you cannot achieve.'

'Where are Sam and Malory?'

Fujisaki sighed. 'Let us walk.'

They headed on round the pond at a measured pace. Fujisaki lit a cigarette and took several thoughtful draws on it.

'If you speak to Mr Twentyman and Miss Hollander before they leave, they will not leave after all, will they? They will stay and try to help you finish what Mr Morahan started.'

'I'll urge them to go. I can do this alone. I just need to find out how they got into so much trouble.'

'I am sorry, Maxted-san, but I do not agree. They will stay. Then all three of you will need my help. And in helping you I will become known to Count Tomura – and to Lemmer – as an enemy.'

'You're afraid you'll end up like Kuroda?'

'Of course. But I would be prepared to risk that if I was convinced you really could stop them.'

'I really can.'

'How?'

'I can't tell you, Commissioner. The fewer who know my plans the better.'

'Mmm. I see.' Fujisaki glanced out across the pond. 'You like lotuses?'

'Very pretty.'

'Some say they have heard the flowers pop when they open. Others say they make no sound. It is not easy to believe they do . . . unless you have heard it.'

'Have you?'

'Not yet. Policemen are too busy to linger by lotus ponds. You must convince me, Maxted-san. Otherwise I will not put your friends' lives – and mine – in danger by telling you all I know of Count Tomura and his German friend. You must convince me you have a weapon to use against them. And I must hear what it is. The letter I received from Kuroda included a message from Marquess Saionji.'

'From *Saionji*?'

'Yes. In Meiji ten – 1877, as you would have it – at the time of Saigo Takamori's rebellion, Saionji was a junior advisor at the Japanese legation in Paris. Saigo tried to buy arms and ammunition for his rebel army from European dealers. Saionji suggested the best way to prevent this was for the legation to outbid Saigo. As a result, his supply was cut off and his army defeated. It is an interesting story. It shows how, even as a young man, Saionji could combat an enemy from a great distance without appearing to do anything.'

'Is he combating Tomura and Lemmer from a great distance?'

'He is trying to. He was born in Kyoto, when it was still the capital. He has a house there, Seifu-so. He told Commissioner Kuroda that you and anyone you vouched for could have sanctuary at Seifu-so if you needed it.'

'Kind of him, I'm sure, but we're a long way from Kyoto.'

'Yet he seems to think you may find yourself there in the future.'

'Why would he think that?'

Fujisaki stopped and looked at Max intently. 'I am listening for the pop of the lotus, Maxted-san. If I do not hear it, I will say no more.'

So Max took the plunge and told him, about the secret son Lemmer had lodged at a Swiss boarding school and how, at word from Max, the boy would be abducted and held until Lemmer had given up the names of his spies and the 'great secret' that would bring down Tomura. And Fujisaki listened, attentively and silently, to every word. And then they walked on.

'How old is the boy?' came Fujisaki's first question.

'Fifteen.'

'You will threaten to kill him?'

'Yes.'

'But you will not, of course, whatever Lemmer does.'

'No. But Lemmer must believe we are willing to kill him.'

'Kuroda was certain Lemmer possessed a letter sent by Prime Minister Terauchi to German Foreign Minister Zimmermann early in 1917 agreeing terms for Japan to change sides in the war.'

134

'He will be required to surrender it.'

'To save the life of his son.'

'His *only* son.'

'Have you any children, Maxted-san?'

'No. You?'

'Yes.' Fujisaki nodded. 'There is nothing else I could imagine that would be effective against a man such as Lemmer. But this . . .' He nodded again, more decisively. 'I will help you as far as I can.'

'Thank you.'

'Thank me when it is over, if we are both still alive. We are putting our heads in the mouth of a tiger. You understand?'

'I do.'

'Very well. Some of the information I will give you I obtained personally, some I obtained from Yamanaka Fumiko. Lemmer entered the country June twentieth. He is staying at the Imperial Hotel under the name of Frederik Boel. He is using a Danish passport. He has been introduced by Count Tomura to several senior government members. Also to the head of the Kempeitai. Two days ago, he visited the Imperial Navy base at Yokosuka. He is accompanied by his secretary, also Danish, according to her passport – Anna Staun.'

'Real name Anna Schmidt.'

'*Arigato gozaimasu.* Anna Schmidt. Count Tomura arrived with them, accompanied by his son and manservant and two other people now staying at his house here in Tokyo: a Russian woman called Natasha Kisleva and a Frenchman called Patrice Brasseur.'

So, Nadia was using the same alias she had in Scotland. As for a Frenchman called Brasseur, there was only one person he could be. Dombreux's failure to meet Max in Lausanne was now explained, though as yet it was unclear whether he had travelled to Japan by choice or by diktat of Lemmer. 'Their real names are Nadia Bukayeva and Pierre Dombreux.'

'*Mata arigato gozaimasu.* Nadia Bukayeva; Pierre Dombreux. Hodgson will have told you that Lewis Everett is the witness who accused Morahan of the murder of Jack Farngold. He and two other men, Albert Duffy and Howard Monteith, have made statements to the police accusing Morahan of killing Farngold as part of a plot to assassinate Prime Minister Hara. I will try to arrange for the investigation of their accusations to proceed very slowly. So far, the only formal charge against Morahan, Djabsu and Ward is murder. Everett, Duffy and Monteith are at the Metropole Hotel in Tsukiji. Count Tomura's house is in Akasaka. I will tell you exactly where presently. It is well guarded. It seems he believes there are people who may wish to harm him or his guests.'

'From what I hear, Tomura's done enough over the years to collect quite a few enemies.'

'Perhaps over the centuries. The Tomuras were feudal lords even before the Tokugawa Shogunate, but it was as allies of the Tokugawas that they grew powerful. Their castle still stands north of Kyoto. Tomura's second wife lives there.'

'He married again?'

'So I understand. A Japanese woman. She is never seen with him in Tokyo. As far as I know, she never comes here.'

'And Sam and Malory? Where are they?'

'At the house of a friend of Yamanaka in Sendagi. Will you go to them there?'

'You said you'd arranged for them to leave Japan tonight.'

'I have. From Yokohama, on a Dutch ship bound for Shanghai.'

'Then I'll see them in Yokohama, before they go. The less time they have to think about staying the better. I want them safely out of the country. Shanghai is perfect.'

'If you want them out of the country, do not let them know you are still alive.'

'I have to, Commissioner. I need to know everything that's happened since they arrived.'

'Also you do not want them to believe you are dead and that Lemmer and Tomura cannot be touched.' Fujisaki glanced at Max knowingly. 'Is that it?'

'I prefer not to leave my friends in needless despair, if that's what you mean.'

Fujisaki did not explain what he meant, though Max suspected he knew. Sentiment was weakness. It was a luxury they could not afford. But without it they were no better than Lemmer. That was the dilemma they would have to live or die by.

'I'm going to give this everything I have, Commissioner.'

Apprehensive though he knew he should have felt, Max was actually possessed by something much closer to satisfaction when he and Fujisaki parted. Whatever he learnt from Sam and Malory before seeing them on their way, there was no reason to hold back now. As when a long-delayed order for action had reached his squadron in France, there was a sense of physical release. At last, he was off the leash.

From the post office next to Ueno station he despatched an urgent cable to box-holder Brown at Evian-les-Bains post office in France. Western Europe was nine hours behind Japan, so Appleby would receive the message in the morning. Max knew he would act on it without delay.

PLEASE CONFIRM ACQUISITION OF ARTICLE ASAP TO BOX SIXTY-SEVEN GPO NIHOMBASHI TOKYO.
GREAVES

The wheels had begun to turn.

Veronica Underwood, nee Edwards, secret service senior cipher clerk, recently reassigned as special assistant to Horace Appleby, emerged from the post office in Evian-les-Bains that morning at an unusually sharp pace.

She was a slim, blonde-haired, fair-featured woman in her late twenties, discreetly dressed, though not discreetly enough to escape an appreciative glance from a man who was entering the post office as she left.

The past fortnight had been a trial for her, but she had borne it without complaint. She respected Appleby and knew if he judged something essential it truly was.

'I can give you no details of what's involved, Mrs Underwood,' he had said to her in the Piccadilly tea-room where they had first discussed the matter one hot June afternoon. 'I need the help of someone I can trust absolutely in an operation crucial to the safety of the realm. Where we're going and why will have to wait. All I can say is you'll never have been involved in anything more important. I know you were fond of Bostridge. Well, this is a chance to bring to book the men responsible for his death. What do you say?'

She said yes, of course, as patriotism and loyalty to the Service demanded. And her husband did his best to accept her decision. She realized, after setting off for Switzerland with Appleby a week later, that he had chosen her not so much because of her deciphering skills (which, though considerable, were not in Bostridge's league) as because he was sure of her. If she had worked for Lemmer, he would not have allowed her to leave the Service, to which she had only recently returned at Appleby's pleading. As it was, Appleby explained, Lemmer had more spies than the most pessimistic assumptions had ever indicated, some – too many – within the Service itself. Their mission was to extort the names of those spies out of Lemmer by the disagreeable recourse of kidnapping his son. 'I don't like it any more than you will, Mrs Underwood. But it has to be done.'

She could only agree. Lemmer had to be stopped. Therefore his son had to be taken. And minding him during however many days they would have to hold him captive would fall partly if not mostly to her. But there it was. With no progress to report in deciphering the Grey File – the impenetrably encoded master-list of Lemmer's agents Max had delivered to Appleby – and therefore no indication as to who was loyal and who was not, drastic action was called for. And this was it.

The team Appleby had assembled for the operation, to be carried out on both the French and Swiss sides of Lake Geneva, was small and, by normal standards, of questionable suitability. It was just as well Veronica was willing to do anything he asked of her. Working with the incorrigibly flirtatious Lionel Brigham, officially on extended leave from the Foreign Office, was by turns irksome and irritating. He reacted as badly to being given orders as was to be expected of a displaced mandarin, but addressing her as 'my girl' and making occasional suggestions she preferred to pretend she did not understand proved a sore test of her forbearance.

The other two members of the team were a French father and son, Michel and André Marmier, Lake Geneva fishermen and boat-repairers, whom Appleby had recruited to buy and crew a motor-launch and do whatever else might be needed without quibbling. For this they were to be generously rewarded. Marmier senior was taciturn even in his native language and spoke no English. Marmier junior was marginally less silent and possessed some facility in English, along with a muscular physique he seized every opportunity to display and which Veronica could not help admiring.

Appleby had rented – technically, Brigham had rented – a lake-side villa west of Evian called Les Saules. He had paid over the odds considering its shabby condition, but it boasted three crucial facilities: a cellar, a telephone line and a landing-stage. Veronica's first task was to render the villa habitable and stock it with food – 'woman's work' as Brigham called it. Really, the man was insufferable, but evidently indispensable.

Appleby had bought two cars, one in Evian, which Veronica drove, one in Lausanne, which he and Brigham used to monitor the comings and goings of the boys at Institut Le Rosey, along the lake at Rolle.

Young Eugen, they discovered, was keen on sports, which led him to cram in solitary cross-country runs between lessons and meals, presumably in order to bolster his physical superiority over his classmates. These runs took him along the hill-top trail above Rolle, which he often had more or less to himself in the late after-noon and early evening. Whether his father would have been happy to learn now vulnerable this made him was hard to say. After all, it was impressive evidence of a Spartan temperament and no one was supposed to know who his father really was.

But Appleby knew.

Veronica emerged into the market square and walked briskly across to the café where locals and visitors were sitting at parasol-shaded tables, with twittering birds competing for any crumbs that fell from late-breakfast croissants.

Appleby was not eating, having already consumed bacon and egg at the villa, fried for him by Veronica. Much to her relief, Brigham had not been staying at Les Saules. Appleby preferred to keep him on hand on the Swiss side of the lake, where he had installed himself, no doubt in some luxury, at the Hôtel Beau-Rivage Palace in Ouchy.

Appleby looked up from his coffee and newspaper as she approached and saw at once the envelope in her hand. 'Is that what I think it is?' he asked.

'A telegram, yes. At last.' She handed it to him and watched as he tore the envelope open. 'It can only be from him.'

'I should say so.' Appleby squinted at the message, then looked up at her. 'And it is.'

'The green light?'

'Yes. The waiting's over.'

She sat down at the table, feeling suddenly and unaccountably nervous. 'My goodness,' was all she managed to say.

Appleby smiled. 'There's time for you to have a cup of coffee.'

'I'd rather have a cigarette.'

'Go ahead.'

She lit one and took a deep draw on it. 'When will it happen?'

Appleby looked thoughtful, as if weighing his answer carefully. Then he nodded. 'Today.'

Appleby was not, as it happened, the only person known to Max who had received a telegram from Japan that morning. Winifred, Lady Maxted, carried hers with her as she travelled up to London, where she had arranged at short notice to have lunch with her brother George.

Her departure from Gresscombe Place had been slightly delayed by the persistence of her daughter-in-law Lydia in demanding to be told what the telegram contained. She had been disappointed, although Winifred knew the subject would be reopened when she returned home that evening.

They met at the Ritz, which George had nominated as really the only place for lunch with a lady, especially when that lady was his sister. 'Champagne always tastes better at the Ritz,' he asserted, before putting his assertion to a thorough test.

But, champagne or no, it was obvious to him from the outset that she was worried about something. 'Why not just come out with what it is, Win?' he suggested after they had ordered their meals.

'This,' she said simply, sliding the telegram across the table for him to read.

She watched George wrestle his reading glasses on to his nose and peruse the brief but telling message. A twitch of his eyebrows was the only immediate sign of his reaction. Then he handed the telegram back to her. 'A bit of a facer, Win,' he said with a grimace.

'Yes.' She nodded and looked down at the stark words printed on the form. 'Indeed.'

YOUR SON IN TOKYO SEEKING TRUTH. PLEASE ADVISE WHAT IF ANYTHING YOU WISH ME TO TELL HIM. HODGSON

'When did this arrive?' George asked.

'This morning.'

'Does Ashley know what it says?'

'No. He was out. And I declined to satisfy Lydia's curiosity on the point.'

'Hodgson's the fellow who . . .'

'Arranged our departure from Tokyo, yes. I had no idea he was still there, but I suppose I shouldn't be surprised. Someone told me he married a Japanese woman.'

'Can you rely on his discretion?'

'Oh yes. He's of the old school. The question he poses is how discreet I want him to be, now James has arrived in the land of his birth.'

'The boy's after Tomura, of course.'

'Yes. That's clear. It's what I've feared all along. I'd hoped persuading Count Tomura to leave Paris would prevent this. There must have been other events we don't know about that prompted James to follow him to Japan. Where he is, as Mr Hodgson says, seeking the truth.'

'But will he find it?'

'I don't know, George. Nor do I know with any certainty what the truth is.'

George frowned in puzzlement. 'Surely—'

'When I spoke to Count Tomura in Paris I had the odd and rather disquieting impression that my threat to reveal all was actually more of a threat than I knew.'

'What do you mean?'

'I told him, quite falsely, of course, that I'd met Jack Farngold a couple of years before the war. The possibility seemed to agitate him. I sensed he was harbouring a secret beyond the secret I implied I was willing to lay bare; that it amounted to more – yes, *even* more – than I was aware of.'

'How could it?'

'I simply don't know. But he gave way to me just a little too easily.'

George mulled her answer over as their first courses arrived. When the waiter had gone, he said, 'Do you want my advice on how to reply to Hodgson?'

She nodded. 'Very much.'

'Tomura's a dangerous man. James is risking his life in Japan, whether he knows it or not.'

'Oh, he knows it.'

'Trying to stop him going was obviously wise. It's a pity you weren't successful. But now he's there, now he's . . . on the scent . . .'

'You think I should help him as much as I can.'

'There's only one thing worse than him learning the truth, Win.'

She sighed. 'Better a living son who may disown me than a dead one who never had the chance?'

George winced. 'I wouldn't have put it quite like that.'

Winifred gazed around the restaurant then, at the brightly dressed parties at the other tables and the decorative murals and the verdancy of Green Park, glimpsed through the open windows. 'Here we sit, amid all this prettiness, while thousands of miles away . . .' She shook her head. 'I wish I could protect James, I truly do. I have always wished that. And I have never been able to. All I have done is . . . delay the inevitable.'

'What will you tell Hodgson?'

She gave a wintry little smile. 'What I must.'

At that moment, on the Swiss shore of Lake Geneva, the ferry from Evian-les-Bains was drawing alongside the pontoon at Ouchy. As the vessel tied up and its passengers began to disembark, Lionel Brigham rose from the nearby bench, where he had been idly smoking a cigarette, and moved forward.

Appleby was one of the first off the boat. He exchanged a nod with Brigham and they marched smartly away.

The day was sunny and warm, the light diamond-sharp, the waters of the lake sparkling. Summer ease had descended on Ouchy. But there was nothing suggestive of ease in the two men's urgent pace and grave expression.

'I gathered from your phone call that Max has been in touch.'

'He has. He's ready for us to move.'

'Today?'

'Assuming the boy obliges us by sticking to his routine, yes.'

'Oh, I think he will. You've alerted the Marmiers?'

'All the arrangements are in place,' Appleby replied, with a hint of curtness.

'I can't tell you what a joy it's been working with you,' said Brigham, with more than a hint of sarcasm.

'We're not here for the pleasure of each other's company, Brigham.'

'I console myself with that thought.'

'So do I.'

WITHIN MINUTES OF HIS REUNION WITH SAM AND MALORY, MAX realized how unrealistic his plan was of learning all he could of the events leading to Jack Farngold's death and Morahan's arrest before seeing his friends aboard the *Star of Batavia* and waving them off on their voyage to safety.

It was not simply that they were dumbstruck and overjoyed to see him. It was the discovery that he too was moved, almost to tears, by the potency of the moment. They had thought him dead, believed him erased from the world. Now, on Yokohama pier, in the soft glow of the gas lamps, he saw their faces and they saw his.

'Is it true, sir?' Sam gasped. 'Is it really you?'

'Oh yes. It's me.'

Sam hugged him, which was something Max could never have imagined him doing. And Malory kissed him. 'I don't understand,' she said. 'How can this be?'

'I got the better of Dombreux in Marseilles. I agreed to let him tell Lemmer he'd killed me so Lemmer would believe I was dead.'

'But Dombreux showed me a photograph, sir,' said Sam. 'He bragged about shooting you.'

'The photograph was faked. I'm sorry it was so convincing, but it had to be. Dombreux wasn't supposed to come to Japan. I don't know how that came about. You were never intended to think I was dead. If everything had gone as I'd hoped, Lemmer would have had no cause to suspect you were even here.'

'There was treachery in the camp, Max,' said Malory. 'We walked

145

into a trap. Everything went wrong, terribly wrong.' Then she smiled. 'But now, at last, something's gone right. So right I can hardly believe it.'

'We don't have long,' said Max, noticing the gesticulations of the Dutch sailor by the gangway. 'I think we should go aboard. I'll get off with the pilot. That'll give us time to talk.'

Malory looked at him in some amazement. 'You surely don't think we're leaving now?'

'You must. You'll be safe from arrest in Shanghai.'

'We were clearing out because we couldn't think of anything we could do here to help Schools, sir,' said Sam. 'But you've thought of something, haven't you? You've thought of a way we can beat the bastards.'

'Maybe I have. But I told Schools I didn't want you involved and you'll recall I wasn't happy about you coming either, Malory. You should both leave. While you have the chance.'

In the end, Max talked them into boarding on the understanding that, if he failed to convince them they should carry on to Shanghai, they could all leave the ship with the pilot at the mouth of the bay. Money had to change hands and the captain's agreement be obtained before the matter was settled. The captain made a brief and exasperated appearance when they reached the deck. He objected, as far as Max could gather, to the alteration of a fixed arrangement. He also muttered ominously about *'het getij'* – the tide, as an English-speaking crewman explained. It was the tide – and the extra money – that finally swung the argument. The *Star of Batavia* set sail.

They stood by the starboard rail as the lights of Yokohama slipped away behind them. Max listened as Sam and Malory related what had happened in the week since their arrival from San Francisco. The extent to which Lemmer had outmanoeuvred them was breathtaking. By seeking to delude Lemmer into believing him dead, Max had unwittingly handed their enemy a weapon to use against them. As for Dombreux, it was impossible to judge what kind of game he was playing, though his own well-funded survival was probably the sum of his ambition.

Max then revealed the move against Lemmer – and through him Tomura – that he and Appleby had prepared. It came close to matching their opponents' ruthlessness. It was bold and it was drastic. It was the only way to win.

'I never imagined we'd have to resort to kidnapping a fifteen-year-old boy,' said Malory when she understood what was involved.

'We can't afford to be squeamish,' said Max. 'We have to strike where Lemmer's weakest. And a son is any man's greatest weakness.'

'Will he realize Dombreux gave you this information?'

'That'll be Dombreux's problem.'

'And not his only problem once Lemmer knows you're alive, sir,' Sam pointed out.

'It's surely better if he continues to think you're dead,' said Malory. 'No one will look for you in Tokyo if they think you were murdered in Marseilles.'

'He'll have to find out soon,' said Max. 'The minute I receive word from Appleby he has the boy, I'll go to Lemmer and deliver our terms for his release.'

'What if he rejects those terms?'

'He won't. His only son; his bloodline; his stake in the next generation: he'll give us what we demand for that.'

'Unless he thinks we're bluffing.'

'I'll make sure he doesn't.'

'You should let me do it.'

Max stared at Malory, dismayed by what she appeared to be proposing. 'It has to be me who faces him, Malory.'

'I'm sorry, but I disagree. I speak enough Japanese to talk my way into his presence. He's never met me, so personal animosity won't cloud the issue. Also, I'm a woman. He'll believe the threat when I deliver it. And I'll make it clear we'd be happy to take his son's life to avenge the taking of yours. He won't think we're bluffing when I've finished with him.'

The force of Malory's argument took Max aback. Capitalizing on the fiction of his death would undeniably give them a stronger hand in their dealings with Lemmer. And it was crucial Lemmer should believe they were willing to kill his son if necessary.

There was a silence. Then Sam said, 'I think she's got you there, sir.'

Max was not altogether sorry to lose the argument, even though he continued to urge them to stay on the ship. He took Malory's point: she probably would handle the confrontation with Lemmer better than him. And if she stayed it was futile to suggest Sam should go. Besides, the reason Morahan had decided to bring Sam to Japan in the first place still held good. A swift escape, in circumstances that could not yet be foreseen, might well be needed. And there was nothing swifter than a plane. Max the pilot and Sam the engineer might yet be back in business together.

It was a much faster return journey across the bay in the pilot's boat than the outward crawl in the freighter, but still there was ample time to ponder the difficult question of where Sam and Malory should go next. Back to Professor Nishikawa's house was the obvious answer, but travelling there without the services of a chauffeur was hazardous. For them to be arrested now would be disastrous, especially if Max was arrested with them. Then Appleby would have no means of communication with Lemmer. For that reason alone, they had to go their separate ways as soon as they left the pier in Yokohama.

As it transpired, however, that moment never came. As they reached the top of the steps after leaving the pilot's launch, a figure stepped into view from the shadow of a storage shed. It was Fujisaki.

Sam and Malory were momentarily alarmed, but Fujisaki set them at their ease once Max had introduced him.

'I was sure you would not persuade your friends to leave, Maxted-san. And I worried about what would happen to them if they stayed. I followed their car from Tokyo. I watched the *Ster van*

Batavia sail. But I was sure you would return soon, together with your friends. And here you are.'

'It seems you're a better judge of us than Max is, Commissioner,' said Malory, with a sidelong glance in Max's direction. 'Despite never having met us before.'

'A policeman becomes familiar with human nature, Miss Hollander. It would not be wise for you and Mr Twentyman to return to Professor Nishikawa's house. Count Tomura may suspect you will have turned to Yamanaka Fumiko for help because of your association with his brother. And Yamanaka's friendship with Professor Nishikawa may become known to him. Therefore I offer you shelter in a small house we use occasionally to lodge witnesses to crimes who are in danger. It is presently empty. I keep the keys and control its use. So, you will be safe there, I think, until your dealings with Herr Lemmer and Count Tomura . . . are determined.'

'It won't need to be long,' said Max, 'one way or the other.'

'I hope it will not be the other way, Maxted-san. Oh, the house has a telephone. You will be able to speak to your friends whenever you wish to. The police are still looking for you, Miss Hollander, and you, Mr Twentyman. But I will ensure the search is ill-directed.' Fujisaki looked at Max. 'We should not travel together. You should return to Tokyo by train. I will drive Miss Hollander and Mr Twentyman to the house. It is close to the entertainment quarter of Shinjuku. They will not be noticed there. Now—' He looked around. 'We should stand here no longer.'

149

THE EVENING LIGHT SPREAD GOLDENLY ACROSS THE PLACID WATERS of Lake Geneva, furrowed only by the wake of a paddle-steamer heading westwards, towards the lowering sun. Appleby drew on his pipe, sparing the view of the lake and the rooftops of Rolle and the vineyards above the town no more than a glance before he returned his attention to the woodland path that crossed the track where he and Brigham stood.

They had pulled the Bugatti on to the verge, virtually blocking the path in the direction from which they confidently expected Eugen Hanckel to appear. The path followed the crest of the hills, with the lake on one side and fields and forests on the other. The track they had driven along led north from Rolle into the countryside.

The bonnet of the Bugatti was up and Brigham stood by it, as if pondering a mechanical mystery. This was all show, intended to persuade young Hanckel their car had broken down. He might stop and offer assistance, helpful boy that perhaps he was. Or he might not. In which case *they* would have to stop *him*.

Appleby consulted his watch and noted there was no cause for concern as yet. According to Brigham, Hanckel ran this way at least every other day and he had missed the previous day, so it was virtually certain they would not be disappointed. If they were, they would have to return the following evening. A delay of twenty-four hours would test everyone's nerves, but Appleby was familiar with such contingencies. It was not a game played to precise rules.

'Have you done this kind of thing often?' Brigham asked between draws on his cigarette.

'Often enough.'

'But the victim's been an adult, I imagine.'

'And I've been assisted by a professional. No two operations are ever the same, Brigham. If you want me to tell you nothing can go wrong, I will. But it wouldn't be true.'

'What a comfort you are.'

'The boy won't get away. That's all you need to know.'

'What if he runs before you can grab him? Will you shoot him down?'

'It won't come to that.'

'But if it does?'

'Be quiet.' Appleby frowned. 'I think I can hear something.'

They both listened intently. There it was: a pattering of running feet some way off. It was Eugen Hanckel. Brigham tossed his cigarette to the ground and stubbed it out. They both took a pace away from the car, further obstructing the path.

They waited as the sound of his running, joined now by his panting breaths, drew closer. Then he appeared. He was wearing what looked like football kit, with plimsolls in place of boots. His dark hair was slicked with sweat, his narrow face flushed. His appearance was not markedly different from that of innumerable other boys at Le Rosey, but his heavy eyebrows and broad shoulders singled him out as their target. He was readily identifiable. Appleby had seen his photograph in Dulière's office and Brigham had heard him addressed as Hanckel by one of his classmates on the streets of Rolle. There was no mistake.

Appleby moved to one side, decanting what he judged was just enough chloroform from the small bottle he held on to a cloth. As he did so, Brigham stepped into Hanckel's path, more or less forcing him to stop.

'*Bonjour, mon garçon,*' said Brigham, smiling.

'Hello,' said the boy, jogging on the spot for a moment.

'Ah! You speak English. Know anything about car engines, young man? Ours has died on us.'

151

Hanckel frowned, no doubt puzzled to be asked such a question by an adult. But he did not remain puzzled for long. Appleby closed on him from behind, wrapped one arm round his chest and with the other clapped the chloroformed cloth to his mouth and nose.

Hanckel was no weakling. He struggled to throw Appleby off and Brigham had to envelop him in a bear-hug to ensure he did not escape. The two men reeled and fought with their victim in the still evening air, Appleby praying no passer-by would chance on the scene. Lemmer, he reflected grimly, would be proud of his son's resistance.

But the older men's weight and strength and the drug itself told in the end. Hanckel's writhings subsided into muscular convulsions Appleby knew signalled he was going under. Eventually, he fell limp in their arms.

Appleby cautiously removed the cloth from the unconscious boy's mouth and they manhandled him into the back of the car, where they covered him with a blanket.

'My God,' gasped Brigham, who looked pale with the shock of what they had done. 'I thought it would be easier.'

'Well, now you know. Start her up. I'll put the bonnet down.'

Brigham climbed unsteadily into the driver's seat and started the engine. Appleby lowered and secured the bonnet, then joined him in the car.

'Let's go,' he declared gruffly.

It was a short drive to the village of Perroy and east from there along the shore of the lake to a patch of woodland at the edge of which André Marmier was waiting, a little too conspicuously for Appleby's liking. He was tossing a knife into the bark of a tree from varying distances, while whistling through the gap in his front teeth.

'Another amateur you have to work with,' said Brigham as they slowed to a halt at the side of the narrow lane.

'I'm paying him and his father too much to call them amateurs,' Appleby growled. He looked ahead, then over his shoulder. Hanckel was not stirring. And there was no other traffic on the road. 'The coast's clear. We'd better get on with it.'

It was the work of a few seconds for the strapping André to lift Hanckel out of the car, still wrapped in the blanket, and carry him off into the cover of the wood. Appleby could not deny he had jumped to it when the time came.

'We'll cope from here,' he said to Brigham before following. They exchanged a nod, then Brigham drove away. He looked heartily relieved his part in the abduction was over. Appleby had instructed him to stay in Lausanne until further notice and keep Dulière under observation, but, if all went well, he would have little else to do.

The motor-boat was waiting at the small landing-stage, obscured by surrounding trees that had clinched using the wood for Hanckel's removal from the Swiss side of the lake. Marmier senior, roll-up cigarette adhering as usual to his lower lip, greeted Appleby wordlessly. The boy was already below in the tiny cabin when Appleby clambered aboard. They moved smartly away from the shore.

'Don't go too fast,' said Appleby, fearing a speedy crossing might attract attention.

There was no response from Michel at the wheel. But André, who was already casually lighting a cigarette, said, 'Leave it to Papa, *monsieur*. 'E knows 'ow to do this.'

Appleby was forced to acknowledge that he probably did. 'How's the boy?' he asked.

André shrugged. *'Il dort.'*

The assessment hardly seemed adequate. Appleby descended the few steps into the cabin and looked at Hanckel, who was lying unconscious on a low bunk, with his head clear of the blanket. The chloroform had caused blisters around his lips and nostrils. They would be painful, but it could not be helped.

'Will 'e wake before we reach the villa?' André asked from the hatchway.

'How long before we get there?'

'Maybe . . . 'alf an hour.'

'Then yes. He may. You'd better tie him up.'

'And a gag? In case 'e tries to call out.'

'Yes. A gag too.'

André's estimate of half an hour was about right, but Hanckel was still unconscious when they reached the French side of the lake. Veronica emerged on to the lawn behind Les Saules as they approached and walked down to the landing-stage to meet them.

The willows that gave the villa its name supplied a handy amount of privacy at this time of the year, other than from out in the lake. And the only craft in sight were a couple of distant yachts.

The villa itself stood halfway up a slope leading from the shore to the lakeside road. It was taller than it was wide, terracotta-tiled and cream-washed, with balconies at most of the windows. Some of the tiles had slipped and paint was peeling from the shutters and balcony railings. It looked neglected, hemmed in by overgrown shrubs and spreading trees. But neglect was halfway to secrecy in Appleby's book. And secrecy would be paramount in the days ahead.

André carried Hanckel down the external steps into the cellar, which Veronica had laboured hard to render suitable for short-term habitation. It still smelt damp, but was a good deal cleaner than when she had first seen it.

They had set up a truckle-bed in one corner, on which the boy was laid. André untied him and removed the gag, then used the manacles Appleby supplied to chain his left wrist to one of several pipes running up into the house from the adjacent boiler.

As far as the Marmiers were aware, the abduction was for ransom money pure and simple. Appleby, whom they knew as Brown, had told them Hanckel's father was a wealthy Zürich businessman, which was easy to believe of a pupil at Le Rosey. They had been paid part of their share in advance, but enough had been held back to ensure their continuing compliance – and assistance, if needed.

''Ow long before 'is father pays?' André asked bluntly as they walked back up the cellar steps at the side of the house.

'I'll give him forty-eight hours,' Appleby replied. 'But there may be delays. He's a businessman. They like to negotiate.'

'You want me to cut off one of the boy's ears and send 'is *papa* that to negotiate with, you tell me, OK?'

'I'll be sure to.'

154

'*Les riches.*' André spat into the bushes as he reached the top of the steps. 'That for them.'

'You can go now.'

'*Oui?*' André gave Appleby a glare. 'We 'ear from you soon, yes?'

'Yes.' Appleby said. 'Soon.'

A few minutes later, the motor-boat pulled away from the landing-stage and headed off, bound for the Marmiers' yard. Veronica did not hide her relief at seeing them go.

'They're a poisonous pair,' she said, almost under her breath.

'They're a necessary pair,' Appleby corrected her. 'With any luck, you won't have to see them again.'

'Keeping the boy chained up down in that cellar doesn't sit well with my conscience, Horace.'

'Nor with mine. But remember who his father is. And what's been done on his orders to people we've worked with and respected. Not to mention what might still be done.'

She nodded grimly. 'I will remember.'

'Now, I must get to the station. The telegraph office will still be open. And the sooner Max hears from us, the sooner young Hanckel will be off that conscience of yours.'

SAM AND MALORY'S FIRST NIGHT IN THE HOUSE IN SHINJUKU WAS FAR from a restful one. A narrow, two-storey building set within a small, enclosed yard, it existed close to the heart of nocturnal entertainment in the district, with a dingy cinema, a Chinese grill-restaurant, a probable brothel and a gambling den as its near neighbours. The hours of darkness in such an area were not hours of quietude.

Malory ventured out early in the morning to buy food. She returned with the ingredients for a breakfast Sam pronounced 'cracking'. It was not long afterwards, however, that he resumed trying to dissuade her from confronting Lemmer, at which he had taken an initial stab the night before.

'We only have one go at this, Sam,' she rejoined. 'I guess you have to ask yourself: do I stand a better chance of intimidating Lemmer than you do?'

It was a question he was reluctant to answer. And he was still havering on the point when the telephone rang. Malory answered it.

'*Moshi-moshi.*'

'It's me.'

Malory mouthed '*Max*' to Sam. 'There's news?'

'A cable. They have him.'

'Good. I'll proceed.'

'Give him twenty-four hours to confirm our claim, but no longer.'

'I understand.'

'And . . . good luck.'

Malory had decided to risk Lemmer being out when she reached the Imperial Hotel rather than forewarn him of her arrival.

Leaving Sam to fret, she walked to Shinjuku station and took a taxi directly to the Imperial. She noted the hotel's size and French-style grandeur. A replacement was under construction on an adjacent site that would be grander still, according to her driver. A *kane-bako*, he called it: a gold mine. And Lemmer, it was true, had come to Japan hoping to mine a rich seam. It was her task to tell him he would see no gold from it.

She was aware, as she crossed the gleaming foyer, that in her worn clothes she did not look like one of the Imperial's natural patrons. Chiyoko had given her a light raincoat to wear over the dress she had left Yokohama in. The coat helped her blend with the crowd on the streets. But here it looked shabby and cheap. Nor had she been able to make herself up as she would have wished.

'Damn appearances, Malory,' she murmured to herself as she approached the desk. 'Manner is all that matters.'

And her manner bore her well. The clerk was rapidly persuaded that 'Boel-san' would want to see her. The name of his visitor? 'Miss Ireton.' The reference to her late employer in Paris would put Lemmer on his mettle without quite knowing who – or what – to expect. The call to Boel-san's suite was not a short one. Malory had the impression the clerk was talking to a woman: Anna Schmidt, presumably. The formulation 'Miss Ireton on urgent business' eventually sufficed. She was asked to go up.

The door was opened by a tall, angular woman with ash-blonde hair and a narrow, sharp-featured face. She was dressed soberly, in shades of brown, and it was hard to imagine a smile coming readily to her thin, pursed lips.

'Frau Schmidt?' Malory asked.

'My name is Staun,' came the reply, in an accent clearly more German than Danish.

157

'Well, may I come in?'

Anna Schmidt stepped back and Malory entered a large, opulently furnished room. There was no one else in it, though a door in the far corner, leading to another room, stood open.

'Your name is Ireton?' Anna Schmidt asked.

'You know who I am, I think. I'm here to see Herr Lemmer.'

'Who?'

'I don't have time to play games. Neither, though he does not know it, does Herr Lemmer. I must speak to him.'

'Herr Boel is a busy man. He sees no one without an appointment.'

'Why ask me to come up, then?'

'So that you may state your business.'

'Very well. It concerns his son.'

Anna Schmidt looked startled. A crack spread across her composure. 'His son?'

'I have no son.'

The voice came from the adjoining room. Turning, Malory saw Lemmer walk through the doorway. He was as he had been described to her: grey-bearded and bespectacled, dignified and deliberate, scholarly in appearance, but with a hint of latent power in his posture and movement.

'Herr Lemmer,' said Malory simply.

'You are Malory Hollander,' he responded. 'A fugitive wanted by the Japanese police. I am about to call down and have the police summoned here to arrest you.'

'You shouldn't do that.'

'Why not?'

'I have already given you the reason. Your son.'

'And I have already said I have no son.'

'Eugen Hanckel.'

There was no change in Lemmer's expression, though something like a gasp escaped from Anna Schmidt. Lemmer moved closer, studying Malory's face intently. She caught the scent of the cologne he was wearing. It carried the aroma of apples.

'He is a pupil at Institut Le Rosey in Switzerland. But he is no longer at the school. We have him.'

'*We?*'

'I'm here to deliver our terms for his release.'

'You admit you have been involved in the kidnapping of this boy who is not my son. That would be another crime you could be arrested for.'

'If you have me arrested, now or later; if I do not leave here when I want; if I am followed when I choose to leave . . .'

'Yes, Miss Hollander? What then?'

'The boy will die.'

Anna Schmidt drew in her breath sharply. Lemmer took another step closer to Malory and stared at her. His self-control was total. She could not but admire that in him. And she had to steel herself not to be cowed by the levelness of his gaze. He was, she knew now, if she had ever doubted it, a formidable force.

'Then you would murder a stranger's child,' he said.

'Eugen Hanckel. Born Berlin, 1904. Not a stranger, Herr Lemmer. Your son. Our prisoner.'

He took a long slow breath. Then: 'What are your terms for the release of this boy who is not my son?'

'The key to the Grey File, authenticated by London; the Terauchi–Zimmermann letter; and Count Tomura's secret.'

'So little? No money? No pot of gold?'

'You heard what I said. We will give you twenty-four hours to consider your answer. That'll allow you to cable the school and confirm the boy's disappearance. Perhaps you'll consult the lawyer Dulière as well. Consult who you wish. But have your answer ready for us.'

'You still have not said who you are working with.'

'I've said what I needed to say.'

'Come, come, Miss Hollander. What are you? A former secretary to a man regarded by your own country as a traitor. Ireton is dead. Max is dead. You and Twentyman are fugitives. And Morahan is in prison. There is only one man whose bidding you can be doing with this charade. Appleby. He is not here, of course. He is not in the line of fire. You are.'

'The terms are as they are.'

159

'*If* Appleby has the boy, he would not dare to kill him.'

'You'll have to be the judge of that. He's your son. Your only son.'

'Why do you not ask for your friends who are in prison to be set free?'

'Because we believe what you can tell us about Tomura will destroy him. And the Grey File won't buy you any favours with the Japanese government once your spies have been identified. So, my friends will be set free as a matter of course.'

'You seem unwarrantably confident, Miss Hollander. Perhaps working for Ireton is to thank for that. You must always have been telling his clients what you knew to be untrue.'

'I know what I'm telling you to be true, Herr Lemmer. We have your son. And he'll be released unharmed only if you accept and honour the terms I've stated.'

'Which I have twenty-four hours to consider?'

'Yes.'

'You'll return for my answer?'

'No. I'll telephone you. Then we'll arrange where and when you're to deliver what we've asked for.'

A long moment of silence elapsed while Lemmer continued to stare at her. She felt her face burning, but she held her nerve and her gaze. Then he said, 'I will expect your call.'

And he said no more.

She took a taxi from the hotel to Tokyo Central station and threaded through the crowds to a small café beneath one of the platforms, where Max was waiting.

'It went well?' he asked, signalling for the waitress to bring her a cup of coffee.

'As well as I could have hoped,' Malory replied, drawing gratefully on a cigarette.

'He has a menacing air about him.'

'I noticed.'

'How did he react?'

'He didn't. Unless you count a cold stare as a reaction.'

'He probably didn't believe you. But he will.'

'I went there to get his attention.' She shuddered. 'And I got it.'

'No one's as invulnerable as he pretends to be, Malory. We've given him a lot to think about. It's really very simple. Is he human or not? If he is, he has to give in.'

Malory's coffee arrived. She took a sip, then looked straight at Max. 'Well, we'll soon know.'

LATER THAT MORNING IN TOKYO, THREE MEN STEPPED FROM A limousine before the entrance to Yasukuni-jinja, the Shinto shrine dedicated to Japan's war dead, set in parkland north of the Imperial Palace.

Two were arrayed in military uniform: Count Tomura Iwazu and his son, Noburo. The Count's uniform, that of a colonel, was noticeably the grander of the two, with gold buttons and braiding and a colourful red and gold sash. He carried it well, with the bullish air of a man who had earnt his decorations. Noburo wore a plainer lieutenant's uniform and looked somehow diminished in the company of his father.

Their companion, dressed in a simple linen three-piece suit, was Fritz Lemmer. He took in the view before them at a glance: the enormous iron *torii*, the gateway to the shrine, the avenue beyond it and the imposingly roofed hall at the end of the avenue, where the names of all those who had died in the service of the Emperor since 1868 were faithfully recorded.

Their destination, beyond the shrine itself, was the military museum in its grounds. Protocol required a foreigner being introduced into senior circles within the Japanese government, as Lemmer was, to pay his respects before displays of ceremonial swords and suits of armour and mementoes of those who had met heroic deaths fighting the Emperor's enemies, be they Russian or Chinese – or German.

'You consider this a waste of your time, Lemmer-san?' Count Tomura asked as they approached the *torii*.

'No, Count. I consider it a duty.'

162

'But not an honour?'

'Are we to argue about this? The Russians were your enemy in 1904. In 1914 they were your ally. Now they are your enemy again. It is the way of the world.'

'Still, you seem impatient. As does my son, I have to say.'

As they passed beneath the *torii*, Noburo protested against this judgement, speaking in his native tongue. The Count's only reaction was to smile.

'You see, Lemmer-san? He denies it also. But I know he would prefer to be with Mademoiselle Pouchert. You will remember her from the ship?'

'There were many Frenchwomen aboard,' said Lemmer none too good-humouredly.

'But only one for Noburo.'

Noburo spoke again in Japanese. His father shot back a retort, also in Japanese.

'It is perhaps more than impatience in your case,' the Count continued, glancing at Lemmer. 'Are you worried about something?'

'What have I to be worried about?'

'Nothing I know of.'

'I do have a request.'

'Of me?'

'When I call at your house later, I wish to bring Everett with me. It is time he understood a little more of the work he will be required to do.'

'Bring him, then. If you have a use for him.'

'I think I do. It may be necessary to bring Duffy and Monteith as well.'

'Whatever you wish. I am at your service.'

'As I am at your service here.'

'For form's sake, we will agree you are. And there is form to be followed.'

They passed through a second, bronze *torii*, then crossed to the *chozuya*, the trough of purifying water, where the Count indicated that Lemmer need not join him and his son in the rinsing of their hands and mouths.

Next they proceeded to the *haiden*, the hall of worship. They walked up the steps to its doorway. There the Tomuras tossed coins into the offerings box, rang the gong, prayed, clapped their hands twice, bowed and backed away.

'What did you pray for, Count?' asked Lemmer, looking at him curiously.

'That must be secret, Lemmer-san. Will you pray also?'

'I am not a believer in any religion.'

'Neither am I.'

'So, this is merely . . . superstition?'

'It is Shinto. There is nothing *merely* about it.'

Lemmer nodded thoughtfully. 'Then I will.' He reached into his pocket, pulled out some coins and was about to toss them into the box when Tomura stopped him.

'Be sure none of the coins is ten sen.'

'Why?'

'Ten is *ju*, which can sometimes sound like *toi* – far. Give ten and what you pray for will only happen far in the future.'

'Could it happen far away in *distance*?'

Tomura considered the point. 'It is possible,' he conceded. 'I had not thought of it.'

'But I am thinking of it,' said Lemmer. He checked his coins, selected one and tossed it in. Then he rang the bell, bowed his head and uttered a silent prayer.

While Lemmer prayed, Eugen Hanckel lay awake on the narrow truckle-bed in the cellar of Les Saules on the French shore of Lake Geneva. It was still the previous night in Europe. The villa was silent, the cellar utterly dark and clammily chill.

Eugen was in pain from blisters on his mouth and nose. His head ached and the manacle fastening his left arm to a pipe was chafing his wrist. He was frightened and confused. The only one of his captors he had seen since being set upon was a young Englishwoman who had told him he would be released when his father had given them 'what we want'.

He did not think what they wanted was money. Whatever it might be, though, he knew his father would resist giving it up. *Vater* was an important man in the world, though the world seemed unaware of it: a great and important man. He had warned Eugen more than once he had enemies who might become Eugen's enemies and now it had happened.

'*Tapfer und treu.*' That was what *Vater* had said Eugen should always be. Brave and true. And he was determined to behave in a way that would make *Vater* proud of him if he ever learnt of it. Yes. He would conquer his fear. And his captors. If he could.

Captivity was also at that moment on the mind of Pierre Dombreux as he walked out of the front door of Count Tomura Iwazu's Tokyo mansion and surveyed the manicured grounds from the shade of the pillared portico. He lit a cigarette and strolled, with every appearance of casualness, out on to the driveway.

Tomura's residence in the capital was a perfect emblem, in its way, of modern Japan. A Gothic pile of excessive size, with a gloomy, dark-wooded interior, it had, attached at the rear, a small and in Dombreux's opinion altogether more elegant Japanese-style home. It embraced the values of the West, while preserving, artfully concealed behind them, the traditions of the East.

The gardens were likewise divided into Western and Japanese sections, the latter requiring a certain amount of exploration to be discovered. Dombreux had had ample time for such exploration since arriving in Japan. Lemmer had required him during those weeks to remain 'on call' at the Tomura mansion. He had left it on only a few occasions, most recently to travel to Yokohama with Nadia Bukayeva and inform Sam Twentyman of Max's death.

Dombreux was painfully well aware that his difficulties were largely of his own creation. He had considered making a run for it after being got the better of by Max in Marseilles. But he had known Lemmer would come looking for him then. The option of going through with the pretence that Max was dead had seemed preferable. What he had not bargained for was that Lemmer would insist he accompany him to Japan. The promise of a new identity and a new, well-funded existence, somewhere of his choosing, had been deferred.

Now a crisis was approaching which he knew he must forestall. Sooner or later, Lemmer would learn Max was alive. He was probably already in Japan. It was simply a matter of time. He had to make a move.

Unfortunately, the Tomura mansion stood within a high-walled boundary more suited to a castle than a house. And it was a well-guarded boundary. No doubt Tomura had good reason to fear intruders. He must have accumulated many enemies in the course of his life. But the precautions he had taken against those enemies served also to confine his guests – if a guest, rather than a prisoner, was what Dombreux really was.

Still, Lemmer had said he would soon have business for Dombreux to transact on his behalf in Osaka. He had not specified what that business was, but the journey there would offer Dombreux his best chance of slipping out of sight – and out of Japan. It still seemed best to await that chance, whatever the strain on his nerves. Max would not want to advertise his survival, after all. His friends were scattered to the four winds. The situation was grave, but not yet, he judged, critical.

He had been in tight spots before. He remembered his confinement in the Peter and Paul Fortress in Petrograd, under threat of execution; his interrogation, sometimes with a gun to his head, in Berlin; his numerous brushes with death on the streets of several European cities. He had always survived. He had never failed to find a way out. And he would not fail again.

He was sure of it.

Eugen stretched his unmanacled right arm down below the bed, to where the pretty Englishwoman had stowed his plimsolls. He grasped the left shoe and slid his forefinger round the outside of the heel. Yes. The strip of plaster was still in place. And he could feel the blunt end of the blade concealed beneath it. '*Tapfer und treu,*' his father had said. '*Tapfer und treu . . . und bereit.*' Brave and true . . . and ready.

And he was.

THEY GATHERED IN THE BASEMENT BILLIARDS ROOM. THE TABLE itself was covered, the game unplayed by the Tomuras, as far as Dombreux could tell. The devotion of a large room to it was another extravagant symbol of deference to a Western style of life.

Lemmer invited Dombreux and Everett to sit on one of the benches supplied for players and spectators. Nadia, curiously, remained standing, stationed by one of the oil paintings of English hunting scenes that graced the wood-panelled walls. Lemmer prowled the rugged space at the baulk-end of the table, in the shadow beyond the glare of the electric chandelier. Daylight seeped in through the small windows set high on one wall, but still it was hard to remember that outside it was a sunny late afternoon.

'You are here to learn what I will require you to do in Osaka next week,' said Lemmer.

Dombreux was disappointed, but not distraught. Nadia and Everett were evidently going to accompany him to Osaka and they would not be leaving for several days. Well, there it was. He backed himself to be able to give them the slip when the time came. And he would just have to wait until then.

'Before we discuss that, however, I need to settle a few outstanding matters. Please leave us, Everett.'

Everett looked surprised and a little disgruntled, but left the room obediently. As the door opened and closed behind him, Dombreux noticed it was being minded by one of the several bulky, impassive manservants Tomura kept about the place. He was not a reassuring sight.

'There has been an incident in Switzerland, Pierre,' Lemmer continued. 'My son Eugen has disappeared from the school where he is a pupil.'

Dombreux displayed only puzzlement, but anxiety began to claw at him inwardly. 'You have a son?' he asked innocently.

'This is the work of Appleby of the British Secret Service. He hopes taking my son will enable him to defeat me. It will not. But that is for another time. For now, I ask: how could he know of Eugen's existence and his relationship with me?'

'I . . . can't imagine.' Dombreux glanced at Nadia. 'Had you heard about this?'

'Yes,' Nadia replied coolly. 'Fritz told me earlier.'

'*Fritz told me earlier.*' Dombreux cursed her silently for her familiarity with Lemmer, her trusted status in his eyes, her untouchability. 'This is awful,' he said. Trying to make Lemmer understand by the force of his gaze that he was genuinely sorry for him. '*C'est épouvantable.*'

'Thank you for the sentiment,' said Lemmer. 'I return to the question. How could Appleby know?'

'I have no idea.'

'No? Well, I do. Only Anna knew before today that I had a son. Now you both know also. Why have I told you? In the case of Nadia it was so that I could consider with her the means by which such information could have reached Appleby. Nadia?'

'There was a report I had not previously mentioned to Fritz, Pierre, about a sighting of you a few months ago . . . in Munich.'

'Munich?' Dombreux could only play the cards he held now. And none of them were trumps.

'Were you there?' pressed Lemmer.

'I . . . don't think so.'

'No?'

'I have taken many journeys. I may have . . . passed through Munich. What if I did?'

'It is through a lawyer there named Koschnick that I arranged

Eugen's education in Switzerland. Did you visit Koschnick's offices, perhaps without his knowledge?'

'*Non, non*. Of course not.'

'But I think someone did, Pierre. I am sure of it. And I must ask: who? And then I must ask: who told Appleby?'

'I have never met Appleby.'

'I believe you. So, someone else told Appleby. But how did that person obtain information about my son?'

'I do not know.'

'No? I think I do. You gave it to them, Pierre. You *sold* it to them.'

Quite where the gun had come from Dombreux could not have said. But Nadia was holding it. And she was pointing it at him.

'I ask myself: who could have done this if it was not you? No one. It is true you have never met Appleby. But you have met Max. You killed him, did you not?'

'Yes. I did.'

'No. You did not. I looked again at the photograph, Pierre. Something about it always troubled me. But the report from Meadows seemed to confirm your account, so I made nothing of it. But now I see. The photograph was faked. The burned body in the Villa Orseis was not Max. You struck a deal with him. In fact, you *bought* a deal with him, using my son.'

Dombreux shook his head. '*Non. Pas du tout!*'

'It is what you did. And I want to know why. I want to know how you came to such an arrangement with him. It was in your interests to kill him. The plan was perfect. What went wrong? How did he defeat you? How did he force you to take his side against me with all the risks you must have known that would entail?'

'I killed Max, as you asked me to. I know nothing of your son.'

'Tell me the truth. Then I may let you live.'

'I have told you the truth.'

'The details of where Eugen Hanckel is being held, Pierre. Give those to me. Then I will see what I can do for you.'

'I know nothing about it.'

'Lie then. Do what you normally do. Invent a story that will win you breathing space. *Pretend* you know something.'

Dombreux understood his situation then. He saw it more clearly in Lemmer's eyes than he heard it in his words. This was the end. This was the maze from which there was no escape.

Lemmer moved to a side-table, where he had placed a briefcase earlier. He opened it and removed a phial of clear liquid and a syringe. He filled the syringe from the phial and began to walk towards Dombreux. Nadia moved closer to him, keeping the gun trained on his head.

'This is the drug Nadia gave you to use on Max, Pierre. I want to be sure it is as effective as I have been told.'

'Do not move,' said Nadia. 'Or I will shoot you.'

Glancing at her, Dombreux did not doubt she meant it. He glanced back at Lemmer, advancing on him round the shrouded billiards table. He saw the needle of the syringe sparkle in the lamplight. And then he decided what to do.

He lunged at Nadia and she fired, once, then twice more in quick succession. He slumped to the floor, blood coursing out of him. '*Quel dommage*,' he murmured weakly, gazing up at her and Lemmer. '*Vous êtes—*' And then he said no more.

Lemmer opened the door and signalled for Everett to enter. The Japanese manservant looked as if he had not even heard the shots, but clearly Everett had. 'What the hell happened?' he gasped, taking in the scene as the door closed again behind him.

'He guessed I had planned a lingering death for him,' said Lemmer. 'He preferred to go quickly. He was a traitor. But he was not a coward.'

Everett wiped his mouth with the back of his hand. Nadia looked at him calmly. She was still holding the gun. 'Do we have a serious problem, boss?' he asked Lemmer.

'We may need to move quickly on several fronts. You are ready for that?'

'Sure.'

'Where are Duffy and Monteith?'

'Waiting in the car, down at the gatehouse.'

'One of them warned Miss Hollander she was about to be arrested.

170

I cannot otherwise explain her escape. Which, do you think?'

'Maybe she just got lucky.' But Lemmer's cold hard stare told Everett that would not suffice as an answer. 'Al wouldn't warn his own mother if there was a rattlesnake in her bed. Howie, on the other hand, has a soft spot for the ladies.'

'Monteith, then?'

Everett nodded.

'Bring him here.'

'You mean to kill him?'

'No. I mean *you* to kill him.'

'He's not working for the other side, boss. If he tipped off Malory, it was just—' Everett stopped. He read in Lemmer's eyes the implacability he had only assumed before. Now it was undisguised. 'I'll do it,' he said in an undertone.

'Proceed, then.'

Everett left the room. A brief silence followed, then Nadia said, 'Do you want me to begin searching for Max?'

Lemmer shook his head. 'No. That will not be necessary. I will send a message to him through Miss Hollander.'

'I am sorry they have found this way to attack you.'

'It is my fault. I should have had a son who died in the war . . . like Appleby.'

'I do not believe Appleby will kill your son. He is not as hard as you.'

'Perhaps not. I would prefer not to find out. I have sent Koschnick to Lausanne to help Dulière learn what he can. But it's a long journey from Munich and Appleby will not have left many clues. There is a limit to what I can achieve at this distance. I've sent Meadows as well. He will arrive sooner. He isn't one of our best, I know. But he is the best available.'

Nadia looked at him in some alarm. 'Will you give Appleby what he demands?'

'No. I will offer Max what he really wants. Then he will have to choose. And I think I know what his choice will be.'

'Will you warn Count Tomura?'

'No. He must not know what has happened to Eugen. He must

not know Eugen even exists. I killed Dombreux because I learnt from Miss Hollander Max is still alive and therefore Dombreux had lied to us. That is all he needs to know.'

Lemmer gave Nadia a tight little smile of encouragement. 'The Japanese government wants what I can supply,' he continued. 'Count Tomura has been useful as a *Mittelsmann*. Now he may be useful to me . . . in another way.'

THURSDAY PASSED SLOWLY AT LES SAULES. VERONICA DELIVERED food and water to the prisoner in the cellar and emptied the bucket he had been supplied with. Eugen Hanckel said little to her beyond, 'You will pay for this.' Anger had replaced his initial fear. She was careful never to step within his reach. He looked as if he wanted to strike her. And she understood why.

Appleby did not visit the boy. He explained he did not want anything he said reported in due course to Lemmer. 'The less he hears about me from his son the better.' Meanwhile, it was best to let Eugen assume they were kidnappers motivated by money and nothing more.

The terms they had set for Eugen's release would by now have been delivered to Lemmer. It would be Friday morning in France before any news of his response could be expected. Until then – and beyond then – it would be a matter of waiting.

As dusk fell softly over the lake, the telephone rang. The Marmiers had been given the number to use in an emergency and only in an emergency. Appleby spoke to André, who claimed a serious problem had arisen which could only safely be discussed face to face. With harrumphing reluctance, Appleby headed off in the Berliet, bound for their yard on the other side of Evian-les-Bains. 'A waste of time, I suspect,' he complained as he left. 'But I have it to waste, I suppose.'

No more than ten minutes after he had left, Veronica's attention was distracted from her latest wrestle with the Grey File cipher by the growl of the Marmiers' motor-launch. She went to the conservatory and saw them tying up at the landing-stage. Her first thought was that they had misunderstood their arrangement with Appleby and believed they had agreed to come to him rather than the other way round.

She walked out into the garden and called to them. 'Why are you here?'

The only response was a wave from André. Leaving his father aboard, with the engine running, he strolled up across the lawn to where she was standing.

'*Bonsoir*, Veronica,' he said with a smile. 'Where is 'Orace?'

'He's gone to your yard. You asked to meet him there.'

'*Non, non*, we meet 'ere.'

'Well, he—'

'*Ça ne fait rien.*' Suddenly, from behind his back André pulled out a gun and levelled it at her. 'Go into the 'ouse, Veronica. Say nothing or I shoot you. *C'est compris?*'

'What . . . are you doing?'

'Another word and I will shoot.' He raised the gun and aimed at her face. 'Go inside. *Tout de suite.*'

Veronica turned and walked slowly back into the house.

'Go to the kitchen,' said André from close behind her.

She headed along the passage past the scullery and into the kitchen, struggling to imagine what the Marmiers thought they were doing – and what she could do to prevent it.

'Sit down.'

There were two chairs in the room, drawn up at the small table she and Appleby used for most of their meals. She sat down on one of them.

Michel Marmier appeared next to her, accompanied by his usual aroma of tar and tobacco. He wound rope round her legs and arms and stomach and tied her fast to the chair, then muttered something to his son she could not understand.

'We 'ave come for the boy, Veronica,' said André. 'Where is the key for *les chaînes*?'

By *les chaînes* he meant the manacles, of course. 'Horace took it with him,' she lied.

'*Non, non.* I do not think so. It is 'ere somewhere. Tell me where. If I have to, I will 'urt you. I will 'urt you bad.'

'I don't know where it is.'

He pulled open several drawers before he found the carving knife. He pushed the tip of it against her front teeth and prised up her lip. 'You 'ave a nice face, Veronica. Don't make me spoil it. Tell me where the key is.'

He meant it. She felt horribly certain of that. He would slash her lip and who knew what else if she forced him to. And since the key was lying in a saucer on the windowsill behind him, he would find it anyway as soon as he troubled to look.

Her gaze must have drifted in the direction of the saucer unconsciously. Michel, who had been watching her from the doorway, pounced on it like a cat on a mouse and clapped the key into his son's hands.

André smiled ironically. '*Merci, papa.*'

'*Dépêche-toi,*' Michel growled at him.

'*Oui, oui.*' André gestured for the old man to leave him to it. And with a scowl Michel left, heading back to the boat, Veronica assumed.

'Tell 'Orace to phone us when he 'ears from the boy's father,' said André. 'Then we will tell him 'ow much of *la rançon* we will let you 'ave. *C'est compris?*'

'You're making a big mistake, André,' said Veronica as coolly as she could.

'*Non, non.* 'Orace makes the big mistake, when he takes us for fools. So, tell him, yes?' He was still holding the knife.

'I'll tell him.'

'*Bravo.*' He tossed the knife on to the draining-board. '*A bientôt,* Veronica.'

André flung open the door that led to the cellar and vanished down the steps. Veronica heard his footsteps on the concrete floor as he strode across it.

'*Allez, mon petit garçon,*' he shouted at Eugen. There was a rattle of the manacles. '*Vous êtes—*'

André suddenly cried out in pain. There was a loud clunk. His cry subsided. Then the gun went off as a loud boom, echoing in the cellar. And something heavy hit the floor.

Veronica could not understand what had happened. She heard racing footsteps on the stairs. Eugen appeared in the doorway, panting heavily, the gun clutched, waggling, in his right hand. They stared at each other.

'Where am I?' Eugen demanded, his voice cracking.

'What?'

'*Where am I?*'

'France,' Veronica replied. 'Near Evian-les-Bains.'

'Evian? Where is Rolle?'

'On the other side of the lake. In Switzerland. Put the gun down, please. Before you hurt someone.'

He gaped at her as if she was mad. She instantly regretted what she had said. It was obvious he had already hurt someone. A strangled moan rose from the cellar behind him.

Eugen Hanckel rushed to the window. From there he could see the landing-stage – and the lake. '*Ein Boot,*' he murmured.

His face was masked with sweat. Veronica noticed for the first time spots of blood on his white football shirt. The gun was waggling even more now. He held it in both hands to steady it and swallowed heavily.

'Listen to me, Eugen,' she said. 'Please.'

He did not seem to hear her. He turned and ran out into the scullery, heading for the garden.

She bent forward and managed to slide the chair closer to the window, until, stretching up, she could see out through it.

Her first glimpse was of Eugen, running towards the launch. Then she saw Michel. He looked round from the wheel, where he was standing, as the boy approached. He must have noticed the gun at once. He brandished the boat-hook and stepped out on to the landing-stage. He could have tried to escape, but concern for his son must have conquered the instinct for self-preservation. In that instant Eugen started firing.

Several bullets flew wide. But one hit Michel in the chest, then another. He staggered and fell.

Eugen jumped past him and into the launch. He untied the mooring-rope and climbed behind the wheel. The craft moved forward, scraping against the landing-stage, then lurched away from the shore.

It slowed and accelerated a couple of times, before Eugen grasped how to control its speed. Then it surged away into the open water of the lake.

APPLEBY SUSPECTED TREACHERY OF SOME KIND AS SOON AS HE found the Marmiers' boatyard deserted, the gate from the road padlocked shut. He raced back to Les Saules. Steam was rising from the Berliet's radiator by the time he arrived. And the light was failing fast.

The scene was better than he had feared in one respect, worse in another. Veronica was mercifully unharmed, though badly shaken. Eugen was gone, not taken by the Marmiers as they had planned, but gone anyway, speeding towards Switzerland in the motor-boat. André lay dead in the cellar, with a large bullet wound in his stomach and a blade embedded in his throat. Michel was sprawled on the landing-stage, dead from two bullets to the chest. The Marmiers' plot to increase their share of the ransom money had led them to their deaths – and Eugen to freedom.

Appleby stood by Michel's body, squinting out across the lake. It was too dark by now to see much and Eugen was almost certainly too far away.

A steamer passed by, heading west, as Appleby watched. As its wake approached the shore, he noticed a rainbow shimmer on the surface of the water. He stooped and shone his torch on the ripples lapping at the support-posts of the landing-stage. It was petrol, enough of it for him to smell. His guess was that one of the bullets Eugen had fired had pierced the motor-boat's fuel tank. How much fuel the tank held and how much it had lost by now he could not say. But suddenly the boy's escape did not look as complete as it had.

Appleby was already turning over in his mind how to deal with the disaster the Marmiers' greed had precipitated. If Eugen told the Swiss police all he knew, there would be nothing for it but to call in *le Deuxième Bureau*. Yet Appleby was far from sure Eugen would tell the Swiss police all he knew. A son of Fritz Lemmer must have been schooled by his father to be reticent as well as resourceful. His resourcefulness had already been demonstrated. His reticence might now save them.

With his customary phlegm, Appleby wasted no time on regrets. The situation was as the situation was. Veronica, for her part, refused to give way to panic. 'What's to be done, Horace?' she asked calmly.

And he had an answer. 'I'll raise Brigham and have him scout along the shore road for signs of the boy landing. But it's virtually dark and there's nothing he can do beyond alerting us to whatever happens over there, if he finds out. I'd guess the boy will make for Rolle. Beyond that . . . I'm not sure. My hope is that Lemmer will give us what we want before word of his son's escape reaches him. Meanwhile, we have to explain to the local police what took place here. This is what I suggest. Three men invaded the house and tied you up. You gathered they'd hidden stolen valuables – jewellery, per-haps – in the cellar while the house was empty. After they retrieved it, there was a falling-out among thieves, leaving two of them dead and the survivor making off with the haul. Eventually, you freed yourself and called the police. I'm afraid I'm going to have to leave you to face them alone. I can't risk being held up answering their questions. I've missed the last ferry, so I'll have to drive round to Lausanne. The journey will take two or three times as long by road, but I've no choice. Tell the police I left for Geneva earlier today and you've no means of contacting me. How does all of that sound?'

'It sounds a long way from how this was supposed to be managed.'

Appleby nodded ruefully. 'It is.'

Brigham was fetched from the dinner table at the Beau-Rivage Palace to take Appleby's call. He began by being irritable, then became reproachful. 'Nothing like this was supposed to happen,' he complained. But at Appleby's insistence he agreed to drive to Rolle and see if there was anything to be seen. He doubted there would be and, privately, Appleby agreed. But they had to try everything. He said nothing about Eugen shooting the Marmiers and left the exact circumstances of the boy's escape unspecified. He judged it best to delay giving Brigham the gruesome details until they met.

When Brigham returned several hours later, Appleby was waiting for him at the Beau-Rivage Palace. He had by then booked himself into the Meurice. He was tired and downcast, but still cleaving to practicalities. Brigham was tired too and clearly rattled as well as disgruntled.

The disgruntlement turned to consternation when Appleby told him all that had occurred at Les Saules. They went to his room, where Brigham heard him out while working his way through a tumbler of Scotch.

'This could hardly be worse,' he pronounced, rubbing his forehead. 'How in God's name did you allow it to happen?'

'I didn't *allow* it, Brigham. An operation like this always has the potential to go wrong.'

'In this case *spectacularly* wrong.'

'Hiring the Marmiers was a calculated risk. They turned out to be greedier than I thought.'

'What are we going to do?'

'You saw nothing on the road?'

'Not a damn thing. I stopped at St-Sulpice, Morges, St-Prex and Nyon as well as Rolle. All quiet as the grave. No police. No motor-boat. Nothing.'

'What about Dulière?'

'I kept an eye on his offices as you asked. He went out this after-noon. I followed him up in the funicular to the station. I was behind him in the queue at the ticket office and distinctly heard him ask for a return to Rolle.'

'Sent there by Lemmer, I imagine, to find out what the school knows.'

'Very probably.'

'He's not likely to hear anything about the boy's escape before tomorrow morning at the earliest. That gives us the better part of a day in Tokyo for Lemmer to conclude he has to give in.'

'You still hope to pull this off?' Brigham's expression was sceptical, if not incredulous.

Appleby looked at him sternly. 'I mean to hold my nerve, Brigham. And I require you to do the same.'

'MISS HOLLANDER,' SAID LEMMER SOFTLY, TAKING THE TELEPHONE from Anna Schmidt. 'You are punctual. As befits a secretary.'

'What is your answer, Herr Lemmer?' Malory asked levelly.

'To your demands? My answer is this. I will discuss them with Max.'

He had instantly wrong-footed her. She did not know how to respond. 'I don't understand. Max is dead, as you well know.'

'But he isn't, is he, Miss Hollander? As *you* well know. I am prepared to make Max an offer. But only face to face. We must meet. Today.'

Malory was struggling to come to grips with the suddenly altered situation. Should she continue to deny Max was alive? Or should she accept Lemmer's proposal? 'Will you agree to the terms I laid before you yesterday?'

'Perhaps. Let Max find out. Send him to me at the Kojunsha Club in Ginza at eleven o'clock. It is comfortable there. And quiet. We can talk in peace.'

'What makes you—'

'Max is alive, Miss Hollander. Please don't pretend otherwise. Dombreux has told me everything. If Max wonders whether he should meet me, tell him this. He was not born in Tokyo.'

'Pardon me?'

'Tell him.'

*

182

And tell him she did.

'It was only a matter of time before he found out I was alive, Malory,' Max assured her. 'I'd hoped it would be longer, but it can't be helped.'

'You'll meet him?'

'Of course. What choice do I have?'

'Do you have any clue what he means by saying you weren't born in Tokyo?'

'None. It might be no more than bait to draw me in. He wants to keep me – us – guessing. That's clear. But we have him, Malory. We have him and he knows it.'

'You will be careful, won't you?'

'I'm always careful.'

'That's not what Sam says.'

'He worries too much.'

'And you worry too little.'

Max approached the Kojunsha Club later that clammily hot morning with more in the way of trepidation than he had been prepared to admit to Malory. What had led Dombreux to tell Lemmer the truth, given how damaging that truth was to his standing in Lemmer's eyes? Max's best guess was that Lemmer had good reason to believe only Dombreux knew of the existence of his son and that he and Max must therefore have struck a deal. If so, Dombreux was in serious danger.

But that was his problem. Max had problems all of his own.

A careful scout around the vicinity of the Kojunsha revealed no sign of surveillance. Max entered the club and found it to be just the sort of cool, quiet haven from the tumult of the city he might have imagined. At that hour, when most of its members would be at their places of business, it was echoingly empty, which Lemmer had no doubt considered an advantage.

Max was expected. According to the elderly porter who greeted him, Lemmer was waiting in the little boardroom. As he escorted Max up the stairs, he said, 'Your father came here often, Maxted-san. I remember him. He was – *sonkei-suru-hito*.' Seeing Max's frown

183

of incomprehension, he added: 'Someone a man can respect.'

Max was tempted to ask if Lemmer was *sonkei-suru-hito*. But he had no wish to embarrass the fellow. 'Thank you,' he said.

The little boardroom was in fact far from little, with three shaded windows' worth of the building's frontage to itself. The table and chairs were made from pale, yellow-brown wood. A fan with vanes as big as propellers was revolving with a deep, thrumming whirr.

Lemmer sat at one end of the table, a Japanese newspaper spread before him, a coffee-cup at his elbow. He was wearing a cream linen suit and looked entirely at ease, unhurried and untroubled.

'Would you like coffee, Max?'

'No.'

'Very well.' Lemmer nodded dismissively to the porter, who withdrew. The door clicked shut behind him. 'Will you sit down?'

Max sat, at a distance of several chairs from Lemmer.

'I've been reading about Marquess Saionji. He seems to be in no hurry to return to Japan. He's currently in England, where he's dined with the King. I wonder what they discussed. The Kaiser, perhaps. They are cousins, after all. Saionji was the Japanese ambassador in Germany when Wilhelm came to the throne. Did you know that?'

'No.'

'1888. *Drei achten, drei Kaiser*, as the schoolchildren say to remember their history. Three eights, three emperors. Wilhelm's father only reigned for a few months. He died of a throat cancer. That was lucky for me. A new young kaiser was my opportunity. I showed him what could be achieved during my time with the embassy here. After that, he trusted me. He believed – still believes, I assume – that the Tsarevich escaped death by my design. Sabotage Russo-Japanese relations, but leave cousin Nikolai alive, though not unscathed. Clever, no?'

'No one will ever doubt your cleverness, Fritz. Sending me to the Orkneys to talk Commander Schmidt into handing over the Grey File was a masterstroke.'

'Thank you.'

'And plotting to sell your network of spies to the Japanese lock,

184

stock and barrel. That was clever too. A fresh start. A new employer. Another world to conquer.'

Lemmer smiled. 'Retirement wouldn't suit me. I have no aptitude for it.'

'Perhaps you should try to develop one.'

'Because of Appleby's ultimatum?'

'We want their names, Fritz. The names of all your spies.'

'I can't give you them.'

'You must.'

Lemmer shook his head. 'No. You ask me to surrender my life's work – the levers of my power. It's too much. I won't do it.'

'Your son's life depends on it.'

'Appleby won't kill Eugen, Max. You and I both know this. His greatest weakness is his lack of ruthlessness. It's a bluff. He will not do it.'

'Are you sure?'

'As sure as I need to be. But what he may do is keep my son from me. Alive, but apart, no longer under my control. I can't have that.'

'Give us the names, then. And Tomura's secret. And the Terauchi–Zimmermann letter.'

Lemmer closed the newspaper and folded it neatly in half, pressing his hands down heavily to crease it. He looked fixedly at Max. Neither man flinched. 'This is my offer to you, Max. Cable Appleby. Tell him you've learnt Eugen isn't my son. He's holding an innocent boy. He has to let him go. Then I will give you Tomura's secret. And the letter. That will enable you to buy Morahan and his two friends out of prison. As for my spies, I keep them. But you – you, Max – learn at last what your father died trying to achieve. And then you have the chance – and the means, which I'll give you – to achieve it.'

'You know I won't agree to this.'

'Think about it. That's all I ask. It's the middle of last night in Europe. It'll be another six hours before there'd be any point cabling Appleby. Take those six hours to consider very carefully what you should do.'

'The answer's no. You take those six hours, Fritz. You consider very carefully what *you* should do.'

'You know I have the secret. Here.' Lemmer tapped a finger against his temple. 'The mystery can be explained. If you accept my offer. Are you armed, by the way?'

Max wondered if there was a tell-tale bulge beneath his left arm, where his gun rested in its shoulder-holster. The Shanghai tailor had assured him there would not be. 'What if I am?'

'If you are, I invite you to draw your gun and hold it to my head and threaten to fire. Then you'll see what I'm willing to tell you to save my life.'

'You'd tell me nothing.'

Lemmer nodded. 'This is true.'

'And I expect you're armed yourself.'

'I don't need to be. The names of my spies; the nature of Tomura's secret; you wouldn't want to erase so much valuable information, would you?'

'How did you get the truth out of Dombreux?'

'I didn't. I *deduced* the truth. Only he could have told you about Eugen. Why did he tell you, Max? Why didn't he kill you?'

'What does he say?'

'Nothing. He's dead.'

Max should have felt neither surprise nor sorrow. Yet, oddly, he felt both. 'It wasn't his fault. He was unlucky. And then . . . he had to give me something.'

'Why do people who try to kill you always seem to be unlucky, Max? Those fellow countrymen of mine who flew against you in the war. Norris's marksman in Paris. Tarn, the master assassin. Fontana. Grattan. Dombreux. There are a lot of heads for you to hang on your wall.'

'Nothing like as many as there are for you to hang on yours.'

'Well, you and I aren't the sort who collect souvenirs, are we, Max? We make mistakes. But more often we don't. Tell Miss Hollander, by the way, that Monteith has paid for his mistake with his life.'

'I never met the man, but I'm sorry to hear that. I'm sure Malory will be too.'

'Yes. The sentimental Miss Hollander. An admirable woman, in

186

her way. But it seems to me she carries too many regrets with her. And regrets aren't helpful, are they?'

'Maybe they're inevitable.'

'Some, perhaps. You'll certainly regret rejecting my offer. If that's what you decide to do. The secret, Max. Your father's secret. *Your* secret. You can have it. You can avenge Henry and Kuroda and Jack Farngold and . . .' Lemmer spread his hands. 'You can do all you've dreamt of doing and more besides.'

'The message you gave Malory for me, Fritz. What did you mean by it? I *was* born in Tokyo.'

Lemmer smiled. 'No. You were not.'

'My birth certificate says I was.'

'Certificates can be forged. Just as photographs can be faked.'

'Where do you say I was born?'

'I don't. I say nothing. Until you accept my offer and send the cable and we hear that Eugen has been freed.'

'What makes you think Appleby would take my word for it that the boy isn't your son?'

'He trusts you. And you will tell him Dombreux has admitted lying to you. I have rejected your demands. I have denied Eugen Hanckel is my son. And Dombreux has confirmed he isn't. That is what you must say. Remember: I was here in Japan in May 1891, when you entered the world. I know your mother and your father. I know exactly what happened. I know everything.'

'I won't do it.'

'You should. You really should. Because otherwise you'll get nothing from me. *Nichts.*'

'We have your son, Fritz. We have him and you'll never see him again if you refuse to give up your spies.'

Lemmer let his gaze dwell on Max for a moment before he responded. 'Then I'll never see him again,' he said quietly.

And Max believed he meant it.

LEMMER'S IMPLACABILITY SHOULD HAVE COME AS NO SURPRISE TO Max. The man was immune to normal human frailties. The logic of what he had said niggled away at Max as he made his way through Ginza to Shimbashi station. Appleby could not have what he wanted. But Max could have what he wanted, or part of it, at any rate – the secret part that was close and personal to him. '*You were not born in Tokyo.*' He would not give ground. But he was tempted to. And Lemmer knew it.

Max turned into the station, bought a ticket and went up on to the southbound platform. Then he turned back abruptly, intending to retrace his steps to the crowded ticket hall. It was a ruse to flush out anyone who was following him, though somehow he did not think Lemmer would have set a tail on him.

Then he saw her, halfway up the stairs he had just started back down. A tall, thin, narrow-faced European woman with ash-blonde hair, wearing a striped, pleated dress and a long pale coat. She was just as Malory had described her.

'Herr Maxted,' Anna Schmidt said. 'We must talk.'

'You followed me from the Kojunsha Club?'

'*Ja.* It is important. Can we . . . go somewhere?'

'I can't imagine we have anything to discuss, Frau Schmidt.'

'But we do.'

'Did Lemmer tell you to come after me?'

'*Nein.*' She shook her head energetically. 'He does not know I am here. Please. Can we talk?'

188

*

They went to a café close to the station and found a secluded booth. Anna Schmidt shakily lit a cigarette and ordered a large brandy with her coffee. She looked around anxiously, as if afraid they had been followed. Max noticed how breathless she was. Whatever her motives, she was acting without Lemmer's consent, a breach of everything she had long lived and worked by.

'What was the answer he gave you?' she asked in a furtive undertone.

'The answer?'

'To your . . . demands.'

'Don't you know?'

'Please, Herr Maxted. Tell me.'

'He won't give up his spies, Frau Schmidt. I'm sure you realize that. He values them more highly than his son's life.'

'*Mein Gott.*' She swallowed hard. 'You met Lothar in Orkney. What did he say . . . about me?'

'That you worship Lemmer. That you believe he can do no wrong.'

'*Ja.*' She nodded. 'I believe that.'

'Then why are we here? What do you want to say to me?'

'I cannot bear it.' She took a gulp of brandy. 'It is . . . *zu wiel.*'

Something was too much for her. But she seemed reluctant to say what it was. Instead, without another word, she took an envelope from her handbag and placed it on the table in front of Max. The flap bore the name and crest of the Imperial Hotel.

'What is this?' he asked.

'*Der Preis.*'

'What do you mean?'

She did not answer. He tore the envelope open and removed the contents: several sheets of Imperial Hotel notepaper covered with writing in slanting capitals. It was a list, arranged in two columns. On the left-hand side were words of German, of no obvious meaning. On the right-hand side were names – surnames followed by Christian names. One leapt out at him immediately: GRIEVESON, NICHOLAS ARTHUR. Grieveson was Political, one of C's senior

189

lieutenants, exposed as a spy working for Lemmer and killed by Nadia in London to stop him revealing what he knew.

'What is this?'

'*Die graue Akte.*' Anna Schmidt stared directly at Max. 'There is no double code. There is his memory and my memory. That is all. Those are the names. *Britisch. Französisch. Amerikanisch. Italienisch. Russisch. Chinesisch. Japanisch.* They are all there. Every one.'

Max could hardly believe she meant it. Yet the names were there before him. Lemmer had said the file was double-encoded to defy decipherment. But Bostridge had speculated about a further private code between Lemmer and Anna Schmidt. And here was the proof of it. They had both memorized the identities that matched the pseudonyms. Lemmer's reference to a double code had been a blind. It was simply a list only two people could read. Until this moment.

'I will give you Count Tomura's secret when you free Eugen. You *will* free him, won't you, now you have the names?'

The bargain was as irresistible as it was incomprehensible. 'Yes,' said Max, awed by the significance of what she had given him. 'We will. But . . . why have you done this?'

'I cannot let my son die.'

'*Your* son?'

'*Ja.* Eugen. Lothar is not my child's father.'

'Lemmer is?'

She bowed her head. '*Ja.*'

'We were told . . . Eugen's mother had killed herself.'

'That was to stop anyone looking for her.'

'And Lothar? He knew?'

'He has known always.' She shook her head dismally. 'He would do anything for Eugen, even though they are not the same blood. He does not know about the school in Switzerland or the name we chose for him: Hanckel. It was to make Eugen safe when the war ended. But it did not make him safe, did it? Dombreux found out. And Dombreux told you.'

'He'll be safe now, Frau Schmidt. I promise.'

She nodded. '*Danke.*'

'His release will take a little while to arrange.'

'But you will arrange it?'

'Yes. I will.'

'*Danke schön.*' She swallowed some more brandy. 'That is all I want.'

Max was left with a bewildering mixture of elation and unease by his encounter with Anna Schmidt. They had agreed to meet again at the same café at the same time the following day. By then Max should have been able to settle with Appleby how, where and when Eugen was to be released. Max would also have cabled the complete list of names to C using the embassy's cipher. Appleby had appointed new, entirely trustworthy code clerks at HQ, with standing orders to communicate incoming messages directly to C himself.

At that point Max judged Anna could be persuaded to take the next step and reveal what Lemmer had offered to tell him about Count Tomura. But did she actually know what that was? Something in her manner made him doubt it. And she had not even mentioned the Terauchi–Zimmermann letter. He foresaw Appleby would resist taking the final step of freeing Eugen until they had everything they wanted. And Max supposed that was the rational, hard-headed way to deal with Anna Schmidt, moved though he had been by her desperation. He did not enjoy playing the role allotted to him, but he knew it served the greater good. It had to be done.

Meanwhile, he had to supply C with the names and Appleby with the news of what had happened. Transmitting the names was the most important step of all. It was the coup de grâce in the battle with Lemmer. But precautions had to be taken. Max could not afford to act hastily.

There was a public telephone inside Shimbashi station. He called the British Embassy from there, using the pseudonym that was now second nature to him.

'Good morning, Mr Greaves,' said Hodgson stiffly, when he answered his extension.

'I need your help.'

'What can I do for you?'

'Meet me at your apartment in half an hour. Make any excuse you like for leaving the office. This is all-important.'

'Well, I—'

'You'll be there?'

'Er, yes. If . . . you think it's necessary.'

'It is. Do you have a typewriter?'

'A typewriter? At home? No.'

'Could you borrow one from the embassy?'

'I . . . suppose I—'

'Bring a machine with you, Cyril. And don't be late.'

BEFORE LEAVING SHIMBASHI STATION, MAX TELEPHONED MALORY and told her she and Sam should sit tight for twenty-four hours. 'The tide's turned in our favour,' he reported.

'Has he agreed to do as we ask?' Malory's tone was disbelieving but hopeful.

'It's not that simple,' Max replied. 'But I think we may win this. Just try to be patient.'

'Easy for you to say.'

'I know. But do your best. I'll be in touch as soon as there's news.'

Max was waiting in the lobby of Uchida Apartments when Hodgson arrived, panting and perspiring. He was not accustomed to hurrying through the midday heat of Tokyo carrying a typewriter in its cumbersome case.

Mrs Hodgson had not responded to the bell, Max explained as they went up. This did not surprise her husband. 'Friday . . . is a . . . shopping day.' And Max was not sorry to hear it. He preferred them to do what had to be done in her absence.

Hodgson was initially incredulous when Max showed him the list. The number of names appalled him. 'All these people . . . are traitors to their country?'

'Yes,' said Max. 'But not for much longer.'

'What do you intend to do?'

'Cable the entire list to C. *After* we've made a copy. That's what

193

the typewriter's for. We'll send the cable this evening, when most of the staff will have left the embassy. Do you know which cipher clerk will be on duty?'

'It'll be . . . Duckett.'

'Let's hope his name's not on the list.'

'It can't be. He's virtually a child. No more than twenty-two or twenty-three.'

'All right. We'll see him later. Now, shall we get on with it? I'll read. You type.'

Hodgson made no immediate move.

'Cyril?'

'Yes, yes. Of course.' Hodgson sat down at his desk and rolled a sheet of paper into the typewriter. 'Fire away.'

While Max's dictation of names proceeded at Hodgson's apartment, a door slid open at Sugamo prison and three prisoners were marched into a large, tatami-matted room, where a shoeless Westerner in a light suit, carrying a briefcase, was awaiting them.

'Good morning, gentlemen,' the man said. 'My name's Gordon Trumper. I'm with the American Embassy.' He was a tall, thin, balding, slightly stooping fellow with glasses, a moustache and a bureaucratic air about him. 'You're Thomas Morahan, Grover Ward and Gazda Djabsu, right?'

'We are,' said Morahan, speaking for the others. Unshaven, unwashed and clad in dull red *yukata*s worn thin to the point of transparency by repeated use, they did not cut imposing figures. 'Sorry we're not looking at our smartest.'

'Don't worry about that.' Trumper spoke in Japanese to the guards who had escorted them in and they left, closing and locking the door as they went.

There was a low table to hunker down round, but they were content to stand and so, it appeared, was Trumper. He set down his briefcase and opened it, pulling out a notebook and some packs of cigarettes. He handed a pack to each of them.

'American,' said Ward. 'How'd you get these?'

'Consignments come in from San Francisco. We have a fixed arrangement.'

'I'll bet you do.'

'Nice,' said Djabsu, lisping slightly on account of a swollen lip, following another fracas with a fellow inmate.

'D'you want to complain about your treatment at all?' Trumper asked, flicking open the notebook.

'No,' said Morahan.

'How'd you come by those bruises?'

'Some of the inmates are a little pugnacious.'

'They have the more bruises,' said Djabsu.

'Well, I'm here to make sure your rights aren't being abused.'

'What rights would those be, Mr Trumper?' asked Ward.

'Ah, to be fed and clothed and . . . not tortured.'

'Then it seems we're basking in the full enjoyment of our rights as guests of the Japanese penal system,' said Morahan.

'I could name a few worse places in Chicago,' said Ward. 'Though the food would be better there.'

Trumper smiled. 'Not much I can do about that.'

'How about legal representation?'

'Oh, that'll be supplied if and when they decide exactly what to charge you with.'

'And when's that likely to be?'

'Hard to say. The process is . . . opaque.'

'*Šta?*' growled Djabsu.

'He doesn't know how long we're going to be here,' Ward explained.

'My apologies, gentlemen,' said Trumper. 'What I can do for you I'll gladly do. Fact is, you're in a tight spot. But my impression is time's on your side. And since little else is, I suggest you sit it out.'

'Are they still intending to accuse us of plotting to assassinate the Prime Minister?'

'Apparently not. Which is good news, believe me.'

'But murdering Jack Farngold?'

'That's the crime you're officially being held in connection with.'

'What about Miss Hollander?'

'Her whereabouts remain unknown. As do those of the Brit, Twentyman. More good news, I'd say.'

'For them it sure as hell is,' said Ward.

'What about our former friends, Everett, Duffy and Monteith?' pressed Morahan.

'I've seen nothing of them,' said Trumper. 'My involvement is limited to supplying you with consular assistance and advice.'

'And your advice is: bide our time.'

Trumper nodded. 'That's about it. Sooner or later, when the Kempeitai's ruffled feathers have been smoothed and the police reckon they can claim to have done enough, the authorities will notify us they'd rather deport you than press charges for which the supporting evidence is . . .'

'Opaque?'

Trumper seemed not to notice Morahan's borrowing of his word. 'Exactly,' he said. 'Look, I don't know what there is between you and Count Tomura and frankly I don't want to know, but this seems to be all about keeping you out of his hair. If we raise a stink, we might embarrass them into taking matters all the way. And embarrassing the Japanese is never a smart idea. So, my recommendation is . . . be stoical. I've seen this kind of thing a few times before.' He treated them to what he clearly imagined would be a reassuring smile. 'It'll come right in the end.'

The typing of the list was complete. Hodgson pulled the last sheet of paper out of the machine and laid it with the others, then looked across at Max. 'How on earth did Lemmer talk all these people into working for him?'

'I doubt he *talked* many of them into it, Cyril. Corruption? Blackmail? Who knows what methods he used? But he sank his claws into them and he never let go.'

'I ought to tell you . . . there's a member of the embassy staff on the list.'

'I know. Reynolds. The Secret Service's man in Japan. We'll have to watch out for him.'

'If he has any inkling we're about to inform C he's a traitor . . .'

'Leave me to worry about Reynolds, Cyril. When will most of the staff go home?'

'The place will be more or less deserted by six o'clock.'

'But Duckett will be there?'

'Yes, yes. He's roster clerk for urgent communications.'

'And he'll follow your orders?'

'Yes.' Hodgson flexed his hands, stiffened by the unfamiliar exercise they had been given. 'Novel though the experience will be for both of us.'

'We'll meet there at six, then. You bring your copy of the list. I'll keep the carbon and the original.' A thought suddenly struck Max: 'Is there anyone else named here who to your knowledge is likely to be in Tokyo?'

'Of course. I was going to mention him. A consular official at the American Embassy. I've met him a few times. Genial sort of fellow. Hard to believe he's—'

'Name?'

'Trumper.' Hodgson sighed. 'Gordon Trumper.'

O N HIS WAY BACK TO THE STATION HOTEL, MAX STOPPED AT THE
post office in Nihombashi and cabled Appleby with the good
news.

HAVE NAMES. CABLING TO LONDON MID MORNING
YOUR TIME. REPLY HERE OR TOKYO STATION HOTEL.
GREAVES.

He assumed Appleby was still sleeping the sleep of the just in
Evian-les-Bains and would find the glad tidings waiting for him at
the post office when he called to check his box. By then the list
might already have reached C. And Lemmer's goose would be
cooked.

The imminence of victory shone in Max's thoughts even as he
threaded his way as anonymously as he could through Tokyo's
crowded streets. It was a matter of hours now; a matter of waiting
– but this time not for long.

Max's assumption of a restful night for Appleby was, in fact, well
wide of the mark. Nor did he pass it in Evian-les-Bains. He woke
early that morning at the Hotel Meurice in Ouchy and immediately
telephoned Veronica to find out what had happened since his
departure from Les Saules. He was relieved to hear her sounding
calmer than many more experienced agents of the Service would
have done in the same circumstances.

'The police were very solicitous, Horace. I don't think it's even crossed their minds that I might have misled them. Apparently, the Marmiers had a shady reputation in the area. I suppose that should come as no surprise. It means the hunt for their murderer will concentrate on the local criminal population, which rather suits us, doesn't it?'

'For the moment, yes.' But pulling the wool over the eyes of the French police was only a stop-gap. If the Swiss authorities contacted them about the claim of a Le Rosey boy to have been kidnapped and held at a villa near Evian-les-Bains, their investigation would take a very different turn.

'What do you want me to do?'

'Nothing, beyond checking for a cable from Max as soon as the post office opens. There's a chance he may yet bring home the bacon.'

'We play for time?'

'That's all we *can* play for.'

It was a game not without hazards, though. Appleby wondered if he should send Veronica back to England. She would be out of harm's way then. But he could not afford to do anything that might make the police doubt her story. For a little longer at least, she had to stay put. 'I need you to hold your nerve, Veronica.'

'Of course.' He admired the self-possession in her tone. 'I understand.'

Appleby had arranged with Brigham to drive out early along the shore road, this time with the advantage of daylight. He had time in hand, even so, and no patience for lingering at the Meurice, so he headed down to the port.

From there he noticed some kind of minor commotion by the pier where the ferries docked. He walked round to see what the fuss was about.

A small tug was towing another boat to a mooring, with several people watching from the pontoon. Appleby recognized the motor-launch at once. It was empty. There was no sign of Eugen.

'*Qu'est-ce qui se passe, monsieur?*' he asked an old fellow in a sailor's cap who looked as if he knew the lake well.

'*Un bateau à la dérive sur le lac.*'

'Drifting, you mean?'

'*Oui, oui.* Drifting.'

'How far out?'

'*A bonne distance.*'

'Anyone aboard?'

The man frowned uncomprehendingly, then grasped the question. '*Ah. Non. Personne à bord.*'

So, the boat had been found empty, adrift on the lake. It must have run out of fuel after all. And some way from the shore. What had Eugen done then? There was no dinghy. He must have swum for it. Which raised the question: how good a swimmer was he?

The British Embassy in Tokyo was, as Hodgson had predicted, thinly staffed and somnolently quiet at six o'clock on a blazing hot Friday afternoon.

Hodgson vouched for Max with the stolid policemanly fellow on the desk, who confirmed Duckett was to be found in the basement code room. 'Should be there, at any rate, unless he's sunbathing on the roof again.'

But sunbathing on the roof he was not. Leslie Duckett, a slightly built, sleepy-eyed young man who could have passed for a schoolboy if kitted out in blazer and short trousers rather than an ill-fitting linen suit, was lounging somewhat sweatily at his post.

'Mr Hodgson,' he said, whipping his feet off his desk. 'This is a surprise.'

'Why do we have someone on duty here twenty-four hours a day, Duckett?' Hodgson responded, with an impressive show of testiness.

'In case of . . . urgent communications.'

'Then you shouldn't be surprised. I *have* an urgent communication.'

'And who's . . . your friend, sir?'

'Mr Greaves. Over from our consulate in Shanghai.'

200

Max gestured for Hodgson to present Duckett with the top copy.

'Encipher this as quickly as you can,' said Hodgson, handing it over.

'Where's it going, sir?'

'Secret Service Headquarters in London.'

'Er . . .'

'Is there some difficulty?'

'Well . . .'

'Out with it.'

'There's a standing instruction from Mr Reynolds that he has to approve anything outgoing to non-FO addressees from staff at or below his level. Which, er, would include, er . . . you, sir.'

'Why don't you phone this Reynolds while Duckett's busy with his cipher-book, Cyril?' suggested Max, smiling casually.

'Yes.' Hodgson caught Max's eye. 'I'll do that from my office.' He glanced at Duckett. 'I'll leave you to make a start.'

'I, er, will need to speak to Mr Reynolds before I can—'

'I'll put him through to you.'

Max followed Hodgson out into the corridor. 'He'll soon spot Reynolds' name on the list,' he whispered. 'And he'll start wondering what sort of a list it is.'

'What are we to do, then?' Hodgson looked worried.

'Let him get on with the enciphering while you're supposedly trying to contact Reynolds.'

'And when he's finished?'

'We'll persuade him to cable the list to C.'

'How?'

'Don't worry, Cyril.' Max smiled. 'I'll see to that.'

Appleby set off with Brigham as planned, though Brigham objected that there was nothing to look for now the boat had been found. 'The boy will have swum ashore and headed for Le Rosey,' he gloomily predicted. 'The game's up.'

'It'll be up when I say so and not before,' Appleby retorted. 'Drive the car and leave the thinking to me.'

'What sort of fix is this going to put Max in?'

'No sort of fix if we can prevent Lemmer learning his son's escaped.'

'How can we hope to do that?'

The answer that had occurred to Appleby was to intimidate Dulière into silence and hope Eugen Hanckel had no means of contacting his father in an emergency. But first he wanted to be sure the boy really had escaped. There was another possibility he did not wish to draw to Brigham's attention. 'I'll explain later,' he barked. 'Just drive.'

'Is the cable ready yet?' Max asked as he entered the code room, with Hodgson trailing behind him.

Duckett looked at Max with a mixture of alarm and suspicion. Who was the stranger from Shanghai to be telling him what to do and demanding to know whether he had done it? 'I've enciphered the document,' he grudgingly admitted. He held up a sheet of paper on which groups of numbers were written out in an apparently random sequence.

'Time to send it, then.'

'Have you, er, spoken to Mr Reynolds, sir?' Duckett asked Hodgson.

'I couldn't get hold of him.'

'Then I, er . . . can't send this.'

'It has to go,' said Max. 'Right away.'

'You see how I'm placed, don't you, sir?' Duckett pleaded. 'Mr Reynolds was emphatic about this kind of thing. And I couldn't help noticing his name is listed here. What exactly—'

'Send it.' Max whipped his gun out of his shoulder-holster and held the barrel a few inches from Duckett's head. The young man blinked and gaped. His mouth fell open and the colour drained from his face. Max smiled down at him. 'There's a good fellow.'

FOR URGENT PERSONAL ATTENTION OF C. LISTED BELOW ALL NAMES KNOWN TO BE COMPROMISED. GREAVES.

With Max standing over him, Duckett added the finishing touches to his encipherment of the message and began tapping it out on the transmitter. Via relay stations strung out across the Indian and Atlantic Oceans, it was on its way to the code room at Whitehall Court in London. Nothing could stop it now. Whatever happened, Max had the satisfaction of knowing he had done what Appleby and C had asked of him. From this moment on, Lemmer's spy network would begin to unravel. It was a certainty. It was victory. Only the cost of that victory had yet to be counted.

While pulses of electricity were carrying Max's message through submarine cables from Tokyo to London, Brigham was driving the Bugatti west along the Swiss shore of Lake Geneva, with Appleby sunk in thought beside him. Neither man had spoken for some time. And Brigham for one had made it clear he did not understand what they could hope to achieve.

Certainty was the only answer Appleby could have supplied, had he been minded to supply it. But he had no wish to explain what form certainty might take in this case. Eugen's escape and his raising of the alarm were not in fact the worst of the eventualities Appleby had considered. The worst was what the emptiness of the drifting motor-boat hinted at.

And at Morges it acquired a horrible solidity.

A police car and an ambulance were drawn up at the side of the road just short of the village. A figure covered by a blanket lay on the lakeside path. A policeman was questioning witnesses. A woman with a small, yapping dog was crying.

'I don't like the look of this,' said Brigham as he stopped the car.

'Your French is better than mine,' said Appleby. 'Find out what's happened.'

Reluctantly, Brigham got out and walked over to where the bystanders were grouped. He engaged one in conversation. While they were talking, another car, coming from the opposite direction, pulled up. The driver looked every inch a doctor. Carrying a

203

Gladstone bag, he climbed out and hurried over to speak to the policeman.

The policeman pulled back the blanket for him to take a look. And there was Eugen Hanckel's grey, dead face, eyes closed, mouth slack, hair plastered to his scalp.

'God forgive me,' Appleby murmured.

Brigham returned glumly to the car. 'Found washed up here this morning,' he said in a gravelly voice. 'Drowned.'

'So I see.'

'It is him, isn't it? There's no—'

'Yes, Brigham.' Appleby nodded. 'It's him.'

DUCKETT WAS TOO INTIMIDATED TO OBSTRUCT MAX AND HODGSON'S departure from the embassy. What he would do once they had gone was another matter, of course, although Hodgson told him he would be well advised to take no action, at least until the following morning. 'I'll be making a full report to H.E.,' Hodgson said, referring, Max assumed, to the Ambassador. 'He'll approve our actions once he knows the importance of that cable.'

'You can count on it,' Max added, putting away his gun.

Outside, walking south beside the moat round the Imperial Palace, Hodgson soon shed the confidence he had displayed for Duckett's benefit. 'Did you really have to threaten to shoot the boy?' he complained, in what was close to a wail.

'Could you have sent the cable?' Max countered.

'Er, no. I haven't been trained to use the machine.'

'Me neither.'

'Is that your answer?'

'Well, the cable's been sent. Frankly, that's all I care about.'

'H.E. will have a fit.'

'He'll have C's fulsome thanks in due course. Followed by congratulations on a vital contribution to the safety of the realm from the Foreign Secretary and probably the Prime Minister. Tell him that and I think the fit will soon pass.'

'What about Reynolds?'

'*Persona non grata* by tomorrow morning along with everyone else on the list. There's nothing for you to worry about, Cyril. They're the ones who should be worrying.'

'What do you suggest I do now, then?'

'Make your report. In person.'

'I'll have to mention you.'

'Of course. Greaves is the name, remember. Sent by C. You don't know where I can be contacted.'

'Well, I don't.'

'That's why you'll sound so convincing. You see? There really is nothing to worry about.'

But there was. And more than a little. Max had failed to give Lemmer the answer he had demanded, which Lemmer was bound to interpret as a rejection of his terms. How he would react Max did not know, but not to react at all would be unlike him.

A greater reaction would follow, however, when he discovered – which tomorrow he was bound to – that his spies had been identified and C was in possession of the uncoded, deciphered names in the Grey File. He would ask who had betrayed him and surely the answer would present itself soon enough.

Max could only hope that before then he was able to persuade Anna Schmidt to reveal Count Tomura's secret. They were to meet at the Lion café at noon. The hours until then stretched out agonizingly before him.

Appleby had still not received Max's cable telling him C would soon receive the decoded list of Lemmer's spies. He was not in Evian-les-Bains, where the cable awaited him, but in Ouchy, standing in the outer office of Marcel Dulière's legal practice, listening as Brigham explained to Dulière's secretary why they needed to see him more or less immediately.

The name Hanckel appeared to clinch the matter. Soon they were ushered into Dulière's dark-wooded inner office. The room was hazy with cigarette smoke and it seemed to Appleby there was a trace of brandy on Dulière's breath. He looked altogether like a man in the throes of regretting at least one of his decisions about what business to take on.

His visitors were weighed down by regrets of their own. Appleby had never intended to carry out his threat to kill Eugen Hanckel. That the boy had died as a result of the kidnap plot Appleby had devised was a burden he knew his conscience would have to bear for the rest of his life. For the present, he had to do all he could to prevent Lemmer learning his son was dead. He knew he needed to concentrate on the task. But it was far from easy. Eugen's lifeless face kept floating into his mind's eye. It was easier for Brigham, in the sense that he enjoyed the luxury of being able to blame Appleby for the tragic outcome. And blame him he did. 'The boy's blood is on your hands,' he had declared. 'I can't imagine why we've ever allowed you Secret Service people so much latitude. This is what comes of it.'

Appleby had been tempted to respond by pointing out that Foreign Office *people* closely resembling Brigham had led Britain into a war that had claimed millions of lives, including his own son's. But he had refrained, reminding Brigham instead that Max's safety depended on them continuing to work together. And Brigham had conceded the point through gritted teeth: 'Very well, God damn it.'

So, here they were, in Dulière's office, with time – though not much of it – to spare before word of Eugen's death could reach his school and be transmitted to the man who sat before them, who could be relied upon to notify Lemmer at once – unless they could dissuade him.

'What can I do for you, *messieurs*?' Dulière asked suspiciously, drawing on a cigarette. He waved them towards a couple of chairs.

'We'll come straight to the point,' said Appleby.

'*Un moment, monsieur.* Which of you is Mr Brown and which is Mr Green?' Dulière smiled awkwardly.

'I'm Brown,' said Appleby. He did not suppose Dulière believed the names they had given to be genuine for a moment. 'You act for the father of a pupil at Institut Le Rosey called Eugen Hanckel. Is that right?'

'How did you come by this . . . information?'

'It doesn't matter. It's true, isn't it?'

Dulière shrugged. 'Perhaps.'

'He went missing two days ago.'

'We know the school will have told you,' said Brigham.

'And we know you'll have told his father,' said Appleby.

Dulière released a sigh of exasperation and stubbed out his cigarette. 'Even if this was true, I could not discuss the matter with . . . *deux étrangers.*'

'You're going to have to. We know who the father is, *maître.* A German spy, sought by every government in Europe.'

'Not *every* government,' objected Dulière, with a hint of self-satisfaction.

'Swiss neutrality won't protect you from the sort of people who'll come calling here, *maître,*' said Appleby. 'I promise you that.'

'And they won't be as polite as us,' said Brigham.

'You're going to hear some news of Eugen later today,' Appleby continued. 'It won't be good.'

Dulière looked alarmed. '*Non?*'

'We don't want you to pass it on to his father. Do nothing. Tell no one. You understand?'

'I cannot do that.'

'You can. If you do, we'll keep your name out of it. There'll be no . . . impolite callers. You'll be able to carry on with your life, quietly and normally. Isn't that what you want to do?'

Dulière's glance flickered between them. 'What happened to the boy?'

'You have a son of your own, don't you? Marcel junior. And a nice house in Avenue de Cour. With a nice wife waiting for you there.'

Dulière's face lost much of its colour. 'Are you . . . threatening my family?'

'You should certainly put their interests first.'

'Mr Brown's giving you good advice, *maître,*' said Brigham. 'You should take it.'

'If you do, you'll never hear from us again,' said Appleby. 'And that would suit us just as well as I imagine it would suit you.' He smiled cautiously. 'So, can we rely on you?'

Dulière said nothing. His hand trembled as he took out another cigarette and lit it. He gave a nod that he may have intended to serve as a sign of agreement. But it was not enough.

'Can we?' Appleby pressed.

Another nod, more emphatic than the first, was followed by the word they needed to hear. '*Oui.*'

There was no cable waiting for Max at the Station Hotel in Tokyo. He was disappointed. Word from Appleby would have been welcome. But it could not be helped. Max knew Appleby would be in touch as soon as practicably possible.

With the list already despatched to C, Max felt free to reclaim the original from the hotel safe. It was a token of the defeat he had inflicted on Lemmer, of which, he hoped, Lemmer was still unaware. A mother's love was stronger than a father's, it seemed. Anna Schmidt's loyalty to Lemmer had surpassed everything except her attachment to her son. That had been Lemmer's undoing.

Max opened the window of his room to let in as much cool air as the evening could supply and turned on the fan. He lay on his bed and smoked a cigarette and tried to find a calm segment of his thoughts to dwell in. The great secret was what he really wanted. He knew that now. Destroying Lemmer's spy ring was his patriotic duty. Avenging his father was his destiny.

'I think that did the trick,' said Appleby as he and Brigham stepped out of Dulière's offices into the bright sunshine of mid-morning Ouchy.

'In which case, I take it you've no more use for me,' said Brigham, with a bitter edge to his voice. 'If it's all the same to you, Appleby, I'd like to go back to Geneva now and try to put this appalling business behind me. I should never have allowed you to talk me into helping you in the first place.'

'I wouldn't recommend Geneva.'

'Why the devil not?'

'If the Swiss authorities ever find out what we did on their territory, they'll be mightily displeased. France is the place for you, Brigham.'

'But what about my League of Nations post?'

'You'll have to wait and see what happens.'

'Wait and see? I—'

'Hold on, isn't that Veronica?'

It *was* Veronica, waving to them from the other side of the road. She was holding a piece of paper in her hand. And she was smiling broadly.

'You were not born in Tokyo.' Max's thoughts returned again and again to Lemmer's tantalizing remark. What did he mean by it? What did he know? *'You were not born in Tokyo.'* If not, then where? Why should his parents have lied to him about such a thing? What was the importance of his place of birth? *'You were not born in Tokyo.'*

Max pictured his parents as they were in the photograph on Hodgson's wall – young, hopeful, happy for all he knew. New Year's Eve, 1889. Before he was even born. Wherever he was born.

He rose from the bed, suddenly in need of any breeze there was to be had by the window. Something slid off his lap on to the floor as he sat up. It was the list of Lemmer's spies, written out by Anna Schmidt on Imperial Hotel notepaper. Max bent down to retrieve it. And then—

And then he saw.

APPLEBY HAD TO GIVE VERONICA THE GRIM NEWS OF EUGEN'S drowning in return for the glad tidings contained in Max's cable. She was shocked and appalled and he did not blame her. He had never considered the boy's death even as a remote possibility and clearly neither had she.

'What are we to do now?' she asked numbly.

'Warn Max what's happened. Confirm C has the list. Start back for London.' He looked at his watch. 'The sooner the better.'

'Won't Lemmer be expecting to hear from you?'

'Yes. And when he doesn't, he'll be suspicious. Silencing Dulière has only delayed the moment Lemmer learns Eugen is dead. We shouldn't be here when he does. And Max shouldn't be in Tokyo.'

Appleby cabled Max from the post office in Ouchy before he and Veronica boarded the next boat back to Evian-les-Bains.

WELL DONE. MUCH REGRET SUBJECT DROWNED.
RECOMMEND YOU LEAVE ASAP. BROWN

Max had left the Tokyo Station Hotel by the time the cable was delivered. It was late on a sultry night, the revellers and wanderers of Ginza moving as in a dream, heat and darkness fused in the shadows beyond the glare of the lamps.

Hodgson was clearly surprised to see him at Uchida Apartments. He waved his wife away and ushered Max towards his study, but

211

Max took the lead and went into the drawing-room, where he immediately noticed a change had been made to the pictures on display.

'I didn't expect to hear from you until tomorrow,' said Hodgson. 'Will you have a drink? Whisky, isn't it?'

'Something occurred to me that I wanted to discuss with you. And no, nothing to drink, thanks.'

'I reported to H.E. He'll be content if he hears from London in the morning, as you predicted. Of course, technically he's not H.E. We're between ambassadors at present, so our Head of Chancery—'

'Where's the photograph?'

Hodgson started back. 'Photograph?'

'New Year's Eve, 1889. It was hanging on your wall when I came here on Tuesday evening. Just where that framed map of China is now.'

Max already knew where the photograph was. He could see the picture had been slipped behind the cabinet to his right. But he was interested to see just how evasive his host would be.

'I'm not sure. My wife, er, moves things around a good deal.'

'Shall we ask her where it is?'

'I, er . . .' Hodgson looked more than flustered. He looked frightened. And Max knew what he was frightened of.

'Come on, Cyril. Show me the photograph.'

A slump of Hodgson's shoulders signalled defeat. He stepped over to the cabinet and pulled out the framed photograph.

'Put it back on the wall. Where it belongs.'

Hodgson took down the map of China and replaced it with the picture Max had seen there on Tuesday evening: the British Embassy staff, adorned in party finery, assembled in the ballroom of the Imperial Hotel on the last night of 1889 – according to Hodgson.

'The list Anna Schmidt gave me is written on Imperial Hotel notepaper,' said Max. 'I have it with me. Here. Take a look.' He pulled the sheets of paper from his jacket and waved them under Hodgson's nose.

'I've already seen it,' said Hodgson in an undertone.

'Really? Did you notice what's printed at the top of each sheet, smartly embossed in gold?'

'I . . . don't think so.'

'Read it.' Max flattened the sheets out. 'Read what it says.'

Hodgson adjusted his glasses and cleared his throat. 'Er, "Imperial Hotel, Tokyo".'

'And under that?'

'"Established . . . 1890".'

'Exactly. 1890. Interesting, wouldn't you say? It seems the Imperial Hotel opened its doors to the public for the first time in the year 1890. Not 1889. So, the photograph of the embassy's New Year's Eve party there can't date from 1889, can it?'

'Um . . .' Hodgson gave a pained frown. 'I suppose not. I must have been mistaken.'

'Since my parents only spent two Decembers in Japan, it follows the photograph must be of the party held on New Year's Eve, 1890. Wouldn't you agree?'

Hodgson's answer barely rose above a whisper. 'Yes.'

'I was born on the fifth of May, 1891.'

'You were?'

'So, at the end of December, 1890, my mother would have been about five months pregnant.

'I . . . suppose she would.'

'But she wasn't, was she? It's quite obvious. Just look at the photograph. That's why you ante-dated it by a year when I asked about it. Because you knew what I'd notice if you gave me the correct date.'

Hodgson sighed. 'I'm sorry,' he murmured.

'She isn't my mother, is she? I wasn't born in Tokyo. And I wasn't born to her at all. Poor old Brigham's barking up the wrong tree.'

'Who?'

'Never mind. You know the truth, Cyril. You were here at the time. And your subterfuge with the photograph proves it.'

'Come to my study. There's something you should see.'

'Something *else*?'

'Yes. Something else.'

Hodgson walked slowly out into the hall and crossed to his study. Max followed. Along the hall he saw Mrs Hodgson watching them anxiously round the edge of a door.

Hodgson lowered himself into the chair behind the desk and signalled for Max to close the door. The study was book-lined and cosy, though uncomfortably hot. A bust of Disraeli spectated from the mantelpiece. An English landscape in the style of Gainsborough hung above it. They could have been in a gentleman's retreat in the Home Counties.

Hodgson pulled open a drawer, took something out and slid it across the desk. Max sat down and picked it up. It was a telegram, tucked inside its ripped-open envelope.

'I cabled your mother two days ago asking her how much of the truth I should tell you,' said Hodgson. 'That's her reply.'

Max took out the telegram and read it.

TELL HIM EVERYTHING IF YOU JUDGE YOU NEED TO.
WINIFRED MAXTED

'The way things seemed to be working out,' said Hodgson, 'I didn't think the need was going to arise.'

Max stared at him. 'Oh, it's arisen.'

'Yes.' Hodgson nodded. 'I see that.'

'I'D BE GRATEFUL IF YOU ALLOWED ME TO SET OUT THE FACTS WITHOUT interruption, Max,' said Hodgson, sipping at a whisky he had poured for himself. 'You should know at the outset your father and mother did what they thought was best for you at every stage. It's hard to see how they could have behaved better, in fact, given the circumstances. Of course, those circumstances were partly of their own making, certainly of Henry's. But perhaps our characters are never more sternly tested than by how we cope with the consequences of our own mistakes.

'Tokyo was a smaller, more Japanese city thirty years ago. It was still at its heart Edo, the city of the Shoguns. Henry's previous postings had been Vienna and Budapest. Nothing can have prepared him or Winifred for the scale of Japan's foreignness. The ways of the people, as you've seen for yourself – their dress, their customs, their codes of honour and behaviour – are utterly different from those encountered in any European country you care to name.

'I was a relative newcomer myself when they arrived and we saw a good deal of each other. Henry and I worked together as well of course, and became friends. The English-speaking community was small and closely knit. One met the same people at every social engagement. There was much mixing with the members and spouses of the other foreign legations as well – American, French, German, Russian, Italian, Dutch. The Japanese we met were mostly of the upper and government classes. Unless you count the courtesans, of course.

215

'I have a Japanese wife. Naturally, I'm biased in an assessment of Japanese women. Some Western men find them supremely attractive. And there's never been the shame attached to . . . the needs of the flesh . . . in this culture. The Japanese are remarkably honest about such things. If you go to the local bath-house, you'll find men and women bathing together, quite unselfconsciously. It's truly a different world.

'Not surprisingly, many Western men took Japanese lovers, sometimes with the benefit of sham marriages. The French were particularly noted for marrying local girls they'd rapidly tire of before going home to France and contracting what they regarded as a genuine marriage to a well-born Frenchwoman. This was before Puccini turned such stories into grand opera, of course. But Madame Butterfly certainly existed.

'I mean to give no offence, but I imagine Winifred would have been prepared to turn a blind eye to a few discreet dalliances on Henry's part. She was – and clearly still is – a pragmatist. Ironically, Henry never required a blind eye to be turned. He wasn't a man who bestowed his affections casually.

'His work in the chancery section required him to meet Japanese politicians, both formally and informally. Baron Tomura Iwazu was one such, a rising star of sorts, though even then it was unclear what his affiliations were. He was unusual in many ways. He was known to have a variety of business interests, for instance, some of them allegedly shady. Also, he had an English wife: Matilda, daughter of Claude Farngold, a Yokohama tea merchant. Henry and Winifred entertained the Tomuras at their home and were entertained in turn at Tomura's residence here in Tokyo. They were soon on friendly terms. Winifred and Matilda met for tea. Tomura enrolled Henry in the Kojunsha Club. They were seen together often.

'I asked Henry once, quite early in our acquaintance – it was more of a warning, really – whether he thought he was in danger of growing too close to Tomura. As I recall, he told me not to be an old woman; Tomura was a rising force who'd repay study. Well, it was convincing enough, if you believed dispassionate scrutiny of the thought processes of a young Japanese politician was what Henry was about. The chief, Fraser, was evidently convinced. But he was a new boy himself, of course. He hadn't quite got the lie of the land.

'Then things started to happen, though it was only later that the shape of events became apparent. There was the assassination attempt against the Foreign Minister, Count Okuma, followed shortly by the death of Claude Farngold. Then there was a change of government. Under the new prime minister, Yamagata, Viscount Aoki became Foreign Minister. And one of Aoki's juniors was . . . Baron Tomura.

'Aoki had a foreign wife himself. She was German. It's probably no coincidence Japanese policy took a turn in favour of Germany around then. Fritz Lemmer popped up at the German legation to encourage the process. He was soon on friendly terms with Tomura himself. Rumours began to circulate that Lemmer exercised a sinister influence on Tomura, and through him on Aoki and other ministers.

'Political life here tends to close down in late July. Everyone heads for the hills. The heat in Tokyo, as you've discovered, can be stifling. Winifred had found her first summer well nigh unbearable. So, Henry took pity on her and sent her to spend the summer of 1890 with friends in Kashmir. As it happened, Tomura was out of the country as well, despatched to China by Aoki on some hush-hush mission: probably to assess how weak the Chinese government was. He was away for a couple of months or more. So was Winifred.

'I was unaware of the growing attachment between Henry and Matilda Tomura. I was out of town rather a lot myself. It's not so surprising it happened. Henry was alone, with time on his hands. Matilda was alone as well, still mourning her father and perhaps harbouring suspicions about her husband's role in his death. She and Henry became lovers. That much is clear. For how long they remained so . . . I don't know. Presumably, when Winifred returned from Kashmir and Tomura from China, or shortly thereafter . . . it ended. Well, it must have done, I think. To have continued would have been madly reckless. Although love, as you may not yet be aware, can inspire madness in the sanest people.

'Matilda was pregnant by Henry, however. Tomura may not have

217

known Henry was responsible, but obviously he would have known he himself wasn't. And he might well have guessed the identity of his wife's summertime lover. The list of suspects can't have been a long one. At all events, the cold rage of a Japanese nobleman betrayed by his English wife would have been a formidable thing. Was it partly revenge for Tomura's murder of her father, I've sometimes wondered. Tomura might have wondered that too. She might even have told him.

'Tomura's family is an ancient clan. They were feudal lords from the beginning of the Tokugawa Shogunate. Some have suggested Tomura hates the Koreans because an ancestor of his was killed during a failed attempt to conquer Korea in 1593. It could be true. Such men think in ways neither you nor I can properly understand. It was that ancestor's son who entered into a well-judged political alliance with Tokugawa Ieyasu, founder of the Shogunate. His reward was a grant of strategically important land north of Kyoto, where he reconstructed an old fort as a massive castle.

'Kawajuki-jo – literally, Kawajuki Castle – is a forbidding place. The architecture is typical of seventeenth-century castle construction, but something about the stonework – dark, unreflective – chills the blood. Well, it chilled mine when I first saw it. It's known generally by another name – Zangai-jo. Zangai's a difficult word to translate. It means the wreck of something, the original shape of which can no longer be discerned. That something could be a human in some renderings. No one seems to know how the name arose. Maybe it refers to some incident in the Tomuras' past that's been forgotten. If so, the name itself would be a zangai. A strange concept. But fitting, somehow.

'When Tomura discovered Matilda was pregnant, he sent her to Zangai-jo. Nothing more was heard of her in Tokyo. Henry kept the secret of their love bottled up. He didn't know she was carrying his child, though he probably suspected he was to blame for her banishment. As you correctly said, you weren't born in Tokyo. You were born in Kawajuki Castle.

'Tomura was in Kyoto at the time, serving as a member of the reception committee preparing for the visit of the Tsarevich. Well, you've read my report. You know I believe – and so did Henry – that Tomura was also preparing an attempt on the Tsarevich's life, with the encouragement and assistance of Lemmer, in order to poison Russo-Japanese relations, greatly to Germany's advantage.

'We never unearthed any proof of that. Neither did Kuroda. Still, Tomura and Lemmer both knew Henry suspected their involvement and Tomura knew Henry had personal reasons for doing everything he could to implicate him. Blocking Kuroda's investigations wasn't enough for him. I suppose he felt Henry was challenging him. And the challenge had to be answered.

'He sent you to Tokyo in the care of a servant called Ishibashi, with instructions to deliver you to Henry's house, accompanied by a letter. I never saw the letter, but I gather in it Tomura made clear his contempt both for Henry and his child, whom Tomura disowned. "Do with him as you please," was the gist of it. "He is no son of mine." And nor were you, of course, for which I suggest you should be grateful.

'It was a time of crisis. Fraser was under mounting pressure because a member of his staff had made allegations against a Japanese nobleman and a German diplomat that couldn't be substantiated. I alone at the legation was privy to the turmoil in that member of staff's private life. Your arrival forced him to confess his infidelity to Winifred. And both were forced to consider what should be done with you. Matilda was beyond help, locked away at Zangai-jo. A scandal was looming of alarming proportions.

'Then the news came. Matilda had died, purportedly of the after-effects of childbirth. A son – a son Tomura was pleased to call his own – had been born. The boy was, in truth, wholly Japanese, the child of one of Tomura's numerous mistresses, who'd accompanied him to China. He fitted the bill, apparently. You've met Noboru. He would never have been acknowledged by Tomura under normal circumstances. But the circumstances were far from normal. And the arrangement defeated any accusation Henry cared to make before he'd even made it.

'When I explained the situation to Fraser, he decided Henry's immediate departure from Japan was essential. I set about arranging it. He and Winifred had come to an understanding by then, reached, I imagine, after many harsh words had been exchanged and both had searched their hearts. They would take you and raise you as their son. The circumstances of your birth weren't your fault. It's greatly to Winifred's credit that she put an innocent child's welfare above the settling of a marital grievance.

'I arranged for them to go home by an indirect route, via Australia, so there'd be no one among the passengers to note the oddity that you arrived in Brisbane as their orphaned nephew and left Fremantle as their son. How they were reconciled in the course of that long journey I don't know. Perhaps you'll tell me they never properly were. However that may be, they both did a noble thing.

'That might seem more obvious in your mother's case than in your father's. But I know he wrestled with his conscience over what to do. He doubted Matilda had died of natural causes. He suspected – and I couldn't blame him – that she'd been killed on Tomura's orders. The rejected child and the murdered mother would be the sum of such a man's response to her betrayal of him. Perhaps he let her live until she'd given birth so that Henry would understand his responsibility for what had happened to her.

'And he did understand it. There was one long, desperate night when I had to talk him out of trying to kill Tomura. I reminded him of his diplomatic duty. Such an act would have handed Lemmer a second triumph. The damage it would have done to Anglo-Japanese relations was incalculable. Henry knew he had to leave. And he knew he had to allow Tomura his victory. With every atom of his being he rebelled against that dismal truth. Yet still he boarded the ship with you and Winifred . . . and left.

'No doubt by then Winifred had already sent a letter to her family – and to your unsuspecting elder brother at his prep school – announcing the birth of her second son. She told me she'd explain that complications with the pregnancy had caused her to keep the news to herself in case of a miscarriage. She'd thought it all through quite thoroughly. It was the version of events she meant to live by.

'I supplied your birth certificate. It's as authentic as any forgery can be, thanks to the advantages a foreign legation enjoys in such matters. The date – the fifth of May – was a guess. It could be wrong by several days. The only man who could tell you is Count Tomura – if he actually remembers. I doubt he'd be willing to tell you, anyway.

'Jack Farngold was at sea when Matilda died. By the time he reached Tokyo, Henry and Winifred – and you – had left. It seemed wise to supply him only with the official version of events. I believe he approached Tomura in hopes of meeting his nephew, as he supposed Noburo to be, and learning something of his sister's final days. I imagine he was given a chilly reception.

'If so, that was a mistake on Tomura's part. Somehow, at some point, Jack Farngold realized – or guessed – that Matilda had been murdered, perhaps along with her child. He asked me to help him bring Tomura to justice. I explained there was nothing I could do for him. Kuroda was obliged to turn him away as well. Kuroda had wheedled the truth out of me after Henry and Winifred's sudden departure and reluctantly agreed what had been done was for the best.

'Yes, we all agreed that. It was for the best. Except Jack Farngold, of course. He was a strange, stubborn, solitary man. He had no one left in the world he cared for, convinced as he was that Noburo wasn't really his nephew at all. He returned to the sea. And I forgot him.

'But he didn't forget. At some point – I don't know when – he began investigating Tomura's affairs. Perhaps in one of the many ports he put into he met someone who'd met someone who'd said, yes, Tomura murdered his English wife to punish her for adultery. Or perhaps it was just Tomura's growing fame after his military exploits in the wars against China and Russia that embittered him in some way. Whatever it was, it set him on his course, searching, always searching, for some way to bring Tomura down.

'Well, Jack Farngold learnt – as you've learnt – that Count Tomura has powerful friends and ample resources. They render him about as invulnerable as a man can be. The Japanese government will want nothing more to do with Lemmer now C can name and expose his spies. But that will damage only Lemmer, not Tomura.

221

He'll brush off the embarrassment and find some other way to pursue his objectives. It's interesting your friend Morahan and his associates were accused of conspiring to assassinate the Prime Minister. If I was Hara and I ever heard about it I'd worry the accusation came from those to whom the idea had already occurred. Dark Ocean isn't the only group plotting to push the government in a militarist direction. Tomura's at the centre of a network of influential people who see expansion and aggression as the fulfilment of Japan's imperial destiny. They're the future. And it isn't a pleasant future to contemplate.

'You've defeated Lemmer and you've inconvenienced Tomura. But you're alive. And the collapse of Tomura's brokerage of Lemmer means it'll seem prudent to him to let the charges against your friends be dropped. You can't help Jack Farngold now. And you certainly can't help his sister, the woman who bore you. She's long dead. I imagine Henry felt he owed it to her to do all he could to rescue her brother. But it's too late to rescue him. It's all too late.

'You know the truth now. There are no more secrets. Despite what they say, injustice does fade with time. The dead can't be brought back to life, Max. Let them rest in peace. You've done a great thing by crushing Lemmer's hopes and plans. Leave it there. And leave Japan. You were born here. Don't die here. You're young. There's a lot of life ahead of you to enjoy. So, enjoy it. I hardly knew her, but I'm sure that's what your mother – your original mother – would want you to do.'

'LIONEL BRIGHAM IS NOT YOUR FATHER. BELIEVE ME IN THIS IF IN nothing else. If I had a Bible with me I would be willing to swear upon it. You are Henry's son. There is no margin for doubt or uncertainty. You are his son and no other man's.'

Max remembered his mother's words – the words of the woman he had always thought of as his mother – as he stood in the Ginza bar he had gone to after leaving Uchida Apartments. He had drunk a lot of sake and *shochu* since then and could hardly recall how he and Hodgson had parted following Hodgson's revelations. What he could recall, very clearly, was standing in the wind and rain on Dover Marine station three months before, listening carefully and incredulously as his mother assured him of what he now knew to be true: he was Henry's son.

But he was not *her* son. Not truly. Not actually. He was the son of Matilda Tomura, born in Kawajuki Castle – Zangai-jo – near Kyoto on some unrecorded day in early May, 1891. She had died soon afterwards, put to death on her husband's orders. Her brother had followed her, also on her husband's orders, twenty-eight years later. And her lover, the father of her child? He was dead too, thanks to Lemmer.

Max had worsted Lemmer. He should have been drinking to celebrate his victory. Instead, he was drinking to drown the bitterness he felt. What satisfaction was there to be had – what peace of mind – if, despite all those things, he allowed Count Tomura Iwazu to dwell in the knowledge of his impunity? No one would call such a man to account. No one would bring him to justice.

Unless Max did. Now. Tonight. Without pause for doubt or reflection or counsels of caution. *Now*.

223

He emptied his glass and studied the steadiness of his hand. Yes. His heart was ice. His mind was clear. Yes. This *was* the right thing to do.

Marcel Dulière returned to his office in Ouchy from a late lunch, with dyspepsia already setting in. He was not surprised. His digestion had never fared well under stress. The two cognacs he had drunk after the wine-accompanied meal had probably been a mistake, as Madame Dulière, who disapproved of spirits, particularly in the middle of the day, would certainly tell him if she ever knew of it.

Dulière's secretary looked as fretful as he felt and promptly doubled his anxieties by reporting that an Englishman called Meadows was waiting in his office, having refused to wait outside. She described him as '*impoli*', which did not surprise Dulière, and '*boiteux*' – lame – which did.

Dulière considered the possibility of flight for a moment before rejecting it. Meadows would certainly come after him, lame or not. He could not run the risk of the man calling on him at home. He summoned what remained of his nerve and went in.

'The boss sent me,' Meadows announced, without rising from the chair Dulière normally occupied at his desk. 'Got any news?'

'*Ah, non. Pas de nouvelles.*'

'Speak English. Where have you been? Your secretary said lunch.'

'*Oui. C'est*—' Meadows' scowl prompted him to switch languages. 'Yes. I was at lunch.'

'The boss will be charmed to hear that. *Lunch*. Something you look as if you could do with missing once in a while, Marcel.' Meadows heaved himself out of the chair and limped round to Dulière's side of the desk. It appeared his right foot was troubling him. He did not look happy. 'Where's the boy?'

'I . . . do not know.'

'You've heard nothing from the school today?'

'*Ah, non.* No. Nothing.' It was a lie he had no choice but to tell.

'So, you've not cabled the boss today?'

'No. I have nothing to tell him.'

'According to your secretary, a couple of Englishmen came to see you this morning. The descriptions she gave made me think I know one of them. What were their names? She didn't have them.'

'Brown . . . and Green.'

'Not Black and White? Or Smith and Jones?'

Dulière grinned awkwardly. 'No.'

'A boy was found drowned on the lake shore this morning at a place called Morges. Did you know that?'

'Er . . . no.'

'Too busy planning lunch to ask around, were you?' Suddenly, from inside his jacket, Meadows pulled a gun and levelled it at Dulière. 'I reckon the police are bound to have contacted the school, them having reported a boy missing. Especially since the word in Morges is that the dead boy was wearing football kit, with a Le Rosey badge on the shirt. So, I'll ask again. Has the school been in touch with you?'

Dulière swallowed hard. He might have foreseen this. He *should* have foreseen this. 'They, er . . .'

'If you give me the wrong answer, Marcel, I *will* shoot you. Your secretary too if she makes a fuss, as I expect she will. So, *has* the school been in touch?'

'Yes,' croaked Dulière.

'What did they tell you?'

'The dead boy is Eugen Hanckel.'

'Why didn't you cable the boss as soon as you heard?'

'Brown . . . and Green . . . threatened me.'

'Well, now I'm threatening you. Was one of them a balding, jowly, self-satisfied type in his late fifties or early sixties?'

'Yes. That would be Brown.'

'OK. Where's your file on the boy?'

'In there.' Dulière pointed waveringly to the cabinet.

'Get it out.'

Dulière unlocked the cabinet and pulled open the drawer holding the file on Eugen Hanckel. He took it out and laid it on the desk in front of Meadows.

'Is that everything?'

Dulière nodded. 'Yes.'

'Best there's nothing left connecting the boy with the boss. The school are bound to refer the police to you in due course, I reckon, don't you?'

'I will say nothing.'

'*C'est vrai, mon ami.*' Meadows raised the gun then and shot Dulière between the eyes.

The Tomura mansion was invisible behind high, broad-stoned walls and tall trees. Akasaka was a quiet part of the city by night. Vehicles were few. The rattle of the trams several streets away was clearly audible in the still, humid air. Max could hear his own rapid foot-falls just as clearly and knew he was making himself conspicuous to anyone who might be watching. But he had tired of creeping in shadows. He meant to present himself at the gate and demand to see Tomura. Somehow he felt certain Tomura would not refuse to face him. The man was too proud for that. So they would meet. And then . . .

There was a single car parked at the side of the street thirty yards or so short of the mansion's main gate. The gate itself was closed, but lights were shining in the small building just inside. The tree-lined drive to the house could be seen sloping upwards beyond it. Max quickened his pace, bracing himself for the events that would be set in motion once he reached the gate.

Then the passenger door of the car opened and a figure jumped out into Max's path: Commissioner Fujisaki.

'What has brought you here, Maxted-san?' he asked breathlessly.

'What's brought *you* here?'

'A telephone call from Hodgson. He was worried about your intentions. He thought you might try to harm Count Tomura.'

'Did he tell you why I might want to?'

'No. But to go in there' – he pointed over his shoulder towards the house – 'as you are now would be crazy. Tomura could have you shot as an intruder. There would be nothing I could do.'

'I'll take my chances.'

'Go back to your hotel. You have been drinking. You are not thinking sensibly.'

'Maybe I'm tired of being sensible.'

'Maybe. And maybe I am sometimes also. But I am a police officer. And I must do my duty.'

Some faint nod of Fujisaki's head was the signal for three men to leap on Max from the deep shadow of the wayside hedge. His reactions, slowed by the amount he had drunk, came far too late for him to evade them. His arms were yanked behind his back. He heard the click of handcuffs round his wrists as he cannoned against the side of the car. And then he heard Fujisaki's voice, soft and regretful, close to his ear.

'I am sorry, Maxted-san. You are under arrest.'

A SAKE/*SHOCHU* HANGOVER WAS NOT A PLEASANT THING TO WAKE TO. Max's head also hurt because of a collision with the doorframe of the unmarked police car he had been bundled into. His throat was as dry and rough as sandpaper. The breakfast he had been roused to confront comprised brackish tea and over-boiled rice. And the cell he was in, deep in the basement of Tokyo Police headquarters, was as hot as an oven, with a mere wisp of marginally less hot air entering through a grille at ceiling height. All in all, Max felt a long way short of his best.

Sobriety and a new day – evident from sallow shafts of light admitted through the grille – cast his discoveries of the previous night in a fresh perspective. His determination to make Tomura suffer for what he had done had not weakened. But he knew – though he might be reluctant to admit as much to Fujisaki – that arresting him had been an act of kindness. It had saved him from himself as much as from Tomura.

Fujisaki's kindness did not extend to the provision of comfortable accommodation, however. The cell was rank with the odour of former occupants, some of whom had scratched messages on the walls. They were all in Japanese, of course, and thus unintelligible to Max, though a sketch of a hanged man was successful in making its point.

Most of the morning had passed, according to Max's watch, when the door of the cell was unlocked and opened for the first time since the removal of his breakfast cup and bowl. The guard signalled for him to come out and escorted him with a few prods of his truncheon by way of direction, along a corridor, up a short flight of steps and into another room.

It was about twice the size of his cell and was furnished with a table and two chairs. Windows set behind bars high in the wall stood open to a faint breeze. The guard gestured for Max to sit down, then closed the door and stationed himself by it, truncheon in hand.

A few minutes passed, then the door opened and Fujisaki came in, carrying a file, which he laid on the table before sitting down opposite Max.

'*Konnichi wa, Maxted-san*,' he said. 'How was your night?'

'Long. Am I still under arrest?'

'Technically, yes. Although it is debatable whether you have been under arrest at all. There will be no official record of your detention. I hope you feel now that I acted in your best interests.'

'Let's say I do.'

'Good. A smoke?' Fujisaki proffered a pack of cigarettes. Max accepted one. Fujisaki lit it for him. Then he lit another for himself.

'When can I leave?'

'Do you still intend to harm Count Tomura?'

'Yes. But not immediately. And not so clumsily.'

'Then you can leave whenever you like. But I suggest we have a talk here first. There is no danger of being overheard.' Fujisaki nodded to the guard. 'He understands no English.'

'All right. What's in the file?'

'Reports on events I must tell you about. Firstly, the dead bodies of two Western men were found in a sewage cart at Shibuya early this morning. Both had been shot. They were naked, so identification will be difficult. As far as we can establish, the sewage was collected from the Akasaka area of the city. Where you were, last night. I wonder, do you know who the men are?'

'Dombreux and Monteith.'

'You are very specific.'

'They were killed on Lemmer's orders. Probably at Tomura's mansion.'

'If that is true, it proves I was right to stop you entering.'

'I suppose it does. From your point of view. A sewage cart, you say?'

'Yes. It seems to me . . . contemptuous.'

'Contemptuousness is something Lemmer and Tomura have in common.'

'And you, of course. They have the problem you pose to them in common. I had a long conversation with Hodgson this morning. He told me everything he told you. About Count Tomura and the Farngolds . . . and you, Maxted-san.'

'Then you know what I mean to make Tomura answer for.'

'Yes. And as a Japanese man I cannot object to a son seeking to avenge his murdered mother. If she *was* murdered.'

'I hold Count Tomura responsible for her death. I don't intend to let him get away with it. It's as simple as that.'

'Yes. I understand.' Fujisaki extinguished his cigarette and lit another. He offered Max one. Max declined with a shake of the head. 'Hodgson also told me you have exposed Lemmer's spy organization. That means his scheme to sell his organization to the Japanese government has failed. A disaster for him. And a defeat for Tomura. This is true, yes?'

'I'm not sure how much of a defeat it is for Tomura. He may actually welcome getting Lemmer out of his hair.'

'Which will only increase your determination to attack him.'

'It'll make no difference to it, Commissioner.'

'No. Of course not. That was stupid of me. Tell me, do you think Lemmer knows yet what you have done to him?'

'Probably not. But he soon will.'

Fujisaki paused for a slow draw on his cigarette, then said, 'I ask because of the other event I must tell you of. Anna Staun – Anna Schmidt – was found dead in her room at the Imperial Hotel this morning. She had slit her wrists in the bath.'

'Good God.' Why? Why should she do such a thing? It made no sense to Max. She was doing all she could to secure her son's release. For her to kill herself at such a time was incomprehensible. 'Did she leave a note?'

'No. That is, no note was found. But it is interesting that Frederik Boel – Lemmer – had already booked out of the hotel by then. We do not know where he is now. He told the hotel manager he planned to travel to Kyoto.'

'Kyoto?'

'That is what we have been told he said. And he did not need to say anything. So, is it a message?'

'Maybe. But what it means . . . I don't know.'

'The collapse of Lemmer's plans makes him no longer a useful ally for Count Tomura. I suspect Tomura will desire a period of . . . discretion . . . in which to recover political credit. This will finally make certain all charges against Morahan, Djabsu and Ward are dropped. Also the charges against Miss Hollander and Mr Twentyman. Their deportation would be the obvious solution to Tomura's problem. What you have discovered is not something that can be used to destroy him, I regret. It is a personal matter between you and him.'

'Yes. It's certainly that.'

'But if you try to settle it personally, Maxted-san, I fear I will have your death to investigate as well as all the others.'

'I don't know how I'll move against him, Commissioner, although I promise you I won't be as bull-headed as I was last night. But I can't walk away. And I'm not going to pretend I'm willing to.'

'No. You are frank, Maxted-san. You are clear. I understand. I even approve. But still . . .' Fujisaki stubbed out his second cigarette and turned to the guard. '*Itte kudasai.*' The guard nodded and left the room.

'I thought he couldn't speak English,' said Max.

'He cannot. But there is a name it may be best he does not hear. A man came here a few hours ago. French, I think. He said he wanted to speak to you.'

'How did he know I was here?'

'I asked. He did not explain. He did not explain much at all. I refused to allow him to see you. He seemed not to be surprised. He asked when you would be released. I did not deny that it would be

231

today. He seemed not to be surprised by that either. He said he would call at your hotel later.'

'He knows where I'm staying?'

'Evidently he does.'

'What name did he give?'

'He insisted I should tell you his name, actually, which is interesting, I think. Laskaris. Viktor Laskaris.'

WELL DONE. MUCH REGRET SUBJECT DROWNED.
RECOMMEND YOU LEAVE ASAP. BROWN

MAX STOOD IN THE FOYER OF THE TOKYO STATION HOTEL, STARING at the telegram that had been waiting for him. He could only imagine Eugen Hanckel had drowned during an escape attempt while being transported across Lake Geneva. It was a terrible turn of events. Max knew how badly Appleby must have taken it. He had certainly never intended the boy to come to any harm.

But to harm the boy had come. Eugen was dead. Anna Schmidt had given away the names of Lemmer's spies for nothing. The news of the drowning must have reached her. That was why she had killed herself. Of the two people she loved most in the world, she had lost one and betrayed the other.

And what of that other? What would Lemmer do now? He would surely seek revenge. Appleby was out of his reach, but Max and Malory and Sam and Morahan were all in Tokyo. Lemmer's rage at such a moment would be a fearsome thing. Max felt sure he would come after them. Appleby clearly thought likewise. Hence his urging. *Leave as soon as possible.*

But Max had no intention of leaving. He was also set upon revenge. And the threat from Lemmer was not going to deflect him.

Malory and Sam were a different matter, however. He would do his best to persuade them to leave. He headed up to his room, meaning to telephone them from there.

But, bemusingly, the telephone was ringing as he entered the room. Cautiously, he picked up the receiver.

'Yes?'

'Mr Maxted. This is Laskaris.'

'Where are you?'

'Downstairs. But I suggest we meet on the station. I will wait for you on the main platform.'

The line went dead. Laskaris, it was clear, did not entertain the possibility that Max would refuse to meet him.

The station was deep in mid-afternoon torpor. Passengers awaiting trains drifted between patches of shade. The women flourished parasols. The men wore wide-brimmed straw hats. The clack-clack of their wooden sandals came at a heat-slowed pace, like the ticking of a clock that needed winding.

The man on the double-sided bench, facing the station building, was the only Westerner of the right age to be Viktor Laskaris, business partner of the late Alphonse Soutine. He was clad in a three-piece cream suit of immaculate cut, though it needed pressing. On his head he wore a smart panama. He was white-haired and generously moustachioed. His face was babyishly soft, as if he had seldom sat out in the sort of sunshine now bathing the platform. He was smoking a fat cigar, with every impression of relish.

On the other side of the bench, behind him, a boy wearing a school cap and red and white check *yukata* was immersed in a comic book. He had slipped off one of his sandals and was flicking it up and down with his toes, producing a sound like the clop-clop-clop of a horse's hoof.

Max sat down next to the white-haired man and nodded towards him. 'Viktor Laskaris?'

'*C'est moi.*' Laskaris touched his hat. 'A pleasure to meet you, Mr Maxted.'

'It's more of a surprise to meet you. I thought you didn't exist.'

'A sleeping partner is not a non-existent partner. Alphonse liked to confuse people about such matters. He was not a naturally honest man.'

234

'What are you doing here?'

'Speaking to you.'

'I meant what are you doing in Japan?'

'The same as you. I am here to avenge a dead man.'

'Soutine?'

'*Mais oui. Un cigare?*' Laskaris took out a case and offered Max a choice of aromatic Havanas.

'No thanks.'

'Smoke a cigarette if you wish. I will not be offended.'

'Perhaps I will.' Max lit up. 'How did you know where to find me?'

'Seddik is with me, Mr Maxted. You know him as le Singe. You will be aware he can find things – including people – that are to others . . . elusive.' Laskaris smiled. 'We travelled here on the same ship as Lemmer and the Tomuras. They know me as Eugène Quinquaud, porcelain collector. They saw nothing of Seddik, though he saw a good deal of them. Since we arrived, I have made extensive enquiries regarding Count Tomura and his collaboration with Lemmer. Seddik has assisted me ably, as you may imagine. I have contacted you because your arrest last night and the death this morning of Anna Schmidt, alias Staun, suggest to me that a crisis is approaching. And I would not want you to meet it . . . unprepared.'

'Le Singe – Seddik – has saved my life twice, *monsieur*. I'd like to have the chance to thank him.'

'He requires no thanks. He bears some responsibility for your father's death. Alphonse should not have allowed him to work for Tarn. But Alphonse always cared for money more than he should have. Helping you to kill Tarn and to escape being killed by Dombreux were honourable actions, however. I hope you agree?'

'Of course. But—'

'Seddik is watching us now. Can you see him?'

Max looked around. 'No.'

'You observe the signal gantry at the end of the platform?'

Max peered towards it, but saw nothing of le Singe. 'Yes.'

'What do you notice?'

'Nothing.'

'That is what you may expect to notice when Seddik watches you. We did not teach him to be so. He was born so, I think. With a gift not to be seen. You, of course, are rather more visible. Which may not be to your advantage.'

'You seem very sure you know what brought me to Japan, *monsieur*.'

'I am. Lemmer, of course. Service of your country. *Le patriotisme*. But also Tomura . . . and the Farngolds.'

'Did you tell Seddik to write their name on the wall in London?'

'*Non, non*. I was in Tunisia when all that happened. Attending to my interests. Seddik had seen the name in the documents he stole from Marquess Saionji. Or more correctly the document Marquess Saionji allowed him to steal. Seddik has, ah . . . *une mémoire visuelle exceptionelle*. He knew Alphonse had drawn your father's attention to references in those documents to the Farngold family. He knew it was important to your father. And therefore to you.'

'How much do you know about the Farngolds?'

'Oh, everything. Everything that can be known, I think. I have the advantage of you. I have read the letter Jack Farngold sent to your father in Petrograd in October 1917. Seddik took it from the villa in Marseilles on my orders. It was actually why I sent him there. Sir Henry had spoken of it to Alphonse. It seemed likely it would give me the answers to many questions.'

'Dombreux said it didn't reveal Tomura's secret.'

'He lied. Which was as natural to him as breathing.'

'You know he's dead?'

'I do. Also I know Matilda Tomura was your mother. I suspect you have discovered that only recently. Perhaps yesterday. Was that why you went to Tomura's house last night?'

'Yes.' Max drew reflectively on his cigarette. For the first time since learning the truth about his parentage, he felt a measure of calm when contemplating the fact that the woman he had always regarded as his mother was not the woman who had given birth to him. 'It came as rather a shock.'

'This is English understatement, I assume.'

'Will you give me the letter, *monsieur*? I am the son of the man it was addressed to, after all.'

'It is rightfully yours, I agree. And I will give it to you. But first a word about the future. The immediate future. Do you know why Lemmer has left Tokyo?'

'I think so, yes.'

'Is it because you have succeeded in identifying his spies, leaving him with nothing to sell to the Japanese government?'

Max looked at Laskaris in some surprise. The man really did seem to know everything.

Laskaris nodded, taking Max's silence for confirmation. 'I thought it must be so. Is that why Anna Schmidt killed herself?'

'In part.'

'So, Lemmer will be like us now – looking for revenge?'

'Quite possibly.'

'But this will not do enough damage to Tomura to satisfy you?'

'Not nearly.'

'Perhaps it will help you to know that I have already devised a scheme that will hurt Tomura – considerably.'

'What sort of scheme?'

'Noburo Tomura met an attractive young Frenchwoman on the voyage from Marseilles and became infatuated with her. Her name is Delphine Pouchert. She works for me. As does Louis Pouchert, who will shortly arrive in Tokyo, looking for his wife. Noburo does not think his mistress is married, of course. Pouchert will play the part of the outraged husband. He will challenge Noburo to a duel.'

'A *duel*?'

'French husbands can be old-fashioned in such matters. Duelling is illegal in Japan, as elsewhere, but what is the law where honour is at stake? Noburo will have a choice. Refuse to fight and be shamed. Or fight and be killed. Pouchert is an expert swordsman. The outcome is certain. So, Noburo will have to choose between disgrace and death. And his father will have to advise him what to do. The hero of two wars and the son who struts in his shadow. They will have to decide the value of their reputation. Difficult, I think.

'But their difficulties do not end there. Count Tomura knows of

Noburo's relationship with Delphine. He regards it as harmless. I think he approves of his son keeping a foreign mistress. But he would not approve of the sport she has with his son. Delphine has enhanced the pleasure she gives Noburo during their encounters by persuading him to take various drugs, including the one his father makes so much profit out of selling to the Koreans: morphine. Noburo is addicted to that now as well as to Delphine. His ruin has already begun.

'When it is complete, I will ensure Count Tomura understands why it has happened. If Noburo had simply killed Alphonse, I would not be here. My friend played too many clever games. They were always likely to lead him to his death. But to torture him as Noburo did? I cannot allow that. So, I will torture Noburo – and his father – in return.'

'I should warn you, *monsieur*,' said Max, dropping the butt of his cigarette and crushing it beneath his shoe, 'that Count Tomura may not be alive to witness his son's ruin.'

'Because you intend to kill him?'

'He killed my mother. What do you expect me to do?'

'Exactly what you propose. But you are likely to fail. So, I hoped you would be pleased to know that, if you do, the Tomuras will still have me to contend with.'

Max smiled ruefully. 'That's a comfort, *monsieur*. I'll keep it in mind.'

'Please do. Of course, you may not feel so murderous towards Count Tomura when you have read Jack Farngold's letter to your father.'

'I doubt that.'

'Naturally.' Laskaris took the letter out of the inside pocket of his jacket and handed it to Max. 'I have some information regarding the Dragonfly which you may wish to hear about when you have had a chance to reflect on the contents of the letter. You can contact me at the Kojimachi Hotel, where I am registered under the name Quinquaud, of course. I will look forward to hearing from you.'

Max hardly heard him. He recognized the envelope at once: frayed manila, addressed to *Sir Henry Maxted, British Embassy,*

Dvortsovaya Naberezhnaya, Petrograd, Soviet Russia, with a green stamp illegibly franked and assorted jottings in Japanese and Russian, along with one word in Russian rubber-stamped in red capitals.

'Not everything is as you suppose,' said Laskaris. 'As you will see.'

MAX DID NOT LOOK AT THE LETTER UNTIL HE HAD RETURNED TO the privacy of his hotel room. He poured himself a tot of whisky from his emergency supply and sat by the window. The turbid late afternoon air carried the rattle of trams and the cawing of crows. He slipped the letter out of the envelope and began to read.

At that moment, several miles away on the outskirts of the city, a car drew up in front of the main gate of Sugamo prison. Gordon Trumper, United States Embassy consular official, was the driver. Beside him sat Lewis Everett and behind him, in the back seat, Al Duffy.

Trumper sucked his teeth anxiously as a guard emerged from the gatehouse and began to walk towards the car. 'Jumpy, are we, pal?' asked Everett.

'You're not, I suppose,' Trumper retorted.

'Why should I be? We're armed and they're not. We know what we're going to do and they don't. Sounds like we have the upper hand. So long as that damn docket of yours gets us in.'

'It'll get us in.'

'Then we can do what we came to do.'

'And get out of this stinking country,' said Duffy.

The guard appeared at the window and inspected Trumper's pass. He asked a couple of questions in Japanese, which Trumper answered fluently. Then he signalled for the gate to be opened and waved them through.

'What did you tell him?' asked Everett as they moved forward.

'That you're consular officials, like I am.'

'Diplomats, hey? Hear that, Al?'

'I heard,' said Duffy.

'Ready for some diplomatic killing, are you?'

'Yup.'

'It has to look like self-defence,' cautioned Trumper.

'And it will,' Everett reassured him. 'Not much like it, maybe. But enough.'

The twenty-four hours Max had asked Malory and Sam to sit tight for had passed without further word from him. They knew he would be in touch as soon as he had definite news. But that did not make sitting out the daylight hours in the clammy heat of the house in Shinjuku any easier. Nor did Malory's attempts to teach Sam the rules of mah-jong – a previous occupant had left a board and tiles behind – do more than exasperate both of them. In the end, they were reduced to swapping apologies for their increasing snappishness.

'It's Saturday afternoon,' Sam complained as he lit his umpteenth cigarette. 'By rights I should be canoodling with my sweetheart under a tree out Chingford way.'

'It's Saturday *morning* in London,' objected Malory. 'Besides, you don't have a sweetheart. You distinctly told me yesterday she married a myopic milkman. If this is Doris the cinema usherette we're talking about.'

'It is,' Sam sighed. 'You're right. She didn't wait for me.'

'And she'd have had to wait several years. So, waiting several hours shouldn't be too much for us, should it?'

'No. It shouldn't.' Sam suddenly brightened. 'Fancy a cup of tea?'

Now it was Malory's turn to sigh. 'Why not?'

Morahan was surprised to hear Trumper had come to see them again so soon. Ward struck an uncharacteristically optimistic note by suggesting he might have good news. Morahan was less confident. But he was happy to go and find out.

241

They were marched towards the room where they had been closeted with Trumper the previous day, but he was waiting for them in the corridor, briefcase in hand, shod for the street and smoking a cigarette.

'I've greased a palm to get us the use of the yard,' he announced with a smile. 'It's not so infernally hot out there.'

None of them raised any objections to a breath of late afternoon air. They had become accustomed to the rank smell and stultifying heat of the cell they shared with nine others. But the exercise yard, a bare rectangle of beaten earth about the size of two tennis courts, flanked by high walls of tightly bound bamboo, was a welcome alternative.

The guard opened the next gate, then fell behind as they headed towards the wide, low-lintelled door leading into the yard. The light outside was dazzling, dust swirling in the glare.

As Morahan stooped to clear the lintel, Trumper stepped close to him and whispered quite distinctly, 'Everett and Duffy are here to kill you.' Then he pressed a gun into Morahan's hand.

Several judgements of risk and probability formed in Morahan's mind during the next few seconds. Ward was first through the door. Morahan and Djabsu were half a pace behind. Trumper slowed, letting them take the lead.

Morahan shaded his eyes with one hand and cocked the gun with the other as he entered the yard. Two men were waiting there, with their backs towards the door: Everett and Duffy. As they turned, he saw the light catch the barrels of the guns they were holding.

The advantage of surprise was lost to them as far as Morahan was concerned. And he was not unarmed, as they would have expected him to be. He closed the gap between them in several long strides, took aim swiftly and fired.

The first bullet took Everett in the chest, the second in the neck. He crumpled and fell with a groan, firing harmlessly into the ground. But concentrating on Everett, as Morahan had done instinctively, exposed him to the threat from Duffy. He heard the shot and felt the impact beneath his raised right arm in the same jolting second.

As he fell, he heard a roar from Djabsu and saw the Serb launch himself bodily at Duffy, whose second shot flew wide as he was flung to the ground, with Djabsu landing on top of him. The breath was knocked out of his body and the gun out of his hand.

Morahan tried to rise, but a wave of pain and weakness swept over him. He saw Ward run into view, stoop and gather up Duffy's gun, then stamp on Duffy's wrist.

'Let me see him, Gazda,' said Ward. Djabsu spat into Duffy's eyes and rolled clear. Duffy opened his mouth to speak, but whether he meant to plead for mercy or curse them defiantly was never to be known. Ward shot him several times in the head and chest, then turned to Everett and shot him several more times as well, for all that he was clearly already dead.

'Trumper slipped me the gun,' Morahan said through gritted teeth, foreseeing that otherwise Ward might shoot their saviour as well.

'I'll want consideration for that,' said Trumper in a faltering voice. 'But for me, you'd all be dead.'

Shouts and rapid footfalls echoed out into the yard from the doorway. Soon, they would be overrun by guards.

'Put the gun down, Grover,' Morahan said, discarding his. 'Don't give them an excuse to shoot you.'

Ward tossed the gun to the ground. 'What happens now?'

'Not sure.'

Morahan stretched his left hand across his chest and felt the wound in his side. Blood was bubbling out of him. Maybe the bullet had pierced his lung. He did not know. For the moment, gazing up at the hazy blue sky above him, he did not especially care. What mattered was that he was alive. While Everett and Duffy – especially Everett – were not.

WHEN MALORY AND SAM'S PATIENCE FINALLY RAN OUT AND Malory called the Station Hotel that evening, she was surprised to be told Max was in his room. And she was even more surprised by his tone when he answered the telephone.

'Hello, Malory.' He sounded subdued or distracted, neither anxious nor exultant. Perhaps he was slightly drunk. She was puzzled. And soon she was confused.

'Have you heard from him?' By *him* she meant Lemmer.

'I should have told you. Sorry. We have the names. I've sent them to London.'

'You have them?'

'Every last one.'

'When were you going to tell us?'

'There have been . . . complications.'

'What kind of complications?'

'I can't go into them over the phone. Maybe we could speak tomorrow.'

'Tomorrow? I—'

She broke off. Sam was tapping on her shoulder. 'There's a car outside,' he said. 'Looks like the police.'

'Coming here?'

As if in answer there came a loud knock at the door. Sam peered through the window. 'It's all right,' he said. 'It's Fujisaki.'

Malory put the receiver back to her ear to speak to Max again. But, to her astonishment, the line was dead. He had hung up.

The mystery of Max's state of mind was forgotten in the wake of what Fujisaki had to tell them. The deaths of Dombreux and Monteith; the suicide of Anna Schmidt; Lemmer's abrupt departure from Tokyo; the shootings at Sugamo prison: tumultuous events that had followed hard on the heels of each other.

Morahan had been taken to the University Hospital on Fujisaki's orders. The Commissioner did not propose to leave him in the prison infirmary. As he explained during their drive to the hospital, Trumper had already made a statement undermining the evidence against them. And their principal accusers were now dead.

It was Fujisaki's opinion that Trumper had got wind of his imminent exposure as a spy of Lemmer's and had decided to sabotage the killings of Morahan, Ward and Djabsu ordered by Lemmer in the hope of gaining some credit with the US Secret Service when they caught up with him.

'This was fortunate for Mr Morahan and his friends,' he said. 'Otherwise they would have been helpless. And we would have had to believe that Everett and Duffy had defended themselves against an attack with knives. We found the weapons on them that they planned to say they had been threatened with.'

As for Morahan's injury, Fujisaki was as reassuring as he could be, praising the expertise of the University Hospital surgeons. But Malory was white with worry. And Fujisaki could not deny he did not really know how serious the injury was.

'At least you are free to visit him, Miss Hollander. I have cancelled the arrest orders against you and Mr Twentyman and I am confident the charges against your friends will soon be dropped. Count Tomura will not object, I think. He will wish to dissociate himself from Lemmer at a time such as this.'

Morahan was still sedated following emergency surgery when they reached the hospital. His surgeon said the operation had gone as well as could be expected. 'He is a strong man. But the injury to his lung is quite severe. And I see . . .' The surgeon hesitated. 'I see . . .

he has had other recent injuries. You should not expect him to recover quickly.'

Malory said she would sit by his bedside until he regained consciousness. She suggested Sam go to the Station Hotel and tell Max what had happened. Fujisaki for his part found a summons awaiting him. The Chief of Police wished to confer with him at headquarters as soon as possible. Fujisaki's expression gave little away. All he said was, 'The Chief does not like cases that involve politics.' Then he left.

Fujisaki had stationed two policemen on the door of Morahan's room, though it was not clear who they might be protecting him from. The ranks of Lemmer's operatives would be thinning fast now they had all been identified. Sam could not help thinking of Nadia and wondering how she would react to the turn of events. He doubted she would be willing to go down with a sinking ship.

Morahan himself looked to be sleeping peacefully, despite being swathed in bandages and attached to an assortment of tubes. Malory wept when she saw him. The sight of this man Sam had come to think of as a tower of indomitability reduced to an unconscious figure in a hospital bed was a reminder of just how foolhardy their decision to challenge Lemmer and Tomura had been. They had never been likely to escape unscathed.

'You heard the doc,' Sam said in an effort to comfort Malory. 'Schools has got what it takes to get over something like this.'

But Malory's expression did not suggest she was comforted at all. 'I hope so, Sam,' she said dolefully. 'I blame myself for talking him into coming to Japan.'

'We all talked ourselves into it. He wouldn't blame you.'

'I know.' Malory clasped Morahan's hand. 'But that doesn't make me feel any better.'

'What would?'

'Schools opening his eyes and smiling at me.'

'Well, he will. You just have to be patient.'

Malory sighed. 'Then I guess that's what I'll be.'

*

246

Sam had been perturbed by Malory's account of her telephone conversation with Max. When he reached the Station Hotel, he was informed 'Mr Greaves' was in the bar. It was thinly populated at that hour of the evening and Max was sitting alone in a booth, staring into a glass of whisky. A drink to celebrate getting the better of Lemmer was understandable, but Max did not look to be in celebratory mood.

This was partly explained by his revelation that Lemmer's son had drowned during the kidnapping operation in Switzerland. An unintended death was something Lemmer himself would probably have dismissed as unimportant if the boot had been on the other foot. Max was not made of such ruthless stuff. Nor was Sam. He had never even met the boy. Neither of them had. But still it was, as Sam said and Max agreed, 'a crying shame'.

It was also the obvious explanation for Lemmer's order to kill Morahan, Ward and Djabsu. He wanted to punish those nearest to hand for his son's death. He was, in the immediate sense, more dangerous than ever.

'You and Malory should probably leave Japan with Schools as soon as he's fit to travel,' said Max, nodding at the wisdom of such advice as if it was obvious to him for the first time. 'None of us is safe with Lemmer looking for revenge and Tomura willing to help him.'

'Maybe Tomura won't be willing to help him, sir,' countered Sam. 'Trumper thought better of it, didn't he? So will a few others. Lemmer could find himself short of friends.'

'Let's hope so. Did Fujisaki tell you what I've learnt about my father and Matilda Farngold?'

'He didn't say anything about that, sir.'

'No? Well, that was decent of him. He probably thought it would come better from me. You have to know. Malory and Schools too.' Max gulped down the last of his whisky. 'Though how . . .' His voice trailed into silence. Sam was astonished to see his eyes welling with tears.

'What's wrong, sir?'

Max shook his head. 'Sorry. I've had a shock. Probably the

247

NIGHT HAD FALLEN, BRINGING RAIN, YET LITTLE RELIEF FROM THE heat. The hospital seemed to have lost most of its population in Sam's absence, its corridors empty and echoing, its courtyards a-splatter from overflowing gutters. Sam could never before recall being worried by Max's state of mind. But now he was. Something had happened beyond the realm of danger and daring where Max normally dwelt, something fundamental to all he was. And Sam could only wait to learn what it might be.

Malory was in much better spirits than when he had left. Schools had regained consciousness and, though drowsy from the pain-killers he had been given, was able to talk, at least for short periods. 'We mustn't tire him,' she instructed them.

Max's appearance at his bedside brought a smile from the patient. 'It's good to see you,' he said, slurring his words slightly. 'I guess you know things haven't exactly gone to plan.'

'There were always lots of ways things could go wrong, Schools. I'm sorry one of them ended like this for you.'

'Don't be. I chose Everett. And I let him choose Duffy and Monteith. They were my mistakes, not yours.'

'There's a lot I have to tell you. But it can wait until you're feeling better.'

'It's true I'm not exactly firing on all cylinders. I can't recommend a bullet in the lung. But I reckon I'll be sitting up and taking notice tomorrow. Nurse Hollander permitting.'

Malory looked sceptical at that, but before she could suggest they leave him to rest, one of the policemen on the door came in, jabbering to the effect that they were wanted outside.

Fujisaki was waiting, newly returned from a grilling by his chief. He ushered them into an empty office and closed the door.

'I have had my instructions,' he announced. 'I hope you understand I have to carry them out.'

'You sound as if we aren't going to like them, Commissioner,' said Malory.

Fujisaki grimaced. 'The incident at Sugamo prison requires a prompt response. The charges against Morahan, Ward and Djabsu cannot be proceeded with, since Everett, Duffy and Monteith are all dead. And Trumper states Everett and Duffy were killed in self-defence. There is also political embarrassment about Count Tomura's involvement in the original arrests following what we gather is the, ah . . . discrediting . . . of his ally Lemmer. So, the Chief has been told what to do and he has told me to do it. Ward and Djabsu will be held at Sugamo until they can be deported to the United States, probably on the next passenger ship to San Francisco. Morahan will be deported with them, or later if he has not sufficiently recovered to leave the hospital at that time. There is no challenge to this ruling. Deportation of any foreigner can be ordered by the Home Ministry without giving any reasons. From their point of view, it is the best solution to the problem.'

'What about us?' asked Sam.

'You and Miss Hollander, Twentyman-san, will also be deported . . . if you come to the attention of the authorities. You were never charged, however, so you cannot be arrested.'

'And me?' put in Max.

'Officially, no one knows you are in Japan, Maxted-san. But you should all leave as soon as possible. That is my advice. Lemmer is defeated. Count Tomura is damaged. Trying to do more . . .' Fujisaki looked intently at Max. 'It is . . . *jisatsu.*'

'Suicide,' murmured Malory.

'He's referring to my pledge to kill Tomura,' said Max. 'I haven't yet told my friends here why he deserves to die, Commissioner.'

'Perhaps you should. Unless . . .'

'I take your advice and persuade them to take it too?'

'What are you talking about?' Malory frowned at Max. 'What's this about a pledge to kill Tomura?'

'Matilda Farngold was my mother,' Max stated simply.

'*What?*'

'She and my father had an affair. After I was born, Tomura sent me to him as a sort of . . . contemptuous gift. My mother – my legal mother, that is – agreed to raise me as her son. And Matilda . . .' Max rubbed his forehead. 'It was said she'd died in childbirth. But my father – and Matilda's brother, Jack Farngold – believed she'd been murdered. Noburo was the son of one of Tomura's mistresses, acknowledged by him in my place.'

'Strewth,' murmured Sam.

Malory stared at Max in amazement. 'And you mean to avenge Matilda's murder?'

'No.' Max slowly shook his head. 'I've thought it over. I never knew her. She's long dead. Her brother's dead too. As is my father. Better there should be no more deaths. Commissioner Fujisaki's right. We should all leave Japan as soon as possible.'

Fujisaki gave Max a small bow. 'I am personally relieved to hear you say this, Maxted-san. It is wise, I think.'

'We'll wait until Schools is able to travel with us, then . . .'

'You're serious, sir?' asked Sam. Something in Max's manner troubled him. Max's words and mood seemed at odds with each other – the one cool and pragmatic, the other dark and turbulent.

'Of course.' But the doubt remained. And Max's expression as he glanced at Sam contained the hint that he wished it to be so, as if there was a truth he needed to conceal from Fujisaki. 'Never more so.'

They left the hospital in a taxi together an hour or so later, Malory having assured herself Schools needed nothing more except a peaceful night's sleep. Fujisaki had added an extra pair of officers to the guard on his room. He was as safe as he could possibly be.

Once they were under way, Max announced he would travel with them to the house in Shinjuku. He said there were plans they needed to make, though this explanation struck Sam as unconvincing and he suspected Malory felt the same, though neither said so. The making of plans to leave Japan could surely best be addressed the following day, when it might become clear how long Schools would have to remain in hospital.

As soon as they were in the house, Max dropped the pretence. 'I'm sorry,' he said. 'There's something I want to tell you that I had to keep from Fujisaki.'

'You mean to pursue Tomura, don't you, Max?' said Malory.

'Not exactly.'

'I don't believe you're willing to put what you've learnt behind you.'

'To be honest, sir,' said Sam, 'neither do I.'

'Nor should you,' Max replied disarmingly. 'But the situation's not what Fujisaki thinks. And it's not what I thought it was when I resolved to make Tomura pay for what he'd done. There's the little matter of this.' He pulled a letter out of his pocket. 'Sent by Jack Farngold to my father in October 1917. I nearly laid hands on it in Marseilles, but le Singe took it before I could read it. He passed it to Viktor Laskaris.'

'Laskaris?' Sam gaped at Max in astonishment. 'He's real?'

'Yes. And he's here in Tokyo, plotting to punish the Tomuras for killing Soutine. I met him this afternoon. That's when he gave me the letter.'

'What does it say?' asked Malory.

'It says why Jack Farngold wanted my father to join him here and what he hoped they could accomplish. It explains why, when my father finally found out what had happened, he made the plans he did. It tells us the truth. And it poses the question: what are we going to do about it?' Max looked intently at them. 'For my own part, I know. But you must decide for yourselves.'

6.X.17

Sir Henry,

You and I have never met, although I expect Matilda mentioned me to you. She is always Tiddy to me. I am her older brother, Jack. I need your help. I think you will agree to give it when you have read this. They say you are an honourable man. I call upon you to prove it.

It was the tea trade that brought Father to Japan. Tiddy and I were both born in Kent, but my earliest memories are of the house on the Bluff in Yokohama where we grew up. I was sent home to England for my education, but I never took to any career that might have led to. Nor to the tea business, much to Father's disgust.

The sea is what I have always loved. The open, limitless ocean. A man is judged aboard ship by what he contributes. If he cannot be relied upon, he is no use. Where he went to school, his accent, his connections – they count for nothing.

Father cut me off when I told him I would make my way in the world as a sailor. Tiddy wrote to me wherever she thought letters would find me. I wrote back whenever I could. I prospered. I worked my way up to captain's rank with the Indo-China Steam Navigation Company. They were a Jardine's operation. To Father, Jardine's were a competitor in the tea business. That drove us further apart. I did not see my family from one year's end to the next. It took many months for a letter from Tiddy to reach me telling me Mother had died. That was how it was. I was my own man, you would say. And I was content to be so.

But I was lonely. Maybe lonesome, as the Yanks would say, fits it better. There were my shipmates, my crew. There was the female company I found ashore. But at heart I was solitary. I never knew how solitary until I got a message through Jardine's that Tiddy was dead.

This is what I found out later. Father had a partner, Daniel Fentiman, who was in charge of the Kobe side of the business. He took to opium and to embezzling money to pay for it. Father suddenly found himself in a tight spot. His profits had already been hit by legislation in the US banning the import of low-quality tea. And he had lost an uninsured shipment in a storm. Bankruptcy threatened.

He was saved by a Japanese investor Fentiman found. Or maybe the investor found Fentiman. Baron Tomura Iwazu. That is how he entered Tiddy's life. Tomura introduced Father to other ways of making money. Then he named the price: Tiddy. It was a piece of commerce between them. Father persuaded her he would be ruined if she did not agree to marry Tomura. It may have been true. And so it was done.

But Father was ruined anyway. It seems he knew too much about Tomura's political activities, in particular an organization he belonged to called Genyosha – Dark Ocean. I know you know about this, Sir Henry. You were a Second Secretary at the Legation. You must have heard about Dark Ocean. They tried to assassinate the Foreign Minister, Count Okuma Shigenobu, in Tokyo on October 18, 1889. His would-be assassin, Kurushima Tsuneki, killed himself straight afterwards. But one of Kurushima's associates, arrested by your friend Kuroda and later released, was a man called Shaku Taisuke. I found him listed in the records of Farngold, Fentiman & Co as a recruiter of seasonal staff, working first in Kobe, then in Yokohama. He joined the

254

company around the time Tomura bailed Father out. He was Tomura's man.

I think Father threatened to report this connection between Tomura and the assassination attempt to Kuroda. That is why Tomura decided to kill him. The fire was no accident. I examined all the reports. Father could have escaped. There was ample time. He did not escape because he was already dead. The fire destroyed the evidence of his murder. Shaku was one of those who suffered minor injuries. I suspect he killed Father. Why else would he have been there?

Father died on October 26, 1889, eight days after the Okuma assassination attempt and just three days after Shaku's release from custody. Shaku Taisuke is dead, by the way. I shall not say how I know that. But you can be sure of it.

Tiddy must have suspected Tomura was responsible for Father's death, though she never said so to me when we met in Yokohama, for what turned out to be the last time, a few months later. Did she say it to you? I have spoken to some of the staff at Tomura's Tokyo house. You can learn much more when you speak their language. It took me a long time to master Japanese and to understand the ways of the Japanese mind. What I am doing they would call *gimu*. It is something I am required to do as my father's son and sister's brother. It has no limit.

I know when your love affair with Tiddy began, Sir Henry. I also know when it ended. I know of the child born to Tiddy and consigned to you by Tomura in his lordly disdain. And I know the child acknowledged by Tomura as his son was not born to Tiddy.

You had already left for England when I reached Tokyo a month after Tiddy's death was reported to me. You had gone, with your wife and orphaned nephew who was to become, in the course of the voyage, your son. It was only much later that I learnt all of that. At first, I did not doubt the explanation that Tiddy had died of complications following

255

childbirth. I travelled to Kyoto to visit her grave and to see the child. But I was turned away from Kawajuki Castle on Tomura's orders. He wanted me to have nothing to do with his son.

That was his mistake. He might have carried it off otherwise. I began to ask questions. And the answers did not satisfy me. There was something wrong – something amiss. It took me years of investigations – that is, months of actual investigation, separated by long voyages – before I was convinced of what had happened. And even then, as I know now, I was wrong.

It was Shaku Taisuke who finally told me, in circumstances where I was sure I could believe him, that Tomura had killed Tiddy – stifled her – shortly after the birth of the child that was not his. That night in Nagasaki, Shaku's last on this earth, was the night I resolved to make Tomura suffer for what he had done.

Know thine enemy, it is said. I know mine. I have studied him well. My intention was not to kill him, but to disgrace him. The hero of two wars, the wearer of many medals, the Butcher of Port Arthur, the great man. What he fears above all things is loss of reputation.

He has good reason to fear it. My investigations have shown his wealth is built on foulness: the working to death of coolies in his Manchurian coal mines; the trafficking of kidnapped Japanese women sold into forced prostitution; the making and selling of drugs to the poor and desperate. Not just opium. Heroin. Cocaine. Morphine. I have seen what they do to people. I have stood in an alley in Keijo and seen an addict knock at a door, wait for a peephole to open, push his arm through with money in hand, be injected with the drug, then walk on. There is an invisible chain that links that man to Count Tomura Iwazu – that man and all others like him.

Commissioner Kuroda believes Tomura was involved in the assassination attempt against the Tsarevich in May 1891 as well as the earlier attempt against Foreign Minister Okuma and the later successful attempt on the life of Queen Min of Korea. He believes it, but he cannot prove it. I believe it, but I do not need to prove it. I have the measure of Tomura. I know him. Power, not wealth, is what drives him. The control of others, by destitution, addiction, subjugation.

He would rather torture than kill his victims. He would rather inflict a miserable life on them than a painful death. That is what I have learnt in the years I have studied him.

So the truth, now that I have it, should not have surprised me as it did. I should have guessed many years ago. The details of the payments I traced through documents I found in the Oriental Development Company's offices in Weihaiwei should have led me to the answer much sooner than they did. But the time has been lost. I cannot help it. Enough time remains, though. That is all that matters.

I am no longer young, though I am younger than you. We will need others to help us. To hire them we will need money. I have some but not enough. That is why I have turned to you, Sir Henry. That is why I am sending you this letter.

We must save the person who has loved us both: your Matilda, my Tiddy. She is not dead, Sir Henry. She did not die of complications following childbirth. Tomura did not kill her. He imprisoned her, in Kawajuki Castle. There she has remained, held captive by him, all these years that number twenty-six. More than a quarter of a century. Nearly half her life. She has been his prisoner all that time.

The castle is said to be impregnable. Tomura seldom goes there, but he keeps it heavily guarded. Some say he hoards treasure there – gold and diamonds to protect him if his other sources of wealth fail. But I know what is really being guarded.

There is a secret way in, a tunnel constructed when the castle was built, but long forgotten. Its location is known to a man who once worked for Tomura. Sickened by what he was required to do, he left and became a monk. He has promised to show me where the entrance to the tunnel is. A way in can be a way out. It is our best chance.

There is a set of apartments within the castle, he told me, cut off from the other rooms, inaccessible unless you know how to reach them. They are protected by a series of traps. No one goes there without Tomura's knowledge and permission. It is called by those who work at the castle *Uchi-gawa* – the Inside. It must be where Tiddy is held.

There is a woman in Keijo who knows how to pass through the traps. It is said she is descended from the man who designed them. It is also said she is no friend of Tomura. I will leave for Keijo tomorrow in the hope of persuading her to tell me how it can be done.

I hope to find a message from you waiting for me when I return, Sir Henry. Cable me at the Merchant Marine Officers' Club, Yokohama. It will not be easy for you to travel to Japan in the current international situation. But the war cannot stand in our way. We must rescue her. You will know that, I think. You will feel it. And you will come, I trust.

We are her only hope, though she cannot know it. She must believe we have abandoned her, or suppose her dead, or are dead ourselves.

Do not let her die his prisoner, Sir Henry.

Help me save her.

J. F.

IT WAS A WARM HIGH SUMMER'S AFTERNOON AT GRESSCOMBE PLACE. Winifred, Lady Maxted, had used the heat as an excuse to retire to her room after luncheon. A reappearance for tea on the lawn would be hard to avoid without arousing suspicion and she was therefore reconciled to it. The return from school of her grandson, Giles, was no incentive, in view of the bullying temperament he seemed to be developing. She could only hope the advanced state of Lydia's pregnancy would have so exhausted her that she would not question Winifred about the telegram she had received that morning – the second within two days.

Winifred was still carrying the telegram, folded away in the small pocket of her dress. She could not decide whether to destroy it or conceal it somewhere. She favoured the former, although she did not delude herself that such action would spare her the eventual need to explain to Ashley – and to Lydia – that James was not her natural son.

James knew already, of course. It was strange to think of him, so distant from her in so many ways, reflecting on his long-delayed discovery of the truth. He might actually have a better opinion of her as a result, now he knew for certain Brigham was not his father. What concerned her most, however, was how he would respond. He would not let Matilda, the mother he had never known, go unavenged. Of that Winifred was quite certain.

It was not obvious from Hodgson's telegram that he had done what she had authorized him to do. YOUR SON NOW IN FULL

POSSESSION OF FACTS. So the message ran. Perhaps James had uncovered the facts himself and merely gone to Hodgson for confirmation. He was such a determined boy that anything was possible.

At twenty-eight, he was hardly a boy any more, of course, though she always thought of him as such. Winifred smiled at the irony that she loved him more dearly than Ashley, the son she had actually borne. They were very different men. And James was the better one by far. It was obvious. It was undeniable.

She regretted now her failure to assure James of her love. The suspicions harboured by him about her relationship with Brigham had always come between them. What she did not regret – what she never would – was agreeing to raise him as her own. He had been a credit to her in all those ways Ashley and Lydia viewed so disapprovingly. He had been a son to be proud of. And proud of him she was.

Whatever he did next, he would do it well, even if it led him to his death. She knew that.

'Take care,' she murmured, laying a finger on his face in the small photograph of him in RFC uniform that stood on her dressing-table. 'Take care, my son.'

Appleby was surprised, yet not surprised, to find C waiting for them when he and Veronica Underwood left the cross-Channel steamer at Dover. C knew when they were due to arrive and, as he explained, he wanted to speak to them before they reached headquarters. 'It's rather hectic there at present, as I'm sure you can imagine.'

Appleby could imagine. The naming of Lemmer's spies was a thunderbolt, unanticipated by all but a few. Many men – and a few women – trusted and relied upon by their governments had been exposed as traitors. They were under arrest now, or soon would be, or on the run, or being sought. They were creatures of the night scurrying in search of a hiding place from the glare of day.

C handed Appleby a copy of the list as they stepped into the first-class compartment he had reserved for their use. The blinds were down on the corridor side. The guard had been spoken to. They would not be disturbed.

'You've done well, Appleby,' said C. 'Extraordinarily well. You've saved the Service. And a good many lives. I'm very grateful. As would your country be, if they ever knew about this, which they won't, until you and I, and probably you too, Mrs Underwood, are long dead.'

'Mrs Underwood has performed admirably throughout, sir,' Appleby said. 'I've had to ask her to carry out some unpleasant tasks. She's never complained or shirked them.'

'Good work, my dear,' said C. 'We'll let you get back to your husband now this is over.'

'Thank you, sir,' said Veronica. 'I was conscious we had to do what we did. The tragic outcome as far as the Hanckel boy is concerned couldn't have been averted by any action of Mr Appleby.'

'I'll await your full report on that, Appleby,' said C. 'There's no question it's damnably unfortunate.'

'Indeed, sir,' said Appleby.

'What about this Foreign Office fellow you used – Brigham?'

'He played his part well, sir. We should acknowledge that. What I asked him to do fell well outside his normal duties.'

'Very good. Now—' The train lurched into motion. As it cleared the canopy of the station, sunlight flooded into the compartment. Shakespeare Cliff was a dazzling wall of white. Appleby lowered the blind to shade their eyes. 'First things first,' C continued. 'Word from our consulate in Geneva. The boy found drowned at Morges has been officially identified as Eugen Hanckel, aged fifteen. Also, the lawyer Dulière and his secretary were found shot dead at his office in Ouchy, Lausanne, last night.'

Appleby gave a fatalistic nod. 'Killed by one of Lemmer's operatives, obviously. My money would be on Meadows.'

'Mine too,' said C. 'The upshot is that Lemmer probably knows by now his son's dead.'

'I've advised Max to leave Japan as soon as possible.'

'And will he?'

'I doubt it. He has personal matters to settle with Count Tomura.'

'Then we can do nothing for him. Lemmer has been defeated and we'd all have wished to settle for that. But the death of his son will have made matters personal for him as well. He'll surely pursue Max.'

'Undoubtedly, sir.'

'We must hope you trained him well in the short time you had at your disposal.'

'We must, sir, yes.'

'As for your activities in Evian-les-Bains, I anticipate the French authorities will drop all inquiries once we've supplied the *Deuxième Bureau* with the names on that list. As for the Swiss, they'll huff and puff if they discover our involvement, but huffing and puffing needn't concern us. Talking of which, please smoke if you wish.'

With every appearance of relief, Appleby lit his pipe.

'Now,' C proceeded, 'I take it there are no means by which Lemmer can establish that Mrs Underwood, or indeed Brigham, assisted you during this mission, Appleby?'

'Definitely not, sir.'

'But he will know you personally organized and carried it out?'

'Yes, sir.'

'Then you must realize he's likely to seek revenge on you too. To expose his spies is one thing. To kill his son . . .'

'There's nothing I can do to stop him coming after me,' said Appleby, puffing philosophically on his pipe.

'You could make yourself hard to find.'

'I'm too old for that game, sir. I'd rather face him, if I have to.'

'You're thinking Max may help you out there?'

'I can't alter what's happened. Or what will happen in Japan. I'd prefer to concentrate on doing useful work in London while we . . . await events.'

'Well, there's plenty of useful work to be done, no question about it. A lot of cleaning of stables is going to be needed in the weeks and months ahead. Not just by us. Other departments. Other countries. The French; the Americans; the Italians: they'll all be seeking your advice as the man who revealed how deeply Lemmer had penetrated their defences. There are bound to be doubts about the terms of the peace treaty now we know some of those who framed them were on

Lemmer's payroll. Though since the treaty was hardly soft on the Germans, that renders his strategy all the more difficult to divine.'

'I think we can say for certain what his strategy was in Japan, sir.'

'Yes. And we've scotched it. Thanks to you.'

'And Max.'

'I haven't forgotten him, Appleby.' C looked thoughtful. 'I never shall. Such men . . . shine brightly.'

Rousing himself almost physically from this brief descent into soulfulness, C smiled across at Veronica. 'I wonder if you'd mind stepping out of the compartment for a while, Mrs Underwood. Appleby and I have matters to discuss which someone about to leave the Service needn't be troubled with.'

Veronica smiled back at him, amused by the gentleness of her dismissal. 'Certainly, sir,' she said.

As the door of the compartment slid shut behind Veronica Underwood on the Dover to London train, the door of another compartment slid open on another train six thousand miles away.

Nadia Bukayeva stepped into Fritz Lemmer's berth on the Tokyo to Kyoto sleeper and closed the door quietly behind her. The bed had not yet been made up and Lemmer's expression, as he looked up from his seat, did not suggest sleep was something he had much use for. His eyes blazed with a fierce energy. His mouth was set in a determined line.

'Is there anything you need?' Nadia asked.

'Nothing you can supply,' he replied, with no implication of rebuke.

'What are you reading?'

'This?' He raised the book he was holding in his left hand, his forefinger marking his place. 'Clausewitz. He clears my mind.'

'Can I ask—'

'What we are to do now my network has been exposed? Now C has the contents of the Grey File before him? Now I am defeated?'

'You are not defeated.'

'I am, Nadia Mikhailovna. Oh yes. I am defeated.' He gestured for her to sit down opposite him. 'But not destroyed. I should have foreseen what Anna would be prepared to do for her son. I should have realized her love of him would outweigh her loyalty to me. When she learnt he was dead, I knew what she would do. I did not try to stop her. She was too weak to live. I am too strong to die. I will not be stopped by this. I will build another network. I will take back what I have lost. You ask yourself: how? Stand by me and you will see. I tried to recruit Appleby, you know. Shortly after his son was killed in the war. I thought the loss would make him vulnerable. I was wrong. It made him stronger. My loss will make me stronger too.' He nodded to her in emphasis. 'It already has.'

MAX ALREADY KNEW LASKARIS WAS A CAUTIOUS MAN, SO PERHAPS the location of their next rendezvous should not have surprised him: the roof garden of the Mitsukoshi department store, Tokyo's answer to Harrods, a little before noon, when the shade of the artfully rigged arbours had drawn shoppers from the floors below to sip tea and nibble bean-paste confections while gazing out across the roofs of Nihombashi.

Laskaris was puffing at one of his ubiquitous cigars when Max joined him by the parapet, high above the traffic of the city, over-looked only by the limply hanging flag of the store.

'You mean to rescue her,' said Laskaris, running a keen-eyed glance over Max. 'I see it in your face.'

'You can't have imagined I'd do anything else.'

'Some might, in view of the impossibility of the task and the fact that you have no memory of her.'

'She's my mother. And I don't believe the task is impossible.'

'No? Kawajuki-jo is a well-guarded fortress. According to Jack Farngold, his sister is confined within an inaccessible inner portion of that fortress. The men you brought here to help you are either dead or under arrest, pending deportation. Your chances of success are close to zero.' Laskaris smiled. 'I take no pleasure in saying this. It is the simple truth.'

'Why did you give me the letter, then?'

'Because you were entitled to read it, as the son of the man it was sent to.'

'You said you could tell me something about the Dragonfly.'

'I can. But it will not help you, if all you have to offer is foolhardiness.'

'It isn't all. You're right, of course. The odds against pulling this off are formidable. But it can be done. If you let le Singe help me.'

Laskaris shook his head. 'I will not send Seddik to his death.'

'Freeing my mother would enrage and humiliate Tomura. I thought that's what you wanted to do.'

'But you can't free her, Max. He has too tight a hold on her. The information I can supply about the Dragonfly counts for nothing if you can't enter the castle. And it's impregnable.'

'We'll go in through the secret tunnel.'

'You know who the monk is that Jack Farngold spoke to?'

Max let the significance of the moment hang between them. Then he said, 'Yes.'

'How?'

'Through his sister. I'm confident he'll agree to help us, just as he agreed to help Jack Farngold.'

'And you want me to allow this "us" to include Seddik?'

'I propose to take her out without anyone knowing. If the place is as well guarded as you say, that's the only way it can be done. In and out through the tunnel. I'll go alone if I have to. But I'd like to have le Singe – Seddik – with me. There's no one better suited for such a mission. You know that.'

'What of your other friends – Twentyman and Miss Hollander?'

'They'll be helping from outside the castle.'

'Just you and Seddik inside?'

'We'd be the perfect team.'

Laskaris took a thoughtful puff at his cigar. His gaze rested on Max for a long moment. Then he spoke decisively. 'The Dragonfly's real name is Hashiguchi Yoko. Her great-grandfather, Hashiguchi Azenbo, is said to be the man who designed and installed the traps around *Uchi-gawa* – the Inside – on the orders of Tomura's great-grandfather. It is also said he had Azenbo killed to ensure the secret of the traps could not be revealed. That would explain why Jack Farngold thought Yoko could be persuaded to help him. As to how she might have come by her great-grandfather's secret, I do not know. You would have to find that out.'

'She betrayed Jack Farngold. She helped Lemmer set a trap for him in Keijo. Why would she do anything for us?'

'Because Tomura doesn't trust her. She supplied Lemmer with information he used to persuade Tomura to help him strike a deal with the Japanese government. Her businesses in Keijo were closed down last year on the orders of Governor General Hasegawa, following complaints about her activities from the Oriental Development Company. And Tomura is—'

'A director of the ODC.'

'Exactly. It was punishment for telling Lemmer what she knew about him, do you think?'

'It's the kind of thing he'd do.'

'Indeed. The Dragonfly was obliged to return home to Kyoto. She lives in a house in the hills west of the city. She has retired, so it is said. But her retirement is probably unwilling. So . . .'

'If she sold information to Lemmer, she might sell it to me.'

'She might, yes.'

'If I can find the tunnel and learn how to defeat the traps inside the castle, then with Seddik's help . . .'

Laskaris pondered the issue, before nodding in evident satisfaction. 'If you can do those things, Max, I will let Seddik help you. If he is willing. As I think he will be. He would feel it atoned for his part – his unwitting part – in your father's murder. But tell me this. Maybe you can get in. Maybe you can get out. With Seddik's assistance. But how do you get away? Once Tomura learns Matilda has escaped, he will pursue her – and you. He will turn all his resources to catching you before you can leave Japan.'

'Then we'll have to leave Japan as quickly as possible.' Max smiled. 'That's where you come in, Viktor.'

Even as Max disclosed to Laskaris the plan he had concocted, the two people he had concocted it with, Malory and Sam, were waiting on the landing-stage in Fukagawa, a few alleys away from the Shimizus' shop. Malory had paid a boy loitering by the adjacent boathouse tavern a few sen to carry a message to Chiyoko. Malory was confident she would come to meet them, as long as she was there to receive the message. Her mother could not be trusted to pass it on.

But soon enough Chiyoko appeared, contriving to smile and frown at the same time when she saw them.

'What are you doing here?' she said anxiously. 'It is not safe . . . for you to be seen.'

'The police are no longer looking for us, Chiyoko,' said Malory.

'But *we're* looking for *you*,' added Sam.

Chiyoko turned her wide eyes on him. 'Why?'

Because some man certainly ought to be, he was surprised to find himself thinking. Before he could frame a more appropriate answer, Malory said, 'Will you come for a short trip with us?' She indicated the *choki-bune* moored at the landing-stage. The boatman was drinking tea and smoking on the verandah of the tavern, swapping gossip with some old men playing Go. Malory had paid him in advance and he was not complaining.

'I cannot leave my mother in the shop for long. Where are we going?'

'Nowhere. But we can talk on the boat without being overheard. The boatman doesn't speak any English.'

'This is important?'

'Very.'

'It's more than that,' Sam put in. 'It's a life's worth of important.'

'We need you, Chiyoko,' said Malory.

'We do,' said Sam.

'Then I go with you,' said Chiyoko, the trust she placed in them lighting her face.

'It is possible, I grant you,' said Laskaris, bestowing a strange, half-surprised look on Max, as if he had not expected a plan that would go so far towards convincing him. 'It might even succeed.'

'We should proceed without delay,' said Max.

'So long as it's understood the failure of one link will signify to me the failure of all. Then Seddik and I will withdraw.'

'It's understood.'

'And you should do the same.'

'I'll do what my conscience dictates, Viktor.'

Laskaris took off his hat then, in a sweeping motion. The strength of the sun made it seem an odd thing to do. Then he nodded in the direction of something – or someone – behind Max.

'*C'est une affaire entendue, Seddik.*'

Max turned. Le Singe was standing close behind him. He was dressed in Japanese clothes, with soft leather boots rather than sandals, striped trousers and sashed tunic beneath a loose, long-tailed, sleeveless coat. He looked neither Asian nor Arab, with a brown cap worn low on his head, though there was something of the desert in his far-seeing gaze.

'He will understand everything you say,' said Laskaris. 'And everything you do. Trust his instincts above your own at all times.'

'I'm pleased to meet you again, Seddik.' Max held out his hand. 'I need your help.'

Very slowly, Seddik Yala stretched out his own hand. He seemed as conscious as Max of the significance of the gesture.

'I have much to tell you.'

'Less than you think,' said Laskaris.

'Thank you for saving my life.'

At this Seddik gave a small bow of acknowledgement.

'And thanks for agreeing to do this.'

Another small bow.

'We must go,' said Laskaris. 'There is much to be arranged.'

Seddik looked at Max expressly. Already it was clear he did not need words to convey his meaning. It was settled. They would go forward together.

The boat returned to the landing-stage after an hour circling the waterways of Fukagawa. Chiyoko disembarked, but Malory and Sam stayed aboard.

'We're sorry if your mother's nose is going to be put out of joint,' said Sam as she looked back at them.

'Her . . . nose?' Chiyoko's English clearly did not extend to such a metaphor.

'We're sorry for the trouble you'll have with her over this,' Malory explained.

'It cannot be avoided,' Chiyoko stated, as if declaring a self-evident philosophical truth. 'My aunt will help her. They will enjoy complaining about me.'

'They wouldn't complain if they knew what you were doing,' said Sam.

'No. They would be too frightened.' Chiyoko smiled gamely. 'Better for them not to know.'

'I'll see you this evening,' said Malory.

'Yes.' Chiyoko nodded decisively. 'I will be there.'

ORAHAN WAS PROPPED UP IN BED AND LOOKING CONSIDERABLY better when Max, Sam and Malory called at the University Hospital late that afternoon. 'As long as I don't move a muscle, I feel just fine,' he said ruefully. A tube was still in place in his side, draining his punctured lung. 'The bullet smashed a rib on its way in and the surgeon didn't do anything by halves. I'm not exactly fighting fit.'

'You should be grateful just to be alive,' said Malory.

'Well, damn it, Malory, I am. Even in a country where I'm not welcome. Your friend Fujisaki looked in earlier, Max. He served me with an official deportation order. Grover, Gazda and I are being shipped back to San Francisco on Thursday.'

'Only if your doctor says you're well enough,' said Malory.

'I'll be well enough. Unless you need me to swing a delay?'

'No,' said Max. 'You should go with Ward and Djabsu on Thursday.'

'With our tails between our legs.'

'We haven't failed yet, Schools.'

'What's that supposed to mean?'

'It means we have a plan,' said Sam brightly.

'A plan to do what?'

'Exactly what we set out to do,' said Max.

'You in on this, Malory?'

She nodded. 'Yes.'

'And the "plan" requires me to beat a humiliating retreat?'

'Why don't you and Malory leave us, Sam?' said Max. 'It's time I put Schools fully in the picture.'

'Yes,' said Malory, so quickly Sam suspected she and Max had already agreed he should speak to Schools alone. 'Good idea.'

The late afternoon had brought a hazy mellowness to the hills east of Kyoto, two hundred miles to the west of Tokyo. The roofs of the ancient capital, the old and the new, the gabled temples and the spired pagodas, stretched out along the lazy curve of the Kamogawa river. From the balcony of his room at the Miyako Hotel, the guest registered as Frederik Boel, citizen of Denmark, gazed across the city, imagining the lives of every one of its inhabitants as part of a natural scheme of things in which his recent misfortunes would eventually reverse themselves. There was no loss, however grievous, he could not recover from. There was no defeat he could not turn by the alchemy of his intellectual superiority into ultimate victory. Only death could undo him. And he was far from dead.

There was a knock at the door of his room. 'Come in,' he called, knowing who his visitor was for the simple reason he had summoned her.

Nadia entered, crossed the room and joined him on the balcony. She looked at him with that concerned, faintly pitying air he had only noticed since the death of his son and the exposure of his spies. He did not want her pity, and he certainly did not want to deserve it.

'I have had a telephone call from Reynolds,' he announced.

'Not Trumper?'

'No. Trumper is in custody. Everett and Duffy are dead. The plan miscarried. Ward and Djabsu remain in prison. Morahan is in hospital. Everett shot him, but not fatally. He is expected to recover.'

'What went wrong?'

'I suspect Trumper betrayed us. To save his own skin. It is what someone in my position must expect. I suspect Reynolds will soon cut loose from me too. Loyalty is not always durable.'

'Mine is.'

He looked at her appreciatively. 'I am grateful for that.'

'What will you do?'

'Adapt, as I must. I may have been hasty in ordering the attack. I was not . . . thinking as clearly as I should have . . . at the time. It is possible Morahan's survival is to our advantage.'

'How?'

'According to Reynolds' police informant, Morahan, Ward and Djabsu are to be deported. They will be put aboard the SS *Woodward*, bound for San Francisco, on Thursday. Ward and Djabsu are still in Sugamo prison, but Morahan is in the University Hospital at Ueno. He is therefore accessible to us. I want you to deliver some material to him. Material damaging to Count Tomura, detailing as it does his involvement in the assassination of Empress Myongsong in 1895 . . . and other matters.'

'You are moving against Tomura?'

'He has discarded me, Nadia Mikhailovna. He believes I have been shorn of my power. He must be reminded he cannot prosper without my assistance. You will tell Morahan you have deserted me and intend by this move to demonstrate you are no longer serving me *or* Tomura. Urge him to hand the material to the newspapers when he reaches San Francisco. Tomura will not enjoy the condemnation that will certainly follow. But he will understand better than he presently does that he cannot renounce our alliance. And he will be able to remind the government that I still have the Terauchi–Zimmermann letter.' Lemmer sighed apologetically. 'I am sorry to send you back to Tokyo when we have only just arrived in Kyoto. The news from Reynolds has obliged me to reconsider our position.'

Nadia shrugged off the inconvenience. 'When do you want me to leave?'

'Tomorrow. I had intended we would visit the Dragonfly together. That will not be possible now. I will go alone.'

'You think Max will contact her?'

'I do. And if he does . . . I want her to be ready for him.'

'It's a long shot,' said Morahan, when Max had finished outlining his plan. 'I guess it always was. But it all hinges on secrecy and surprise now. You'll have no fire-power.'

273

'I'll have le Singe,' Max responded. He was standing by the window of Morahan's room and could see Malory and Sam down in the courtyard, walking slowly, dust thrown up in puffs by their heels. There was a thin layer of dust on the window as well, visible where the sunlight struck it. He looked back at Morahan. 'I sense this is my only chance.'

'I wish I could help.'

'You can. By telling anyone who asks we've decided to head for Shanghai without waiting to see you off on the boat to San Francisco.'

'Damned unfeeling of you.'

'No one must have any reason to suspect the truth.'

'I'll give them none. But I reckon Fujisaki suspects already. He asked me to tell you Chief Inspector Wada of the Kyoto Police is a man you can trust.'

'So's Fujisaki. He'll play along. Let's hope I don't need Chief Inspector Wada's assistance.'

'When will you leave?'

'Malory and Chiyoko will take this evening's sleeper. Sam and I follow tomorrow. As for Laskaris and le Singe, that's up to them. But I have Laskaris's word they'll be in Kobe by Wednesday. And I don't intend to make a move before you leave the country.'

'And you also don't intend to make a move if either Chiyoko's brother or the Dragonfly lets you down?'

'Those are Laskaris's terms for agreeing to le Singe's involvement.'

'And are they *your* terms for going ahead?'

Max said nothing. He and Morahan exchanged a long, frank look.

'I thought not.'

'She's my mother, Schools. What do you expect me to do?'

'Go it alone if you have to. Not that Sam will let you. But here's the thing, Max. What about Malory? She'll probably stick by you however suicidal the attempt ends up being.'

'I promise you I'll get her to safety.'

'You can't promise that.'

'I'll make sure she's not in danger. You have my word.'

'That'd be worth more if we didn't both know she's well capable of putting herself in danger whatever you do. But let's shake on it anyhow.'

Max walked across to the bed and took Morahan's hand.

'Good luck, Max.'

'Thanks.'

'I can't imagine how you must feel after discovering it's your own mother Henry was setting out to rescue. It's a helluva thing.'

'Yes.' Max nodded. 'A hell of a thing is exactly what it is.'

MALORY AND CHIYOKO CAUGHT THE SLEEPER TRAIN TO KYOTO that evening. No one saw them off. Their plan relied on making themselves as inconspicuous as possible. Malory suspected Chiyoko's mother had argued violently against her going, but it had done no good, as Malory could have predicted. A strong vein of stubbornness ran through Chiyoko's small frame. She recognized the rightness of what they were doing.

They did not speak of Junzaburo during the journey, though he was much in Malory's thoughts, as she felt sure he was in Chiyoko's. Neither had seen him in more than a decade, in Malory's case more than two decades. He was a monk now, at the temple of Joyaku-ji, in Nara. He had made peace with the life he had left behind, the life in which he had served Tomura's devious ends – and had loved Malory.

It was cruel, in its way, to wrench him out of the sanctuary he had found. But there was no choice. They could not stand aside. And Junzaburo had already agreed to help Jack Farngold. He would agree to help them as well. Malory was sure of it.

But helping Jack Farngold would not have involved meeting Malory again. There was an infinity of good reasons why they should not meet again. But what mattered was the one good reason why they should.

Max and Sam left Tokyo the following morning. They had plenty of time to talk on the train, but were content mostly to smoke and watch the scenery drift by in companionable silence.

Sam devoted a good deal of attention to a map of Japan and its near neighbours he had insisted they buy, with place names marked in English as well as Japanese. Max noticed him plotting distances by reference to the scale and knew exactly what he was trying to calculate. But neither spoke of the eventuality he was preparing for.

'I'm glad you're here, Sam,' Max said, when they left the train to stretch their legs during a lengthy stop at Hamamatsu.

'Me too, sir.'

'Still hoping we'll open that flying school?'

'Haven't ruled it out.'

'I think you must have been born optimistic, you know.'

'Born hungry, my ma says. Talking of which, why don't we buy a couple of those lunch boxes they're hawking?' He pointed to the vendors walking along the platform, offering refreshments to the passengers on the train. 'Oh, cripes. Sorry, sir. Gassing on about my mother like that. It was . . .'

'Don't worry.' Max clapped him on the back. 'I'm not about to crack up over this.'

'No. 'Course not. Malory and Chiyoko should be in Nara by now.'

'That they should. So, to stop you wondering how they're getting on, let's get some lunch. Just think, Sam. There might be some beer in those boxes.'

Sam brightened. 'I suppose there might.'

'See what I mean? Born optimistic.'

From Kyoto, Malory and Chiyoko took a local train south to Nara. Malory had been there once in the company of Miss Dubb. She remembered it as peculiarly infertile ground for Lutheran missionaries, rich as it was in Buddhist temples and Shinto shrines. It had been the Japanese capital for a while, back in early medieval times, and wore an air of placid antiquity.

Several of the temples, including Joyaku-ji, were located in Nara Park, a sprawling expanse of ponds, groves and deer-cropped lawns east of the railway station. Chiyoko confessed as they approached Joyaku-ji that she did not know how her request to see Junzaburo would be received. It would never have occurred to her to visit him there in normal circumstances. But these were not – as she intended to emphasize – normal circumstances.

Joyaku-ji was typical of many Buddhist temples Malory had seen, with grand gateways, sweeping gables and a magnificent five-storey pagoda at its centre. A pair of fearsome, snarling *Nio* guardians flanked the main gate. They encountered an orange-robed monk just inside and Chiyoko explained why they were there. The monk looked solicitous and fretful in equal measures. He bustled off.

'He said we should wait here,' Chiyoko revealed.

And wait they did, for ten or more minutes, watched by the statues. This allowed ample time to wonder what they would do if Junzaburo simply refused to see them. Chiyoko had identified herself as his sister, but had not revealed Malory's name to the monk. Surely Junzaburo would never guess she of all people had come in search of him.

At one point, she had the disquieting impression Junzaburo was observing them from some spy-hole in one of the surrounding buildings. She tried to dismiss the idea as absurd, with only limited success. Eventually, the monk returned.

He pointed back along the avenue by which they had approached the temple as he spoke and Chiyoko glanced in that direction as he did so. Malory thought she caught the words *ike* – pond – but also *ikemasen* – must not; do not. The monk was not smiling, as he had initially, which hardly seemed a good omen.

He had already turned and begun to walk away when Chiyoko supplied a translation. 'He says we are to wait on the far side of the pond beside the maple grove we passed. Junzaburo will come to us there. *If* he comes. There was something . . . disapproving . . . in the way the monk spoke. I am not sure I understand. But I think Junzaburo will come.'

For her part, Malory did not know what to think. She would very much have liked to smoke a cigarette to calm her nerves, but somehow it seemed the wrong thing to do. They retreated along the avenue to the pond.

It was a rounded square of peaceful lily-patched water in which the adjacent maples were brightly mirrored. Malory and Chiyoko took up their station, as instructed, on the side farthest from the temple, and waited.

The wait turned out to be more than sufficient for Malory to recall many long-forgotten incidents from her relationship with Junzaburo. The sunlight shafting through the maples reminded her of the sunlight shafting through the window of their room at the *onsen* hotel in Hakone; and of the smile on Junzaburo's face as he woke and realized she was there.

The early autumn of 1895: such a long, long time ago. She found it hard to imagine she had ever been so young. But she had. So had Junzaburo.

The orange-robed, shaven-headed figure who eventually approached the other side of the pond was not young, however. At that distance, with the light between them thrown up from the water, she could not have said with any certainty that it was Junzaburo. His face was in shadow. Only the set of his shoulders told her it was him.

They stood, regarding each other. More minutes slowly passed. Junzaburo made no move. 'We should walk round to him,' Malory whispered.

'*Hai*,' Chiyoko responded, forgetting to speak English in the stress of the moment.

They started moving. Immediately, Junzaburo responded with a loud clap that brought them to a halt. He pointed at them and raised his index finger.

'I think he means . . . only one of us should go,' said Chiyoko.

'Yes,' said Malory. And it was clear to her which one it was to be. 'You go. I'll stay here . . . until he calls for me.'

And so she stayed, while Chiyoko walked slowly round the perimeter of the pond to where Junzaburo was waiting.

The reunion of brother and sister was a strange and hesitant coming together. They did not cry out or embrace. They spoke with

279

heads bowed but close together. Malory had no clue as to what was passing between them. Then Chiyoko laid her head briefly on Junzaburo's shoulder. He raised his hand, as if to stroke her hair. But he did not do so. He glanced across the pond at Malory, his expression unreadable, his thoughts veiled.

Brother and sister stood a little apart then and talked, it seemed, with greater intensity.

Malory did not know how long this continued. It seemed like only a few minutes, but might well have been more. Then Junzaburo bowed, turned and walked away.

Malory watched him striding towards the sanctuary of the temple. He did not once look back. He was stronger than the Junzaburo she had known. He was a remade man. She was glad of that. But, somewhere within herself, she was also sorry.

'He will do it.' Chiyoko's words made Malory start, unaware she had already rejoined her.

'He will?'

'He will lead Max to the tunnel. He will show him the way in. He will travel to Kyoto tomorrow and lodge at the temple of Minami Hongan-ji. Max can find him there.'

'He'll willingly do this?'

'Oh yes. As he would have done for Jack Farngold. It is . . . *tadashi*. It is his duty. He cannot act against Tomura himself. But he will help the son of Tomura's wife as he would have helped her brother.'

'Why wouldn't he speak to me?'

'He had little time. He could not—'

'Please tell me the truth, Chiyoko.'

'I am sorry.' Chiyoko fell silent for a moment. Her gaze dropped. Then she looked at Malory directly. 'He is an enlightened one now, Malory. Perhaps you do not understand. He is free of anger and desire. He has found peace. You – your presence – disturbs that. He said . . .'

'What did he say?'

'That once he would have rejoiced to see you again. Once it was all he dreamt of. But that was *samsara* – the wheel of suffering. And he is no longer bound to the wheel. He will help Max. But he will not speak to you. I am sorry.'

'So am I. But we shouldn't be, should we?' Malory glanced towards the temple where the orange-robed figure of Junzaburo was walking in through the gate. Sunlight glittered on the spire of the pagoda above him. 'We should be glad for him.'

MAX AND SAM SPENT THAT NIGHT AT NAGOYA, IN THE SAME *RYOKAN* where Max had stayed on his way to Tokyo from Nagasaki the week before. He did not fail to be amused by Sam's consternation at the bathing arrangements.

'There's a young lady in there who I swear hasn't got a stitch on, sir,' Sam complained, retreating from a first foray to the bathroom.

'Are you planning to climb in in your underpants, then?'

''Course not.'

'Well, there you are. When in Rome, Sam.'

They were en route, but they had not arrived. Max found the thought strangely comforting as he drifted off to sleep, with Sam already snoring on the other side of the room. He did not know what awaited them in Kyoto. It was impossible even to guess. But he knew *who* awaited them.

They resumed their journey early the following morning, reaching Kyoto in the early afternoon. They found Malory and Chiyoko in the station waiting room, where they had whiled away a couple of hours since arriving from Nara.

It was Max's first meeting with Chiyoko. And it began with the most vital question of all: would her brother help them?

'Yes, Maxted-san. He will.'

'Then we're in business. And please call me Max.'

'Very well . . . Max.'

'You know Sam.'

'Of course.'

'I think he may have some work for you to do.'

'I'll tell you about it later, Chiyoko,' said Sam.

She frowned at him in puzzlement, then at Max. 'Malory says we are going to Seifu-so. Is that true?'

'Yes. And the sooner we go the better. We shouldn't be seen together in public places.'

'But nobody knows we are here.'

'Then let's keep it that way.'

They took a motor-taxi to Marquess Saionji's villa. Unlike Tokyo, Kyoto's streets were laid out in a grid pattern. They followed one of the tram routes due north through the jumbled cityscape, following the boundary wall of the old Imperial Palace in the latter part of the journey.

'You sure about this, sir?' Sam whispered to Max at some point. 'I mean, you've never actually met Grand Duke Saionji, have you?'

'Marquess. And yes, I'm sure we need to lie low. He told Kuroda we could stay under his roof. Anywhere else we'll be conspicuous. And that we can't afford to be.'

Sam sighed. 'Right you are, sir.'

Seifu-so lay on the other side of the Kamo-gawa river from the old Imperial Palace, but not far from it, as befitted the residence of a man who had, according to Chiyoko, been a childhood playmate of the Meiji Emperor. She was astonished at the idea of enjoying such an eminent man's hospitality. And her astonishment did not end there. 'He must have known you would come here.'

'Yes,' murmured Max. 'Before I knew myself.'

The villa lay behind a high wall, surrounded by a verdant garden, manicured in the Japanese style. It comprised several linked buildings spread out across the property, elegantly proportioned, with wide verandahs and mellow-wooded pillars. They were received at the gate by a senior servant called Umezu, a portly, impassive fellow who spoke only rudimentary English. Chiyoko explained to him who they were, but, despite much bowing, it was clear he required sight of Max's passport before admitting them. Once satisfied as to Max's identity, he overflowed with solicitude, arranging tea while guest quarters were prepared. Marquess Saionji had sent word that James Maxted and any companions travelling with him were to be shown every consideration.

Max was at pains to emphasize, through Chiyoko, that their presence at Seifu-so, above all their identities, must remain secret. Umezu assured him everything that occurred at Marquess Saionji's direction was *naisho* – confidential. All his staff knew that and abided by it religiously.

Max asked how easy it would be to hire a couple of cars for their use. Umezu did not bat an eyelid. He thought he could arrange for a local garage to deliver a pair the following morning.

'We've fallen on our feet here, sir,' Sam remarked when they were shown their accommodation. There appeared to be any number of rooms at their disposal and several servants to cater for their every want.

One vital modern amenity the villa possessed was a functioning telephone, as Max had hoped. His first call was to the Oriental Hotel in Kobe, where Laskaris had arrived the previous day, registering as Quinquaud. 'I have arranged for an ocean-going vessel, with crew, to be available,' he reported. 'Will we have reason to use it?'

Max replied in guarded language, confirming Shimizu Junzaburo's agreement to lead them to the secret tunnel.

'And as for the interior?'

Uchi-gawa: the Inside. Everything hinged now on the Dragonfly. But Tomura's orchestration of the closure of her Korean business gave her a powerful motive to help them. Max was confident. 'I'm going to seek an appointment for tomorrow.'

'We will be close at hand by then, in case swift action is called for. I will leave word of how I can be contacted.'

Umezu supplied Hashiguchi Yoko's telephone number. He seemed well informed about the circumstances of her return from Korea.

He seemed altogether well informed, though tight-lipped, about many things, in fact. He confirmed Max's assumption that the woman spoke good English and described her, with a poker face, as *kanyo* – translated by Chiyoko as broad-minded.

Whether that was good or bad Max was about to find out. A man answered the telephone and responded gruffly, in Japanese, to Max's request to speak to her. At length, a female voice came on the line.

'This is Hashiguchi Yoko.'

'*Konnichi wa, Hashiguchi-san.* My name is Greaves. James Greaves.'

'You are English?'

'Yes.'

'What can I do for you, Mr Greaves?'

'It's more a question of what we can do for each other. I'm experiencing some business difficulties in Korea – Chosen – and I—'

'What is your business?'

'Import-export.'

She laughed at that. 'And what are your difficulties?'

'Obstacles placed in my path by the Oriental Development Company.'

'You do not surprise me.'

'No? Well, maybe I can interest you in, er . . . a commercial opportunity . . . that would be greatly to your advantage and greatly to the ODC's *dis*advantage.'

There was a lengthy pause, during which Max thought he detected a draw on a cigarette. Then: 'Tell me more, Mr Greaves.'

'I'd be happy to, if we could meet.'

'Are you in Kyoto?'

'Yes. I'd prefer to come to your villa rather than meet anywhere in the city. Absolute discretion is vital. Tomorrow, perhaps?'

'Tomorrow?'

'The opportunity will only exist for a limited period.'

'Very well. Tomorrow. Come at noon.'

Max decided to take Malory with him when he visited the Dragonfly. Malory seemed able to read people better than he could and she also spoke a certain amount of Japanese. The encounter was bound to be challenging given how extensively he had misrepresented himself. He sensed Malory would succeed in steering the discussion on to the right path where he might fail.

She readily agreed, but with little of her usual gusto. She had been subdued since their arrival and, as evening encroached on Seifu-so, he found her standing on one of the bridges across the two ponds in the garden, smoking a cigarette and gazing pensively at a reflection of herself in the still water.

'You haven't said much about your meeting with Junzaburo,' Max ventured.

'There's nothing to say.' She smiled wryly. 'He refused to speak to me.'

'But—'

'He said everything that needed to be said to Chiyoko. He wouldn't allow me anywhere near him. I'm afraid you'll have to keep us apart.'

Max touched her shoulder. 'I'm sorry.'

'I wanted him out of my life and I succeeded. I have nothing to complain about.'

'But still . . .'

'I'd never have seen him again in normal circumstances. I wish I *hadn't* seen him again. You think you've neatly stored your past away and then you find . . . it isn't really past at all.' She pushed back her shoulders and took a deep breath. 'Never mind. There are more important matters to consider, aren't there? I believe I'll try to put a call through to the hospital in Tokyo and ask how Schools is.'

'Good idea.'

'Thank you, Max.'

With that she bustled off, leaving Max to wonder what he had said or done to deserve her thanks.

Schools was reported to be recovering well. There was no reason why he, Ward and Djabsu should not be embarking for San Francisco on Thursday. By then, with luck, Max would be ready to strike. It would not be long now. It would not be long at all.

286

THE CARS, DELIVERED EARLY THE FOLLOWING MORNING, WERE A PAIR of barrel-nosed Appersons imported from the United States. The proprietor of the garage oversaw the delivery and appeared beside himself with joy at hiring them out to Marquess Saionji's household.

Sam was less impressed. 'They look overpowered to me.'

'Don't worry, Sam,' said Max. 'I'll take it steadily. You be sure to do the same.'

'I'd better take a look at the engines.'

'No time. We both have a lot to do. Let's go.'

'Hold on. You're not due at the Dragonfly's villa till midday. And you said it isn't far away.'

'It isn't. But I want to go somewhere else first. Mind he doesn't speed, Chiyoko. Come along, Malory.'

Malory had, in fact, already guessed where she and Max were bound: Kawajuki Castle – Zangai-jo. Max was eager for a first sight of his birthplace and the place of Matilda Tomura's long imprisonment. Malory suspected Sam would guess that soon enough himself. And she was curious for her part about what Sam had been detailed to attend to, with Chiyoko's assistance. He had been uncharacteristically reticent on the subject.

Umezu had supplied directions to the castle. It overlooked a valley twenty-five miles or so north of Kyoto. The road through the valley led ultimately to the Sea of Japan coast. It might have been a route of some importance before the coming of the railways, but there was little traffic on it that morning. After leaving Kyoto it threaded its dusty way steadily north through thickly wooded hills. Mist was lifting slowly from the peaks. A Japan untouched by the modernizing spirit of Meiji seemed to creep in around them. There were rice-fields on the few level stretches of land, stands of bamboo and pine, carpets of wild flowers, clusters of thatch-roofed farm buildings.

Then they reached the valley. As the car rounded a corner, the castle revealed itself to them. It reared above the village of Kawajuki on a rocky spur projecting from the surrounding hills.

Where natural rock ended and the bailey wall of the castle began was hard to tell. The two coalesced into a soaring barrier of stone, turreted at its corners. There was another, higher wall within, then the keep and lower towers at the heart of the structure, all multi-storeyed, with successions of wide, swooping gables and deep upturned eaves.

It might have looked a little like a wedding cake but for the colour of the stonework: dark, tinged with a bronze, metallic sheen. The sunlight found in its surfaces only shadow and blankness. Hodgson had described the effect as chilling and Max could not suppress the same reaction. Zangai-jo was a forbidding place, as no doubt it was meant to be.

'My Lord,' said Malory. 'I'd no idea it would be so . . .'

'Penitential?' The word was out of Max's mouth before he had weighed its full meaning.

Malory looked at him oddly. 'Whose penance are we talking about, Max?'

'I don't know. But a lot of penance is owing, one way or another.'

'I asked once if the men you've killed in your life weigh on your conscience. You said no. Then I asked what would. And you said, "This, if I didn't do it." '

Max returned her look. 'I remember.'

'Neither of us knew then what "this" really meant, did we? We had no idea. We couldn't have imagined.'

'No.' He glanced towards the castle. 'But we know now. It's there. Right in front of us.'

He turned the car round then. And drove away.

The Dragonfly's villa was in a hilly, sylvan setting overlooking the Hozu-gawa river, a few miles west of Kyoto. The lane up to it was narrow, hemmed in by bamboo forest on either side. Only Malory's educated guess that the *kanji* on a sign at the foot of the lane represented Hashiguchi gave Max the confidence to follow it to the end.

The gate stood open, seeming to confirm they had come to the right place. Max pulled the car in and stopped. The roof of the villa was visible through the trees ahead of them. They climbed out, Max carrying a briefcase containing what he hoped would be enough money to satisfy their hostess. They followed a footpath that traced the curve of the hill, leading to a smaller gateway into an ornamental garden centred on a lawn in front of the villa – low-roofed and handsome.

A paper door slid open and Hashiguchi Yoko walked out on to the broad verandah. Max did not doubt who she was for a moment. She was not wearing a kimono, as he had subconsciously expected, but a loose, long-sleeved tunic over wide trousers, with flat-soled sandals: an outfit that was neither Japanese nor Western. Her fine-boned face, framed by grey hair, carried an expression not so much of haughtiness as superiority. She looked down at them with neither disdain nor humility. But the tilt of her head did suggest curiosity.

'Good day, Mr Greaves,' she said.

Max bowed. '*Konnichi wa, Hashiguchi-san.*'

'Who is your companion?'

'My secretary, Miss Bowles. She speaks rather better Japanese than I do.'

'Indeed?' The Dragonfly spoke to Malory then, in rapid-fire Japanese.

'*Wakarimasen,*' Malory responded. '*Motto yukkuri hanashite kudasaimasen ka?*'

The Dragonfly laughed. '*Kamaimasen.* You will not need your slow Japanese here. Come.' She waved for them to join her.

A table and two chairs, made of bamboo, were set out on the verandah. She clapped her hands and a bowing, kimono-clad maid appeared. The Dragonfly issued orders. A third chair was fetched. Tea seemed certain to follow.

They sat down. 'This is a lovely setting,' said Max, nodding towards the tree-walled valley below them.

'It is lovely if it is where you want to be,' said the Dragonfly.

'It's an ideal place to retire to,' said Malory.

'Exactly. To *retire* to. But I do not wish to retire. I enjoy doing business. Now, what is *your* business, Mr Greaves?'

'Like I said on the phone, import-export.'

'This is not a telephone conversation. I have no time for vagueness or pretence. What is your business?'

The arrival of tea gave Max a breathing space. The maid fluttered around in a tinkling of porcelain and a rustling of fabric. Then she was gone.

'Mr Greaves?' The Dragonfly studied Max over the rim of her teacup.

He sensed the direct approach would serve them best. 'I'm here to offer you the chance to hurt Count Tomura and make a profit into the bargain.'

There was no flicker of reaction in her expression. 'Why should I want to hurt Count Tomura?'

'Because you do not wish to retire,' said Malory.

'Are you American, Miss Bowles?'

'Yes.'

'But you are English, Mr Greaves?'

'I am.'

'What are your real names?'

Max tried to look mildly offended. 'Are you suggesting we're using aliases?'

'It would be surprising if you were not.' The Dragonfly smiled. 'What you want. And what you are willing to pay for it. You should tell me simply. I do not share my countrymen's fondness for indirectness. The appeal of the bargain will not be increased by a delay in setting out its terms.'

'The Inside, Hashiguchi-san,' said Max. 'The traps installed round part of the interior of Kawajuki-jo – Zangai-jo – by your great-grandfather on the orders of Count Tomura's great-grandfather. We're told you can equip us to defeat them. In return, I'd be willing to pay a great deal of money.'

'A way round – or through – the traps? That is what you want?'

'Yes.'

'Who told you I could supply this information?'

'Jack Farngold.'

'Jack Farngold?'

'He came to you in Keijo. You didn't sell to him. Instead, you sold *him* to Lemmer, who handed him over to Tomura.'

'And Tomura rewarded you by closing down your business in Korea,' added Malory.

'It must be strange to be an American woman,' said the Dragonfly, frowning at Malory. 'To speak so freely is a wonderful and a terrible thing.'

'Is it true Count Tomura's ancestor had your great-grandfather killed after he'd finished the job?' asked Max.

'So my grandfather told me. And he did not lie.' The Dragonfly bowed her head, as if reflecting on the injustices her family had suffered at the Tomuras' hands. 'I hear Jack Farngold is dead.'

'Yes,' said Max. 'He is.'

'Murdered by an American.'

'Murdered by Tomura,' said Malory.

The Dragonfly nodded. 'It was always certain.'

'Nothing's certain,' said Max. 'Except money.'

'Why would you want this information you offer to buy from me?'

'Why did Jack Farngold want it?'

'Are you a Farngold, Mr Greaves? Are you another one with their blood in your veins?'

'Will you sell me the information?'

'What price will you offer?'

'What price will you ask?'

The Dragonfly relaxed in her chair, considering the point. Half a minute or so slowly passed. Then, suddenly, a door behind them slid violently open, banging and rattling against its stop. A tall, broad-shouldered, raven-haired Japanese man in Western dress burst on to the verandah and glared at them. He had a moustache worthy of a Mexican bandit, with a deep tan to match it.

He shouted at the Dragonfly in Japanese. She responded with cold hauteur, waving her hand at him dismissively. He rounded the table, jabbing his finger at Max and Malory, still shouting. Max was about to stand up and tackle him, but the pressure of Malory's hand on his forearm kept him where he was.

Silence fell suddenly, broken only by the man's stertorous breathing. He stared at the Dragonfly and she stared back at him, then he turned on his heel and stalked back into the villa.

'Please close the door, Mr Greaves,' the Dragonfly said when he had gone. Max leant out of his chair and pushed it shut. 'Did you understand any of that, Miss Bowles?'

'A little,' Malory replied. 'He mentioned Count Tomura. He said you should throw us out. And he said that if you didn't you were . . . *ki-chigai*. Which means . . . mad, I think.'

'Yes. Mad. Maybe I am, to keep him in luxury and tolerate his outbursts. He is not always so ill-mannered. Sometimes he is charming. Sometimes he is even considerate. I would have intro-duced him if he had given me the chance. Terada Dentaro. He wants to be an actor.'

'Was he acting just now?' asked Max.

The Dragonfly smiled wintrily. 'No. That was all Dentaro.'

'You were about to name your price when he interrupted us.'

'Fifty thousand yen.' She looked at Max frankly. 'Can you afford it, Mr Greaves?'

'Yes. I can.'

'Half today. Half when you have the information.'

'When will that be?'

'It can be tomorrow. If you agree to my terms.'

'What are they?'

'Dentaro is worried about what Count Tomura will do if he learns I have helped you. He is right to be. There is—'

292

A crash somewhere in the villa set the panels shaking. The sound came to them of heavily shod feet striking the stones of the path across the garden. Looking round, they saw Terada striding towards the gate.

'Ah,' said the Dragonfly. 'I think he may be going for a walk. That will be good for him.'

'Your terms, Hashiguchi-san?' Max prompted.

She smiled at him. 'You should not be so eager, Mr Greaves. It is bad to look eager in business. Lucky for you I hate Count Tomura enough not to raise my price.'

'That's not luck,' said Malory. 'That's why we're here.'

'True.' The Dragonfly acknowledged the point with a courtly bow. 'So, I—' She broke off as the throaty roar of an engine rumbled through the still air. 'Ah, not a walk. The motorcycle.' The machine growled away. She seemed relieved to know her darling Dentaro had left them to it. 'I will soothe him later. Now . . . *Uchi-gawa*. The Inside. The Kansei era was a difficult time in Japan. Tomura Munetada – Count Tomura's great-grandfather – had many enemies. He wanted a place within his castle where he would be completely safe. Also where he could hold a prisoner beyond the possibility of escape if he needed to do so. My great-grandfather designed and built it for him. And then he was killed. Kansei Ten was the year. 1798, by your reckoning. My grandfather was eight when his father died. He never forgot what happened to him. He kept many papers and other things – left behind by his father. Come. There is something you must see.'

The Dragonfly rose and led the way down from the verandah and round the villa towards the rear. There were several outhouses in this shadier reach of the property. One was built of stone, with narrow, barred windows and a stout iron door.

'When my grandfather built this villa, he wanted to be sure his father's records would be safe from fire. They are stored in that building. Hundreds of documents. All the details of all the work he did. And models he made of his designs.'

'There's a model of the Inside?' Max asked urgently.

She nodded. 'The model is as it really is, but smaller, naturally. It is complete. It is accurate. It is better than any guide. Though you will need a guide – and a better one than any I know – to get into the castle. Only when you have done so will the model be of use to you.'

'Leave me to worry about that.'

'Gladly.'

'The model is ours for fifty thousand yen?'

'Yes. But this transaction cannot become known to Count Tomura. I must be able to say the model was stolen from me. I will leave the door of the storehouse unlocked tonight. I will say later someone must have opened it. How? A Ninja trick, maybe. Or they picked the lock. Who knows? The models are stored in wooden boxes, identified by labels recording the names of the buildings they matched. The intruder will steal the chest labelled *Zangai-jo*. You cannot read Japanese, of course. That fact will divert suspicion from you, if you escape . . . with whatever you seek there.'

'And it *is* a fact, Hashiguchi-san. I can't read Japanese.'

'Have you paper?'

Max tore a sheet from the notebook he carried and handed it to her, along with a pencil. He watched the swift and intricate movements of her fingers as she wrote down the symbols. Then she passed the sheet of paper back to him.

残

骸

城

'*Zangai-jo*,' said the Dragonfly. 'That is what the label will show.'

'Won't there be other labels looking remarkably similar – to the untrained eye?' said Malory.

'There will, Miss Bowles. You have a sharp mind. My great-grandfather made many models. Some were built, some not. He worked in many places, though nothing he did was quite as unusual as the installation at Zangai-jo. Naturally, the intruder must be sure to take the right box.'

294

'Maybe you could show us where it is,' said Max.

The Dragonfly frowned at him. 'And risk you taking it now? Then you may never pay me a sen. Do you think me a fool?'

'Not at all.'

'The box you want is on the third shelf up from the floor on the left side as you enter the storehouse. That should be enough for you.'

'We'll manage,' said Max, catching Malory's eye. Already, he had thought of the surest way to identify the correct box. 'What if it can't be done tonight?'

'I will leave the door unlocked each night until it *is* done. Or you tell me you have changed your mind. Which would be wise. I spoke of a Ninja trick. You will need a great many of those to enter Zangai-jo and leave again unharmed. If you do change your mind . . .'

'The twenty-five thousand isn't refundable.'

The Dragonfly smiled. 'I see you already understand me, Mr Greaves. That makes doing business with you much easier. The money must be in my account at the Kyoto branch of the Bank of Japan in Sanjo-dori before they close their books this afternoon. It is agreed?'

Max bowed. 'It is agreed.'

THEY WERE AT THE BANK WITHIN THE HOUR. IT WAS A GRAND, Baroque building, replete with dark wood and high ceilings. The staff were unfailingly polite and helpful. Max did not have ¥25,000, but he did have sterling of more than equivalent value. After much stamping of dockets and inscribing of chits, the money was deposited in the account of Hashiguchi Yoko.

They drove back to Seifu-so, to be told Laskaris had rung and left the telephone number of the inn where he was staying. Max called him straight away.

An hour later, Max was striding along a hot and dusty avenue of the park surrounding the old Imperial Palace, heading for the pond at its southern end.

Laskaris was waiting there, as promised, squinting with apparently fixed concentration at a flotilla of carp, while puffing at one of the cigars that were his constant companions.

'I judge from your expression, Max,' he said, 'that your visit to the Dragonfly went well.'

'We have a deal with her, yes.' Max at once set out the terms. 'The model can be in our hands by tomorrow. That, together with Shimizu Junzaburo's services as guide, will get us into the castle, into the Inside – and out again.'

'As simple as that?'

'I never said it would be simple, Viktor. But it's feasible. Feasible *enough*, I think.'

Laskaris went on studying the carp for a moment, then said, 'I agree. But I detect in your tone a need to ask rather more of me than I have so far offered.'

'It's true. First, there's the money. I don't have enough left to fund the entire fifty thousand yen.'

Laskaris chuckled. '*Une bagatelle.* I will supply as much as you need.'

'Thank you.'

'Is that all?'

'No. There's the question of readily identifying the Zangai-jo box.' Max took out the piece of paper which the Dragonfly had given him and handed it to Laskaris. 'That's what appears on the label.'

'There are many boxes in the storehouse, also labelled?'

'Yes. She has told me where the one we want is. But even so . . .'

'It would be easy for a *gaijin* – a foreigner such as you or I – to become confused and take the wrong box.'

'The Dragonfly's told me where to look. But yes, I fear it would.'

'Show this once to Seddik, however, and he would know it again at a glance.' Laskaris smiled at Max. 'That is what has occurred to you, of course.'

'I confess it has.'

'When do you plan to do this?'

'First light tomorrow. There are thick bamboo forests around the villa and there's cloud coming over. By night, I reckon it'll be impossibly dark. Just before dawn would be the time.'

'Yes.' Laskaris nodded. 'That would be sensible.'

'I'll go with him, of course. I could go alone, but it'll be quicker and surer if Seddik retrieves the box. And it'll be a useful rehearsal for our visit to Zangai-jo.'

'Which will be the night after?'

'I'll take advice from the monk, but I imagine so, yes. Schools and the other two will be on their way to San Francisco by then.'

'And you can leave from Kobe later in the day.'

'Don't you mean *we* can leave?'

297

'I shall stay, Max. This will hurt Tomura. But not enough for my purposes.'

'As you please.'

'It's settled, then. Seddik will go with you tonight.'

'Shouldn't we ask him first?'

'My consent is his consent. He will go with you. When will you leave?'

'Three ack emma.'

'Ack emma?'

'Sorry. Buzzers' slang. From the war.' Max smiled, as much as anything because of how strangely distant – and how simple – his wartime life now felt to him. 'Three a.m. From Seifu-so.'

'He'll be there.' Laskaris held up the piece of paper. 'I'll keep this for him.'

There was little of Kyoto south of the railway station. The city dribbled out into rice-fields and dusty vistas. The temple of Minami Hongan-ji stood close to the railway tracks, tranquil and rustic on one side, noisy and modern on the other, with trains rumbling past.

Max was not kept waiting long at the gate. The monks of Minami Hongan-ji wore red. Shimizu Junzaburo was instantly identifiable by his orange robe. Max knew he must be in his mid-forties, but he looked younger, with his shaven head and his placid expression. Whatever he had once been, he was armed now with the shield of Buddhist enlightenment. But he could not shrug off his past and the obligations it imposed on him. Nor, clearly, did he intend to try.

'You are Max,' he said with a bow.

'Chiyoko said you would be here.'

'I am where I have known long I would one day be. The prisoner of Zangai-jo is not forgotten.'

'You know who she is – and what she is to me?'

'Yes. Also what she was to Jack Farngold.'

'You agreed to help him.'

'Yes. Then he went to Chosen to learn the secret of *Uchi-gawa*. But he did not return.'

'The Dragonfly betrayed him. Tomura held him captive, before killing him. He died nine days ago, in Tokyo.'

'I am sorry for him. Also for his sister. And for you. Man does not live to strive and suffer. There is a higher path.'

'And I'll happily tread it once I've set my mother free.'

Junzaburo's large, lambent eyes seemed to look into Max's very soul. 'No,' he said softly. 'You are a warrior. You will not turn away. Even if there is no enemy left to fight. I will pray I am wrong.' He smiled beneficently. 'But I am not.'

'You'll lead us into the castle?'

'I will. But I cannot fight for her, Max. I cannot kill. That is behind me.'

'I'm not asking you to fight.'

'You have what Jack Farngold sought from the Dragonfly?'

'I will have, by tomorrow. A model of the Inside, made by the man who designed and constructed it.'

'I have never been there. Few who served Tomura were ever allowed to go there. But I know where it is. I will lead you as far as its entrance. Then . . .'

'We're on our own?'

'How many will you be?'

'Two.'

'The other?'

'Is highly gifted.'

'But not a warrior?'

'Not in the sense you mean.'

'Maybe that is best. Maybe you will succeed. I will pray you do.'

'Malory—'

'I cannot speak of her.' For the first time, Junzaburo's composure faltered. 'I wish her everything good. But I am still not strong enough in my heart to hear her voice or know what she thinks. You understand?'

Max nodded. 'Yes.'

'When shall we do this, Max?'

'Tomorrow night.'

Junzaburo gazed up at the sky, in which clouds were building, and appeared to speak, though no words were audible. Then he looked at Max and said, 'We must be in the hills by early evening. It is an hour's climb from the nearest road. We should pass the night in the tunnel and enter the castle at dawn.'

'You think that's the best time?'

'The night watch will be tired. And there will be just enough light for you to see by. I do not know the hazards you will meet. There will be many. But any other time is worse.'

'Dawn it is, then. I have a car. It won't take us long to reach the area. Wait for me in front of the railway station at five o'clock tomorrow afternoon.'

'I will be there. And I will be ready.' With that he bowed and walked away.

'There and ready,' Max murmured to himself. 'Well, I can't ask more than that.'

Max had walked to Minami Hongan-ji. He boarded a tram to return to Seifu-so, knowing the route would take him to the northern end of the Imperial Park. It was crowded with people going home from work, hot and tired from their labours. Many fell asleep as the journey proceeded through the centre of the city. Conversation was limited, conducted in whispers. The vehicle rattled and swayed onward, its bell jangling at intervals.

Max found himself thinking of another tram-ride, in Paris earlier in the year, when his father had suddenly seen Lemmer, standing close to him in the car. But for that one glimpse, Sir Henry might have lived to mount his own rescue mission in Japan. Max himself might be in Surrey, running the fabled flying school he and Sam had dreamt of. The secrets he had uncovered would be unknown to him. He would be leading a different life.

But chance had decreed otherwise. And he was not sorry.

Sam and Chiyoko had returned in his absence and Malory had elicited far more from them about their activities than she had from Max.

'A plane, Max? I thought the plan was to leave by sea.'

300

'You and Sam are leaving by sea, Malory. But unlike a plane, a boat can be overhauled and stopped. If it is, you'll have nothing to hide. I'm a pilot. This is the best way, believe me.'

'Why didn't you mention it before?'

'I wanted to be sure we could lay our hands on a suitable machine. Can we, Sam?'

'Yes and no, sir.'

Max sighed. 'Take a turn with me in the garden and explain what the hell that means, would you?'

'I'd have got ruddy nowhere without Chiyoko, sir, and that's a fact. No one in these parts seems to speak a word of English. She did all the talking. We went to the only aerodrome round here, south of the city. Fookoo something. An Army base, with a small civilian operation tacked on. I was hoping they'd be getting rid of surplus planes at a knock-down price, like at Hendon. No such luck. Nothing doing. But Chiyoko charmed some bloke into suggesting we try a boatyard on a lake east of here.'

'Lake Biwa?'

'That'd be it.'

'What use is a boatyard to us, Sam?'

'They've got a plane for sale. But that's where we come to the snag. She's a seaplane, sir. And you've never flown one, have you?'

'It can't be that difficult.'

'I was hoping you'd say that, sir. My thoughts exactly. This machine could be just what we're looking for. Japanese Navy surplus. Two-seater biplane, twin main floats, built for reconnaissance. Engine in good condition. Range of nearly eight hundred kilometres. I make that about five hundred miles. Now, I've checked and double-checked the map. Your nearest friendly port is Why-high-why, one of our colonies on the Chinese coast. The Royal Navy'll look after you there. That's about eight hundred miles. Shanghai's closer to a thousand. Either way—'

'It's too far.'

'Extra fuel's the answer, sir. We can strap tanks to the fuselage. The plane was designed to carry a machine-gun, so we'll be all right for weight. You just have to put down somewhere halfway and fill her up.'

'By somewhere halfway you mean in the middle of the Yellow Sea?'

'I was thinking more of an inlet on the Korean coast, sir. The route to Why-high-why takes you straight across Korea. Originally, I was reckoning on you putting down in a field. It'll have to be the sea now. A quiet stretch, obviously.'

'And a calm one.'

'It's not perfect, sir, I know, but what is? At least you don't have to worry about a runway this end. You'll have the lake. I reckon it should work. The plane's ours for a thousand yen. A fair price, according to Chiyoko. Though what she knows about the price of second-hand planes . . .'

Max smiled. At a fiftieth of the price of Hashiguchi Azenbo's model of his design for Zangai-jo, it sounded not so much fair as extraordinarily generous. Max clapped Sam on the shoulder. 'You've done well, Sam. Better than I could have asked for. Tomorrow, you and I are going to buy a seaplane.'

SCHOOLS MORAHAN SHIFTED UNCOMFORTABLY IN THE CHAIR HE HAD walked to from the bed in his room at the University Hospital in Tokyo. He was feeling much better today, no question about it, but even so the journey from the bed had left him breathing in a fashion reminiscent of his emphysemic old dad in the Lower East Side tenement that was the scene of his earliest memories.

He was contemplating a walk to the window to see how his patched lung coped with the effort when the door opened and Takatsuki came in. He was the only policeman Fujisaki had sent to guard Schools who spoke any English.

'You have a visitor, Morahan-san. She has not been before. *Roshia-jin*, I think.'

'*Roshia-jin?*'

'From *Roshia*.'

A Russian. And a woman. There was only one person it could be. They had never met before, though, in a sense, they knew each other quite well. 'What's her name?'

'Kisleva, she say.'

Schools reminded himself that Nadia Bukayeva was a hardened killer. He was unarmed and none too robust. He could not afford to take any risks. But he was curious – as doubtless she had known he would be.

'I told her to go away,' Takatsuki continued. 'But she say she has something for you.'

'A bullet, maybe.'

Takatsuki frowned. '*Wakarimasen.*'

Schools mimed firing a pistol.

The frown became a grin. 'You like us search her?'

Schools nodded. '*Hai.* Yes. Search her. And do a thorough job. Thorough? All over?'

The grin broadened. 'You no worry, Morahan-san. We search her good.'

Fully ten minutes passed after Takatsuki left the room. Then the door opened again and Nadia Bukayeva walked in. She was not beautiful, but she was vital and alluring. Schools felt sure Takatsuki had enjoyed searching her and that he had indeed done a thorough job of it.

She appeared unruffled, however, and, above all, undeflected. The directness with which she looked at Schools was a statement of intent.

'What can I do for you, Nadia?' Schools asked. 'It is Nadia, right?'

'And you are Schools Morahan, the big man. Leaving Japan tomorrow, I hear.'

'What's that to you?'

'I have this for you.' She dropped a well-filled foolscap envelope on the bed. 'To take to America with you.'

'You're a little young to be writing your memoirs.'

'The envelope contains information obtained by Lemmer about Count Tomura's part in various incidents, including the assassination of Korean Empress Myongsong in October of 1895.'

'Queen Min? Kinda old news, I'd say.'

'Read it and you will not think that. The assassins did not just kill her. They raped her. They burned her. They beheaded her. And Tomura was there. He was one of them.'

'He's your friend, Nadia, not mine. And I judge people by the people they choose to associate with. That doesn't leave you smelling of violets.'

'He is not my friend.'

'He's Lemmer's friend. And you serve Lemmer.'

'No longer.'

'No?'

'You know what has happened. Lemmer is finished. He is over. I am not with him any more.'

'Who are you with?'

'No one. That is why I have brought this to you. To prove I no longer serve Lemmer *or* Tomura.'

'What d'you want me to do with it?'

'Take it with you to San Francisco. Give it to the newspapers. Use it to damage Tomura.'

'Well, if it's as sensational as you say, I guess the papers'll want to print it. What d'you get out of it?'

'I want Max to tell Appleby I am out of the game. I want to be forgotten.'

'If I see him, I'll pass your message on.'

'And when will you see him?'

'Couldn't say. He's already out of the country. Shanghai-bound.'

Nadia sighed. 'We both know where Max is. Also why he is there. But I do not know *exactly* where he is. Therefore I cannot warn him. Only you can.'

'Warn him of what?'

'I have a source of information in Count Tomura's house. I have learnt something today that Max should be told of.'

'What would that be?'

'Tomura has left Tokyo. He has taken his son and Ishibashi with him. They are travelling to his castle north of Kyoto. Kawajuki-jo. Zangai-jo. That is where they are going. They will arrive tomorrow.'

Nadia was right about the need to warn Max of such a development. But Schools did not intend to tell her so. 'Why should Max care where the Tomuras go? Like I told you, he's left the country.'

She gave Schools a tight little smile. 'Warn him. He is your friend. He must know of this. It makes what he plans to do more dangerous. And it was already dangerous enough.'

'Well, I—'

'I have told you and you will tell him. That is the truth. I say no more. *Do svidaniya.*' She turned and walked swiftly from the room.

'Where are you going, Nadia?' he called after her.

But she did not reply.

Schools waited a strategic few minutes, then heaved himself out of the chair and went to the door.

'Takatsuki?' he called.

Takatsuki appeared. 'She gone, Morahan-san. Nice, huh?'

'I need to make a telephone call to a Kyoto number.'

'Telephone? *Sumimasen*, Morahan-san. No telephone calls unless *Chokan* says.'

By *Chokan*, Takatsuki meant his boss, Commissioner Fujisaki. Schools sighed heavily. 'Better call *Chokan*, then.'

It took over an hour to contact Fujisaki, though he readily gave his consent once Schools had assured him the call would have no effect on his deportation the following day. 'I'll go quietly, Commissioner. You have my word.' And his word was evidently good enough.

After Takatsuki had authorized the operator to put him through, Schools was connected with Seifu-so.

'Seifu-so.'

'Schools Morahan calling. For Max.'

'Max? Er . . . Wait, please.'

A moment passed. Then:

'Schools?'

'There's news, Max. I had a visit from Nadia Bukayeva.'

'You did?'

'She claims to have split from Lemmer.'

'That wouldn't surprise me.'

'She wants you to put in a good word for her with Appleby.'

'Why would I do that?'

'Because she's done you a favour. She told me something you need to know. Tomura's heading your way, with his son in tow.'

'Is he, by God?'

'They'll reach the castle tomorrow. That swings the odds against you.'

'Maybe.'

'To hell with maybe, Max. They'll be *there*.'

'*If* Nadia told you the truth. It could be a ruse to scare me off. Some move by Lemmer to persuade Tomura he still needs him. It won't work.'

'You'll go ahead?'

'Of course.'

Of course. Max would go through with it however slim his chances were. He knew no other way. 'How are your preparations going?'

'Just as I'd hoped.'

'Then all I can do is wish you the luck you'll surely need.'

'Thanks, Schools. Listen, Malory will want to speak to you, I know. A last word before you get on that ship tomorrow. Don't mention Nadia's visit, will you, or this news about Tomura? There's no sense worrying her unnecessarily.'

It seemed to Schools that Max had a strange definition of *unnecessarily*. But arguing with him was futile. His certainty was evident in his voice even down a crackling telephone line. He was committed. He was determined. Nothing – absolutely nothing – was going to stop him.

MAX BARELY SLEPT THAT NIGHT. WELL BEFORE THREE O'CLOCK, HE was up, waiting by the gate for le Singe to arrive. He walked out into the lane that led down to Imadegawa-dori. The darkness beneath the bamboos that fringed the lane was sprinkled with fireflies. The air was sweet and warm, the silence velvety.

Then le Singe was there, beside him, announcing himself as a sensation before Max was properly aware of the darker patch of shadow at his elbow that was a human presence.

'Seddik?'

A hand, placed lightly on Max's shoulder, was le Singe's answer. He had arrived.

'Follow me.'

Max walked back in through the gate and round to the rear of the villa, where the Appersons were stowed. A lantern was shining there, held by Sam, who had got up to see them off.

'Thought I'd better be here, in case you had trouble with the car, sir,' he explained, not altogether convincingly. 'They can be temperamental, these Yank motors.'

'We'll be fine, Sam,' said Max. 'There's nothing to worry about. This is just a little pantomime to oblige the Dragonfly.'

'You be careful, even so.'

'Aren't I always?'

Nodding to le Singe, Sam said, 'Pleased to meet you again.'

There was no immediate response. After an awkward few seconds, le Singe nodded back.

'I was at Soutine's apartment, in Paris.'

Another nod. That was all. 'He knows, Sam,' said Max. 'He knows.'

Max drove west through the empty night as far as the village of Arashiyama and a little way beyond.

Le Singe was a disconcerting travelling companion, by virtue of his stillness as much as his silence. He gave no clue to his thoughts or intentions. He was there, as Laskaris had said he would be. His collaboration with Max had begun. There was nothing more.

Max pulled the car off the road close to the lane leading to the Dragonfly's villa and stopped. The new day was dawning. The shadows remained deep in the bamboo forest around them. But at least he could now see le Singe's face.

'Ready?'

Le Singe took a deep draught of air and gazed about him, widening his eyes, as if to accustom them to the level of the light. Then he nodded. And they both got out of the car.

It was a swift march up the bamboo-tunnelled lane to the outer gate of the villa. They climbed over and Max led the way along the foot-path he had followed with Malory the day before.

Screened by the trees bounding the property, to the rear of the villa itself, stood the outhouses. The light was still thin, the outlines of buildings and hedges blurry, but the way ahead was readily discernible. After entering the garden, they diverted left, avoiding the lawn, where they might have been glimpsed by an early-rising servant.

They paused twenty yards or so short of the storehouse, beneath some ginkgo trees. All was quiet. Nothing stirred in the villa. The time had come to discover whether the Dragonfly had been as good as her word.

'The box is in there,' said Max, pointing. 'It's on the third shelf up on the left as you enter. We need to be certain we have the right one.'

Le Singe smiled, as if the matter was simplicity itself. He slipped the piece of paper Laskaris had given him out of his tunic and handed it to Max without even glancing at it. The *kanji* were imprinted on his mind. Max wondered how many times he had actually looked at them. Once? Twice? It did not matter. They were there. There would be no mistake.

'Let's go,' said Max, starting forward.

But le Singe grasped his arm and held him back. He was still smiling. But he was also shaking his head, signalling for Max to stay where he was. He could do this alone. He *wanted* to do this alone.

Max shrugged his consent and le Singe moved away from the trees. Watching him go, Max wondered if his motive was to demonstrate his expertise in advance of their raid on Zangai-jo. It was unnecessary. His expertise was not in doubt. But perhaps he thought Max would be reassured to see it in action.

Just as le Singe reached the door, there was a drift of smoke from the far side of the outhouse. The source of the smoke was out of sight. Max could not have explained why it disturbed him. But, suddenly, he was uneasy.

Le Singe hesitated. He had smelt the smoke as well. But there was not a lot of it. Perhaps there was no cause for alarm. He stretched forward and turned the door handle.

It was not locked. There was a creak as the heavy iron door swung open. Le Singe stepped over the threshold.

In that instant, there were three powerful gunshots in quick succession. Le Singe staggered back. He was hit. He took two faltering steps, then fell.

Max had his gun in his hand and was racing towards the storehouse. It was a trap, he realized too late, intended for him. And le Singe had walked straight into it.

Terada Dentaro appeared in the doorway, holding a short rifle. The barrel was smoking. He looked down at le Singe and frowned. The Arab boy's grimacing face was not the face he had expected to see. Then he saw Max.

But not soon enough. Max pumped four bullets into his chest. Terada was jolted back against the doorframe. He gave a spluttering groan and tried to raise the rifle. Max shot him through the head then. He slid down, blood smearing the post behind him. And toppled to one side.

Max crouched over le Singe and saw the pool of blood spreading beneath him. His coat and tunic were dark with it. His eyes rolled. He tried to raise his right arm. He seemed to be pointing at something, trying to focus on it.

Max turned and looked up. The object of le Singe's attention was the figure of a dragon, carved on the ridge of the storehouse roof above the door, copper-green, taloned and fanged, jaws gaping in a silent snarl.

When Max looked back, the light had gone out behind le Singe's eyes. He could see the dragon no longer.

Cursing himself for his failure to anticipate treachery, Max hurried round to the side of the building. The ashes of a fire were heaped there, fragments of wood still smouldering, smoke rising from them fitfully. An empty wooden chest lay discarded nearby.

Suddenly, what had happened was horribly clear. Terada had burnt the model of the Inside, then lain in wait to kill Max. No doubt he had hoped for a lot in the way of career advancement from Tomura in return for such distinguished service. Whether the Dragonfly was party to what he had done Max did not know.

But he meant to find out.

He ran to the villa and wrenched open one of the doors. Where the Dragonfly might be he could only guess. He strode along passages, flinging doors wide, seeing empty rooms beyond empty rooms, hanging lanterns and calligraphic scrolls stirring in the moving air.

Then he heard a scream. It was from some way off, unconnected, as far as he could tell, to his invasion of the house. It became a high, keening wail. He raced towards it, through the maze of rooms.

Its source was the room in which the Dragonfly evidently slept. Beneath a screen-painting of herons and cherry blossom, she lay stretched across a futon, pink-robed and motionless, her face frozen in the blankness of death. The maid who had served tea the

311

previous afternoon was kneeling beside her, sobbing and howling, unaware of Max's presence.

An argument; a struggle; strangulation; stifling. How Terada had killed her hardly mattered. They were both dead now.

And so was le Singe.

THE GUILT MAX FELT AT LE SINGE'S DEATH WAS ROOTED IN KNOWING he had persuaded Laskaris to let the boy help him. It was only made worse by the fact that he had kept to himself Morahan's warning that Tomura was heading for Zangai-jo. He should have considered why Tomura had left Tokyo, of course, though even if he had guessed Terada was the reason . . .

Sam, Malory and Chiyoko were waiting for him at Seifu-so. He told them as plainly as he could what had happened. He saw the shock blanch their faces. It was not supposed to have been like this. His plan had miscarried. And clearly, in their view, little of it remained. But that was not how he saw it. That was not how he saw it at all.

He telephoned Laskaris and broke the news. He heard the old man gasp and stifle a sob. Whatever Seddik Yala had been to Soutine, to Laskaris he was something close to a son. This was a loss he would find hard to bear, all the more so for being unexpected, if not unbelievable.

'*Mon Dieu*,' Laskaris groaned. 'I thought he was immortal.'

An hour later, Laskaris was at Seifu-so, listening face to face to Max's account of how le Singe had met his death. There was no cigar this time. Laskaris was grey and grave and sombrely spoken.

They stood in the garden, where the crows cawed and the breeze moved dark shadows across the surface of the pond. Many silent moments passed after Max had finished before Laskaris spoke. When he did, his voice was gravelly, his tone leaden.

'I must go to the police. Seddik needs me more in death than in life. I will have to arrange his burial. I will say he told me he was going to meet Terada Dentaro. I will say I do not know why. I will say nothing about you.'

'You should ask for Chief Inspector Wada. Fujisaki said he was a good man. He's probably already been called to the villa.'

Laskaris nodded. 'Wada. I will remember.' He looked at Max, his expression tautening. 'Tomura is responsible for this. I will make him pay.'

'He's due at Zangai-jo later today.'

'How do you know that?'

'A phone call from Morahan.'

'When?'

'Last night.'

'And yet still you went ahead.'

'It never occurred to me Terada had contacted him. It was supposed to be just a make-believe burglary.'

'But once Tomura reached Zangai-jo, your chances of success would be much reduced, even with Seddik and the model of the Inside. When did you intend to inform me of the change in circumstances?'

'I—'

'You didn't, did you? You were not willing to be deflected. And now, Max? With Seddik dead, the model destroyed and Tomura on his way to the castle, will you still not be deflected?'

Max said nothing. No reply he could offer seemed to fit the moment.

'You will die in there. They will kill you. It is suicide to attempt a rescue with so little – with nothing – in your favour.'

'It is my duty, Viktor. It's as simple as that.'

'*Your* duty? Not Seddik's, you would agree?'

'I'm truly sorry. If I'd known what Terada was up to . . . Seddik would still be alive.'

Laskaris turned away. He took and held a long breath, then

314

slowly released it. He turned back and looked at Max again. 'You should leave Japan tomorrow, from Kobe, in the vessel I have engaged. The *Ptarmigan*. The captain is a Scot named McFarland.' He handed Max a sealed letter. 'This directs McFarland to take instructions from you or Twentyman or Miss Hollander. He will convey you to Shanghai. He will be carrying a cargo of furniture, but he is at your disposal.'

'Thank you. Sam and Malory will be aboard.'

'But not you?'

'Nor you, Viktor. We both have unfinished business here.'

'I may be risking my life by remaining. You will be throwing yours away.'

'He looked a broken man, sir,' said Sam, coming out to meet Max on the verandah after Laskaris had left.

'He thought le Singe was untouchable. So did I, if it comes to it. I never imagined – neither did Laskaris – that he could be killed by one fool with a gun.'

'If a bullet's got your name on it . . .'

'We should be leaving.'

'To go where, sir?'

'Lake Biwa.'

Sam frowned in obvious dismay. 'You mean . . .'

'I'm not giving up.'

'But . . . without le Singe and the model . . .'

'After we've bought the seaplane and checked it over and fitted the spare fuel tanks, I want you to put Chiyoko on the next train to Tokyo. Then I want you and Malory to travel to Kobe. Stay there overnight. The ship Laskaris has engaged is the *Ptarmigan*, waiting in the harbour. I have a letter authorizing the skipper to take instructions from you or Malory. Go aboard tomorrow morning and tell him to make for Shanghai. We'll meet there in a week or so. I'll stand you a drink at the Astor House.'

'That's whistling in the wind, sir, and you know it.'

'I have to do this, Sam. And I'm going to.'

'I'll come with you.'

'No. I'd be worried about you and you'd be worried about me. It wouldn't work. I'll go in alone after Junzaburo's shown me the way. I need your help to fix up the plane and make sure Malory and Chiyoko are safe. Will you do that for me?'

''Course I will, but—'

'Say no more, Sam. This is how it has to be.' Max gave Sam a look that willed him to understand and accept his decision. 'And we have work to do. So, let's get on with it.'

Before they left for Lake Biwa, the argument was repeated, in an only slightly different form, between Max and Malory. But she was wasting her breath.

He dwelt in a place slightly apart from all of them now. He existed where previously only a fighter plane had taken him: the solitude of his own judgement.

'Isn't what happened to le Singe a warning to you, Max? Tomura knows you're coming. You have no idea how the Inside is designed. You've lost every advantage you had.'

'Not every one, Malory. There's still Junzaburo.'

'He can get you in. But no one can get you out.'

'I'm backing myself to do that.'

'Sam doesn't want to lose you. *I* don't want to lose you. Leave with us. Talk to Schools. Devise some other way to rescue your mother.'

'There is no other way. Le Singe can't be brought back to life. The model can't be *un*burned. I have the resources I have. And I'm going to use them.'

IN THE END, THEY DROVE TO THE BOATYARD TOGETHER – MAX, SAM, Malory and Chiyoko – prior to going their separate ways.

The yard was on the western shore of Lake Biwa, north of Ohtsu. The proprietor, Mr Muchaku, was a small, wrinkled, taciturn fellow, only moderately susceptible to Chiyoko's charm. His susceptibility to a thousand yen, however, was never in any doubt. The plane was towed out of its shed, its propellers uncovered and its wings unfolded for Max to inspect.

'What d'you reckon, sir?' Sam enquired nervously after Max had looked her over.

'She'll do.'

'Maybe you should ask to try her out.'

'No. We don't want to attract the attention of the locals. You passed her fit to fly?'

'I turned the engine over. She's sound enough. 'Course, the instructions in the cockpit are in Japanese, but a dial's a dial when all's said and done and the controls won't give you any problems.'

'What about the extra fuel?'

'Included in the price. I'll fix the tanks on as soon as you pay the man.'

Without further ado, Max paid. Muchaku's mouth curled in a smile. He obviously reckoned he had struck a good deal. He had a brief conversation with Chiyoko, then bustled off to his ramshackle office.

'He will give you a receipt,' she explained.

'It's good to know I won't be accused of theft, I suppose,' said Max.

'Also he will give you – ah! There is what he will give you.'

Muchaku reappeared, cradling two sets of flying jackets, boots, gloves, helmets and goggles.

'You'll be needing those, sir,' said Sam. 'However hot it is down here, it'll be cold up top, specially over the sea.'

'So it will.' Almost for the first time, Max considered the practicalities of cladding Matilda Tomura in flying kit, loading her into the plane and taking off. She had been a prisoner for close to thirty years. She might well be frail and feeble, sick in mind as well as body. She might be incapable of even leaving the castle. Then what would he do?

'Second thoughts, sir?' asked Sam.

'None at all,' Max replied firmly. 'You'd better see to those fuel tanks.'

While Sam busied himself with the tanks, cack-handedly assisted by one of Muchaku's employees, with Chiyoko standing by to translate his instructions, Max waited with Malory by the yard's slipway. Sunlight glistened on the surface of the lake and burnished the peaks that tracked its western shore. The seaplane stirred gently at its mooring.

'You're not going to try to talk me out of it again, Malory?' Max asked.

'What would be the point?'

'None, of course.'

'There you are, then.'

'The *Woodward* will be setting sail around about now.'

'Taking Schools to safety. And tomorrow the *Ptarmigan* will take Sam and me to safety as well. I know. We're leaving. But you're staying.'

'Not for long.'

'One way or another?'

'Tell Chiyoko I won't put her brother's life at risk, would you? I don't want her to worry about that after all she's done for us.'

'You don't want anyone to worry, Max. Isn't that right? You don't want them to, but they will. What you're doing is suicidal and you know it. Chances are we'll never—'

'Don't say that.' Max pressed his fingers against Malory's lips, silencing her. 'Just wish me luck. That's all I need.' He lifted his hand away then, freeing her to speak.

She looked at him for a long time, then shook her head sadly. 'You're impossible, Max. Of course I wish you luck. All the luck in the world. But it's not enough, is it?'

He smiled softly. 'It is for me.'

She turned away. 'I'm trying very hard not to cry,' she said, her voice thick with the effort.

'By the time I was shot down, in April of seventeen, Malory, the life expectancy of a fighter pilot on the Western Front could be measured in weeks. Ask Sam. He never expected to see me again every time I took off. Yet here I am. I beat the odds. And I'll go on beating them. I promise.'

'Sam's waving to you.' Malory pointed towards the seaplane. Sam and his helper were standing on the floats, with the tanks hoisted into position. It seemed Max's approval of something was required.

'I'd better go.'

Max set off without waiting for another word from Malory. She watched him stride away. 'Yes, of course,' she murmured to herself – and, in a sense, to him. 'You have to go.'

Max was right about the SS *Woodward*. At that moment, the last of her ropes was falling away as she cleared the pier-side in Yokohama and moved out into the harbour. Watching her leave was Commissioner Fujisaki, standing impassively among the onlookers. He raised a hand in muted farewell to Schools Morahan, who responded in kind from one of the open midship decks.

Schools was leaning on a walking stick, supplied to him before he left the hospital. He was not happy to need one and did not look it. He was not happy about any of the circumstances of his departure from Japan, in fact, but he and Fujisaki both knew going quietly was the only choice open to him.

319

Ward and Djabsu had already gone in search of a drink – more likely several drinks – to celebrate their release from prison.

Schools had undertaken to join them later, though he was not sure he would when it came to it. His mind dwelt fretfully on what might be happening in Kyoto. Max had promised to protect Malory, but Max was not master of his own destiny, far less Malory's. The future could not be predicted, only hoped for. And there would be no news, good or bad, during the three-week voyage to San Francisco. Limbo was all Schools had to look forward to.

That and the day he regained enough mobility to toss his Japanese walking stick into the Pacific Ocean. Summoning a smile in anticipation of the moment, he moved as adroitly as he could away from the rail. And left the view of Yokohama behind him.

After leaving the boatyard, Max drove Sam, Malory and Chiyoko to Ohtsu station. From there Chiyoko was to catch a train to Tokyo via Nagoya, Malory and Sam a train to Kobe. No one would be looking for them at Ohtsu, whereas Tomura might conceivably have set a watch on the station at Kyoto. He must know by now Max had not been caught in the trap set for him at the Dragonfly's villa.

The time had come for brisk goodbyes and summonings of false optimism. Max thanked Chiyoko for her help and assured Malory and Sam he would meet them in Shanghai.

He saw the truth in their faces, though – the fear, if not the conviction, that there would be no meeting in Shanghai; that this time he would not win through. He saw it. But he pretended not to. And they joined him in the pretence.

Final farewells were exchanged. And then he drove away.

MAX DID NOT RETURN TO SEIFU-SO, RECKONING IT POSSIBLE Tomura would soon have Saionji's villa watched. Nor did he want there to be any possibility of becoming entangled with the police. Before leaving Shanghai, he had bought plenty of ammunition for his gun and a bandoleer to carry it in, together with a knife. Even then, he had foreseen a moment such as this would arrive. He could not turn away from it. And he did not intend to try.

He would not have chosen such a public place as the railway station to collect Junzaburo if he had thought Tomura might learn he was in Kyoto. Accordingly, he drove to Minami Hongan-ji, arriving more than half an hour before the time of their rendezvous, parked near the gate of the temple and waited for Junzaburo to emerge.

Passers-by in that part of the city late on a hot afternoon were few. Max smoked a couple of cigarettes to ward off gnats from the nearby rice-fields. He was not surprised by how calm he felt, how undismayed by what lay before him. He had discovered his aptitude for taking risks early in the war. 'You should be more careful, sir,' Sam had said to him more than once. And Max had always given the same reply. 'Being careful is what gets a chap killed.' Eventually, he had come to believe that. And it was a belief that had served him well. So far.

*

'You have changed the plan,' said Junzaburo, making Max jump by his sudden, soft-footed arrival from somewhere other than the main gate of the temple.

Max turned round to face him and was surprised by what he saw. The orange robe was gone. Junzaburo was clad in a dark green hooded tunic and loose trousers. He was wearing a conical straw hat and had a well-filled rope-handled bag slung on one shoulder.

'Why are you not waiting at the station, Max?'

'Get in. I'll explain on the way.'

Junzaburo climbed in and they set off. Max went back the way he had come, under the railway line, then headed north on the western side of the city.

'Where is your friend?' Junzaburo asked, when the promised explanation did not promptly follow.

'He's dead,' said Max.

Junzaburo did not respond at first. Then he nodded, as if the news confirmed some prognostication of his. 'I am sorry,' he said.

'I don't have the model either.'

'Have you seen it?'

'No. It was destroyed by a man who lives – lived – with the Dragonfly.'

'Is he dead also?'

'Yes. As is the Dragonfly. He killed her.'

'And you killed him?'

'Does it matter?'

'Perhaps not. But the Dragonfly is gone?'

'Yes.'

'All the advantages you thought you would have – the model of *Uchi-gawa*, the gifted companion – are lost to you?'

'They are.'

'Then it is hopeless.'

'That's for me to decide.'

'*Hai, hai.* Yes. For you to decide.'

Silence yawned between them as the Apperson growled on through the arrow-straight intersections of Kyoto's dusty streets, past cyclists and carts and slower-moving cars and vans.

'They say Kyoto is laid out like a Go board,' said Junzaburo suddenly. 'The representation is not perfect, of course. You know the game of Go, Max?'

'Something like chess?'

'Nothing like chess. There are no moves. The players place their stones on the intersections of the lines on the board. There are three hundred and sixty-one intersections. The game is won by building territory and surrounding and capturing the enemy's stones.'

'What are you telling me, Junzaburo? That I'm surrounded?'

'You already know that.'

'Then what?'

'The game ends when all the stones have been played, even if it is obvious who has won long before the last stone is played. And often it is obvious. As it is for you.'

'Lucky for me I'm not a Go player, then.'

'Do not finish the game, Max. Walk away from the board.'

'I can't do that.'

'Then you are wrong. You are a Go player. And you will lose the match.'

'We'll see.'

'Does Tomura know what you mean to do?'

'Maybe.'

'Is he at the castle?'

'Probably.'

'You have nothing in your favour.'

Max glanced at Junzaburo then and smiled. 'I have you.'

'Not enough.'

'And I have the nerve, which Tomura may think I lack, to go through with this.'

'Still not enough.'

'You promised to get me in there.'

'And I will.'

'Then don't worry. I won't complain later I wasn't warned.'

Silence fell again between them. It was obvious what Junzaburo was thinking. For Max, he did not believe there would be a later.

323

The car climbed into the hills as the sun slipped towards the horizon. The green of the cedar-cloaked peaks deepened in the mellowing light. The shadows lengthened. The only words spoken by Junzaburo for the next hour were simple instructions. 'Go on.' 'Turn here.' 'It is not far.'

They stopped on a saddle of land between two narrow valleys, with rugged slopes above them, where clumps of trees clung to the earth between aprons of scree. The road had become little more than a track. They pushed the car off it into the cover of some bushes, cutting several long branches to lay across it for extra camouflage. Then they started to climb, up through the ramrod-straight cedars and the loose scree, where Max several times lost his footing, but Junzaburo looked as assured as a mountain goat in his simple leather moccasins.

It grew chill as evening encroached, Max's breath clouding around him as he struggled up the pathways that Junzaburo's eye alone detected. The light thinned and grew misty, the hilltops around them dissolving in murk.

The entrance to the cave was concealed by a jumble of boulders, at the end of a gully invisible from below. 'How did you first find this?' Max panted as he caught up with Junzaburo, who was breathing as easily as if he had done no more than take a stroll in the park.

'I was told of it by an old man who had served Tomura's father. He saw something in me he liked. He said there might come a time when I would need to escape from Zangai-jo – from Tomura. He was right. But I did not need to use a tunnel. I became useless to Tomura. I cannot say now if I turned away from him or he turned away from me. I was . . . discarded.' Junzaburo sighed. 'As for the tunnel, this end is a natural cave, as you see. It is the same for much of its length. The rest was built as an escape route for the Tomuras if the castle ever fell. They have always had enemies. And they have always feared that one day their enemies would be stronger than them. But that day has never come.'

'Yet.'

'As you say, Max. Yet.' Junzaburo moved towards the dark mouth of the cave, stooping to clear the low overhang of rock. 'Follow me,' he called back softly over his shoulder.

MAX HAD BROUGHT A TORCH WITH HIM, BUT JUNZABURO ADVISED him to use one of the two torches he had brought instead. They comprised metal brackets fixed to wooden handles and wrapped in resin-soaked cloth, extra rolls of which Junzaburo carried in a bamboo cylinder fastened to his waist. They produced an impressive amount of light, casting a chaos of shadows ahead into the cave.

It was a slow, scrambling descent, along a twisting path of sorts between tumbled boulders. The roof grew lower, then higher, then lower again. Bats disturbed by the light swooped past them, sometimes brushing Max's shoulder. Water dripped and trickled unseen through crevices in the rocks. The air was cold and damp, the echoes of their uneven footfalls dogging their progress.

No words were exchanged as the journey continued. Time compressed itself into the confines of the cave, measured only by their breaths and their stubborn, onward steps. Max began to consider once more the feasibility of what he was attempting. Could Matilda Tomura return this way with him? Could she even walk? Or might he have to carry her?

At length the descent ceased. The cave levelled out and closed in around them, funnelling towards its end. A wall of rock loomed ahead.

'There is a way through,' said Junzaburo. 'See? To the right.'

What looked no more than a vertical crack in the rock revealed itself on closer inspection to be a narrow gap through which a man could squeeze sideways. And beyond?

'That is where the tunnel begins.'

It was no easy matter to force themselves through, pulling their bags behind them. Only certainty of an onward route would have prompted anyone to persist.

On the other side was a low-roofed but solidly constructed tunnel of stone blocks, expertly worked. The air was dryer than in the cave, though if anything colder. The tunnel curved slightly ahead of them, with no end in sight.

'We wait here till an hour before dawn,' said Junzaburo. 'You have food?'

At Chiyoko's bidding, Umezu had supplied Max with some rice and bean-paste cakes. Max had them in his knapsack, along with a flask of water, woollen gloves and a comforter. Junzaburo had food too – rather more of it – and sake as well as water, enough for several tots each. He was also carrying a blanket, which he spread for them to sit on.

The torchlight revealed a column of Japanese characters carved in one of the stones forming the wall of the tunnel. Max asked Junzaburo what the inscription said.

'It records the date of the completion of the tunnel. "Finished in the year of the death of Tokugawa Ieyasu." He was the first Shogun. That means 1616 in the Western calendar. Three hundred and three years ago.'

'Perfect craftsmanship,' said Max, gazing up at the arched, interlocking stones, irregular in size but fitted together perfectly.

'Nothing less would have been tolerated.'

'Why is the castle called Zangai-jo?'

'Eat your food. Soon we must put out the torches. There will be time to talk in the dark. More time than you could want.'

When the torches were extinguished, the darkness was total. There was no glimmer of light anywhere. There was no sound either, except when they shifted on the blanket or spoke. Whispering came naturally. There was no need to speak any more loudly than that.

327

'You asked why the castle is called Zangai-jo,' said Junzaburo. 'It is because Tomura's ancestors were even more brutal than he is. The most brutal of them all was his grandfather's father, Tomura Munetada. I heard the story from the old man who told me of this tunnel. Munetada would not allow the family of anyone he punished with death to bury the body. It was left to rot where it lay, beneath the wall of the castle, on the mountainside. *Zangai* is a body that has lost its form. *Zangai* is what his victims became.

'The fear of ending like that bound men to Tomura Munetada. And the memory of it – never spoken of among us, but known, *always* known – bound men like me to Tomura Iwazu. Fear, Max. Pure fear, distilled like a potion. It is how he governed us. It is how he governs still.

'There are things I did – so many things – that shame me. If the brother of one of the women I tricked into boarding Tomura's brothel-ships held a knife to my throat, I would say, "Kill me if you wish; I deserve to die." I remember the face of one of the women so clearly. She could not have been more than sixteen or seventeen. And so beautiful. So very beautiful. I told her she could earn seven yen a month as a barmaid in Hong Kong – riches to her. I saw trust and hope in her eyes. I loaded her on to a ship at Kagoshima that night. She soon must have realized she wasn't going to Hong Kong but to one of our . . . *jinniku no ichi* – whore-markets, as they were called.

'I am glad it is dark so you cannot see my face as I tell you this. And there is worse I could tell you. If I could force the words from my mouth.'

'You don't owe me a confession, Junzaburo,' said Max, to break the silence that followed.

'Not you, no. But the girl. I owe it to her. She is dead, probably. One of Tomura's *zangai*. Out there somewhere. In Korea. Or Manchuria. Forgotten, except by those who loved her.'

'You walked away from it. You renounced that life.'

'Yes. But it did not renounce me.'

'What kind of difficulties am I likely to encounter inside the castle?' Max asked, eager to lure his companion away from guilt-laden melancholy.

'Difficulties?' Junzaburo savoured the word. 'I would not call them that, exactly. But what are they? They are many, Max. They are many.'

'Any information you can give me would help.'

'*Hai, hai.* Information. The tunnel enters the castle at the first floor level below ground. *Uchi-gawa* is on the second level below ground. There is a passage you will have to walk along from the point where you enter. It has one turn in it. Then you will reach the stairs to the lower level. Those stairs may be guarded. At the bottom, there is another passage – no turn – leading to the door into *Uchi-gawa*. I have seen the door once only. It is barred so that no one can come out without knocking for the guard to open. Going *in* is easier, if the guard is not there or can be distracted.

'The corridor leading to *Uchi-gawa*, to the right from the bottom of the stairs, has a nightingale floor. It was made so that the nails squeak – like a bird calling – when walked on. It can only be defeated by shuffling, so your weight on the boards is always the same. That means you must move very slowly.

'Within *Uchi-gawa*, where I have never been, I suspect there are false turnings, trap-doors and other snares. The guards will be armed with guns as well as swords. I do not see how you can get past them. If Tomura knows what you intend, they will be more watchful than usual. Of course, Tomura does not know that you know of this tunnel. Approach from this direction will not be expected. Still, for one man – you, a European, with no Ninja training – to enter and leave with the prisoner of Zangai-jo? It is . . .'

'Impossible?'

'Yes. I should say it is impossible. But it is impossible also for a son to abandon his mother. So, you are here. She is there. Closer to you than she has been since the day you were carried from her. You cannot succeed. You know that, of course. But you cannot turn away. You may be able to enter. You will not be able to leave. You understand this?'

'I understand I have to try.'

'Then I must help you.'

'To get into the castle. That's all. I promised Chiyoko I wouldn't put your life at risk.'

'My life is not yours to promise.'

'I already have too many deaths on my conscience, Junzaburo. I don't want to add yours.'

'You are thinking of the friend who should have been with you tonight?'

Max was. Le Singe had saved his life twice and then lost his. His unspoken words – '*I have done what I can for you*' – echoed in Max's mind. His smile formed anew in the darkness in front of him. 'Which is more important to you?' Junzaburo asked. 'To see your mother? Or to rescue her?'

'I intend to do both.'

'But if you can do only one?'

'I'll let fortune make the choice.'

'I cannot kill anyone. I cannot hurt anyone. I am pledged to that. You understand?'

'Yes.'

'If I could help you enter *Uchi-gawa* without causing you to break your promise to Chiyoko and without raising my hand against another man? What would you say to that?'

'I'd say: how?'

'*Kasai*. That is the answer. Fire.'

SLEEP IN THE TUNNEL WAS A CHILLY, FITFUL THING. MAX MOVED between wakefulness and shallow, troubling dreams, of le Singe and his father and Corinne Dombreux. There was neither pattern nor meaning to the dreams, only uneasy familiarity. He was relieved when Junzaburo roused him with the announcement that it was time for them to move.

They walked for a while along the slowly curving, gently descending tunnel, carved out three centuries before to save the Tomuras from their enemies. Eventually, the light from their torches showed the end ahead of them: a solid stone wall.

As they drew closer, Max saw the outline of some form of door in the wall, constructed of the same stone. It was low and arched and fitted with neither handle nor hinges.

'I hope this is what you were expecting,' he said.

'It is what the old man told me to expect,' said Junzaburo.

He knelt in front of the door and began pressing his hands against it, working his way methodically down and across the surface. Max could do nothing but watch.

A barely audible scraping noise signalled Junzaburo's success. The door opened by an inch or so, swivelling at the centre, so that one side moved towards them as the other moved away.

Junzaburo sat back on his haunches and looked up at Max. 'Are you sure you want to go on? It is still possible to turn back.'

'You know I'm not going to do that.'

'I do.'

Junzaburo stood up then, took a small wooden hairpin from his pocket and dropped it into Max's pocket.

'What's that for?' Max asked suspiciously.

'Invisibility. It was carved during an eclipse. It holds the darkness and makes it hard for your enemies to see you.'

'You don't expect me to believe that, do you?'

'If you do not believe it, they will see you better than if you do not carry it.'

Max felt the force of Junzaburo's conviction. He could not have explained why, but, in that moment, as they stood together in the torchlight, belief in such a talisman did not seem absurd. 'I'll carry it,' he said.

Junzaburo nodded in acknowledgement. Then he pushed the door further open and Max followed him through.

Beyond lay a cramped, low-ceilinged chamber, boarded and panelled in wood. It appeared to be empty. But Junzaburo cast the light of his torch across the floor, looking for something. And soon enough he found it: a spy-hole into the room below. He slid back the cover and peered down through it.

'No one is there, I think,' he announced. 'Stand here.' He waved Max forward, then moved to the wall on his left and pressed one of the floorboards.

There was a click and a length of the floor slid downwards, revealing itself as a narrow ramp, ridged to supply footholds. Junzaburo lowered it by a rope to form a stairway.

'We should move fast now,' he murmured, leading the way down the stairs. Max scrambled after him.

They were in the passage Junzaburo had described to Max the night before, in the basement of the castle. A distant glimmer of lamplight gave shadowy form to the walls and floor. The lamp itself was out of sight, beyond the turn in the passage Junzaburo had mentioned.

Max helped him push the stairway back up into the ceiling, where it clicked into place. From below, it looked no different from the other stretch of boarding between the supporting beams.

'You must push it up to open,' Junzaburo whispered urgently. 'At this end. See?'

'Yes.'

'Direct above this spot. Count your paces from here to the turn. So that you can find your way back when you leave. Now follow me.'

They extinguished their torches and moved cautiously along the passage. Max counted his paces carefully as he went. They stopped where it took a right-angled turn and Junzaburo peered round the corner.

'The light is from a lantern above the stairs,' he reported. 'No guard there. But there will be one guard at least at the door to *Uchi-gawa*. That is certain. Go down and hide under the stairs. Remember the nightingale floor. I will set a fire at the top. Then I will go back to the tunnel. The guard will come when they smell burning. That will be your chance. Kill no one if you can avoid it. It is better always not to be seen.'

'And I'm invisible, of course.'

'I see you, Max. You see me. Now we part. That is all.'

'Shake my hand.'

'If you wish it.'

Junzaburo followed the handshake with a bow. No other word was spoken between them. Max stepped round the corner and headed for the stairs.

They were wide, with open treads, leading down to the passage that led to the Inside. He was near his goal now. He took each step carefully, keeping close to the wall to avoid causing creaks.

At the bottom, he set his feet down with painful caution. There was no bird-call. He shuffled slowly round the newel-post and into the deep shadow beneath the stairs, avoiding the bars of light from the lantern.

A single squeak betrayed him then, for all his care. He froze. But almost in the same moment he heard a crackle of something tindery above him. The fire had been lit.

The crackle became quickly noisier. There was a flickering shadow of flame cast down the stairs. Suddenly, there was a burst of squeaking and the sound of running feet. A darkly clad figure appeared from the direction of the Inside. He hesitated at the foot of the stairs and looked up, then shouted, '*Kaji da!*', and began bounding up them. Another darkly clad figure appeared from the same direction and raced up after him.

This was Max's chance. There would surely not be more than two guards on the door. And in the commotion, he did not need to worry about the nightingale floor. He emerged from his hiding-place.

As he did so, a third guard loomed out of the shadows from a different direction. They almost collided. But the man did not seem to see Max. He bounded past him and up the stairs. And only then did Max realize his hand was in his pocket, his fingers closed round the hairpin. He shook his head in wonderment.

Then he started along the passage at a run, the tell-tale bird-calls drowned out by the shouts and thumps above and behind him.

It was not far to the door, illuminated by a lantern. It was in fact more of a gate: a pair of high wooden doors sealed by a stout locking bar.

Max needed all his strength to raise one end of the bar over a retaining bracket. Then it slid across smoothly, clearing one door. Max turned the handle and entered.

Dim lanterns lit the way between gulfs of shadow. There was at once a choice of turnings. Along the one Max took, the level of the floor rose by a step, then fell. Then the passage turned back almost completely on itself. Suddenly, thanks to a lucky sliver of light, Max saw a rectangular hole in the floor directly ahead of him. He edged round it. A draught rose from the hole, whose depth Max could not judge, though the coolness of the air made him wonder if it led to some sheer flank of the castle's wall. He hurried on.

He came to what seemed a dead end. Switching on his electric torch, he found himself confronted by two doors. Both led to empty cupboard-like spaces. He wondered if he should retrace his steps. '*False turnings, trap-doors and other snares.*' That had been Junzaburo's best guess about the nature of the Inside.

He took a closer look at the cupboards and tapped the rear wall of one. It was nothing more than a hollow-sounding panel. There was a groove close to the ceiling that could serve as a finger-hold. Using that, he was able to slide the panel open.

Another passage, with light beyond a corner. He switched off his torch and tiptoed towards it.

Beyond the corner was a sliding door and beyond that a large room. It looked like several Japanese rooms Max had seen, with wooden beams and decorated walls, a dais and an alcove at one end, next to a sliding door that led to some other room beyond. There were wall-paintings of herons and pine trees, much glittering metal-work and intricate patterning on the coffered ceiling. But there were also bars, fashioned like the bars of a jail-cell, confining access to a walkway running round two sides of the room. Within was a gilded cage – a prison.

There were no windows, of course. The Inside was below ground. No natural light appeared to reach this part of the castle. Oil lamps, burning low, cast their sallow glow over the elegantly decorated dungeon.

Max took several paces along the walkway towards the door set in the bars. He did not have long. As soon as the guards doused the fire and returned to their post, they would realize someone had entered. He called out softly, 'Is anyone there?'

There was no response. He called a second time, more loudly. 'Is anyone there? *Konnichi wa?*'

There was a movement, a shifting of a shadow beyond the paper-panelled sliding door at the rear of the cell.

'*Konnichi wa?*'

The door slid open. A woman gazed out at him. She was thin, grey-haired and stooped, wearing a frayed yellow *yukata*. Her face was gaunt and hollow-cheeked, her eyes deeply sunk, but pale blue – like his own. She opened her mouth to speak, but no words came.

The woman looked all of sixty or seventy, though Max knew Matilda Tomura was actually in her early fifties. He did not doubt it was her. He did not doubt that, for the first time since he was newly born, he was looking at his mother.

'Hello? Are you . . . Matilda?'

The use of English seemed to amaze her. She gaped at him in speechless astonishment. Max imagined she was amazed as much as

335

anything by the fact that she did not know who he was. A new face in the long years of her imprisonment had to be a rarity.

He reached for the handle of the door. It would surely be locked. But he would try to open it anyway.

As he pulled the handle down, he saw the woman raise her hand and look alarmed.

But the warning was too late. The section of floor he was standing on vanished beneath him. And he fell.

MAX WAS STILL SEMI-CONSCIOUS WHEN THE GUARDS PULLED HIM out, more aware of the throbbing in his head, which had struck the wall of the pit as he fell, than of the manhandling he received. They bundled him into the cell and handcuffed him by his right wrist to one of the bars.

There they left him for some tract of time he could not measure as he drifted in and out of consciousness. Awareness slowly returned, along with the knowledge that they had taken his gun, knife and bandoleer, along with his knapsack. He probably still had his invisibility pin, though. He wondered if it had sensed his scepticism.

A face formed blurrily in front of him, then dissolved, then formed again. Once his eyes had regained the ability to focus, he realized the woman he now shared the cell with – Matilda Tomura, née Farngold, his mother – was sitting on the edge of the dais, staring at him.

'Do you . . . know who I am?' he slurred.

He had to repeat himself several times before she understood. And then she merely shook her head. She did not know.

'My name . . . is James Maxted. James . . . Maxted.'

That also took an age to sink in. But she recognized the name. He saw her mouth it and nod.

'I was born . . . in May 1891.'

Her eyes widened.

'I was born here. In this castle. You remember that . . . don't you?'

'Maxted?' She formed the name awkwardly, as if unused to speaking. 'James . . . Maxted?'

337

'Yes.'

'Born . . . here?'

'Yes.'

'Then—'

The sliding door from the passage was suddenly opened. The cell filled with torchlight. Matilda Tomura scurried back to the doorway of the room at the rear. Max turned and saw Count Tomura Iwazu, flanked by guards, glaring through the bars at him.

He was dressed in a dark red kimono, loose trousers and a black outer coat. His bearing was as Max recalled from their encounter in Marseilles – straight-backed and square-shouldered. So was his demeanour – proud, scornful, simmering with violent inclinations. Behind him, shrinking back, dressed in a similar outfit, was the Count's arrogant, insecure son, Noburo. And at the rear of the group stood Ishibashi, the ever-present factotum, bulky and impassive, also in a kimono.

'Lieutenant Maxted,' said Tomura levelly. 'Will you not stand to speak to me?'

With some effort, Max rose. He slid the handcuff up the bar until it struck a cross-bar and would go no further. He had to bend to one side to accommodate it.

'How did you enter the castle?' Tomura demanded.

'By the main gate. I don't think you pay your men enough, Count. They're surprisingly bribable.'

'You lie. Was it the tunnel?'

'What tunnel? I don't know what you're talking about.'

'It does not matter. We have you now.'

'Congratulations.'

'You should have given up after your Arab friend died and Hashiguchi Azenbo's model was destroyed. It was madness to continue.'

'I never could take no for an answer.'

'We will find out who helped you enter. When we do, we will kill them. But we will not kill you, Lieutenant Maxted. There is no death for you here. Except the death of old age.'

'You mean to keep two prisoners now, Count? Is that it?'

'Yes.' Tomura smiled at Max. 'You came for your mother. You have her.' He looked towards Matilda. 'Old above her years. Shrivelled in her mind and her body. She cannot look at me. She cannot speak to me. She is broken. As you will be broken.'

'She's your *wife*.'

'No. Noburo's mother is my wife. This creature is nothing to me.'

'Let her go, then.'

Tomura laughed. 'I will let no one go. Her punishment and your punishment are the same. Life – the whole of the rest of it – buried here.'

Max looked at Noburo. 'Your father's mad. You know that, don't you?'

Noburo said nothing. He stared at Max with a mixture of horror and hatred. The arrogance Schools had spoken of was there too. But there was vulnerability as well. Perhaps Delphine Pouchert had already wrought a change in him. Perhaps Laskaris's road to revenge had always been the better one to tread.

But revenge had not brought Max to Zangai-jo. He understood that about himself. The primal urge to answer the question his very existence posed was what had brought him, in the teeth of reason. Where had he come from? *Where?* The castle he stood in; the woman he was imprisoned with: they were the grid references of his quest. He was there at last. He had found it. And, having found it, he would never be free of it.

'It would have been better for you to die in Marseilles,' said Count Tomura. 'That would have been clean and quick. This will not be. This will be slow extinction. You will watch your mother live another ten years or twenty years and then die. And then you will live on here alone. Until you die also.'

'You'll be dead yourself by then, Count.'

'Yes. I will. But Noburo will not release you. You can be sure of that. You were born here. You will die here.'

'I don't think so. I have friends who'll come after me.'

'You have no friends who can rescue you from this. Morahan and his people have left Japan. I defeated them. And I have defeated you.'

339

'So you think. Tell me, why didn't you just stifle me at birth?'

'That would have been too easy. I wanted your mother to know you had been taken away, to be raised as another woman's child, without any knowledge of her. That was harder for her to bear than your death would have been.'

'I have knowledge of her now.'

'But the price you have paid for it is too high. You have learnt the truth. But you have become its prisoner.' Tomura inclined his head sideways and squinted at Max, observing him as if he were some exotic specimen in a zoo. 'These bars, Lieutenant Maxted. Study them well. Study them closely. They will be in your sight every day. Every one of the many days I will keep you here, alive, while to the world you will be . . . dead.'

Max kept up a bold front until Count Tomura and the others left. Then he sat down at the foot of the bars and contemplated his situation. He had brought his present plight on himself. He knew that. He had gone on when all sense suggested he should stop. He had refused to turn back. He had forced his way into what was now his prison. *That* was his situation.

Matilda Tomura crept over and sat down beside him. 'James,' she whispered, gazing at him in awe and disbelief. 'My . . . son?'

'Yes,' he said. 'That is who I am.'

She pressed her hand – small, cold and trembling – into his. She looked into his eyes. Eventually, he would have to tell her how her brother had died and all he had done to find her. He would have to tell her everything.

And, if Count Tomura was to be believed, as Max feared he was, there would be ample time to do that. In fact, there would be nothing but time.

MATILDA MOVED AND SPOKE – WHEN SHE SPOKE – SLOWLY AND hesitantly. She stroked Max's hand and, on one occasion, his cheek. She stared at him for silent minute after minute. It was clear to Max it would take her many days simply to believe he was present. Perhaps she thought he was a hallucination. Perhaps hallucinations had troubled her before. She had been there, in that room, and the room beyond, for twenty-eight years. What effect such protracted confinement would have on someone Max could only guess.

Or, alternatively, he could wait to find out.

How long he would be kept handcuffed to the bars was also a matter of guesswork. A pail was supplied for his use, which suggested it might be for some time. Tomura no doubt intended to prove to him from the outset that he had forfeited all forms of liberty.

The absence of daylight in the castle's basement was not, in fact, as complete as Max had assumed. Grilles in the ceiling admitted some light, channelled from above, as the day progressed. Activities in the rest of the building reached him as creaks and muffled percussions.

Minutes became hours. His head hurt. He was hungry and thirsty. He was also very tired. At some point, he fell asleep.

He was roused by a rumbling noise he could not identify. Its source, he eventually realized, was a dumb waiter in the wall next to the sliding door he had entered by. Ishibashi appeared a few minutes later and removed from it a tray bearing beakers of tea and bowls of

341

rice. He slid the tray into the cell through a flap and, ignoring Max, called to Matilda, whom he addressed respectfully as *Oku-sama*.

She came and collected her tea and rice with a humble nod of gratitude, then retreated to the rear room. Max took several gulps of tea and ate a handful of rice. He stared at Ishibashi, willing the man to react. But no reaction came.

'Do you remember taking me to Tokyo after I was born?' Max asked, as much as anything to break the silence.

Ishibashi's reply took a long time to emerge. 'I remember,' he said, in a low, sonorous voice.

'Maybe you can tell me when I was born. Was it the fifth of May?'

'Fifth?' Ishibashi's tone suggested he did not understand the word.

'Yes. The fifth of May, 1891. Is that right?'

Ishibashi shook his head. 'Not fifth.' He raised three fingers. 'Three May. *Go-gatsu mikka, Meiji ni-jyu yon.* Then you born.'

Max, it seemed, was two days older than he had supposed. All his birthdays had been late. 'How long have you worked for Count Tomura?' he asked, keen to prolong the conversation.

But Ishibashi did not share his keenness. Perhaps he felt he had already said too much. He pointed to Max's rice bowl. 'Eat. No speak. *Subayaku.*'

So Max ate. And drank his tea. He had barely finished when Matilda returned, walking in the halting, stooping way he feared he would become used to. Imprisonment had made her apprehensive and subservient. It had hollowed out the core of her, so that the self-possessed and vivacious young woman Max imagined his father had fallen in love with no longer existed.

She replaced her beaker and bowl on the tray, then replaced Max's as well. She bowed to Ishibashi and thanked him. '*Arigato gozaimasen.*' He, the servant, had become one of her masters. Max felt bottomlessly sorry for her then. He longed to restore to her all she had lost. But he knew he could not.

Ishibashi took the tray back to the dumb waiter, loaded it in and pulled the bell next to the compartment. A rumbling ascent to some part of the castle's kitchen began.

Ishibashi paused and looked at Max thoughtfully, though what he was thinking was utterly unknowable. He stood there for a full minute or so, statuesquely still.

Then he turned and left.

The day faded into night. Two guards came to trim the lamps and replace the pail. They did not speak. Max lay down and searched the shadows and patterns on the ceiling for a way out of the trap into which he had blundered. His defiant words to Count Tomura meant nothing inside his own head. He had found his mother, but she was a confused, prematurely old woman who did not know him any more than he knew her. Blood was not always thicker than water. He had thought he could rescue her and shoot his way out if they could not escape undetected. He knew now the idea was exactly what Tomura had called it: madness. His arrogance and his stubbornness had brought him there. And he would probably still be there when they had changed to humility and acquiescence. But the changes, when they came, would avail him nothing. Tomura would show him no mercy. He listened to Matilda, shuffling around the rear room, muttering to herself too quietly for him to catch the words. Occasionally, it sounded as if she was singing, though what the song was Max could not discern. He felt the cold hand of despair on his shoulder. What a fool he had been. What a damned fool.

Max was actually grateful when Noburo came to see him. Taunting an enemy was preferable to contemplating defeat by him. Although, in this case, Noburo clearly intended to do some taunting of his own.

'You have lost, Maxted. You have *lost*. You are like all Westerners. You think you are superior to us. You think you can come here and take what you want. You are wrong. You will learn that now. You will learn what losing really means.'

Max longed to tell Noburo that Delphine Pouchert was not in thrall to him, as he doubtless supposed, and Louis Pouchert would soon be coming to demand satisfaction. But those surprises would have to wait. The past was a safer topic. 'When did you find out you were illegitimate, Noburo? It must have been quite a shock. More to the point, when did you find out your father had a legitimate son – but it wasn't you?'

'I *am* his son. *You* are not.'

'I don't know how Japanese law works, but in English law a son born in wedlock is the legitimate offspring of his mother's husband whoever actually fathered him.'

Noburo stepped closer to the bars and spat at Max. 'You are no one here, Maxted. Nothing. Dirt under my boot. Shit of a dog.'

Seizing the moment, Max grabbed at Noburo with his unfettered left hand. But his fingers only brushed the shoulder of Noburo's kimono as he sprang away. He was alarmed, though, and a little frightened. Max could read that much in his eyes.

He pulled out a knife and pointed it at Max. 'Put your throat to the bars, Maxted. Maybe I will slit it for you.'

'And disobey Daddy? I doubt it.'

'One day you will beg me to do it.'

'No. I can promise you, Noburo, I'll never beg you for anything.'

'You think you are better than me.'

'I *am* better than you. And you know it. Your father knows it, too.'

The knife was trembling in Noburo's hand. He was angry as well as frightened. He was angry *because* he was frightened. 'One day I will kill you.'

Max smiled, confident it would infuriate Noburo to see he could not be cowed. 'Try,' he said. 'Any day you like.'

Rue du Verger, Montparnasse, Paris, early morning, Wednesday 19th February, 1919

A MAN STEPS OUT OF AN APARTMENT BUILDING INTO THE COLD grey light of a winter's dawn. He is Sir Henry Maxted, a sixty-six-year-old British diplomat with a seemingly unremarkable career behind him, recalled from retirement to act as one of many advisors on technical issues within the British delegation to the Paris Peace Conference. He looks the part: broadly built, bewhiskered, firm of gaze and bearing. He is the very model of reticence and respectability.

The gathering of the weary victors of the Great War has filled Paris with such men as Sir Henry – the politicians and functionaries of dozens of governments, along with the journalists, spies, mistresses, chancers, schemers and suppliers of unspecified services drawn to the councils of the powerful as are flies to a dung-heap.

Sir Henry has few illusions about the true nature of the peace conference, which he sees as an unseemly scramble for the spoils of war. He has few illusions about anything, in fact, least of all himself. But his long training in the art and wiles of diplomacy would have disposed him, in the normal course of events, to play his small part in the proceedings obediently and unobtrusively. Events, however, have not followed anything close to their normal course since his arrival in Paris a month ago.

He could and perhaps he should have declined the invitation to join the British delegation. His specialist knowledge of Latin American affairs is hardly crucial. He is very far from indispensable

345

and he knows it. The truth is that his primary motive for coming to Paris was to renew his acquaintance with Corinne Dombreux. What that renewal has led to is a reappearance in his life of something he thought he would never experience again: joy.

How strange it is – how confoundingly odd – to rediscover passion at an age when it might be supposed to have withered. He lights a cigar as he reaches the starburst intersection of roads at Carrefour Vavin and glances across at Hazard, the grocery store on the opposite corner, where innumerable delicacies from around the world – grapefruit, caviar, anchovy paste, Turkish delight – seem always to be available. *Lait garanti pur*, the sign above its window reads. *25c.* Milk, guaranteed pure, for twenty-five centimes. He knows nowhere else where purity is available on such reasonable terms.

The morning is chill and overcast, but dry, which decides him against using the Métro to reach the Hôtel Astoria, where he will be expected to make at least a token appearance in the corner of Herbert Norris's outer office set aside for him. He will take the number 2 tram from Gare Montparnasse to l'Etoile and stroll round from there to the building that has become the British delegation's administrative hub.

He heads west along Boulevard du Montparnasse, puffing thoughtfully at his cigar. He has in truth a great deal to think about, though none of it concerns his negligible duties for the delegation. He is a man assailed as well as transformed by all that has intruded into his life of late. Falling in love with Corinne and discovering, to his delight and disbelief, that she was falling in love with him is more than enough to contend with. Social stigma and family turbulence are bound to ensue if they are to live together when the conference ends, as it eventually must. But he has more than that to dwell upon – much more.

It is still possible, he tells himself, to ignore what he has recently learnt, or to conclude that it is untrue. He has succeeded over the decades in largely forgetting the tragedy in which he featured. He has never once supposed he could have misunderstood it in the way it now seems he may have done.

The cities he has lived in press around him in his imagination as

346

he walks: Vienna, Budapest, Tokyo, Constantinople, Rio de Janeiro, Petrograd; but Tokyo most of all. The city's magical qualities have grown in the nearly thirty years since he left, to the point where now he experiences his memories of it as if recalling a dream – unreal, blurred, fragmentary.

But the memories are potent for all that. They are the glittering shards of his shattered younger self. And Tokyo is a city, as Japan is a country, so unlike all others that it might exist on another planet: the maze of crowded streets and silent temples and stone walls and wooden bridges; the swarming inhabitants with their strange clothes and sing-song language; the hawkers of balloons and kites and noodles; the silvery rain and the cherry blossom and the cornflower blue of the domed sky. '*Moyaya-moya*,' he remembers the kindling-women calling, as if it were an incantation. '*Moyaya-moya*.' They were calling that morning long ago when he met Matilda Tomura by chance on Nihombashi Bridge and let her persuade him to accompany her to the Shirokiya department store, where, she said, she wanted to see the latest Western fashions to have reached the Orient.

He had never been alone with her before. They had met at balls and receptions and formal dinners – and once at her husband's gloomy Western-style house in Akasaka – but never otherwise. They had never laughed and caught their breath at the look in each other's eyes. All this was new to them that spring morning in Nihombashi – new and magical.

It should have ended there. For a British diplomat to enter into a dalliance with the English wife of a Japanese politician was the sheerest folly. It was also a gross dereliction of duty. But the heart is capable of many derelictions.

The price he paid for what happened in the course of the long, hot summer that followed their springtime encounter was considerable. But for Matilda it was worse, far worse. For most of the intervening years he has condemned himself for letting her murder – as he felt sure it was – go unavenged, though how he could have done otherwise remains unclear. It is a stain on his conscience nonetheless. It is a scar that will never fade.

Lately, however, the suspicion has formed in his mind that Matilda may have suffered a worse fate even than death – that her husband, Count Tomura, has punished her infidelity with imprisonment in a basement dungeon at his castle north of Kyoto.

It hardly seems credible. Yet the evidence that it is true has mounted to the point where Sir Henry is close to being convinced. It began with his visit to Pierre Dombreux during the Frenchman's confinement in the Peter and Paul Fortress in Petrograd. It was a bone-numbingly cold day in early December, 1917, when the Neva was sheeted with ice. Dombreux said he wanted to tell Sir Henry something in case the Bolsheviks decided to shoot him. He had intercepted a letter sent to Sir Henry by Matilda's brother, Jack Farngold, claiming that 'Things did not happen as you believe they happened' and that he needed Sir Henry's help to 'undo what Tomura has done'.

According to Dombreux, the letter had been taken from him by his interrogators. But Sir Henry's liking for the man did not blind him to his duplicitous nature. Pierre Dombreux was a player of many devious games. How he subsequently extricated himself from the Cheka's custody Sir Henry did not know. He had left Petrograd by then, evacuated with the Ambassador early in the New Year. And a few months later Dombreux, denounced by the French as a traitor, was reported dead. Unable to learn more of Jack Farngold's supposed letter, Sir Henry tried to forget it.

In Paris, though, the possibility of investigating the matter further presented itself to him. Through Alphonse Soutine and his tame Arab cat burglar, le Singe, Sir Henry has obtained information culled from documents held by the Japanese delegation to the peace conference. This, and further information reluctantly revealed by his old Japanese police acquaintance from Tokyo days, Kuroda Masataka, who has owned to meeting Jack Farngold on several occasions, has strengthened his suspicion that Matilda is not dead after all, but a prisoner in Kawajuki Castle.

What to do? If he is to attempt a rescue, it must stand a good chance of success. Failure might be worse than inaction. Schools Morahan, whom he has consulted in confidence without entering

348

into any details, has given him a rough idea of how expensive such an operation, if properly mounted, would be. The cost is simply beyond Sir Henry's means, short of taking steps that would risk alerting others – notably his wife – to what he was doing. And Winifred must under no circumstances know anything of this. Without the necessary funds, therefore—

'Damn,' he says, suddenly noticing that cigar ash has fallen on his sleeve. He realizes he has been unaware of his surroundings since leaving Carrefour Vavin. Blowing the ash away, he presses on.

The cobbled breadth of Place de Rennes opens before him, loud with the rumble of carts and the squeal of trams. Looking to his left, he notes the time shown on the station clock and takes out his watch to check it by. There is no discrepancy.

He stares at the watch-face, letting its Swiss-perfected representation of time confer some clarity and precision on his thoughts. He needs both. He needs them as never before. He cannot hesitate for long. He either acts or he does not. He either stakes his all on this or he turns his back on it and grasps the chance of happiness with Corinne.

If he does act – and he can raise the money he needs to act – no one close to him must know. That is clear to him. Not Corinne, not Winifred, not Ashley. Above all, not James. What James would do if he learnt the truth does not bear contemplation.

Normally, Sir Henry would amble along to the Café de Versailles, just across from the station, and sip a milky coffee while nibbling a croissant and flicking through the pages of one of the establishment's cane-bound newspapers to see what the French press make of the doings of Wilson and Lloyd George and their very own Clemenceau. Only then would he go on to the Astoria. He would be in no hurry – no hurry at all.

But his mood is unsettled, his mind abuzz with whether and what and how. Loitering holds no appeal. He sees a number 2 tram entering the square and knows it will stop to take on passengers. He discards his cigar and heads towards it at a rapid stride.

A fateful intersection becomes certain in that moment. The

lifelines of two men who have not met for nearly three decades turn towards each other . . . and converge.

Sir Henry boards the tram just as it moves away from the stop. There is barely space for him to slip into the car. He catches a drift of cologne from one of the other occupants. It carries the scent of apples and is familiar in the vague, unsettling way smells can be.

As the tram takes a gentle curve into the continuation of Boulevard du Montparnasse, the passengers sway with it, to varying degrees. And in that variation a figure reveals itself to Sir Henry's sight: a man, standing only a few feet from him, overcoated and hatted, one arm raised to grasp the rail, the other buried in his pocket. He is bearded and bespectacled, his expression calm, his gaze confident yet withdrawn.

Sir Henry's mouth falls open in surprise. They know each other. Better than either would care to admit. The encounter should not be so shocking. The world has come to Paris. It was predictable – though Sir Henry failed to predict it – that Fritz Lemmer should have come too. He is not likely to have admitted defeat, however many of his countrymen have. He is here, where the future is at stake. Of course he is. Sir Henry almost smiles then, at the chance – and the irony – of their meeting once more.

There is not even the hint of a smile on Lemmer's face, however. It is expressionless. No one could guess they are old acquaintances. He takes his gloved hand from his pocket and draws it sideways through the air. It is a gesture of conciliation as well as caution. *Leave me alone* is the message it conveys. *Leave me alone and I will leave you alone.*

Sir Henry obliges him by looking away. The conciliatory note puzzles him, however. It is uncharacteristic. Perhaps the war – and especially the manner of its ending – has dented even this man's legendary sangfroid.

A tempting but dangerous idea forms in Sir Henry's mind in that moment. It is a sign, he knows, of his desperation. But this is surely an opportunity he should not let slip. There are many who would be willing to pay handsomely for information concerning the whereabouts of the Kaiser's fugitive spymaster, the ever elusive Fritz Lemmer. Sir Henry is one of very few people who know what Lemmer looks like, thanks to their paths crossing in Tokyo. And now he has seen him again. Here, in Paris. Where he should not be. Providence has shown its hand.

Fine judgement is required, however. Sir Henry knows he must be seen to yield. He must give Lemmer no cause to think him a threat. To move against such an opponent will be perilous. It would be madness to forewarn him in any way.

Accordingly, Sir Henry drops his head slightly and turns aside, his show of submissiveness intended to convey acceptance: *I will leave you alone*. He looks out through the rear of the tram. It is slowing for its next stop. No one else is edging forward to leave, since they have only just boarded. He steps out alone on to the platform.

A few moments later, he is walking back along the boulevard towards Place de Rennes, considering what he should do next. Money is the key, which Lemmer has just unwittingly handed to him. And there may be other ways to raise money, given le Singe's capabilities and the market for secrets that Schools Morahan and his partner, Travis Ireton, actively trade in. There is much to think about.

He hears the tram trundling away behind him. But he does not look back. His eyes – and his thoughts – are directed straight ahead. He has made his decision. He glances up at the blank grey sky and the mansarded rooftops on either side and follows with his eye the flight of a pigeon across the space between them.

The bird does not fear falling. The bird has wings. And so does hope.

Sir Henry Maxted, retired diplomat, reborn avenger, smiles at the thought and lengthens his stride.

It has begun.

And five months later to the day, six thousand miles away, it will end.

351

Max could not have said what time it was when he woke. His watch had been taken from him, as had everything bar the clothes he lay in. The sickly glow from the oil lamp in the walkway was the same at all hours. It was the rumble of the dumb waiter that had roused him. He wondered if some form of breakfast was going to be supplied, though he could hardly believe it was yet morning.

Five minutes or so passed, then the door opened and Ishibashi came in, carrying a lantern. He was moving faster than when he had last brought food and there was a change in his expression, or rather the appearance of an expression where before he had been stony-faced. Now he was frowning and, it seemed to Max, anxious. He made no move towards the dumb waiter. And, at that point, Max noticed he was holding a pair of long-handled metal-cutters.

To Max's astonishment, Ishibashi took a key from the folds of his kimono and unlocked the door of the cell. He stepped inside and gestured for Max to stretch the chain on his handcuffs. He fixed a link close to Max's wrist in the jaws of the cutters and grimaced as he applied pressure. The chain snapped and one end swung free. Max caught it just before it made a clanging impact with the bars.

'What's going on?' he said, scrambling to his feet and staring at Ishibashi in amazement.

'You hear sound?' Ishibashi nodded in the direction of the dumb waiter.

'Yes. But—'

352

'Put Oku-sama in. I pull up, send down again. Then pull up you.'

'In the dumb waiter?'

'*Erebe ta. Hai.*'

'I'll never fit. I'm surely' – Max raised his hands – 'too big.'

'I take out shelf. You fit. Get Oku-sama now. I go up.'

'Where are you taking us?'

'*Soto.* Out of Zangai-jo.'

'Why are you doing this?'

'See you born here. Not want see you die here. We go now. *Subayaku.*'

'All right. OK. Yes.'

'Pull bell when ready. *Hai?*'

'*Hai.*'

Without further ado, Ishibashi hurried out of the cell, heading for wherever the dumb waiter was sent down from. The turn of events was bewildering, but Max knew better than to waste time trying to understand the workings of Ishibashi's conscience. A chance of escape was a chance he had to take.

He ran into the rear room, where a small globe-lantern was burning. Matilda was sitting up on her futon, looking alarmed. '*Nan-da,*' she began. Then: 'What? What is it?'

'We're leaving.'

'Leaving?'

It was not surprising she could not grasp the concept. She had been there more than long enough to assume she would remain for ever. Trying hard not to panic her, Max lifted her gently to her feet. She was spectrally thin and seemed to weigh no more than a babe in arms. 'You must trust me,' he said, willing her to do so as he gazed into her sunken eyes.

A long moment followed, during which Max had to force himself to await her response. Then she said, 'I trust you . . . James.'

'Do you have some warm clothes?'

'In the closet.' She pointed towards it.

Max wrenched the closet door open and was confronted by garments from a bygone era: long gowns and dresses of the Victorian period. He grabbed a scarf and a fur-lined hooded cloak, imagining his father helping Matilda on with it at the conclusion of some winter ball long in the mislaid past, when she was young and beautiful – and light of heart.

Turning back, he saw her pick up a small silver-framed photograph and slip it into a pouch which she secured inside the belt of her *yukata*.

'Where are we going?' she asked.

'Home,' said Max.

'Yoko . . . Yokohama?'

'No. England.'

Why he had said that he could not properly have explained. She stared at him in disbelief. How long was it, he wondered, since she had been in England? Could she even remember her homeland?

'We must go.'

He looped the scarf round her neck. She slid her hand down the fabric and frowned, as if surprised by its familiarity. Carrying the cloak, Max led her as quickly as she was able to move out through the cell to the dumb waiter. He opened the door and judged at once she would be able to squeeze into it. As for him . . .

'You must get in,' he said. 'This is how we escape.'

'Truly?'

'Truly. Ishibashi is helping us. He'll be waiting for you upstairs. Let me . . .'

He lifted her in. She folded her legs and dropped her head on to her knees to fit into the compartment. He pushed the cloak in beside her.

'I'll see you soon. OK?'

To that she nodded and cast him a look in which fear and faith were fused. He felt his heart jump. Then he closed the door on her and yanked the bell-pull next to it.

He could not hear the bell ring at the top of the shaft, but almost immediately the dumb waiter began to move, rumbling up and away from him.

Several minutes passed in silence, quite long enough for him to wonder if what was happening was merely an elaborate hoax.

Then the dumb waiter began to descend again, the belts it moved on slapping against the inside of the shaft. The rumbling grew louder as it approached, then stopped. It had arrived.

He opened the door and was instantly convinced he would never fit inside. He sat up on the lip and manoeuvred his head and torso into the compartment, then tried to pull his legs in after him. It seemed it could simply not be done. He was much taller than Matilda and considerably wider in the shoulder. Somehow, though, scraping his knees on the roof against which the back of his head was already jammed, he compressed himself just enough to fit. Then he stretched out his left hand to pull the bell and slid the door shut.

A second later, he began to move.

The dumb waiter rose unsteadily through the shaft, creaking as well as rumbling, probably because it was not designed for a load of such weight. How many floors it rose through he could not tell. Two was his best guess.

Then it stopped. The door was wrenched open. Max was momentarily dazzled by a blaze of torchlight, then he was pulled violently from the compartment.

He crashed to the floor, his shoulder taking most of the impact. He rolled over on to his back and saw Noburo standing above him, grinning crazily, with a sword clasped in his hand. And there was blood on the blade.

Glancing to his left, Max saw Ishibashi's slumped figure beside him on the floor. His face was locked in a rictus of pain. Blood was pooling beneath him, flowing from a deep wound in his stomach.

Somewhere in the gloom beyond Ishibashi, Matilda was crouching against a pillar, her arms clasped round her knees. She was rocking slightly and whimpering in shock and fear.

'No escape, Maxted,' Noburo hissed through gritted teeth. 'You die here. Beside the traitor Ishibashi.' He tossed the knife he had threatened Max with earlier on to the floor, a foot or so from Max's right hand. 'Reach for it. Go on. I give you this chance. Reach for the knife.'

There was instantaneous clarity in Max's mind. Noburo had

discovered Ishibashi's loyalty could no longer be relied upon. He had let Ishibashi put his plan into operation before intervening and without telling anyone else so that he could claim all the credit for defeating it. This was to be his personal triumph, his route to long-withheld paternal approval. He would not harm Matilda. That would be to frustrate his father's intentions. But killing Max in fair combat, using a traditional Samurai weapon, was something he would never have to justify or apologize for. On the contrary, it was something he would be able to glory in.

'Reach for the knife.' Noburo's voice cracked. 'Or I will kill you where you lie.'

And put the knife in my hand afterwards, Max did not doubt. This was the confrontation Noburo had foreseen as he raised the dumb waiter, with Ishibashi already despatched and his next and principal victim on the way. This was to be Noburo's transfiguration.

Or not. Max feinted to the right, then immediately rolled to the left. He felt the draught of the descending sword-blade as he propelled himself upright and heard the splintering impact with the stretch of flooring where his head had been resting a fraction of a second earlier.

Then he was on his feet. He flicked the remaining links of the handcuff chain round his fingers to form a knuckle-duster. As Noburo swung towards him, Max struck him heavily across the brow. There was a cracking sound of fracturing bone and a burst of blood. Noburo cried out and slashed at Max with the sword. Max ducked out of the way and charged him head first.

Noburo was propelled back against the wall. A second after he hit it, Max struck him again in his injured eye, then grabbed the hilt of the sword and pulled it from Noburo's weakened grasp. He swivelled round, knowing he was going to sink the blade into Noburo's stomach. He knew it with a cold, hard certainty he was surprised to find he possessed.

Then it was done. And the hot blood was flowing. Noburo was choking and gasping as Max ground the blade into him. His faltering breath was warm on Max's face, his right eye blinded, his left filled with pain. He tried to push Max away, but all his strength was draining out of him. He tried to speak, but only bubbles of bloody phlegm formed on his lips. For Tomura Noburo, son of Iwazu, scion of an ancient line, this was the end.

'You lose,' said Max.

And those were the last words Noburo heard.

THE NEXT COUPLE OF HOURS WERE FOR MAX A BLUR. INSTINCT became his master. He had killed Noburo. His clothes bore the copious stains of his blood. And Ishibashi was also dead. But Max and Matilda were out of the cell where Count Tomura had decreed they should spend the rest of their lives. Max's only thought now was to get out of Kawajuki Castle as well. They would not be safe until they were beyond the walls of Zangai-jo.

Matilda was virtually paralysed with shock at what she had seen. She still trusted Max, but she was frightened by the violence he had shown himself capable of. He realized he would have to carry her for much of the journey that lay ahead. The power of speech seemed to have deserted her.

The room in which Ishibashi and Noburo had died was a pantry of some kind. The corridor outside led who knew where. In one direction the kitchen, presumably. Max's sense of orientation suggested the entrance to the tunnel could not be far away, though certainly it was one floor below them. There was no reason to think it would be guarded, since Tomura believed them both to be securely locked away. And Max felt sure Noburo had acted alone, in search of accolades he would never now receive. The sword was too cumbersome to manage along with Matilda and Ishibashi's lantern, which they needed to light their way, so Max armed himself only with Noburo's knife. They set off.

*

358

Finding the tunnel and avoiding other occupants of the castle, while carrying Matilda, was an exhausting struggle, both physically and mentally. Max had to force his brain to keep his fear of pursuit in check. He did not know what time it was and therefore how soon the bodies in the pantry were likely to be discovered. Once they were, though, a hunt would begin. And the hunters would know where to look.

Max kept the shutter closed on the lantern as often as he could. He halted at intervals to check his bearings and listen for raised voices or the sound of running feet. He heard none. The descent to the floor below was the most hazardous stage of all, which, after much hesitation, he simply charged through. He took several wrong turns in search of the tunnel and had to double back each time. Finally, he found the right panel in the right ceiling. He set Matilda down, lowered the stairway and carried her up.

His strength began to fail him as they made their way along the tunnel. He staggered and stumbled. On one occasion, he fell. Matilda wept and mumbled. To her, he sensed, salvation had become a nightmare of blood and flight. He could hardly have disagreed. Everything he did now, however thinly his resources were stretched, was governed by one imperative: escape.

A new day had dawned. Max saw it initially as thin grey light ahead of them after they had passed from the tunnel into the cave. It grew and strengthened. And then they were out, beyond the mouth of the cave, beyond the last of Zangai-jo.

He set Matilda down and rested for a moment against a boulder, gazing at the hills and valleys spread before him, limned in shades of pink and purple. The sun was rising, fat and golden, behind bruised hummocks of cloud. It looked as if it would be a good day for flying.

Now he allowed himself to believe for the first time. They were going to make it. What he had pledged to do was within his grasp. Freedom beckoned.

He urged Matilda on. 'One last push,' he told her, though she hardly seemed to register the words. 'We're nearly there.'

*

He slipped and slid down the steep slope of scree and rock with Matilda on his back.

It was a relief to reach the first stand of cedars and to be able to use their trunks for support. He looked back several times, but only the clouds were moving. There was no pursuit. Not yet.

They reached the track, then the car. The key had been taken from Max with all his other possessions, so he had to start the vehicle with the crank-handle, something he began to fear would be beyond him. But, eventually, it fired. He lowered Matilda gently into the passenger seat, then started off.

He began to relax as they descended. All he had to do was reach the boatyard and take off in the seaplane. The worst was behind them.

Then, round a sharp bend in the track, overhung by trees and boulders, he came suddenly on another car, blocking the way. Its engine was not running and its driver was nowhere in sight. Max pulled up close behind it, yanked on the brake and climbed out.

The bonnet of the other car was cool. It had evidently been there for some time, slewed across the track, effectively ensuring no one could pass in either direction. Max did not like the look of it. He found it hard to believe the obstruction was not deliberate. Logically, he should have sounded the Apperson's horn in the hope the driver – wherever he was – would hear him. But something held him back.

He turned round and smiled at Matilda, raising his hand to reassure her all was well, though he was far from sure it was. She did not react. She had seemed dazed since leaving the castle, over-whelmed, he guessed, by the avalanche of events and the shock of re-entering the outside world. She sat hunched in the car, gazing ahead without focusing, engulfed in the folds of the cloak.

He decided to push the other car off the track. That would send it down a rocky slope, where it would certainly be stranded, even if its radiator did not burst or its axle break. But he was not inclined to worry about that. He reached in to release the brake.

'Don't do that, Max,' came a voice.

Max whirled round. Lemmer was there, in front of him, standing by the rear off-side of the Apperson, clad in a duster coat and travelling cap. In his right hand he held a long-barrelled revolver. It was trained on Matilda.

She did not turn to see who had spoken. She bent her head slightly and squeezed her eyes shut, as if she could bear no more tumult and disorder, as if another stranger's voice was one too many.

'What do you want?' Max demanded.

'Where is Ishibashi?' Lemmer asked.

'What's he to you?'

'He has worked for me for many years. An informant within Tomura's household has proved invaluable to me. His name never appeared in the Grey File. Anna knew much, but not everything.'

'Ishibashi was acting on your orders?'

'Yes. It was not in my interests for you to languish in captivity in Kawajuki Castle. So, where is Ishibashi, Max? Is that his blood I see on you?'

'No. But he is dead. Killed by Noburo.'

'And Noburo?'

'Also dead.'

'Killed by you?'

'Yes.'

'So, now you have slain Tomura's son as well as mine.'

'Eugen's death was an accident. You know Appleby would never have meant to kill him. As for Noburo, it was him or me.'

'And it is always you who survives.'

'So far.'

'Tomura will pursue you to the ends of the Earth to avenge his son. You should understand that. It is his nature. But it is not mine.'

'Why did you want me free?'

'I wanted you *and* Countess Tomura free, Max. Both of you. Because you are to blame for Eugen's death, whether it was accidental or not. So, why should I not kill the mother you have striven so hard to rescue?' Lemmer cocked the gun and pointed it at the back of Matilda's head. 'Why should—'

361

'*Don't!*' pleaded Max. 'Please. She's never harmed you in any way.'

'Nor did Eugen ever harm you.'

'I'm begging you. Don't kill her.'

'There is no need to beg, Max.' Lemmer smiled at him knowingly. 'You can save your mother's life. If you agree to my terms.'

'Your *terms*?'

'I will spare her, if you swear to do as I ask.'

'What do you want me to do?'

'Nothing. Yet. But one day, months or more likely years from now, I will ask you to do something for me. And you will pledge yourself now to do it. Without question. Without hesitation. Whatever it is.'

'You can't be serious.'

'But I am. I will spare Appleby as well as your mother. In return, I may ask anything of you. And you will do it. Because you will owe me your mother's life. And Appleby's too.'

'Are you mad?'

'I believe not. We must each do the best for ourselves in this world. You have defeated me. But I choose not to surrender. I choose to fight on. Revenge will not help me prepare for the challenges ahead. But I will take it, if that is all you offer me. So, what is your answer?'

Max could not find one. If the promise Lemmer demanded was what it would take to save Matilda, he had to give it. Yet he knew he would come to regret it if he did. Desperately, he played for time. 'How can you be sure I'd honour such a promise?'

'Because of that word, Max. Honour. It means everything to you. I know I can trust you to keep your word, when you have solemnly given it. If not, what ground can you stand on? What justification can you offer for the things you have done? You are not like the rest of us, are you? For you, the struggle must be for more than survival. It must be for a cause. It must be for honour. Your father's; your own; your country's. So, the choice is before you. I advise you not to deliberate too long. When Tomura finds that you have killed his son, he will respond with all his strength. And he will do it quickly. I do not know what plan you have for leaving Japan, but I hope you can leave speedily. You certainly need to. And I will not stop you, once we have concluded our business here. Which you can do by uttering a single word. Yes. Or no. Which is it to be?'

SAM HAD KNOWN FROM THE OUTSET HE WOULD NOT BE LEAVING WITH Malory from Kobe. It was clear to him his place was with the seaplane. Only then could he guarantee it would be ready for use when Max returned from Kawajuki Castle, as Sam had not allowed himself to doubt he would.

Malory had tried to talk him out of it, before realizing the hopelessness of the task. Sam's plan was simple. He would see Max and his mother off, then travel by train to Nagasaki, where Malory would arrange for the *Ptarmigan* to call and wait for him, before sailing on to Shanghai.

Sam was not prepared to countenance the possibility that anything would go wrong. 'It took Max three days to get from Nagasaki to Yokohama, so I should be able to make it there from here in closer to two. That means Monday. Tuesday at the latest. You can count on it.'

'I wish I could, Sam,' Malory had said. 'You know Max wouldn't want you to do this, don't you?'

'I don't trust that Muchaku geezer. I want to be sure the plane won't let Max down. He'll complain. But he'll be glad of my help in the end.'

Malory could have warned Sam he might find himself waiting at the boatyard in vain. The truth, of which both were well aware, was that Max's raid on Kawajuki Castle was appallingly dangerous, even with Junzaburo's help. But Sam believed, as Malory clearly realized, that to prepare for anything other than success was halfway to admitting defeat.

364

'I can't stop you, can I?' she had said, shaking her head at him.

'Not a chance. Don't worry, though. You'll see me in Nagasaki. And I'll have good news when you do. Just you wait and see.'

He left the Kobe train at Osaka and was back in Ohtsu by early evening. He walked out to the boatyard in the fading lakeside light, wondering how Max was faring up in the mountains, away to the north. He had eaten a meal of sorts on the train, promising himself that one day soon he would dine on pie and mash and a pint of Bass.

The boatyard was deserted, save for a caretaker, a spindly, wizened, glittery-eyed old fellow who naturally spoke no English. But Muchaku had told him about the buyer of the seaplane and Sam had taken the trouble to glean a few key phrases from Chiyoko, which, even in his mangled delivery, persuaded the caretaker of his bona fides. Soon, Sam was on first name terms with Soho, as the old man was apparently called. Then he was sampling Soho's sake, essential, much miming of shivering implied, to survive a night's caretaking.

The night was in truth quite balmy. Soho allowed him to sleep for a few hours on his futon in the boatyard office in return for keeping watch while Soho took a nap of his own. He evidently did not expect anything to happen. And it did not.

Muchaku was less welcoming when he encountered Sam the following morning. But he could hardly object to a friend of the seaplane's new owner tinkering with it, so reluctantly he let Sam carry on.

Sam brought the plane out of its shed, opened out the wings and applied oil to just about every moving part. With each hour that passed, he expected Max to arrive, but he did not. The day elapsed slowly and ever more anxiously. Sam exhausted his supply of cigarettes and eventually paid the boy who had assisted him the previous day to go and buy him more, along with some food. The pot of eel and noodles the boy returned with tasted surprisingly good, the Japanese cigarettes unsurprisingly not.

When the working day came to an end, Muchaku made it obvious he wanted rid of Sam. Shooing gestures were accompanied by the word '*Ashita*', uttered with much emphasis. Sam had picked up enough Japanese to know what it meant. *Tomorrow*. But he did not admit to understanding, appeasing Muchaku with repeated apologies. '*Sumimasen. Sumimasen* with knobs on.' Muchaku looked irritated, but helpless. He had been paid well. The discussion ended inconclusively.

Tomorrow weighed on Sam's mind every bit as much as on Muchaku's. Something had gone wrong. Even Sam's excessive optimism could not resist that realization. Max was in trouble, held captive, perhaps, or worse. At some point in the small hours, during one of his chain-smoking spells as stand-in caretaker, Sam decided he would have to seek help if Max did not arrive by noon the following day. He would go to the temple in Kyoto and find out what Junzaburo knew. If Junzaburo had also failed to return, he would go to Laskaris and ask him to persuade the police to search the castle. Max had said Fujisaki had vouched for a Kyoto chief inspector called Wada. He was the man to turn to. Wada would probably be in awe of Count Tomura, of course. But he would have to be talked round. It was as simple as that.

But it would not be simple, as Sam well knew. And whatever he accomplished might not be enough. It might already be too late for Max. Which was not a cheering thought to be alone with, in the middle of the night, in a foreign land.

Worried though he was, Sam slept soundly when given the chance, exhausted by his own anxiety. It was dawn when Soho woke him. And it was immediately obvious he had not woken him merely to say goodbye. He was gabbling and gesticulating, in an attempt to communicate something of importance. And he was smiling, as if the something was not bad news.

Nor was it. The Apperson was parked in the yard. And Max was standing beside it. In the passenger seat of the car sat a tiny, frail woman Sam would have judged to be seventy or so, wearing a fur-lined cloak, with the hood raised, over a *yukata*.

Max looked tired and strained. There were bloodstains on his shirt. His clothes were dusty and torn. There was a bruise on his forehead and a short length of chain was hanging from a handcuff attached to his right wrist.

'Bloody hell, sir,' said Sam.

'Bloody hell indeed,' Max responded. 'What are you doing here?'

'Reckoned you'd get off safer with my help.'

'You're supposed to be aboard the *Ptarmigan*, for God's sake, heading for Shanghai.'

'I will be once you've left, sir. You and . . .' Sam approached the car. 'Countess Tomura, is it?'

The woman in the cloak looked at Sam and smiled feebly, though whether she was smiling at him was unclear. A veil seemed to hang between her and the world.

'Pleased to meet you,' said Sam. The greeting drew no reaction. He turned to Max. 'I've been having kittens, sir. What kept you?'

'I'll tell you later.'

'This is . . . who you went after?'

'Yes. Matilda Tomura, née Farngold.' Max looked bemusedly at the woman who was his mother but also a stranger. 'I've done what Pa died trying to do. I've freed the prisoner of Zangai-jo.'

'I knew you would, sir.'

'But we're not out of the woods yet. Is Malory safe?'

'She'll have left on the *Ptarmigan* yesterday, as planned. She's going to have them put in at Nagasaki to wait for me. I'll go there by train as soon as—'

'You can't do that, Sam. It's too risky. Tomura will be after my blood. And yours, if he finds out you're still in the country. I killed his son, you see. I killed Noburo Tomura.'

Somehow, Sam was not surprised. 'He had it coming, sir.'

'Yes,' Max nodded. 'He did.'

'But it's a two-seater plane. Room for you and the Countess only.'

'The Countess is as light as a feather, Sam. You'll have to squeeze in with her. We can cable Malory from Weihaiwei and tell her not to wait for you at Nagasaki. We need to be out of Japan as soon as possible. I'm not leaving without you.'

A SINGLE JOY-RIDE FROM HENDON AERODROME IN THE SUMMER OF 1911, during his first Cambridge long vacation, was enough for Max to fall in love with flying. The ardour cooled to some degree during the war, but he remembered his early experiences with a keen edge of nostalgia. He talked his way into the Royal Flying Corps before he had even graduated and took his first solo flight at Upavon, on Salisbury Plain, one warm September afternoon in 1913, when the skylarks were singing and the cotton-wool clouds were scattered across a vault of pure, enticing sapphire.

It seemed longer ago to him than six years as he steered the seaplane away from the boatyard pontoon that morning on Lake Biwa. The caretaker watched him with rising curiosity from the lee of the tumble-down office building. A heron took to the wing from a nearby perch as the engine growled. Max eased the machine out into the clear water and swung her nose round to face the open lake.

He had not flown a plane since going down behind German lines in Flanders in April 1917. He had worried he might be rusty after two years with his feet on the ground, but he felt no sign of it. He felt, as he always had, at one with the machine he sat in. Floats in place of wheels made no difference. It was an aeroplane. And he was a pilot. He was born to it.

He glanced over his shoulder and exchanged a thumbs-up with Sam. Matilda, swaddled in the cloak and cradled in Sam's lap as if she were a child, did not seem to see him. Whether she understood what they were about to do he rather doubted. But Sam understood, grinning gamely at him as he fastened his flying helmet. A lot could go wrong. But they could not fritter away their time debating what that might be. They had to go.

Others had taken their chance and died in the course of Max's pursuit of the truth. He thought of Kuroda and le Singe in particular and wondered if their lives were worth what he had achieved. It was too late for such wondering, of course. He had striven to finish what his father had started and they had suffered for it. Nor were they the only ones. His path to this moment was drenched in the blood of the deserving and the undeserving alike.

What the future held he could not guess. He did not feel able to look beyond the flight to Weihaiwei. The journey would be difficult, especially when it came to refuelling. There would be all manner of hazards. There always were. The weather was set fair, but it was a long way, he was unfamiliar with the plane and much of the navigation would have to be done by eye. Sam's presence was a welcome reassurance. On the spur of the moment, he decided to say so.

'I'm glad you're here, Sam,' he shouted over his shoulder.

'Me too, sir,' Sam shouted back.

'Shall we get this bird in the air, then?'

To that Sam replied with a double thumbs-up.

Max turned back to the controls and tightened the chin-strap on his flying helmet. He thought of his father then and the flight together they had never taken. He would surely be proud of what Max had accomplished on his behalf.

It was not over. It would never be over while Tomura and Lemmer and Matilda lived. Tomura would seek to avenge his son's death at Max's hands. One day Lemmer would call upon him to fulfil the promise he had reluctantly given. Matilda, the woman who had given birth to him, would have a place to find for herself in a world she hardly knew. And she too would have Tomura to fear. The things Max had done would never be far from him. The past lay ahead as well as behind.

But in the present, *this* present, he could savour the satisfaction of beating the odds. 'I did it, Pa,' he murmured. 'Not bad, hey? Not bad at all.'

He started taxi-ing, accustoming himself to the feel of a plane on water. Everything seemed to be working – throttle, rudder, elevator, ailerons. Sam had done his work well. The machine was as ready as Max – primed, set, eager. And the lake was clear and still. He opened the throttle.

Speed and noise stirred his memory. This was how it had always been. There was nothing like it. This was his element.

The plane accelerated across the lake, a flotilla of ducks scattering from its path, the waves it was making thumping against the fuselage. There was a boat in the distance, but Max reckoned they would clear it with ease. He glanced at the tachometer. The revs were right. Everything was right. His touch on the stick was gentle. The nose came up. They were off.

And climbing. Into the wide blue sky.

AUTHOR'S NOTE

In *The Ends of the Earth*, as in the first two volumes of this trilogy, *The Ways of the World* and *The Corners of the Globe*, I have made no alterations to recorded history. Real people, places and events have been depicted as accurately as possible. Tokyo, where much of the action of *The Ends of the Earth* is set, has changed utterly – arguably, several times – since 1919. Anyone seeking to picture the city as it was before the Great Kanto Earthquake of 1923 is indebted, as I am, to Edward Seidensticker, author of *Low City, High City* and *Tokyo Rising*. I am also very grateful to Masahiro Wakabayashi of the Kyoto Prefectural Library & Archive for supplying invaluable information about Japan's former capital, a city that has changed much less than Tokyo, and to my good friend Toru Sasaki for helping me in innumerable ways during research for this book.